PORTRAIT IN SEPIA

"A storyteller of resounding wit and gusto, Allende's . . . passion is for her indefatigable, eccentric characters. . . . *Portrait* is allusive, sensuous, often blisteringly atmospheric and turbulent with secrets and self-discovery. . . . [It] moves, thrills, and delights."   —*Miami Herald*

"Spectacular storytelling. . . . The author's elaborate skill in weaving intimate emotional detail into the broad canvas of history is in fantastic display."   —*Atlanta Journal-Constitution*

"Allende's imagination is a spectacle unto itself—she infects her readers with her own colossal dreams."   —*Book* magazine

"Rich and complex. . . . Allende exercises her supreme storytelling abilities, of which strong, passionate characters are paramount. . . . A grand installment in an already impressive repertoire."   —*Publishers Weekly*

"A vision. . . . Rich in tones, shadows, and light. . . . Allende's eloquently layered descriptions breathe life into her characters."
—*People* magazine

"Complex, intriguing, ambitious. . . . It's Allende's remarkable flair for character that makes it all come alive."   —*Kirkus Reviews*

"Allende's craft and skill at storytelling, her temperance and restraint, and the straightforwardness and honesty of her prose shape [*Portrait in Sepia*] into an engaging novel."   —*St. Petersburg Times*

PORTRAIT
IN SEPIA

ALSO BY ISABEL ALLENDE

Isabel Allende

PORTRAIT IN SEPIA

A Novel

Translated from the Spanish by Margaret Sayers Peden

HARPER**PERENNIAL** MODERN**CLASSICS**

NEW YORK • LONDON • TORONTO • SYDNEY • NEW DELHI • AUCKLAND

HARPER**PERENNIAL** ● MODERN**CLASSICS**

A hardcover edition of this book was published in 2001 by HarperCollins Publishers.

P.S.™ is a trademark of HarperCollins Publishers.

HarperCollins books may be purchased for educational, business, or sales promotional use. For information please write: Special Markets Department, Harper-Collins Publishers, 10 East 53rd Street, New York, NY 10022.

FIRST PERENNIAL EDITION PUBLISHED 2002.
FIRST HARPER PERENNIAL EDITION PUBLISHED 2006.
FIRST HARPER PERENNIAL MODERN CLASSICS DELUXE EDITION PUBLISHED 2010.

Designed by Barbara DuPree Knowles/BDK Books

The Library of Congress has catalogued the hardcover edition as follows:
Allende, Isabel.
[Retrato en sepia. English]
    Portrait in sepia / by Isabel Allende ; translated from the Spanish by Margaret Sayers Peden.—1st ed.
        p. cm
    ISBN 0-06-621161-1
    1.Peden, Margaret Sayers.   II. Title.
PQ8098.1.L54 R4813 2001
863'.64—dc21   00-054127

ISBN 978-0-06-199153-0 (deluxe edition)

10 11 12 13 14   ID/RRD   10 9 8 7 6 5 4 3 2 1

For Carmen Balcells and Ramón Huidobro,
two lions born on the same day,
forever alive

And that's why I have to go back
to so many places in the future,
there to find myself
and constantly examine myself
with no witness but the moon
and then whistle with joy,
ambling over rocks and clods of earth,
with no task but to live,
with no family but the road.

—PABLO NERUDA, *End of the World* (Wind)

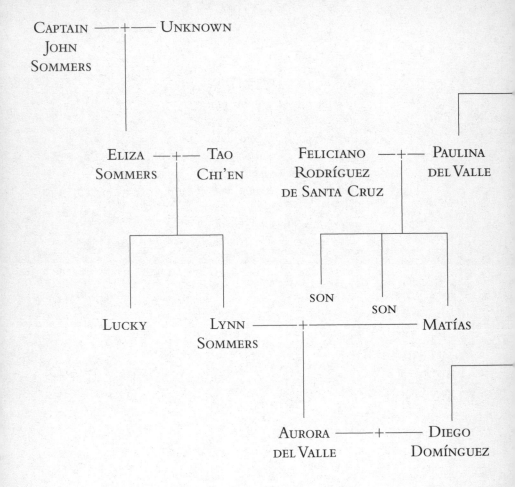

CAPTAIN JOHN SOMMERS —+— UNKNOWN

ELIZA SOMMERS —+— TAO CHI'EN

FELICIANO RODRÍGUEZ DE SANTA CRUZ —+— PAULINA DEL VALLE

SON

SON

LUCKY

LYNN SOMMERS —+— MATÍAS

AURORA DEL VALLE —+— DIEGO DOMÍNGUEZ

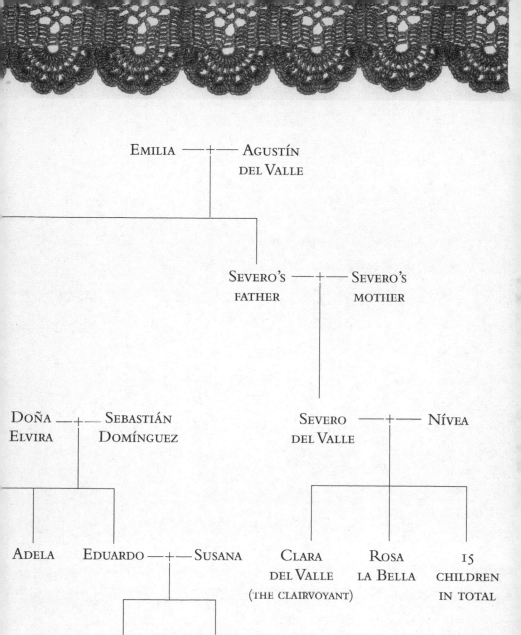

EMILIA ——+—— AGUSTÍN
DEL VALLE

SEVERO'S ——+—— SEVERO'S
FATHER   MOTHER

DOÑA ——+—— SEBASTIÁN   SEVERO ——+—— NÍVEA
ELVIRA   DOMÍNGUEZ   DEL VALLE

ADELA   EDUARDO ——+—— SUSANA   CLARA   ROSA   15
                                         DEL VALLE   LA BELLA   CHILDREN
                                         (THE CLAIRVOYANT)   IN TOTAL

CHILD   CHILD

PART ONE

1862–1880

I came into the world one Tuesday in the autumn of 1880, in San Francisco, in the home of my maternal grandparents. While inside that labyrinthine wood house my mother panted and pushed, her valiant heart and desperate bones laboring to open a way out to me, the savage life of the Chinese quarter was seething outside, with its unforgettable aroma of exotic food, its deafening torrent of shouted dialects, its inexhaustible swarms of human bees hurrying back and forth. I was born in the early morning, but in Chinatown the clocks obey no rules, and at that hour the market, the cart traffic, the woeful barking of caged dogs awaiting the butcher's cleaver, were beginning to heat up. I have come to know the details of my birth rather late in life, but it would have been worse not to discover them at all, they could have been lost forever in the cracks and crannies of oblivion. There are so many secrets in my family that I may never have time to unveil them all: truth is short-lived, watered down by torrents of rain. My maternal grandparents welcomed me with emotion—even though according to several witnesses I was ugly as sin—and placed me at my mother's breast, where I lay cuddled for a few minutes, the only ones I was to have with her. Afterward my uncle Lucky blew his breath in my face to pass his good luck on to me. His intention was generous and the method infallible, because at least for these first thirty years of my life, things have gone well. But careful! I don't want to get ahead of myself. This is a long story, and it begins before my birth; it requires patience in the telling and even more in the listening. If I lose the thread along the way, don't despair, because you can count on picking it up a few pages further on. Since we have to

begin at some date, let's make it 1862, and let's say, to choose something at random, that the story begins with a piece of furniture of unlikely proportions.

Paulina del Valle's bed was ordered from Florence the year following the coronation of Victor Emmanuel, when in the new kingdom
of Italy the echoes of Garibaldi's cannon shots were still reverberating.
It crossed the ocean, dismantled, in a Genoese vessel, was unloaded in
New York in the midst of a bloody strike, and was transferred to one
of the steamships of the shipping line of my paternal grandparents, the
Rodríguez de Santa Cruzes, Chileans residing in the United States. It
was the task of Captain John Sommers to receive the crates marked in
Italian with a single word: *naiads*. That robust English seaman, of
whom all that remains is a faded portrait and a leather trunk badly
scuffed from infinite sea journeys and filled with strange manuscripts,
was my great-grandfather, as I found out recently when my past finally
began to come clear after many years of mystery. I never met Captain
John Sommers, the father of Eliza Sommers, my maternal grandmother, but from him I inherited a certain bent for wandering. To
that man of the sea, pure horizon and salt, fell the task of transporting
the Florentine bed in the hold of his ship to the other side of the
American continent. He had to make his way through the Yankee
blockade and Confederate attacks, sail to the southern limits of the At-
lantic, pass through the treacherous waters of the Strait of Magellan,
sail into the Pacific Ocean, and then, after putting in briefly at several
South American ports, point the bow of his ship toward northern
California, that venerable land of gold. He had precise orders to open
the crates on the pier in San Francisco, supervise the ship's carpenter
while he assembled the pieces of the jigsaw puzzle, taking care not to
nick the carvings, install the mattress and ruby-colored canopy, set the
whole construction on a cart, and dispatch it at a leisurely pace to the
heart of the city. The coachman was to make two complete turns
around Union Square, and another two—while jingling a little bell—
before the balcony of my grandfather's concubine, before depositing it

at its final destination, the home of Paulina del Valle. This fanfaronade was to be performed in the midst of the Civil War, when Yankee and Confederate armies were massacring each other in the South and no one was in any mood for jokes or little bells. John Sommers fulfilled the instructions cursing, because during months of sailing that bed had come to symbolize what he most detested about his job: the whims of his employer, Paulina del Valle. When he saw the bed displayed on the cart, he sighed and decided that that would be the last thing he would ever do for her. He had spent twelve years following her orders and had reached the limits of his patience. That bed still exists, intact. It is a weighty dinosaur of polychrome wood; the headboard is presided over by the god Neptune surrounded by foaming waves and undersea creatures in bas-relief, and the foot, frolicking dolphins and cavorting sirens. Within a few hours, half of San Francisco had the opportunity to appreciate that Olympian bed. My grandfather's amour, however, the one to whom the spectacle was dedicated, hid as the cart went by, and then went by a second time with its little bell.

"My triumph lasted about a minute," Paulina confessed to me many years later, when I insisted on photographing the bed and knowing all the details. "The joke backfired on me. I thought everyone would make fun of Feliciano, but they turned it on me. I misjudged. Who would have imagined such hypocrisy? In those days San Francisco was a hornet's nest of corrupt politicians, bandits, and loose women."

"They didn't like your defiance," I suggested.

"No, they didn't. It's expected that we women will protect our husband's reputation, no matter how vile."

"Your husband wasn't vile," I rebutted.

"No, but he did a lot of stupid things. In any case, I'm not sorry about the famous bed, I've slept in it for forty years."

"What did your husband do when he found he was discovered?"

"He told me that while the country was bleeding through a civil war, I was buying furniture fit for Caligula. And he denied everything, of course. No one with an ounce of sense admits an infidelity, even if they catch you in bed."

"Do you say that from experience?"

"I wish it were so, Aurora!" replied Paulina del Valle unhesitatingly.

In the first photograph I took of her, when I was thirteen, Paulina is in her mythological bed, propped up on pillows of embroidered satin, wearing a lace nightgown, and decked out in a pound of jewels. That's how I saw her many times, and that's how I would have liked to see her at her wake, but she wanted to go to the grave in the somber habit of the Carmelites and for several years have masses sung for the repose of her soul. "I've created plenty of scandal, it's time to pay the piper," was her explanation when she sank into the wintry melancholy of her last days. Seeing herself so near the end, she became terrified. She banished the bed to the cellar and in its place installed a wooden platform with a horsehair mattress, to die without luxuries after living with such excess, and see if Saint Peter would start a new account in the book of her sins, as she said. Her fear, nevertheless, was not so far-reaching that she gave up other material goods, and up to her last breath she held the reins of her financial empire, by then very reduced, in her hands. Of the bravura of her youth very little was left at the end, even her irony was wearing thin, but my grandmother created her own legend, and no horsehair mattress or Carmelite habit could stand in her way. The Florentine bed, which she granted herself the pleasure of parading through the main streets to mortify her husband, was one of her most glorious moments. At that time the family was living in San Francisco, using another name—Cross—because no North American could pronounce the rotund syllables of Rodríguez de Santa Cruz y del Valle, a true shame since their authentic name carried centuries-old resonances of the Inquisition. They had just moved to Nob Hill, where they had constructed an outlandish mansion, one of the most opulent in the city, a delirium conceived by a number of competing architects contracted and dismissed every other day. The family had not made its fortune during the gold rush in 1849, as Feliciano claimed, but, rather, thanks to the unequaled entrepreneurial instincts of his wife, who had come up with the idea of transporting fresh produce packed in beds of Antarctic ice from Chile to California. During that tumultuous era a peach fetched an ounce of gold, and Paulina knew how to capitalize on those circumstances. Her enterprise prospered, and the family came to own a flotilla of ships sailing between Valparaíso and San Francisco. At first they had returned empty, but soon they were retracing their route laden with California flour. In the process they ruined several Chilean agriculturists, including Paulina's father, the daunting Agustín del Valle, whose wheat rotted in warehouses because he could not compete with the Yankee's finely ground white flour. His liver rotted as well, from rage. At the end of the gold fever, after losing their health and soul in pursuit of a dream, thousands and thousands of adventurers returned home poorer than when they had left, but Paulina and Feliciano made a fortune. They took their place at the apogee of San Francisco society, despite the almost insuperable obstacle of having a Spanish accent. "In California everyone is newly rich and lowborn," Paulina always muttered in the days before she folded her tent and went back to Chile, "whereas our genealogical tree goes back to the time of the Crusades." Titles of nobility or bank accounts were not, however, the only thing that opened doors to them; there was also the congeniality of Feliciano, who made friends among the most powerful men of the city. It was quite difficult, in contrast, to swallow his wife, who was ostentatious, foulmouthed, and irreverent, a woman who trampled over everyone in her path. No way to deny it: at first Paulina inspired the mixture of fascination and fear you feel when you see an iguana; only when you knew her better did you discover her sentimental side. In 1862 she launched her husband in a commercial enterprise linked with the transcontinental railroad— one that made them enormously wealthy. I can't explain where that woman got her nose for business. She came from a family of Chilean landowners, rigid in judgment and limited of spirit. She was raised in her father's family home in Valparaíso, saying the rosary and embroidering, because her father believed that ignorance guaranteed the submission of women and the poor. She barely mastered the rudiments of writing and arithmetic, she never read a book in her life, and she added on her fingers—she never subtracted—yet everything she touched made money. Had it not been for her spendthrift sons and relatives, she would have died with all the splendor of an empress. Those were the years the railroad connecting the east and the west coasts of the United States was being built. While everyone was investing in the stocks of the two companies and betting on which could lay rails the faster, she, indifferent to that frivolous race, spread a map on the dining room table and with a topographer's patience studied the future route of the train along with locations where abundant water was to be found. Long before the humble Chinese laborers drove the last nail joining the tracks in Promontory, Utah, and the first locomotive crossed the continent with its clashing iron and volcanic smoke, bawling like a ship in distress, she had convinced her husband to buy land at the places marked on her map with crosses in red ink.

"That's where they'll build towns, because there's water, and in each one of those towns we will have a store," she explained.

"That's a lot of money," Feliciano exclaimed, horrified.

"Then borrow it, that's what banks are for. Why should we risk our own money if we can use someone else's?" Paulina replied, as she always did in such cases.

That was where they were, negotiating with banks and buying land across half the country, when the matter of the concubine exploded. The lady in question was an actress named Amanda Lowell, a delicious Scottish mouthful with milky flesh, spinach-colored eyes, and peach flavor, according to those who had tasted her. She sang and danced badly but with enthusiasm; she acted in inconsequential plays and enlivened wealthy men's parties. She had a snake of Panamanian pedigree, long, fat, and tame but spine-tingling in appearance, that she wound around her body during her exotic dances. It had never given any sign of aggression until one unfortunate night when La Lowell showed up with a feather diadem in her hair and the beastie, confusing the headdress for a distracted parrot, came close to strangling its mistress in its determination to swallow the bird. The beautiful Lowell was far from being one of the thousands of so-called soiled doves in the amatory landscape of California. She was a high-class courtesan whose favors were not attained simply with money: good manners and charm were also called for. Thanks to the generosity of her protectors, she lived well and had more than sufficient means to support an entourage of artists with no talent. She was condemned to die poor because she spent as much as a small nation's gross product and gave away what was left over. In the flower of her youth, she stopped traffic in the street with the grace of her bearing and her red lion's mane of hair, but her taste for scandal had undercut her luck: with one fit she could ruin a good name and a family. To Feliciano, the risk was but a further incentive; he had the soul of a pirate and the idea of playing with fire seduced him as much as La Lowell's incomparable buttocks. He installed her in an apartment in the heart of San Francisco, but he never appeared in public with her because he knew the nature of his wife, who once in a fit of jealousy had cut off the arms and legs of all his suits and left them in a heap at the door of his office. For a man as elegant as he, a man who ordered his clothing from Prince Albert's tailor in London, that was a mortal blow.

In San Francisco, a man's city, the wife was always the last to learn of a conjugal infidelity, but in this case it was La Lowell herself who divulged it. The minute her protector turned his back, she began carving notches on the pillars of her bed, one for each lover received. She was a collector; she wasn't interested in men for their own merits, only the number of marks. It was her goal to surpass the myth of the fascinating Lola Montez, the Irish courtesan who had breezed through San Francisco during the gold fever. Word of La Lowell's notches flew from mouth to mouth, and local gallants fought to visit her, as much for the beauty's charms, whom many already knew in the biblical sense, as for the amusement of bedding the mistress of one of the city's most illustrious citizens. The news reached Paulina del Valle after it had made the complete circuit of California.

"Most humiliating of all is that the bitch has been cuckolding you, and now everyone is saying that I'm married to a rooster with no cock-a-doodle-do," Paulina rebuked her husband—she had a tongue like a Saracen scimitar at such moments.

Feliciano Rodríguez de Santa Cruz had known nothing of La Lowell's collecting tendencies, and his vexation nearly killed him. He had never imagined that friends, acquaintances, and men who owed him tremendous favors would mock him in that way. On the other hand, he never blamed his lover because he accepted with resignation the caprices of the fair sex, delicious creatures with little moral fiber, always ready to yield to temptation. Whereas they were bound to the earth, humus, blood, and organic functions, men were destined for heroism, great ideas, and—though not in his case—sainthood. Confronted by his wife, he defended himself as best he could, and took advantage of a moment of truce to throw in her face the business of the bolt she used to lock the door of her room. Did she think a man like him could live in abstinence? It was all her fault for having turned him away, he alleged. The business of the bolt was true. Paulina had renounced their carnal romps, not for lack of desire, as she confessed to me forty years later, but out of pride. It revolted her to look at herself in the mirror, and she assumed that any man would feel the same if he saw her naked. She remembered the exact moment she became aware that her body was becoming her enemy. A few years before, when Feliciano returned from a long business trip to Chile, he had caught her by the waist and with his usual hearty good humor tried to sweep her off her feet and carry her to bed, but was unable to budge her.

"Shit, Paulina! Do you have rocks in your underdrawers?" He laughed.

"It's fat," she sighed sadly.

"I want to see it!"

"Absolutely not. From now on, you can come to my room only at night and with the lamp out."

For a while those two, who had frolicked without restraint, made love in the dark. Paulina stood firm, impervious to the pleas and rages of her husband, who never got used to finding her beneath a pile of covers in the blackness of her room, or to embracing her with missionary haste while she held his hands to keep him from filling them with her flesh. That tug of war left them exhausted and with nerves screaming. Finally, using the pretext of the move to the new mansion on Nob Hill, Paulina installed her husband at the other end of the house and shot the bolt on the door to her bedroom. Disgust for her own body outweighed the desire she felt for her husband. Her neck disappeared behind her double chin, her breasts and belly were a single episcopal promontory, her feet could not bear her weight for more than a few minutes, she could not dress herself alone or fasten her shoes, but in her silk dresses and splendid jewels, which were what she nearly always wore, she presented a prodigious spectacle. Her greatest worry was sweat in the folds of her fat, and she used to ask me in whispers if she smelled bad, although I never perceived any aroma but eau de gardenia and talcum. Despite the widely held belief that water and soap were bad for the bronchial tubes, Paulina spent hours floating in her tub of enameled iron, where she felt as light as in her youth. At eighteen she had fallen in love with Feliciano when he was a handsome and ambitious young man, the owner of silver mines in the north of Chile. For the sake of his love, she defied her father, Agustín del Valle, who figures in the history books of Chile as the founder of a small and miserly, ultraconservative political party that disappeared more than two decades ago but every so often revives like a bald, pathetic phoenix. That same love for Feliciano sustained her when she decided to forbid him entry to her bedroom at an age when her nature called more than ever for his embrace. Unlike her, he matured gracefully. His hair had turned gray, but he was still the same happy, passionate, free-spending, and lusty man. Paulina liked his common side; the idea that this gentleman with the resonant family names came from a line of Sephardic Jews, and that beneath the silk shirts with embroidered initials was a devil-may-care tattoo acquired in a port during a binge. She longed to hear again the dirty words he'd whispered in the days they were still paddling about the bed with all the lights on and would have given anything to sleep once more with her head resting on the indelible blue ink dragon on her husband's shoulder. She could never believe that he wanted the same. To Feliciano, Paulina was always the daring young sweetheart he had run away with in his youth, the only woman he admired and feared. It occurs to me that those two never stopped loving each other, despite the cyclonic force of their fights, which left everyone in the house trembling. The embraces that once made them so happy turned into battles that culminated in long periods of truce and such memorable revenge as the Florentine bed, but nothing ever destroyed their relationship, and until the end, when Feliciano was fatally felled by a stroke, they were joined by the enviable complicity of true scoundrels.

Once Captain John Sommers had assured himself that the mythic bed was on the cart and that the coachman understood his instructions, he set off on foot in the direction of Chinatown, as he did each time he visited San Francisco. On this occasion, however, grit alone wasn't enough to get him there, and after two blocks he had to call for a rented coach. He climbed in with difficulty, gave the driver the address, and leaned back in the seat, panting. His symptoms had begun a year ago, but in recent weeks they had become more acute. His legs were too weak to hold him, and his head was filled with fog; he had to battle constantly the temptation to abandon himself to the cottony indifference that was seeping into his soul. His sister Rose had been the first to notice that something was not going well, back before he felt any pain. He smiled as he thought of her: she was the person closest and dearest to him, the guiding light of his wandering existence, more real in his affections than his daughter Eliza or any of the women he had held in his arms during his long pilgrimage from port to port.

Rose Sommers had spent her youth in Chile at the side of her older brother, Jeremy. At his death, however, she had returned to England to grow old in her own country. She lived in London in a small house a few blocks from theaters and the opera, a slightly down-at-the-heels neighborhood where she could live as she pleased. She was no longer the proper mistress of the house for Jeremy; now she could give free rein to her eccentric bent. She liked to dress as an out-of-luck actress and take tea at the Savoy, or as a Russian countess when she walked her dog; among her friends were beggars and street musicians, and she spent her money on trinkets and charities. "Nothing is as liberating as age," she would say, happily counting her wrinkles. "It isn't age, sister, it's the economic freedom you've won with your pen," John Sommers would reply. This white-haired spinster had made a small fortune writing pornography. The true irony, thought the captain, was that now that Rose had no need to hide, as she had when she lived in the shadow of her brother Jeremy, she had stopped writing erotic stories and devoted herself to turning out romantic novels at an exhausting pace, and with unparalleled success. There was no woman alive whose mother tongue was English, including Queen Victoria, who hadn't read at least one of the romances written by Dame Rose Sommers. Her distinguished title merely legalized a position that Rose had taken by assault years before. Had Queen Victoria suspected that her favorite author, one upon whom she had personally bestowed the rank of dame, was responsible for a vast body of salacious books signed "An Anonymous Lady," she would have swooned. It was the captain's opinion that the pornography was delicious but that Rose's love novels were pure trash. For years he had taken on the task of arranging publication and distribution of the forbidden stories Rose produced right under the nose of her elder brother, who died convinced that she was a virtuous maiden whose only mission was to make life agreeable for him. "Look after yourself, John. You know you can't leave me alone in this world. You're losing weight, and your color isn't good," Rose had repeated every day the captain visited her in London. Since then, a relentless metamorphosis had been transforming him into a lizard.

Tao Chi'en had just removed his acupuncture needles from a patient's ears and arms when his assistant advised him that his father-in-law had arrived. The *zhong-yi* carefully placed his gold needles in pure alcohol, washed his hands in a basin, put on his jacket, and went out to welcome his visitor, amazed that Eliza had not informed him that her father would be arriving that day. Captain Sommers's every visit created a commotion. The family would await him eagerly, especially the children, who never tired of admiring his exotic gifts and hearing stories about sea monsters and Malaysian pirates from their colossal grandfather. Tall, solid, skin leathery from the salt of the seven seas, beard untamed, with a voice like thunder and a babe's innocent blue eyes, the captain cut an imposing figure in his blue uniform, but the man Tao Chi'en saw seated in a chair in his clinic was so diminished that he had difficulty recognizing him. He greeted the captain with respect, having never overcome the habit of bowing before him in the Chinese manner. Tao had met John Sommers in his youth, when he was working as cook on his ship. "You address me as sir! Is that clear, Chinaman?" he had ordered the first time he spoke to Tao. Their hair was black then, thought Tao Chi'en, with a stab of anguish as he regarded the announcement of death standing before him. Laboriously the Englishman got to his feet, held out his hand, and then clasped Tao Chi'en in a brief embrace. The *zhong-yi* realized that now he was the taller and heavier of the two.

"Did Eliza know that you were coming today, sir?" Tao asked.

"No. You and I need to speak alone, Tao. I am dying."

The *zhong-yi* had known that the moment he saw him. Without a word he led the captain to the consulting room, where he helped him undress and lie down on a cot. His naked father-in-law presented a pathetic sight: dry, thickened skin, coppery in color, yellowed nails, bloodshot eyes, swollen belly. Tao began by palpating his body, and then he took the captain's pulse at his wrists, neck, and ankles, to verify what he already knew.

"Your liver is ruined, sir. Are you still drinking?"

"You can't ask me to give up the habit of a lifetime, Tao. Do you think anyone can endure a life at sea without taking a drink from time to time?"

Tao Chi'en smiled. The Englishman drank half a bottle of gin on normal days— an entire bottle if there was something to mourn or celebrate—without its seeming to affect him in the least. He never even smelled of liquor because his strong, cheap tobacco permeated his breath and clothing.

"Besides, it's a little late to repent, don't you think?" added John Sommers.

"You can live longer, and in better condition, if you stop drinking. Why don't you take a rest? Come live with us for a while. Eliza and I will take care of you until you recover," the *zhong-yi* proposed, looking away so the captain would not see his emotion. As so often happened in his role as a physician, he had to fight against the feeling of terrible impotence that overcame him when he was forced to confront how limited the resources of his science were and how immense man's suffering.

"What makes you think that of my own free will I would place myself in Eliza's hands and let her condemn me to abstinence! How much time do I have left, Tao?" asked John Sommers.

"I cannot tell you exactly. You should get another opinion."

"Yours is the only opinion I respect. Ever since you pulled my tooth halfway between Indonesia and the coast of Africa and I didn't feel a thing, no other doctor has laid his damned hands on me. How long ago was that?"

"About fifteen years. I appreciate your confidence, sir."

"Only fifteen years? Why does it seem to me that we have known each other all our lives?"

"Perhaps we knew one another in another lifetime."

"The idea of reincarnation terrifies me, Tao. Imagine if in my next life I turned out to be a Muslim. Do you know that those poor wretches don't touch alcohol?"

"That surely is your karma. In every incarnation we must resolve what we left unfinished in the previous one," Tao joked.

"I prefer the Christian hell, it's less cruel. Well, we'll say nothing of this to Eliza," John Sommers concluded as he dressed, struggling with the buttons that escaped his trembling fingers. "Since this may be my last visit, it's only right that she and my grandchildren remember me happy and healthy. I leave with a calm heart, Tao, because no one could look after my daughter Eliza better than you."

"No one could love her more than I do, sir."

"When I'm no longer here, someone must look to my sister. You know that Rose was like a mother to Eliza."

"Don't worry. Eliza and I will always be in touch with her," his son-in-law assured him.

"My death . . . I mean . . . will it be quick, and with dignity? How will I know when the end is coming?"

"When you vomit blood, sir," Tao Chi'en said sadly.

That happened three weeks later, in the middle of the Pacific, in the privacy of the captain's cabin. As soon as he could stand, the old seaman cleaned up the traces of his vomit, rinsed out his mouth, changed his bloody shirt, lighted his pipe, and went to the bow of his ship, where he stood and looked for the last time at the stars winking in a sky of black velvet. Several sailors saw him and waited at a distance, caps in hand. When he had smoked the last of the tobacco, Captain John Sommers put his legs over the rail and noiselessly dropped into the sea.

Severo del Valle met Lynn Sommers in 1872 during a trip he made with his father from Chile to California to visit his aunt Paulina and uncle Feliciano, who were the subjects of the family's finest gossip. Severo had seen his aunt Paulina once or twice during her sporadic appearances in Valparaíso, but not until he knew her in her North American surroundings did he understand his family's sighs of Christian intolerance. Far away from the religious and conservative milieu of Chile, from his grandfather Agustín, confined to his paralytic's wheelchair, from his grandmother Emilia with her lugubrious laces and linseed enemas, from the rest of his envious and timid relatives, Paulina had reached her true Amazonian proportions. On his first journey, Severo del Valle was too young to measure either the power or the fortune of that famous aunt and uncle, although the differences between them and the rest of the del Valle tribe did not escape him. It was when he returned years later that he would realize that they were among the richest families in San Francisco, along with the silver, railroad, bank, and stagecoach barons. On that first trip, at fifteen, sitting at the foot of his aunt Paulina's polychrome bed while she planned the strategy of her mercantile wars, Severo had decided his own future.

"You should be a lawyer, so you can use all the power of the law to help me demolish my enemies," Paulina counseled that day between bites of a cream-filled pastry.

"Yes, Aunt. Grandfather Agustín says that every respectable family must have a lawyer, a doctor, and a bishop," her nephew replied.

"You also need a head for business."

"Grandfather believes that commerce is not a profession for gentlemen."

"Tell him that gentlemanliness doesn't put food on the table, and he can stick it up his ass."

The youth had heard that phrase only in the mouth of their coachman, a Spaniard from Madrid who had escaped from prison in Tenerife, and who for incomprehensible reasons also said he shit on God and milk. Who could explain the Spanish?

"Don't be so goody-goody, dear boy," Paulina shouted, rolling with laughter at her nephew's expression. "We all have asses."

That same afternoon she took him to Eliza Sommers's pastry shop. San Francisco had dazzled Severo with his first glimpse from the ship: a luminous city set in a green landscape of tree-covered hills descending in waves to the edge of a bay of calm waters. From a distance it looked severe, with its Spanish plan of a grid of streets, but on closer look it had all the charm of the unexpected. Accustomed to the sleepy aspect of the port of Valparaíso, where he had grown up, the boy was stunned by the dementia of houses and buildings in many styles, of luxury and poverty, all mixed together as if it had sprung up overnight. He saw a dead, fly-covered horse in front of an elegant shop selling violins and grand pianos. Through the noisy traffic of animals and coaches streamed a cosmopolitan throng of Americans, Spanish and Spanish Americans, French, Irish, Italians, Germans, a few American Indians, and former black slaves, freed now but still poor and rejected. They turned toward Chinatown and in the blink of an eye found themselves in a country inhabited by Celestials, as the Chinese were called, whom the coachman scattered with cracks of his whip as he drove the fiacre toward Union Square. He stopped before a Victorian-style house, simple in comparison to the delirium of molding, bas-relief, and rosettes prevalent in that neighborhood.

"This is Mrs. Sommers's tea shop, the only one around," Paulina explained. "You can get coffee anywhere you please, but for a cup of tea you have to come here. The Yankees have abominated this noble brew ever since their war of independence, which began when rebels burned the Englishmen's tea in Boston."

"But wasn't that a century ago?"

"Yes. You see, Severo, how stupid patriotism can be."

Tea wasn't the reason for Paulina's frequent visits to this shop, it was Eliza Sommers's famous pastries, which filled the room with a delicious aroma of sugar and vanilla. The house, one of many imported from England during the early days of San Francisco along with a manual of instructions for putting it together, like a toy, had two stories and was topped with a tower that gave it the air of a country church. On the first floor, two rooms had been combined to enlarge the dining room, which contained several chairs with twisted feet and five round tables covered with white cloths. On the second floor they sold boxes of hand-dipped candies made of the best Belgian chocolate, almond marzipan, and several kinds of Chilean sweets, Paulina del Valle's personal favorites. Two Mexican employees with long braids and white aprons and starched coifs served as waitresses, telepathically directed by the tiny Mrs. Sommers, who in comparison with Paulina's impetuous presence seemed barely to exist. The wasp-waisted, foaming underskirted fashions favored the former but magnified the bulk of the latter, in addition to which, Paulina del Valle was never known to scrimp on yardage, flounces, pompoms, or pleats. That day she was costumed like a queen bee, in black and yellow from head to toe, with a feather-topped hat and bodice of stripes. Many stripes. She invaded the tea shop, swallowing up all the air and with every step setting cups to rattling and making fragile wood walls moan. When the servants saw her enter, they ran to change one of the delicate caned chairs for one more solid, into which the grande dame settled herself with grace. Paulina always moved deliberately, for she considered that nothing made one as unattractive as haste; she also avoided all the noises of old age, never allowing any panting, coughing, groaning, or sighs of exhaustion to escape in public, even though her feet were killing her. "I don't want to have a fat woman's voice," she would say, and she gargled with lemon juice and honey every day to keep her voice "slim." Eliza Sommers, tiny and straight-backed as a sword, dressed in a dark blue skirt and melon-colored blouse buttoned at the neck and wrist, and with a modest pearl necklace as her only adornment, looked distinctly young. She spoke a Spanish rusty for lack of use and a British-accented English, jumping from one tongue to the other in the same sentence, just like Paulina. Señora del Valle's fortune and her aristocratic blood placed her far above Eliza's social level. A woman who worked for pleasure could only be accused of being mannish, but Paulina knew that Eliza no longer belonged to the class in which she had grown up in Chile, and worked because she needed to, not for pleasure. Paulina had also heard that Eliza lived with a Chinaman, but even her devastating indiscretion was not sufficient to allow asking Eliza directly.

"Mrs. Eliza Sommers and I met in Chile in 1840," Paulina explained to her nephew. "She was eight years old at the time and I was sixteen, but now we are the same age."

While the waitresses were serving tea, an amused Eliza Sommers listened to Paulina's incessant chatter, interrupted barely long enough for her to gobble another bite. Severo forgot about the women when at the next table he discovered a precious little girl pasting pictures into an album by the light of the gas lamps and the soft glow of the stained-glass windowpanes that dappled her with sparks of gold. The girl was Lynn Sommers, Eliza's daughter, a creature of such rare beauty that even then, though she was only twelve years old, several of the city's photographers were using her as a model: her face illustrated postcards, posters, and calendars of angels plucking lyres and naughty nymphs in forests of cardboard trees. Severo was still of an age when girls are a slightly repugnant mystery to boys, but now he gave in to fascination. Standing beside her, he contemplated her openmouthed, not understanding why he felt a tightness in his chest and a desire to weep. Eliza Sommers interrupted his trance by calling the youngsters to have a cup of chocolate. The little girl closed the album without paying any attention to Severo, as if she didn't see him, and stood up lightly, floating. She sat down to her cup of chocolate without speaking a word or looking up, resigned to the boy's impertinent gaze and fully aware that her looks separated her from other mortals. She carried her beauty like a deformity, with the secret hope that with time it would go away.

A few weeks later Severo sailed back to Chile with his father, carrying in his memory the vastness of California and with the vision of Lynn Sommers firmly entrenched in his heart.

Severo del Valle did not see Lynn again until several years later. He returned to California at the end of 1876 to live with his aunt Paulina, but he did not renew his acquaintance with Lynn until one winter Wednesday in 1879, and by then it was already too late for both of them. By the time of his second visit to San Francisco, the young man had reached his definitive height, but he was still bone thin, pale, ungainly, and uncomfortable in his skin, as if he had too many elbows and knees. Three years later, when he stood mute before Lynn, he was a mature man, with the noble features of his Spanish ancestors, the flexible build of an Andalusian bullfighter, and the ascetic air of a seminarian. Much had changed in his life since the first time he saw Lynn. The image of that silent little girl with the languor of a relaxed cat had accompanied him throughout the difficult years of his adolescence and the grief of his mourning. His father, whom he had adored, had died, still comparatively young, in Chile, and his mother, confounded by her immature but overly lucid and irreverent son, had sent him to finish his studies in a Catholic school in Santiago. Soon, however, he returned home with a letter explaining in no uncertain terms that one bad apple spoils all the others in the barrel, or something of that nature. Then the self-sacrificing mother made a pilgrimage on her knees to a miraculous grotto where the Virgin, always ingenious, whispered the solution to her: pack him off to the military service and let a sergeant deal with the problem. For one year Severo marched with the troops, endured the rigor and stupidity of the regiment, and emerged with the rank of reserve officer, determined never again in his lifetime to go near a barracks. He had no more than set his foot out the door when he returned to his old friendships and erratic moods. This time his uncles got into the act. They met in council in the austere dining room in the home of Severo's grandfather Agustín, without the presence of the youth and his mother, who had no vote at the patriarchal table. In that same room thirty-five years earlier Paulina del Valle, her head shaved but crowned with a diamond tiara, had defied the males of her family to marry Feliciano Rodríguez de Santa Cruz, the man she had chosen for herself. There, that day, the charges against Severo were being presented to his grandfather: he refused to confess or take Communion; he ran around with bohemians; books on the blacklist had been discovered in his possession; in short, it was suspected that he had been recruited by the Masons or, worse yet, the liberals. Chile was going through a period of battles between irreconcilable ideologies, and the more government posts the liberals won, the greater the ire of ultraconservatives imbued with messianic fervor like the del Valles, all of whom were attempting to implant their ideas by means of excommunication and pistols, crush the Masons and anticlerics, and wipe out the liberals once and for all. The del Valles were not disposed to tolerate a dissident in the very bosom of the family and of their own blood. The idea of sending Severo to the United States came from Grandfather Agustín. "The Yankees will cure him of his hankering to run around raising hell," he predicted. So without asking his opinion, Severo was sent off to California, dressed in mourning and carrying his deceased father's gold watch in his jacket pocket, a meager array of luggage—including a huge Christ with a crown of thorns—and a sealed letter for his uncle Feliciano and aunt Paulina.

Severo's protests were merely formal, because that voyage fit right in with his own plans. His only regret was leaving Nívea, the girl whom everyone expected him to marry someday, in accord with the Chilean oligarchy's venerable custom of marriage among cousins. Severo was suffocating in Chile. He had grown up a prisoner in a thicket of dogmas and prejudices, but contact with other students at the school in Santiago had fed his imagination and awakened his patriotic fervor. Until that time he had thought there were only two social classes: his and that of the poor, separated by a fuzzy gray area of functionaries and masses of "the common people," as his grandfather Agustín called them. In the barracks he had come to realize that the members of his class, with their white skin and economic power, were but a handful, and that the vast majority of Chileans were poor and of mixed blood. It was in Santiago, however, that he had discovered a vigorous and growing middle class, educated and with political ambitions, that was in truth the backbone of the nation, among whom were immigrants fleeing from war and poverty, scientists, educators, philosophers, booksellers—people with modern ideas. He was awed by the oratory of his new friends, like someone in love for the first time. He wanted to change Chile, to turn it completely around, purify it. He became convinced that the conservatives—with the exception of the members of his own family, who in his eyes were acting out of error, not evil—belonged to the hordes of the devil, in the hypothetical case that the devil were something more than a colorful invention, and he was prepared to participate in politics as soon as he became independent of his family. He understood that it would be several years before that happened, which was why he considered the trip to the United States a breath of fresh air; there he could observe the enviable democracy of the North Americans and learn from it, read whatever he pleased without worrying about Catholic censorship, and become acquainted with the advances of the modern age. While in the rest of the world monarchies were being toppled, new states born, continents colonized, and marvels invented, in Chile the parliament was discussing the right of adulterers to be buried in consecrated cemeteries. In his grandfather's presence it was forbidden to mention the theory of Darwin that was revolutionizing human knowledge; on the other hand, one could spend an afternoon arguing about the improbable miracles of saints and martyrs. Another incentive for the voyage was Severo's memory of the girl Lynn Sommers, which with oppressive persistence kept infiltrating his affection for Nívea, although he never admitted that, not even in the most secret places of his heart.

Severo del Valle had no idea when or how the idea of marrying Nívea had come up; it may have been that they didn't decide it, the family did, but neither of them rebelled against their fate because they had known and loved each other from childhood. Nívea belonged to a branch of the family that had been well off when her father was alive but that at his death found itself impoverished. A wealthy uncle who was to be a prominent figure in the war, Don Francisco José Vergara, helped educate his nieces and nephews. "There is no poverty worse than that of people who have come down in the world, because they have to give the appearance of having more than they do," Nívea had confessed to Severo in one of her characteristic moments of sudden lucidity. She was four years younger, but much more mature than he; it was she who set the tone for their childhood affection, with a firm hand leading him toward the romantic relationship they shared when Severo set sail for the United States. In the enormous houses where they lived their lives, there were more than enough corners to play at love. Groping in the shadows, and with the clumsiness of pups, the cousins discovered the secrets of their bodies. They caressed one another with curiosity, verifying their differences, not knowing why he had this and she had that, dazed by modesty and guilt, never speaking: if they didn't put it into words, it was as if it had never happened, and was therefore less sinful. They explored one another with haste and fear, aware that they couldn't admit these cousinly games even in the confessional, though it meant being condemned to hell. There were a thousand eyes spying on them. The old maidservants who had seen them born protected that innocent love, but spinster aunts watched them like crows: nothing escaped those scaly eyes whose only function was to register every instant of family life or those crepuscular tongues that divulged secrets and aggravated quarrels—though always within the bosom of the clan. Nothing left the walls of those houses. It was everyone's first duty to preserve the honor and good name of the family. Nívea had developed late and at fifteen still had an innocent face and the body of a girl. Nothing in her appearance revealed her strength of character: short, plump, with large dark eyes that were her only memorable feature, she seemed insignificant until she opened her mouth. While her sisters were assuring their way to heaven by reading pious books, she was, on the sly, reading the articles and books her cousin Severo slipped her beneath the table, and the classics lent to her by her uncle José Francisco Vergara. When almost no one in her social setting was speaking of it, Nívea pulled out of her sleeve the idea of women's suffrage. The first time she mentioned it at a family dinner in the home of Agustín del Valle, she sparked a conflagration. "When are women and the poor going to have the vote in this country?" Nívea had blurted out, forgetting that children were not to open their mouths in the company of adults. The aged patriarch of the del Valles thumped the table so hard that the cups danced, and ordered Nívea to go immediately to confess. Nívea quietly fulfilled the penance imposed by the priest, then wrote in her diary, with her usual passion, that she did not plan to rest until women won their basic rights, even if she were expelled from the family. She had been fortunate enough to have an exceptional teacher, Sor María Escapulario, a nun with the heart of a lioness hidden beneath her habit, who had taken note of Nívea's intelligence. With this girl who avidly absorbed everything she was taught, who questioned what even Sor María Escapulario herself had never questioned, who challenged her with reasoning unexpected in her years, and who seemed about to explode with vitality and health inside her horrible uniform, the nun felt well rewarded as a teacher. All by herself, Nívea was worth the effort of having for years taught a multitude of rich girls with poor minds. Because of her affection for the girl, Sor María Escapulario systematically violated the rules of the school, which had been created for the specific purpose of turning students into docile creatures. With Nívea she held conversations that would have horrified the mother superior and spiritual director of the school.

"When I was your age," said Sor María Escapulario, "I had only two choices: marry or enter the convent."

"Why did you choose the second, Mother?"

"Because it gave me more freedom. Christ is a tolerant husband. . . ."

"Women have a raw deal, Mother. Have children and obey, and that's all," sighed Nívea.

"It doesn't have to be like that. You can change things," the nun replied.

"By myself?"

"Not by yourself, no. There are other girls like you, with a clear head for thinking. I read in a newspaper that now there are women who are doctors. Imagine."

"Where?"

"In England."

"But that's very far away."

"That's true, but if they can do it there, someday it can be done in Chile. Don't lose heart, Nívea."

"My confessor says I think too much and pray too little, Mother."

"God gave you a brain for you to use; but I warn you that the path of rebellion is strewn with danger and sorrow; it takes a great deal of courage to travel it. It is not too much to ask divine providence to help you a little," Sor María Escapulario counseled.

So firm did Nívea's determination become that she wrote in her diary that she would give up marriage in order to devote herself completely to the struggle for women's suffrage. She was not aware that such a sacrifice would not be necessary, and that she would marry a man for love who would back her up in her political goals.

Severo boarded the ship with a wronged air so that his relatives would not suspect how happy he was to be leaving Chile—he didn't want them to change the plan—and how ready to get the best possible benefit from this adventure. He told his cousin Nívea good-bye with a stolen kiss, after swearing that he would send her interesting books through a friend, to elude the family's censorship, and that he would write her every week. She had resigned herself to a separation of a year, never suspecting that he planned to stay in the United States as long as possible. He would explain that to Nívea by letter; he decided, he didn't want to make their farewells even more difficult by announcing those intentions before he left. At any rate, both were too young to marry. He saw her standing on the dock of Valparaíso in her olive-colored dress and bonnet, surrounded by the rest of the family, waving good-bye and forcing herself to smile. "She's not crying and not complaining; that's why I love her and always will,"

Severo said aloud to the wind, prepared to overcome the whims of his heart and the temptations of the world through pure tenacity. "Most Holy Virgin, bring him back to me safe and sound," Nívea pleaded, biting her lips, weak with love, not remembering for a minute that she had sworn to remain celibate until she fulfilled her duty as a suffragist.

The young del Valle fingered his grandfather Agustín's letter all the way from Valparaíso to Panama, desperate to open it but not daring to because it had been instilled in him by blood and fire that no gentleman puts an eye on another's letter or a hand on another's money. Finally curiosity was stronger than honor—this was a matter of his destiny, he reasoned—and with his straight razor he cautiously broke the seal, then held the envelope over the steam from a kettle and opened it using a thousand precautions. That was how he discovered that his grandfather's plan included sending him to a North American military school. It was a shame, his grandfather added, that Chile was not at war with some neighboring country so that his grandson could pick up his weapon and become a man, the way he was supposed to. Severo threw that letter into the ocean and wrote another in his own words, placed it in the same envelope, and dribbled sealing wax over the broken seal. In San Francisco his aunt Paulina was waiting for him on the dock, accompanied by two servants and Williams, her pompous butler. She was attired in an outrageous hat with so many veils flying in the wind that had she not been so heavy she would have blown away. She burst into gales of laughter when she saw her nephew descending the gangplank with the Christ in his arms, then clasped him to her soprano's bosom, suffocating him in the mountain of her breasts and her gardenia perfume.

"The first thing we do will be to get rid of that monstrosity," she said, pointing to the Christ. "And we'll have to buy you some clothes; no one here goes around in an outfit like that."

"This was my father's suit," Severo clarified, humiliated.

"You can tell, you look like a grave digger," Paulina commented, and as soon as she said it remembered that the boy had lost his father only a short time before. "Forgive me, Severo, I didn't mean to offend you. Your father was my favorite brother, the only one in the family I could talk to."

"They altered several of his suits to fit me, in order not to waste them," Severo explained, his voice quavering.

"We got off to a bad start. Can you forgive me?"

"It's all right, Aunt."

At the first opportunity, the young man gave his aunt the purported letter from his grandfather Agustín. Paulina gave it a cursory look.

"What did the other one say?" she asked.

Severo's ears turned red, and he tried to deny what he had done, but his aunt didn't give him the opportunity to trip himself up in lies.

"I would have done the same, nephew. I want to know what my father's letter said so I can answer him, not to pay any attention to what he says."

"It said to send me to a military school, or to war, if you have any around here."

"You came too late, they already had it. But now they're massacring Indians, in case you're interested. The Indians are doing a pretty good job defending themselves; they just killed General Custer and more than two hundred soldiers of the Seventh Cavalry in Wyoming. That's all anyone is talking about. They say that an Indian named Rain in Your Face—now there's a poetic name for you!—had sworn vengeance against General Custer's brother, and that during the battle he tore out his heart and ate it. Are you still interested in being a soldier?" And Paulina del Valle laughed quietly.

"I've never wanted to be in the military—those are my grandfather Agustín's ideas."

"In the letter you forged you say you want to be a lawyer; I see that the advice I gave you years ago did not fall on barren ground. I would like that, dear boy. American laws are different from Chilean ones, but that doesn't matter. You will be a lawyer. You will read law with the best firm in California— my influence should be good for something."

"I will be indebted to you for the rest of my life, Aunt," said Severo, impressed.

"Of course you will. I hope you don't forget that; after all, in a long life you never know when I might need to ask you a favor."

"Count on me, Aunt."

The next day Paulina del Valle appeared with Severo in the offices of her lawyers, the same who for more than twenty-five years had been earning her enormous commissions, and without preamble announced to them that beginning the next Monday she expected to see her nephew working with them and learning the profession. They could not deny her. The aunt took the youth into her home, gave him a sunny room on the second floor, bought him a good horse, provided him an allowance, hired an English teacher for him, and proceeded to introduce him to society, because according to her there was no better capital than good connections.

"I expect two things from you: loyalty and good humor."

"Don't you also expect me to study?"

"That's your problem, my boy. What you do with your life is not incumbent on me."

Nevertheless, in the next months Severo was aware that Paulina was closely following his progress in the legal firm, keeping a close eye on his friendships and a close accounting of his expenses, and anticipating his every step even before he took it. How she knew so much was a mystery, unless Williams, the inscrutable butler, had organized a network of spies. The man directed an army of servants who discharged their duties like silent shadows; they lived in separate quarters at the back of the grounds and were forbidden to speak to the master and mistress of the family unless they were rung for. Nor could they speak to the butler without first passing through the head housekeeper. Severo had difficulty understanding such hierarchies, because in Chile things were much simpler. The *patrones*, even the most despotic like his grandfather, treated their employees harshly but attended to their needs and considered them part of the family. Severo had never known a maidservant to be dismissed; those women came to work in their home at puberty and stayed until they died. The small palace on Nob Hill was very different from the monastic homes of his childhood, with their thick adobe walls and lugubrious iron gates, and their sparse furniture lined up against bare walls. In his aunt Paulina's home it would have been an impossible task to compile an inventory of contents, from the heavy silver door latches and faucets in the bathroom to the collections of porcelain figurines, lacquered Russian boxes, Chinese ivories, and whatever objet d'art or whim of greed was in vogue. Feliciano Rodríguez de Santa Cruz bought things to impress his visitors, but he was not a barbarian like others of his wealthy friends who bought books by the pound and paintings to match the upholstery. As for Paulina, she was not in the least attached to those treasures: the only piece of furniture she had ordered in her life was her bed, and she had done that for reasons that had nothing to do with aesthetics or ostentation. What interested Paulina was money, pure and simple; her challenge lay in earning it astutely, accumulating it tenaciously, and investing it wisely. She paid no attention to the things her husband acquired or to where they were displayed, so the result was a grandiose house in which the residents felt like strangers. The paintings were enormous, the frames massive, the themes intrepid—*Alexander the Great at the Conquest of Persia*—and there were also hundreds of lesser paintings, organized by subject, for which various rooms were named: the hunting salon, the marine salon, the watercolor salon. The drapes were heavy velvet weighed down with fringe, and the Venetian mirrors reflected to infinity: marble columns, tall Sèvres vases, bronze statuary, and urns overflowing with flowers and fruit. There was a two-story library and two music salons filled with fine Italian instruments, although no one in the family knew how to play them and music gave

Paulina a headache. Gold-initialed silver spittoons sat in every corner, because in that frontier city it was perfectly acceptable to spit in public. Feliciano had his suite in the Oriental wing, and his wife had hers on the same floor but at the opposite end of the mansion. Between the two, joined by a broad corridor, were the children's bedrooms and guest rooms, all empty except for Severo's and one occupied by Matías, the eldest son, the only one still living at home. Severo del Valle, accustomed to the discomfort and cold that in Chile were considered good for one's health, spent several weeks becoming accustomed to the oppressive embrace of the feather mattress and pillows, the eternal summer of the stoves, and the daily surprise of turning the bathroom tap and being rewarded by a stream of warm water. In his grandfather's house the toilets were stinking privies at the back of the patio, and on early winter mornings there was a film of ice in the washbasins.

The hours of the siesta often found the young nephew and his incomparable aunt on the mythological bed, she under the covers, with her account books on one side and her pastries on the other, and he, sitting at her feet between the naiad and the dolphin, discussing family and business affairs. Only with Severo did Paulina permit such a level of intimacy; very few people had access to her private rooms, but with him she felt totally at ease in her nightgown. This nephew gave her the satisfaction she never received from her children. The two younger sons lived the life of heirs, luxuriating in symbolic employment as directors of the clan's enterprises, one in London, the other in Boston. Matías, the firstborn, was destined to head the line of the Rodríguez de Santa Cruz y del Valles, but he didn't have the least vocation for it. Far from following in the footsteps of his spirited parents, taking an interest in their empire, or fathering male sons to prolong the family name, he had made hedonism and celibacy an art form. "He's little more than a well-dressed fool," Paulina described him once to Severo, but when she learned how well her son and her nephew got on, she worked diligently to foster that emerging friendship. "My mother never takes a stitch with an unthreaded needle," Matías joked. "She must be planning for you to save me from a life of dissipation." Severo had no thought of taking on the task of changing his cousin. Just the opposite—he would have been happy to be like him; by comparison he felt stiff and funereal. Everything about Matías astounded him: his impeccable style, his glacial irony, the ease with which he threw money around.

"I want you to be familiar with my business dealings. This is a vulgar and materialistic society, with very little respect for women. Here nothing matters except fortune and contacts—that's why I need you," Paulina announced to her nephew a few months after he arrived. "You will be my eyes and ears."

"I don't know anything about business."

"But I do. I'm not asking you to think, that's my job. You keep your mouth shut, watch, listen, and report to me. Then you do what I tell you, without asking too many questions. Are we clear on this?"

"Don't ask me to play any tricks, Aunt," Severo replied with dignity.

"I see you've heard gossip about me. Look, my boy, laws were invented by the strong in order to dominate the weak—there are so many more of them. But I have no obligation to respect those laws. I need a lawyer I have complete confidence in so I can do whatever I please without getting into trouble."

"In an honorable fashion, I hope," Severo warned.

"Oh, child! We won't get anywhere that way. Your honor will be safe, as long as you don't exaggerate."

So they sealed a pact as strong as the blood ties that united them. Paulina, who had taken him in with no expectations, convinced that he was a rogue or they would never have sent him to her from Chile, was happily surprised by this clever nephew with the noble sentiments. Within a few years, Severo had learned to speak English with a facility no one else in the family had shown; he had come to know his aunt's various undertakings like the palm of his hand, had traveled

twice across the United States by train—one of them attacked by
Mexican bandits—and even had time to complete his legal training.
Severo maintained a weekly correspondence with his cousin Nívea,
which with the passing years was becoming more intellectual than
romantic. She wrote him about the family and Chilean politics; he
bought her books and clipped articles about the advances of the suffragettes in Europe and the United States. The news that an amend-
ment to authorize the vote for women had been presented before the
North American Congress was celebrated by both, long distance, although they were in agreement that to imagine anything similar in
Chile was madness. "What do I gain by studying and reading so
much, Cousin," wrote his sweetheart, "if there is no place for action
in a woman's life? My mother says it will be impossible to marry me
off because I frighten men away, and that I should make myself pretty
and keep my mouth closed if I want a husband. My family applauds
the least sign of learning in my brothers—I say *least* because you already know how dim-witted they are—but in me the same achieve-
ment is considered boastful. The one person who tolerates me is my
uncle José Francisco, because I offer him the opportunity to talk
about science, astronomy, and politics, subjects he likes to hold forth
on, although my opinions don't matter to him. You cannot imagine
how I envy men like you, who have the world for a stage." Love
never took up more than a couple of lines in Nívea's letters and a
couple of words in Severo's, as if they had a tacit agreement to erase
their intense and hasty caresses in the corners. Twice a year, Nívea
sent Severo her photograph, so he could see that she was becoming a
woman; he promised to send her one but always forgot, as he also
forgot to tell her that he would not be coming home that Christmas.
Another girl, one in greater haste to marry than Nívea, would have
angled her antennae to locate a less evasive sweetheart, but she never
doubted that Severo del Valle would be her husband. So sure was she
that their separation, which dragged on for years, did not overly concern her; she was prepared to wait to the end of time. As for Severo,

he held the memory of his cousin as a symbol of everything good, noble, and pure.

Matías's appearance possibly justified his mother's opinion that he was nothing but a well-dressed fool, but there was nothing of the fool about him. He had visited all the important museums of Europe, he knew about art, he could recite every classical poet who ever lived, and he was the one person who used the library in their home. He cultivated his own style, a mixture of bohemian and dandy: of the former he had the habit of nightlife and of the latter his mania for details of haberdashery. He was considered the best catch in San Francisco, but he made no bones about being a confirmed bachelor; he preferred a trivial conversation with the worst of his male enemies to a tryst with the most attractive of his female admirers. The only place his life might coincide with a woman's was for procreation, he said, a proposition absurd in itself. To answer the demands of nature he preferred a professional from among the many who were available. A late night among gentlemen that did not end with a brandy at the bar and a visit to a brothel was inconceivable; there were more than a quarter million prostitutes in the country, and a good percentage of them earned their living in San Francisco, from the miserable Singsong Girls of Chinatown to refined ladies from southern states forced by the Civil War into life as courtesans. The young heir, so little tolerant of feminine weaknesses, was a model of patience with the gross behavior of his bohemian friends; that was another of his eccentricities, like his taste for thin black cigarettes, which he ordered from Egypt, and for real and literary crimes. He lived in his parents' palatial home on Nob Hill and maintained a luxurious apartment in the heart of the city, crowned by a spacious garret he called the *garçonnière*, where he occasionally painted and frequently hosted soirées. He mixed with the bohemian underworld, poor devils sunk in stoic and inescapable poverty: poets, journalists, photographers, aspiring writers and artists, men without families who spent their lives half ill, coughing and conversing, and who lived on credit and never wore a watch because time had not been invented for them. Behind the back of the aristocratic Chilean, they made fun of his clothes and his manners, but they put up with him because they could always come to him for a few dollars, a drink of whiskey, or a spot in his garret to spend a foggy night.

"Have you noticed that Matías has the mannerisms of a sodomite?" Paulina commented to her husband.

"How could you even think of saying such a barbarous thing about your own son!" protested Feliciano. "We've never had one of those in my family, or in yours!"

"Do you know any normal man who matches the color of his muffler to his wallpaper?" snorted Paulina.

"All right, goddammit! You're his mother, and it's up to you to find a sweetheart for him! This boy is already thirty and is still a bachelor. You'd better be finding one soon, before we have a tubercular alcoholic on our hands, or worse," warned Feliciano, unaware that it was already too late for lukewarm measures of salvation.

On one of those nights of chilling winds so typical of summer in San Francisco, Williams, the butler of the swallowtail coat, knocked at the door of Severo del Valle's room.

"Forgive the intrusion, sir," he murmured with a discreet cough, entering with a three-candle candelabrum in his gloved hand.

"What is it, Williams?" asked Severo, alarmed because it was the first time anyone had interrupted his sleep in that house.

"I fear we have a small difficulty on our hands. It's Mr. Matías," said Williams, with that pompous British deference, unknown in California, that always sounded more ironic than respectful. At that late hour, he explained, a message had been delivered to the house, sent by a lady of doubtful reputation, one Amanda Lowell, whom the young gentleman often visited, one of those people from "a different ambience," as Williams put it. Severo read the note by the light of the candles: only three lines, seeking immediate help for Matías.

"We must advise my aunt and uncle—Matías may have had an accident," Severo del Valle decided.

"Look at the address, sir. Right in the very center of Chinatown. It seems to me that it would be better if the master and his lady were not informed," suggested the butler.

"Really! I thought you had no secrets from my aunt Paulina."

"I try to avoid upsetting her, sir."

"What do you suggest we do?"

"If it is not asking too much, that you don your clothing, collect your weapon, and come with me."

Williams had waked a stable boy to ready one of the coaches, but since he wanted to keep the matter as quiet as possible, he himself took the reins and drove purposefully through the dark, empty streets toward the Chinese quarter, guided by the instinct of the horses after the wind kept blowing out the lamps on the carriage. Severo had the impression that this was not the first time the man had driven through these alleyways. Soon they got out of the coach and on foot plunged into a passageway that opened onto a shadowy courtyard filled with a strange, sweetish odor like roasted nuts. There was not a soul to be seen and no sound but the wind, and the only light filtered through the chinks in a pair of small windows at street level. Williams struck a match, once more read the address on the paper, and without cere-mony pushed one of the doors that opened onto the courtyard. Severo, with his hand on his weapon, followed. They walked into a small, unventilated though clean and neat room in which they could barely breathe for the dense aroma of opium. Around a center table, lined against the walls, were wooden compartments, one above another like berths on a ship, covered by a mat and with a block of hollowed-out wood in way of a pillow. These spaces were occupied by Chinese, sometimes two in a cubicle, lying on one side facing small trays con-taining a box with a black paste and a small lighted lamp. It was long past midnight, and the drug had already exerted its effect on most. Lethargic, the men lay wandering through their dreams; only two or three still had the strength to dip a thin metal rod into the opium, heat it over the lamp, fill the tiny thimble of the pipe, and inhale through the bamboo stem.

"Good God!" murmured Severo, who had heard of this but never seen it.

"It is less harmful than alcohol, if you will allow me to say so," replied Williams. "It does not induce violence, and it does no harm to others, only the person who smokes it. You may note how much calmer and cleaner this place is than any drinking establishment."

An ancient Chinese man dressed in a tunic and wide-legged cotton trousers limped forward to meet them. His red-rimmed eyes peered from between deep wrinkles; he had a sparse mustache, gray like the thin queue hanging down his back, and all his fingernails, except for thumb and index, were so long that they turned back on themselves, like the tail of some antediluvian mollusk. His mouth was a black hollow, and his few remaining teeth were stained by tobacco and opium. This lame great-grandfather spoke to the new arrivals in Chinese, and to Severo's surprise the English butler answered with a couple of barks in the same tongue. There was a very long pause in which no one moved. The Chinese man locked eyes with William, as if he were studying him, and finally he held out his hand, into which Williams deposited a few dollars the old man stowed beneath his tunic next to his heart. Then he picked up a candle stub and made signs that they should follow him. They passed through a second room, and then a third and a fourth, all similar to the first; they walked the length of a twisting corridor, went down a short staircase, and found themselves in another hallway. Their guide indicated that they should wait, and disappeared for a time that seemed endless. Severo, sweating, kept his finger on the trigger of his cocked weapon, alert and afraid to say a word. Finally the great-grandfather returned to lead them through a labyrinth to a closed door, which he contemplated with absurd attention, like someone deciphering a map, until Williams handed him an additional couple of dollars. Then he opened it. They entered a room smaller even than the others, darker, more smoke-filled, and more oppressive, because it was below street level and there was no ventilation; in all other details it was identical to the previous ones. On wooden litters lay five white Americans, four men and a middle-aged but still splendid woman with a cascade of red hair spilling out around her like an incandescent mantle. To judge by their fine clothing, these were well-to-do people. All were in the same state of happy stupor, except one who lay on his back barely breathing, his shirt ripped, his arms spread wide, his skin the color of chalk, and his eyes turned back in his head. It was Matías Rodríguez de Santa Cruz.

"Come, sir, assist me," Williams ordered Severo del Valle.

Between them, they succeeded in lifting him; each placed one of the unconscious man's arms around his neck, and that was how they carried him, like someone crucified: head hanging, body limp, feet dragging the dirt floor. They retraced the long way back through narrow passageways and suffocating rooms, one after the other, until suddenly they were out in the open air, in the incredible purity of the night, where they could take deep, eager, dazed breaths. They made Matías as comfortable as they could in the carriage, and Williams drove them to the *garçonnière,* which Severo had supposed his aunt's employee knew nothing about. Even greater was his surprise when Williams pulled out a key, opened the main door to the building, and then another to open the door to the garret.

"Then this isn't the first time you've rescued my cousin, Williams?"

"Let us say that it will not be the last," he replied.

They laid Matías on a bed in the corner of the room, behind a Japanese screen, and Severo proceeded to moisten his face with damp cloths and shake him to bring him back from the nirvana in which he was floating, while Williams went out to look for the family doctor, after warning that it would not be a good plan to notify Severo's aunt and uncle of what had occurred.

"My cousin may die!" exclaimed Severo, still trembling.

"In that eventuality we may have to inform the master and mistress," Williams conceded courteously.

Matías lay five days struggling through spasms of agony, poisoned to the marrow. Williams brought a nurse to the garret to look after him and made arrangements so that his absence would not be a cause of scandal at home. This incident created a strange bond between Severo and Williams, a tacit complicity that was never translated into actions or words. With another individual less hermetic than the butler, Severo would have thought he shared a kind of friendship, or at least that they liked each other, but the Englishman raised an impenetrable wall of reserve around himself. Severo began to observe him. He treated the employees under his orders with the same cool and impeccable civility he extended to his employers, and in that way succeeded in terrorizing them. Nothing escaped his vigilance, from the gleam of the ornate silver tableware to the secrets of each resident in that immense house. It was impossible to calculate his age or origins; he seemed eternally stalled in his forties and, except for the British accent, gave no hint of his past. He changed his white gloves thirty times a day, his black wool suit seemed always recently pressed, his snow-white shirt of the best Dutch linen was starched like cardboard, and his shoes gleamed like mirrors. He sucked mint pastilles for his breath and used eau de cologne, but he did so with such discretion that the only time Severo perceived the scent of mint and lavender was the time in the opium den when he had brushed against him as they lifted the unconscious Matías. On that occasion, Severo had also noticed the wood-hard muscles beneath the swallowtail coat, the tense tendons in his neck, as well as the man's strength and flexibility, none of which fit in with the picture of an English lord down on his luck.

As cousins, Severo and Matías had in common only their patrician features and a taste for sports and literature. In all else they seemed not to be of the same blood: the former was as noble, fearless, and naive as the latter was cynical, indolent, and libertine. But despite their contrasting temperaments and the years that separated them, they formed a friendship. Matías made a great effort to teach Severo to fence—though he lacked the elegance and quickness indispensable for that art—and to initiate him into the pleasures of San Francisco, but the younger man turned out to be a bad companion in revelry because he tended to fall asleep on his feet. He worked fourteen hours a day in the law office and spent the remaining hours reading and studying. The two cousins often swam naked in the pool in the mansion, and challenged each other to contests of Greco-Roman wrestling. They would dance about each other, alert, preparing to spring, and finally they would attack, scrambling for balance, rolling until one succeeded in subduing the other, pinning him to the floor. They would be wet with sweat, panting, excited. Severo would push away, perturbed, as if the competition had been an unconfessable embrace. They talked about books and commented on the classics. Matías loved poetry, and when they were alone recited from memory, so moved by the beauty of the verses that tears ran down his cheeks. Severo was also disturbed on those occasions because his cousin's intense emotion seemed to him a kind of intimacy forbidden between men. He lived for news of scientific advances and journeys of exploration, which he told Matías about in a vain attempt to interest him, but the only news that managed to dent his cousin's armor of indifference had to do with local crimes. Matías had a curious relationship, based on liters of whiskey, with Jacob Freemont, an old and unscrupulous journalist always short of funds, with whom he shared a morbid fascination for criminal behavior. Freemont still worked the police beat for the newspapers, but he had lost his reputation many years before when he invented the story of Joaquín Murieta, a supposed Mexican bandit during the days of the gold rush. His articles had created a myth and fueled the hatred of the white population toward Spanish-speaking peoples. To calm things, the authorities offered a reward to a certain Captain Harry Love to hunt down Murieta.

After three months of riding around California in hot pursuit, the captain chose an expeditious solution: he killed seven Mexicans in an ambush and brought back a head and a hand. No one could identify the remains, but Love's exploit reassured the whites. The macabre trophies were still being exhibited in a museum, though there was a consensus that Joaquín Murieta was a monstrous creation of the press in general and of Jacob Freemont in particular. That and other episodes in which the newspaperman's guileful pen muddied reality finally won him the reputation of being a liar, and closed doors to him. Thanks to his strange connection with Freemont, the crime reporter, Matías was able to view murder victims before their bodies were removed and to witness autopsies at the morgue, spectacles that repelled as much as excited him. He would emerge from those adventures in the underworld of crime drunk with horror, proceed directly to the Turkish bath, where he spent hours sweating out the stench of death clinging to his skin, and then close himself in his *garçonnière* to paint disastrous scenes of people chopped into bits.

"What does all this mean?" asked Severo, the first time he saw those Dantesque paintings.

"Aren't you fascinated by the idea of death? Homicide is a tremendous adventure, and suicide is a practical solution. I toy with the idea of both. Some people deserve to be murdered, don't you agree? And as for me, cousin, well, I don't plan to die a decrepit old man. I would rather end my days with the same care I use in choosing my suits, and that's why I study crimes, as training."

"You're mad. And, besides, you have no talent," Severo concluded.

"You don't need talent to be an artist, just audacity. Have you heard of the Impressionists?"

"No, but if this is what those poor devils paint, they won't get far. Couldn't you find a more agreeable subject? A pretty girl, for example?"

Matías burst out laughing and announced that on Wednesday

there would be a truly pretty young girl at his *garçonnière*, the most beautiful in San Francisco according to popular opinion, he added. She was a model his friends fought to immortalize in clay, on canvas, and on photographic plates, with the additional hope of making love to her. They exchanged bets to see who would be the first, but for the moment no one had succeeded in so much as touching her hand.

"She suffers from a detestable defect: virtue. She's the only virgin left in California, although that's easy to cure. Would you like to meet her?"

And that was how Severo del Valle came to see Lynn Sommers again. Until that day he had limited himself to secretly buying post-cards with her image in shops for tourists and hiding them in the pages of his law books, like a shameful treasure. Many times he hung around the street on Union Square where the tea shop was located, hoping to see her from afar, and he made discreet inquiries of the coachman who drove every day to pick up pastries for Paulina del Valle, but he had never dared introduce himself honorably to Eliza Sommers and ask permission to visit her daughter. Any direct action seemed an irreparable betrayal of Nívea, his cherished lifetime sweet-heart. It would be a different matter, he had decided, if he ran into Lynn accidentally, since in that case a meeting would be a prank of fate, and no one could blame him. It had never crossed his mind that he would see her in his cousin Matías's studio under such strange circumstances.

Lynn Sommers was the happy product of mixed races. Her name should have been Lin Chi'en, but her parents decided to Anglicize the names of their children and give them their mother's surname, Sommers, to make life easier for them in the United States, where the Chinese were treated like dogs. They named the older child Ebanizer, in honor of an old friend of his father, but called him Lucky because he had the best luck of anyone who had ever lived in Chinatown. Their younger child, a girl, born six years after their son, they named Lin in honor of her father's first wife, buried many years before in

Hong Kong, but when they filled out her birth certificate they used the English spelling: Lynn. Tao Chi'en's first wife, who bequeathed her name to the girl, had been a fragile creature with tiny bound feet, adored by her husband but crushed by consumption. Eliza Sommers learned to live with the ever-present memory of Lin, and came to think of her as just another member of the family, a kind of invisible protectress who looked out for the well-being of her home. Twenty years earlier, when Eliza had found she was pregnant again, she had asked Lin to help her carry the baby to term; she had already had several miscarriages, and she did not have much hope that her depleted body could sustain the pregnancy. That was how she explained it to Tao Chi'en, who each time before had placed all his resources as a *zhong-yi* at his wife's disposal, in addition to taking her to the best Western medicine specialists in California.

"This time we will have a healthy baby," Eliza assured him.

"How do you know," he asked.

"Because I asked Lin."

Eliza always believed that Tao's first wife had been by her side during the pregnancy and given her the strength to give birth to her daughter; then—like a good fairy—she had leaned over the cradle to offer the baby the gift of beauty. "She will be called Lin," the exhausted mother had announced when at last she held her daughter in her arms, but Tao Chi'en was frightened. It was not a good idea, he said, to give the child the name of a woman who had died so young. Finally they changed the spelling to keep from tempting fate. "It's pronounced the same," Eliza concluded. "That's all that counts."

On her mother's side, Lynn Sommers had English and Chilean blood, and from her father the genes of the tall Chinese of the north. Tao Chi'en's grandfather, a humble healer, had handed down to his male descendents his knowledge of medicinal plants and magic incantations for curing various ills of the body and mind. Tao Chi'en, the last of that line, had enriched the paternal legacy by training to be a *zhong-yi* with a wise man from Canton, and also through a lifetime of study, not only of traditional Chinese medicine but of everything that fell into his hands concerning Western medical science. He had built a solid reputation in San Francisco, and though he was consulted by American doctors and had patients of several races, he was not allowed to work in their hospitals; his practice was limited to the Chinese quarter, where he had bought a house large enough to install his clinic on the first floor and his residence on the second. His reputation protected him; no one interfered in his activities with the Singsong Girls, as those pathetic sex slaves, all children really, were known in Chinatown. Tao Chi'en had taken on his shoulders the mission of rescuing as many of them as he could from the brothels. The tongs that controlled and sold protection in the Chinese community knew that he was buying the tiny prostitutes to give them a second chance far away from California. He had been threatened a couple of times, but nothing drastic had happened to him because sooner or later some member of a tong might need the services of the famed *zhong-yi*. As long as Tao Chi'en didn't go to the American authorities, acted discreetly, and rescued the girls one by one with antlike patience, he was tolerated because his actions did not make a dent in the enormous profits of the enterprise. The one person who looked on Tao Chi'en as a public menace was Ah Toy, the most successful madam in San Francisco and the owner of several houses that specialized in adolescent Asian girls. She alone imported hundreds of young victims every year, right past the American customs officers, who, duly bribed, looked the other way. Ah Toy detested Tao Chi'en and, as she had often said, would rather die than consult him again. She had done that once when very ill from a cough no one could cure, but on that occasion both had understood that they would always be mortal enemies.

Every Singsong Girl Tao Chi'en saved was a bamboo shoot driven under Ah Toy's fingernail, whether or not the girl belonged to her. To Ah Toy, as well as to Tao Chi'en, the Singsong Girls' fate was a matter of principle.

• • •

Tao Chi'en always rose before dawn and went out into the garden, where he performed martial exercises to keep his body in shape and his mind clear. After that he meditated for thirty minutes and then lit the fire for the kettle. He would wake Eliza with a kiss and a cup of green tea, which she slowly sipped in bed. That moment was sacred for them both; the cups of tea they drank together sealed the night they had shared tightly embraced. What happened between them behind the closed door of their room compensated for all the day's efforts. Their love had begun as a gentle friendship, subtly woven in the midst of a tangle of obstacles ranging from being able to communicate only in English and having to overcome prejudices of culture and race to the difference in their ages. They had lived and worked together under the same roof for more than three years before they dared cross the invisible frontier that separated them. Eliza had been driven to wander in circles for thousands of miles of an endless journey pursuing a hypothetical lover who slipped through her fingers like a shadow. Along that road she would leave her past and her innocence in tatters and confront her obsessions before the decapitated, gin-preserved head of the legendary bandit Joaquín Murieta finally to understand that her destiny was Tao Chi'en. The *zhong-yi*, in contrast, had known that long before, and had waited for Eliza with the quiet tenacity of his mature love.

The night when finally Eliza dared travel the twenty-four feet of corridor that separated her room from that of Tao Chi'en, their lives changed completely, as if the past had been chopped off with one swipe of a hatchet. Beginning with that ardent night there was not the least hint of temptation to turn back, only the challenge of carving out a space in a world that did not tolerate the mixing of races. Eliza went there barefoot, in her nightgown, feeling her way in the shadow; she pushed Tao Chi'en's door, certain she would find it unlocked, because she sensed that he wanted her as much as she wanted him, but despite that certainty she was frightened by the finality of her decision. She had hesitated for a long time before taking that step because the *zhong-yi* was her protector, her father, her brother, her best friend, her only family in that foreign land. She was afraid she would lose everything when he became her lover, but she was standing at Tao's threshold and her eagerness to touch him was stronger than the sophistries of reason. She went into the room, and in the candlelight she saw Tao sitting cross-legged on the bed, dressed in white cotton tunic and trousers, waiting for her. Eliza did not have time to wonder how many nights he had spent that way, listening for the sound of her footsteps in the corridor, dazed as she was by her own boldness, trembling with shyness and anticipation. Tao Chi'en did not give her the opportunity to retreat. He came to meet her, opened his arms to her, and she walked forward blindly until she bumped against his chest, in which she buried her face, breathing the familiar salty sea scent of that man, clinging with both hands to his tunic because her knees were buckling beneath her, while a river of explanations poured from her lips and blended with the words of love he was murmuring in Chinese. She felt arms lifting her from the floor and gently placing her on the bed; she felt warm breath on her neck, and hands holding her, then she was seized by an uncontainable anxiety and she began to shiver, frightened and contrite.

From the time his wife died in Hong Kong, Tao Chi'en had occasionally consoled himself in the hasty embraces of paid women. He had not made loving love for more than six years, but he did not allow his eagerness to run away with him. So many times he had gone over Eliza's body in his thoughts, and he knew her so well that it was like exploring her soft valleys and gentle hills with a map. She thought she had known love in the arms of her first lover, but intimacy with Tao Chi'en revealed to her the extent of her ignorance. The passion that had swept over her at sixteen, a passion for which she had traveled halfway across the world and more than once risked her life, had been a mirage that seemed absurd by comparison. Then she had been in love with love, making do with the crumbs given her by a man more interested in leaving than in staying with her. She had searched for him four years, convinced that the young idealist she had known in Chile had in California been transformed into the fabled bandit Joaquín Murieta. During that time Tao Chi'en had waited with his proverbial calm, sure that sooner or later Eliza would cross the threshold that separated them. It was he who had accompanied her when the head of Joaquín Murieta had been exhibited as entertainment for Americans and as a warning to Latins. He had thought that Eliza would not be able to bear the sight of that repulsive trophy, but she had stopped before the large jar containing the head of the supposed criminal and looked at it without emotion, as if it were a marinated head of cabbage, until she was very sure that it was not the man whom she had followed for years. In truth, it didn't matter; on the long trail of an impossible romance, Eliza had acquired something as precious as love: freedom. "I am free," was all she had said when she viewed the head. Tao Chi'en understood that at last she had shed the burden of her former lover, that it didn't matter whether he was alive or had died looking for gold in the foothills of the Sierra Nevada; in any case she would not be searching any longer, and if one day the man appeared she would be able to see him in his true light. Tao Chi'en had taken Eliza's hand and they had left that sinister exhibition. Outside, they breathed the fresh air and walked away, at peace and ready to begin a new stage in their lives.

The night that Eliza went into Tao Chi'en's room was very different from the nights of secret and hurried embraces with her first lover in Chile. With Tao she discovered some of the many possibilities of pleasure and was initiated into the fathomless love that was to be hers for the rest of her life. With complete serenity, Tao Chi'en began freeing her from layers of accumulated fears and useless memories, caressing her with inexhaustible dedication until she stopped trembling and opened her eyes, until she relaxed beneath his wise fingers, until he felt her move like waves under his hands, open to him, illuminated from within. He heard her moan, call to him, plead with

him: he saw her yielding, moist, eager to give herself and take him
with complete abandon, until neither knew where they found themselves or who they were, where he ended and she began. Tao Chi'en
led her beyond orgasm to a mysterious dimension where love and
death are interchangeable. They felt their spirits were expanding, that
desires and memory had disappeared, that they gave themselves to
one another in an enormous pool of bright light. They held each
other in that extraordinary space, recognizing each other, perhaps because they had been there in earlier lives and would be many times
more in future lives, as Tao Chi'en suggested. They were lovers for all
eternity; their karma, he said with emotion, was to seek and find each
other, but Eliza laughed and replied that it was nothing as solemn as
karma, only a simple urge to fornicate, that to tell the truth she had
been dying to do that with him for several years and was hoping that
in the future Tao's enthusiasm would not flag because that was going
to be her priority in life. They pleasured themselves that night and a
good part of the following day, until hunger and thirst forced them to
stagger from the room, drunken and happy, holding hands for fear
that they would suddenly wake and discover that they had been wandering lost in an hallucination.

The passion that joined them from that night, and that they nourished with extraordinary care, sustained and protected them in their
inevitable moments of adversity. With time that passion resolved into
tenderness and laughter; they ceased to explore the two hundred
twenty-two ways to make love because they were satisfied with three
or four, and now they felt no compulsion to surprise each other. The
better they came to know each other, the greater was their affection.
From that first night of love, they slept in a tight knot, breathing the
same breaths and dreaming the same dreams. That did not mean their
lives were easy. They had been together for almost thirty years in a
world that had no place for a couple like them. Over the course of the
years, the small white woman and the tall Chinese man became a familiar sight in Chinatown, but they were never completely accepted.

They learned not to touch in public, to sit apart in the theater, and to walk down the street with some distance between them. In certain restaurants and hotels they could not go in together, and when they went to England—she to visit her adoptive mother, Rose Sommers, and he to give lectures on acupuncture at the Hobbs clinic—they could not travel in the first-class section of the ship or share a stateroom, although at night she would slip stealthily down the hall to sleep with him. They were married in a discreet Buddhist ceremony, but their union had no legal standing. Lucky and Lynn were registered as illegitimate children recognized by the father. Tao Chi'en had managed to become a citizen after an infinite number of negotiations and bribes; he was one of the few who escaped the Chinese Exclusion Act, another of the discriminatory laws of California. His admiration for and loyalty to his adoptive country was unconditional, as he had demonstrated during the Civil War, when he traveled across the continent to offer himself as a volunteer at the front and work as aid to Yankee medics for the four years of the conflict, but he felt profoundly foreign, and although he had spent all his life in America, he wanted his body to be buried in Hong Kong.

The family of Eliza Sommers and Tao Chi'en lived in a spacious and comfortable house more solid and of better construction than most in Chinatown. All around them the main language was Cantonese, and everything from food to newspapers was Chinese. Several blocks away was La Misión, where the Spanish speakers lived and where Eliza Sommers used to stroll for the sole pleasure of hearing her language, but her day was spent among Americans in the vicinity of Union Square, where her elegant tea room was located. With her pastries, Eliza had from the beginning contributed to the upkeep of the family. A major part of Tao Chi'en's income ended up in the hands of others: what didn't go toward helping poor Chinese laborers in times of sickness or misfortune would likely be spent at the clandestine auctions of child slaves. Saving those creatures from a life of ignominy had become Tao Chi'en's sacred mission; Eliza Sommers knew that from the beginning and accepted it as characteristic of her husband, another of the many reasons she loved him. She set up her pastry shop so she would not have to torment him by asking for money; she needed independence to give her children the best American education, for she wanted them to integrate completely in the United States and live without the limitations imposed on either Chinese or Chileans. With Lynn she succeeded, but her plans went awry with Lucky—the boy was proud of his origins and had no intention of ever leaving Chinatown.

Lynn adored her father—impossible not to love that gentle, generous man—but she was ashamed of her race. She realized at an early age that the only place for Chinese was their quarter; they were detested in the rest of the city. The favorite sport of white youths was to stone the Celestials or cut off their queues after beating them up. Like her mother, Lynn lived with one foot in China and the other in the United States; they both spoke English and dressed in the American style, even though at home they usually wore silk tunics and trousers. Lynn had little of her father about her, except for her long bones and Oriental eyes, and even less of her mother. No one knew where her rare beauty had come from. Her parents never let her play outdoors, as they had her brother Lucky, because in Chinatown women and girls from proper families were recluses. On the rare occasions that she walked through the quarter, she held her father's hand and kept her eyes lowered to keep from provoking the almost exclusively male throngs. Father and daughter attracted attention: she for her beauty and he because he dressed like an American. Tao Chi'en had years before renounced the typical queue of his people, and he wore his hair short and combed straight back; he dressed in an impeccable black suit, a shirt with a celluloid collar, and a top hat. Outside Chinatown, however, Lynn went around as free as any white girl. She attended a Presbyterian school where she learned the rudiments of Christianity, which, added to the Buddhist practices of her father, eventually convinced her that Christ was the reincarnation of Buddha. She went shopping alone, as she did to her piano lessons and to visit her school friends; in the afternoons she sat in her mother's tearoom, where she did her homework and entertained herself rereading the romantic novels she bought for ten cents or that her aunt Rose sent her from London. Eliza Sommers's efforts to interest Lynn in the kitchen or in other domestic activities were futile: her daughter did not seem cut out for everyday chores.

As she grew older, Lynn kept her exotic angel face, but her body began to round with perturbing curves. For years her photographs had circulated without major consequences, but everything changed when by fifteen she was fully developed and had become aware of the devastating effect she had on men. Her mother, terrified by the consequences of that tremendous power, tried to tame her daughter's bent for seduction, driving home the norms of modesty and teaching her to walk like a soldier, without moving her shoulders or hips. But to no avail; men of every age, race, and condition turned to stare at her. Once Lynn understood the advantages of her beauty, she stopped cursing it, as she had when she was young, and decided that she would be an artist's model for a while until a prince on a winged horse came along to lead her to matrimonial bliss. During her childhood, her parents had tolerated the photographs of fairies and swings, thinking of them as an innocent caprice, but they considered it an enormous risk to let her show off her new womanly image in front of the cameras. "This business of posing isn't decent work, it will be her ruination," Eliza Sommers determined sadly; she knew that she could not dissuade her daughter from fantasies or protect her from the trap of beauty. She presented her qualms to Tao Chi'en in one of those perfect moments when they were resting after making love. He explained to her that every person has his or her karma, that it isn't possible to direct others' lives, only sometimes to amend the direction of one's own, but Eliza was not prepared to allow misfortune to catch her daughter off guard. She had always accompanied Lynn when she posed for photographs, making sure of their decency—no bare calves using the excuse of art—and now that the girl was nineteen, she was ready to redouble her zeal.

"There's this painter following Lynn around. He wants her to pose for a painting of Salome," she announced to her husband one day.

"Who?"

"Salome. The one with the seven veils, Tao. Read the Bible."

"If she's in the Bible, I suppose it's all right," he murmured absentmindedly.

"Do you know what the fashion was in the time of Saint John the Baptist? If I don't keep an eye on her, they'll be painting your daughter with her breasts bared!"

"Then keep an eye on her." Tao smiled. He caught his wife about the waist and pulled her down onto the large book open on his knees, telling her she shouldn't be frightened by tricks of the imagination.

"Oh, Tao! What are we going to do about Lynn?"

"Nothing, Eliza. She will marry one day and give us grandchildren."

"She's still a child!"

"In China she would already be too old to get a bridegroom."

"We're in America, and she's not going to marry a Chinese man," she said with conviction.

"Why? Don't you like Chinese?" the *zhong-yi* teased.

"There isn't another man like you in all the world, Tao, but I think Lynn will marry a white man."

"Americans don't know how to make love, I'm told."

"Maybe you could teach them." Eliza blushed, her nose in her husband's neck.

Lynn posed for the portrait of Salome wearing flesh-colored tights beneath her veils and scrupulously supervised by her mother, but Eliza Sommers could not take the same firm stand when her daughter was offered the enormous honor of modeling for the statue of the Republic that was to be displayed in the center of Union

Square. The campaign to raise funds had lasted for months, and people contributed what they were able: schoolchildren their pennies, widows a few dollars, and magnates like Feliciano Rodríguez de Santa Cruz fat checks. Every day the newspapers published the amount raised the day before, until enough had been gathered to commission the monument from a famous sculptor brought especially from Philadelphia to carry out that ambitious project. The most distinguished families in the city competed by giving parties and balls to allow the artist the opportunity of choosing their daughters; it was known that the model for the Republic would be the symbol of all San Francisco, and every young girl aspired to the distinction. The sculptor, a modern man with bold ideas, looked for weeks for the ideal girl, but none satisfied him. To represent this vigorous American nation composed of valiant immigrants from the four corners of the world, he announced, he wanted a model of mixed blood. The financiers of the project and the city officials were alarmed: whites could not imagine that people of another color were entirely human, and no one wanted to hear of a mulatto girl presiding over the city from atop the obelisque in Union Square, as the artist intended. California was in the vanguard in questions of art, said the newspaper editorials, but the business of the mulatto was a lot to ask. The sculptor was at the point of succumbing to the pressure and selecting a descendant of some Danes when by chance one day he went into Eliza Summers's pastry shop, planning to console himself with a chocolate éclair, and saw Lynn. There was the woman he had been seeking to pose for his sculpture: tall, beautifully proportioned, with perfect bones, and not only did she have the dignity of an empress and a face with classic features, she also had the stamp of exoticism he desired. There was something about her beyond mere harmony, something unique, a blend of East and West, of sensuality and innocence, of strength and delicacy, that seduced him completely. When he informed Eliza that he had chosen her daughter to be his model, convinced that he was bestowing a tremendous honor on that modest family of pastry makers, he encountered firm resistance. Eliza Sommers was fed up with wasting her time chaperoning Lynn in the studios of photographers whose only task consisted of pressing a button; just the idea of having to do that for this little man who would be creating a bronze sculpture several meters tall exhausted her. Lynn, however, was so proud of the possibility of being the Republic that Eliza could not refuse her. The sculptor found he had to pull out all the stops to convince the mother that a brief tunic was the appropriate attire for this work, because she couldn't see the relation between a North American republic and the clothing of ancient Greece, but finally they agreed that Lynn would pose with bare arms and legs, though with her breasts covered.

Lynn was indifferent to her mother's worries about protecting her virtue, lost as she was in her world of romantic fantasies. Except for her dazzling looks, Lynn was not outstanding; she was an ordinary young girl who collected china figurines and copied poems into notebooks with pink pages. Her languor was not elegance but laziness, and her melancholy shallowness, not mystery. "Just leave her alone; as long as I'm alive Lynn will never want for anything," Lucky had promised again and again, because he was the only one who fully understood how silly his sister was.

Lucky, several years older than Lynn, was a hundred percent Chinese. Except on the rare occasions when he had to sign some legal document or have his picture taken, he dressed in a smock, loose trousers, a sash at his waist, and slippers with wooden soles, but he also always wore a cowboy hat. He did not have his father's distinguished bearing, his mother's delicacy, or his sister's beauty; he had short legs, a square head, and a slightly greenish complexion. People found him attractive, nevertheless, because of his irresistible smile and contagious optimism, which came from the certainty that he was marked by good luck. Nothing bad could happen to him, he believed; his happiness and fortune had been guaranteed from birth. He had discovered that gift when he was nine years old, playing fan-tan with other boys; that day he had run into the house announcing that from that moment his name would be Lucky—instead of Ebanizer—and that he would not answer to any other name. Good luck had followed him everywhere; he won at every game of chance, and although he was rebellious and impertinent, he had never had problems with the tongs or the white authorities. Even the Irish policemen fell victim to his charm, and while his buddies got beatings, he got out of jams with a joke or a magic trick, one of the many he performed with his prodigious prestidigitator's hands. Tao Chi'en could not resign himself to the happy-go-lucky attitude of his only son and cursed the good star that allowed him to escape the hard work of ordinary mortals. It was not happiness he wished for him, but transcendence. He worried when he saw Lucky passing through this world like a songbird; with that attitude, he would damage his karma. Tao believed that the soul makes its way toward heaven through compassion and suffering, overcoming obstacles with nobility and generosity, but if Lucky's road was easy all the way, what would he have to overcome? In his next incarnation Tao feared his son would come back as a flea. His firstborn, whose duty was to help him in his old age and honor his memory after his death, should continue the noble family tradition of healing; he even dreamed of seeing him become the first Chinese-American physician with a diploma. Lucky, however, was horrified by foul-smelling potions and acupuncture needles; nothing repelled him as much as others' illnesses, and he could not understand his father's pleasure when faced with an infected bladder or face spotted with pustules. Until he was sixteen and out on his own, he had to assist in the consulting room, where Tao Chi'en drummed in the names of remedies and their applications and tried to teach Lucky the indefinable art of taking pulses, balancing energy, and identifying humors, subtleties that went in one ear and out the other. At least Lucky was not traumatized by those chores, as he was by the scientific tomes of Western medicine his father studied so faithfully. The surgical operations described in cruelest detail horrified him, as did the illustrations of bodies with peeled-back skin, their muscles, veins, and bones revealed, though not their modestly covered private parts. He never ran short of excuses for getting away from the clinic, but he was always available when it was time to hide one of the miserable Singsong Girls his father often brought to their house. That secret and dangerous activity was made to his measure. No one better than he for moving the lifeless girls under the very noses of the tongs; no one more skillful for spiriting them out of the quarter as soon as they had recovered a little; no one more ingenious in making them disappear forever on the four winds of freedom. He didn't do these things for reasons of compassion, as Tao Chi'en did, but rather for the excitement of taking risks and putting his good luck to the test.

Before she was nineteen, Lynn Sommers had rejected a number of suitors and was accustomed to male attentions, which she received with queenly disdain, for none of her admirers fit her image of a romantic prince, and none spoke the words her aunt Rose Sommers wrote in her novels; she judged every one of them to be ordinary, unworthy of her. She believed she had found the sublime destiny she so richly deserved when she met the one man who never looked at her twice, Matías Rodríguez de Santa Cruz. She had seen him several times from a distance, in the street or in a coach with Paulina del Valle, but they had never exchanged a word. He was older, and he moved in circles to which Lynn had no entrée; and had it not been for the statue of the Republic, they might never have crossed paths.

Under the pretext of supervising the costly project, the politicians and magnates who had contributed to the cost of the statue often met in the sculptor's studio. The artist basked in fame and loved the good life; while he worked, seemingly absorbed in fashioning the mold into which the bronze would be poured, he enjoyed the boisterous male companionship, along with the bottles of champagne, the fresh oysters, and the good cigars his visitors brought with them. On a platform, illuminated by a skylight in the ceiling where natural light filtered through, Lynn Sommers balanced on tiptoe, arms upraised, in a pose impossible to maintain for more than a few minutes; dressed in a light pleated tunic that hung from one shoulder to her knees, revealing her body as much as covering it, she held a laurel wreath in one hand and a parchment with the U.S. Constitution in the other. San Francisco was a good market for the female nude: all the bars displayed paintings of voluptuous odalisques, photographs of courtesans with exposed buttocks, and plaster frescoes on which nymphs were chased by tireless satyrs. A totally naked model would have provoked less curiosity than this girl who refused to remove her clothes and was never free of her mother's eagle eye. Eliza Sommers, in a dark dress, sitting stiffly in a chair beside the platform where her daughter was posing, kept watch, refusing the oysters and champagne offered in an attempt to distract her. Those foolish old men were motivated by lust, not love of art—that was clear as water. Eliza couldn't keep them from being there, but at least she could be sure that her daughter did not accept any invitations and, when possible, that she didn't laugh at their jokes or respond to their indiscreet questions. "Nothing is free in this world. You would pay a very dear price for those trinkets," she warned whenever her daughter grumbled about refusing a gift. Posing for the statue was an interminable and boring process that left Lynn numb with cold and with cramps in her legs. It was early January, and the stoves in the corners were far from successful in warming the high-ceilinged room with its swirling air currents. The sculptor worked in his coat, progressing at a maddening pace, undoing today what he had done yesterday, as if he really had no final concept despite the hundreds of sketches of the Republic pinned to the walls.

One fateful Tuesday, Feliciano Rodríguez de Santa Cruz appeared with his son Matías. Feliciano had heard of the exotic model, and he thought he should meet her before the monument was installed on the square and the girl's name came out in the newspaper, making her an inaccessible prey; that is, assuming that the monument was ever dedicated. At the rate things were going, it could well happen that before the bronze was poured, the opponents of the project would win the battle, and the whole thing would fade away. There were still many who were uncomfortable with the idea of a Republic that wasn't Anglo-Saxon. Feliciano's aging scoundrel's heart still fluttered at the scent of a conquest, which was why he was there. He was over sixty, but it didn't seem to him that the model's being under twenty was an insuperable obstacle; he was convinced that there was very little that money couldn't buy. All he needed was an instant to evaluate the situation when he saw Lynn on the platform, so young and vulnerable, shivering in her daring tunic in front of a studio of machos hoping to devour her. It wasn't compassion for the girl, however, or fear of the rivalry among the cannibals that stopped his initial impulse; it was Eliza Sommers. He recognized her at once, despite having seen her only a few times. He had never suspected that the model about whom he had heard so much was the daughter of one of his wife's old friends.

Lynn Sommers didn't notice Matías's presence until half an hour later, when the sculptor called an end to the session and she could hand over the laurel wreath and parchment and climb down from the platform. Her mother threw a blanket over her shoulders and poured her a cup of chocolate, leading her behind the screen where she would change her clothes. Matías was near the window, absentmindedly gazing out on the street. His were the only eyes that were not fixed on the girl. Lynn immediately noticed the man's virile good looks, his youth and breeding, his exquisite clothes and haughty bearing, the lock of chestnut hair falling carelessly onto his forehead, the perfect hands with gold rings on the little fingers. Amazed to find herself ignored, Lynn pretended to trip to draw his attention. Several hands hurried to support her, but not those of the dandy at the window, who barely swept his eyes over her, totally indifferent, as if she were part of the furniture. And then Lynn, her imagination galloping, decided without the least reason that this was the gallant promised for years in her romance novels. At last she had met her destiny. As she dressed behind the screen, her nipples were hard as pebbles.

Matías's indifference wasn't feigned; in fact he didn't notice the girl. He was there for reasons very distant from lust. He needed to talk with his father about money, and he hadn't found another opportunity to do so. He was up to his neck in trouble and needed a check that very day to cover his debts in a gambling house in Chinatown. His father had warned him that he didn't intend to continue paying for such diversions, and had it not been a matter of life or death, as Matías's creditors had let him know in no uncertain terms, he would have got the money little by little from his mother. This time, however, the Celestials were not disposed to wait, and Matías guessed, correctly, that the visit to the sculptor's studio would put his father in a good humor and it would be easy to get what he needed from him. It was several days later that, out carousing with his bohemian friends, he realized he had been in the same room with Lynn Sommers, the most sought-after girl of the moment. He had to make an effort to remember her, and even wondered whether he would be able to recognize her if he saw her in the street. When the bets began to fly as to who would be the first to seduce her, he listened out of inertia and then, with his habitual insolence, announced that he would do it in three steps. The first, he said, would be to get her to come alone to the *garçonnière* so he could introduce her to his friends; the second would be to convince her to pose nude before them; and the third would be to make love to her—all in the period of one month. When he had invited his cousin Severo del Valle to meet the prettiest woman in San Francisco that Wednesday afternoon, he was carrying out the first part of the bet. It had been easy to get Lynn's attention through the window of her mother's tea shop, then wait for her at the corner when she came out, using some invented pretext, walk with her a couple of blocks down the street, pay her a few compliments that would have sent a more experienced woman into gales of laughter, and set a rendezvous with her at his studio, warning her to come alone. He felt frustrated; he had supposed she would offer a more interesting challenge. Before the Wednesday of the rendezvous he didn't even have to expend much effort to seduce her: a few languid gazes, a brush of his lips upon her cheek, a few sighs and stock phrases in her ear were enough to disarm the girl-child trembling before him, swooning with love. To Matías, this feminine penchant for suffering and surrender was pathetic; it was precisely what he most detested about women, which was why he got along so well with Amanda Lowell, who shared the same attitude: a contempt for sentiment and a reverence for pleasure. Lynn, hypnotized like a mouse facing a cobra, at last had a target for the florid art of her love letters and her pictures of faint damsels and slick-haired gallants. She never suspected that Matías shared those romantic missives with his unsavory friends. When Matías tried to show them to Severo del Valle, his cousin refused. He still wasn't aware that the notes were sent by Lynn Sommers, but the idea of making fun of the love of an ingenuous young girl repelled him. "Apparently you are yet a gentleman, Cousin, but don't worry, curing that is as easy as curing virginity," commented Matías.

That memorable Wednesday, Severo del Valle accepted his cousin's invitation to meet the prettiest girl in San Francisco, as he had proclaimed her, and found that he was not the only person summoned for the occasion. There were at least a half dozen bohemians drinking and smoking at the *garçonnière*, along with the same red-haired woman he had seen for a few seconds two or so years before when he went with Williams to rescue Matías from the opium den. He knew who she was because his cousin had spoken of her, and her name circulated in the world of frivolous night revels. She was Amanda Lowell, a great friend of Matías, with whom he joked about the scandal she had unleashed in the days when she was Feliciano Rodríguez de Santa Cruz's lover. Matías had promised her that upon his parents' death he would give her the Neptune bed Paulina del Valle had ordered from Florence to spite her. La Lowell had little connection anymore with the life of a courtesan—in her mature years she had discovered how petulant and boring most men are— but she felt a deep affinity with Matías, despite their fundamental differences. That Wednesday she was sitting by herself, reclining on a sofa and drinking champagne, aware that for once she was not the center of attention. She had been invited so that at this first meeting Lynn Sommers would not be the only woman among men, lest she feel intimidated and leave.

After a few minutes there was a knock at the door; it was the famous model for the Republic, swathed in a heavy wool cape with a hood over her head. When she removed the mantle her virginal face was revealed; her black hair was parted in the middle and combed back into a simple bun. Severo del Valle felt his heart leap as all his blood rushed to his head, pounding at his temples like a regimental drum. He had never dreamed that the victim of his cousin's bet was Lynn Sommers. He couldn't speak, he didn't even greet her as the others did; he backed into a corner, and there he stayed through the hour of the girl's visit, paralyzed with anguish, his eyes never leaving her. He hadn't the slightest doubt about the outcome of the bet among this group of men. He saw Lynn Sommers as a lamb laid out on a sacrificial stone but still ignorant of its fate. A wave of loathing for Matías and his cohorts welled through his body, mixed with a deafening rage against Lynn. He could not comprehend how the girl could fail to recognize what was happening, why she didn't see the trap of that double entendre flattery, of the glass of champagne filled again and again, of the perfect red rose Matías pinned in her hair, all of it so predictable and vulgar that it nauseated him. "She must be hopelessly stupid," he thought, as sickened by her as by the others, but annihilated by the overflowing love that had for years been awaiting its chance to germinate and now exploded, leaving him stultified.

"Is anything wrong, Cousin?" Matías teased, handing Severo a glass.

Severo couldn't answer, and had to turn his head to hide his murderous state of mind, but his cousin had guessed his feelings and was prepared to carry the joke even further. When Lynn Sommers announced that she had to leave, after promising she would return the next week to pose for the cameras of the "artists," Matías asked his cousin to see her home. So that was how Severo del Valle found himself alone with the woman who had succeeded in holding at bay his long love for Nívea. He walked with Lynn the few blocks that separated Matías's studio from Eliza Sommers's tearoom, so upset that he couldn't even start a polite conversation. It was too late to tell Lynn about the bet; he knew that she had fallen in love with Matías with the same terrible obsession that he felt for her. She wouldn't believe him; she would feel insulted, and even if he explained that to Matías she was just a plaything, she would still march straight to the slaughterhouse, blinded by love. She was the one who broke the uncomfortable silence to ask if he was the Chilean cousin Matías had mentioned to her. Severo realized with absolute finality that the girl hadn't the least recollection of their first meeting years ago, when she was pasting pictures into an album by the light of the stained-glass window; she could not suspect that he had loved her from that moment with the tenacity of first love, nor could she have known that he hovered around the pastry shop, or that they had often passed in the street. Her eyes simply hadn't registered his presence. When they said good-bye, he handed her his calling card, bowed with the gesture of kissing her hand, and mumbled that if she ever needed him, please not to hesitate to call. From that day he avoided Matías and buried himself in study and work, hoping to get Lynn Sommers and the humiliating wager out of his mind. When his cousin invited him the following Wednesday to the second session, in which it was foreseen that the girl would take off her clothes, he insulted him. For several weeks he couldn't write a single line to Nívea, or read her letters, which he kept without opening, crushed with guilt. He felt filthy, as if he too were participating in soiling Lynn Sommers, and boasting about it.

Matías Rodríguez de Santa Cruz won his bet with little effort, but along the way his cynicism deserted him, and without wishing it he found himself trapped in the thing he feared most in this world: a sentimental entanglement. He didn't actually fall in love with the beautiful Lynn Sommers, but the unconditional love and innocence with which she gave herself to him actually moved him. The girl placed herself in his hands with total confidence, willing to do anything he asked, never judging his intentions or calculating the consequences. Matías gauged the measure of the absolute power he exercised over her when he saw her standing naked in his garret, red with confusion, covering her pubis and breasts with arms and hands in the center of a circle formed by his cronies, who were pretending to photograph her without veiling the rutting-dog excitement their cruel game aroused. Lynn did not have the hourglass body so much in vogue at the time, no hips and opulent breasts separated by an impossible waist; she was slim and sinuous, with long legs and round breasts tipped with dark nipples. Her skin was the color of summer fruit, and a mantle of smooth black hair fell to the middle of her back. Matías admired her as one more of the many objets d'art he collected; he thought she was exquisite, but congratulated himself that he wasn't attracted to her. Unmindful of her feelings, simply to show off before his friends and as an exercise in cruelty, he asked Lynn to open her arms. She looked at him a few seconds and then slowly obeyed, as tears of shame rolled down her cheeks. With her unexpected weeping, a frozen silence fell over the room; the men looked away and stood with cameras in hand, not knowing what to do, for what seemed a very long time. Then Matías, mortified for the first time in his life, picked up an overcoat and covered Lynn, wrapping her in his arms. "Everyone out! The party's over," he commanded his guests, who began to leave, one by one, perturbed.

Alone with Lynn, Matías sat her in his lap and began to rock her like a child, mentally asking her to forgive him but incapable of forming the words, as the girl kept weeping silently. At last he led her gently behind the screen to his bed and lay down with her, enfolding her like a brother, stroking her head, kissing her brow, moved by an unknown and powerful sentiment he could not name. He did not desire her, he wanted only to protect her and restore her innocence, but the impossible softness of Lynn's skin, the shining hair falling over him, her apple scent, undid him. The unreserved surrender of the nubile body opening at the touch of his hands surprised him, and without knowing how he found himself exploring her, kissing her with an anxiety no woman had ever evoked, placing his tongue in her mouth, her ears, on every inch of her body, crushing her, penetrating her in a storm of passion he could not control, riding her mercilessly, blind, unbridled, until he exploded in a devastating orgasm. For a brief instant they met in another dimension, defenseless, naked in body and mind. Matías had experienced an intimacy that until then he had avoided without knowing even that it existed; he had crossed a last frontier and found himself on the other side, stripped of will. He had had more lovers— female and male—than he liked to remember, but he had never lost control in that way, lost irony, distance, the notion of his own inviolable individuality to fuse so simply with another human being. In a certain way, he had yielded *his* virginity in that embrace. The journey lasted only a fraction of time, but it was enough to terrify him; he returned to his body exhausted, and immediately began assuming the armor of his habitual sarcasm. When Lynn opened her eyes he was already not the same man with whom she had made love but the one he had always been—though she lacked the experience to know that. Aching, bleeding, happy, she had abandoned herself to the mirage of an illusory love; Matías continued to hold her, though his mind was already far away. They lay like that until light faded from the window and Lynn realized she had to hurry back to her mother. Matías helped her dress and walked with her to within sight of the tearoom. "Wait for me, I'll come tomorrow at the same time," she whispered as they said good-bye.

· · ·

Severo del Valle knew nothing about what had happened that day, or the events that followed, until three months later. In April 1879 Chile declared war on her neighbors, Peru and Bolivia, in a dispute over land, nitrates, and pride. The War of the Pacific had begun. When the news reached San Francisco, Severo went to his aunt and uncle to notify them that he was leaving to join the fight.

"Didn't we agree that you were never going near a barracks again?" his aunt Paulina reminded him.

"This is different—my country is in danger."

"You're a civilian."

"I'm a sergeant in the reserves," he corrected.

"The war will be over before you can get to Chile. Let's see what the newspapers have to say, and what your family thinks. Don't rush into this," his aunt counseled.

"It is my duty." Severo was thinking about his grandfather, the patriarch Agustín del Valle, who had recently died, shrunken to the size of a chimpanzee but with his bad disposition intact.

"Your duty is here, with me. The war is good for business. This is the moment to speculate in sugar," Paulina argued.

"Sugar?"

"None of those three countries produces it, and in times of trouble people eat more sweets."

"How do you know that, Aunt?"

"Personal experience, my boy."

Severo left to pack his suitcases, though he would not leave on the ship that sailed for the south days later, as he had planned, but at the end of October. That same night he packed his aunt told him they were expecting a strange visit and she wanted him to be present because her husband was on a trip and the matter might require the counsel of a lawyer. At seven that evening Williams, with the air of disdain he adopted when obliged to serve people of inferior social rank, showed in a tall, gray-haired Chinese man dressed in severe black and a small woman with a youthful and inoffensive appearance, but haughty as Williams himself. Tao Chi'en and Eliza Sommers found themselves in the wild game salon, as it was called, surrounded by lions, elephants, and other African beasts staring down at them from their gilded frames. Paulina frequently saw Eliza at her pastry shop but she had never come across her anywhere else; they belonged to separate worlds. Nor did she know the Celestial who, to judge by the way he was holding Eliza's arm, must be her husband or her lover. Paulina felt ridiculous in her forty-five-room palace, dressed in black silk and dripping with diamonds, facing that modest couple who greeted her with simplicity, maintaining their distance. She noticed that her son Matías acknowledged them nervously with only a nod, without offering his hand, and took a seat apart from the group behind a jacaranda wood desk, apparently absorbed in cleaning his pipe. Severo del Valle hadn't a glimmer of doubt as to why Lynn Sommers's parents were in the house, and he wished he were a thousand leagues away. Intrigued, on her guard, Paulina did not waste time by offering them something to drink but gestured to Williams to retire and close the doors. "What can I do for you?" she asked. Then Tao Chi'en began to explain, with no change of expression, that his daughter Lynn was pregnant, that the author of that offense was Matías, and that he expected the only possible restitution. For once in her life, the del Valle matriarch lost her tongue. She sat stunned, gasping like a beached whale, and when finally she got her voice back, it was to squawk like a crow.

"Mother, I have no connection with these people. I do not know them, and I do not know what they are talking about," said Matías from the desk, carved ivory pipe in hand.

"Lynn has told us everything," Eliza interrupted, getting to her feet, her voice quivering but holding back the tears.

"If it's money you want—" Matías began, but his mother cut him off with a ferocious glare.

"You must forgive us," Paulina said, speaking to Tao Chi'en and Eliza Sommers. "My son is as surprised as I am. I'm sure we can work this out in a decent way, whatever's right."

"Lynn wishes to marry, of course. She has told us that you two are in love," said Tao Chi'en, also standing by now, speaking to Matías, who responded with a curt laugh that sounded like a dog barking.

"You seem like respectable people," said Matías. "Nonetheless, your daughter is not, as any of my friends can attest. I don't know which of them is responsible for your unhappy circumstance, but certainly I am not."

Eliza Sommers had completely lost her color. She was as pale as plaster and trembling so hard she seemed about to fall. Tao Chi'en took her firmly by the arm and, supporting her as he would an invalid, led her toward the door. Severo del Valle thought he would die of anguish and shame, as if he were the one responsible for what had happened. He hurried to open the door for them and accompanied them outside, where a hired carriage was waiting. He could not think of anything to say to them. He returned to the salon in time to hear the end of an argument.

"I will not tolerate having bastards of my blood strewn about the landscape!" Paulina screamed.

"Define your loyalties, Mother. Whom are you going to believe, your own son or a pastry shop owner and a Chinaman?" Matías fired back, slamming the door as he left.

That night Severo del Valle confronted Matías. He had enough information to be able to deduce events and he intended to disarm his cousin through tenacious questioning, but that wasn't necessary; Matías immediately told him everything. He felt trapped in an absurd situation for which he was not responsible, he said. Lynn Sommers had pursued him and handed herself to him on a tray. He never really intended to seduce her—the bet had been nothing but bombast. For two months he had been trying to wean her away without destroying her. He was afraid she would do something foolish; she was one of those hysterical young girls capable of throwing herself into the sea for love, he explained. He admitted that Lynn was little more than a child and that she had come to his arms a virgin, her head filled with sugary poems and completely ignorant of the rudiments of sex, but he repeated that he had no obligation to her, and that he had never mentioned the word *love* to her, much less *marriage*. Girls like her always brought complications, he added, which was why he avoided them like the plague. He had never imagined that his brief meeting with Lynn would have such consequences. They had been together a handful of times, he said, and he had recommended that afterward she douche with vinegar and mustard; how could he know that she was so astoundingly fertile? In any case, he was willing to pay the expenses of the baby, the money was the least of it, but he did not plan to give the child his name because there was no proof it was his. "I will not marry now, or ever, Severo. Do you know anyone with less vocation for bourgeois life than I?" he concluded.

One week later, Severo del Valle went to the clinic of Tao Chi'en, after having mulled for hours the scabrous mission his cousin had assigned him. The *zhong-yi* had attended his last patient for the day, and he received Severo alone in the small waiting room of his office on the first floor. He listened impassively to Severo's offer.

"Lynn does not need money, that is why she has parents," he said, reflecting no emotion. "In any case, I appreciate your concern, Mr. del Valle."

"How is Miss Sommers?" asked Severo, humiliated by the other man's dignity.

"My daughter still believes there has been a misunderstanding. She is sure that soon Mr. Rodríguez de Santa Cruz will come to ask her to marry him, and out of love, not duty."

"Mr. Chi'en, I can't tell you what I would give to change these circumstances. The truth is that my cousin is not in good health, he cannot marry. I regret it more than I can say," murmured Severo del Valle.

"We regret it much more. Lynn is merely a diversion for your cousin. To Lynn, he is her life," Tao Chi'en said softly.

"I would like to explain to your daughter, Mr. Chi'en. May I see her, please?"

"I must ask Lynn. At the moment she does not want to see any-one, but I will let you know if she changes her mind," the *zhong-yi* replied, walking Severo to the door.

Severo del Valle waited three weeks without news of Lynn, until he couldn't contain his impatience any longer and went to the tea shop to ask Eliza Sommers to allow him to speak with her daughter. He expected to be met with unyielding resistance, but Eliza, enveloped in her aroma of sugar and vanilla, received him with the same serenity Tao Chi'en had shown when he spoke with him. At first Eliza had blamed herself for what happened: she had been careless, she hadn't been capable of protecting her daughter, and now the girl's life was ruined. She wept in her husband's arms until he reminded her that when she was sixteen she had suffered a similar experience: the same excessive love, abandonment by her lover, pregnancy, terror. The dif-ference was that Lynn was not alone; she would not have to run away from home and sail half the length of the hemisphere in the hold of a ship to follow an unworthy man, as Eliza had done. Lynn had come to her parents, and it was their great good fortune that they were able to help her, Tao Chi'en had said. In China or in Chile, their daughter would be lost, society would have no forgiveness, but in California, a land without tradition, there was room for everyone. The *zhong-yi* gathered his small family together and told them that the baby was a gift from heaven and that they should await it with joy; tears were bad for karma, they harmed the creature in the mother's womb and marked it for a life of uncertainty. This infant boy or girl would be welcome. Its uncle Lucky, and he himself, its grandfather, would be worthy substitutes for the absent father. And as for Lynn's thwarted love, well, they would think about that later. He seemed so enthusiastic about the prospect of being a grandfather that Eliza was embarrassed about her prudish concerns; she dried her tears and never again blamed herself. If to Tao Chi'en the compassion he felt for his daughter counted more than family honor, the same should be true for her, she decided; her duty was to protect Lynn and nothing else mattered. That was what she calmly told Severo del Valle that day in the tearoom. She did not understand the Chilean's reasons for insisting on speaking with her daughter, but she interceded in his behalf, and finally Lynn agreed to see him. She barely remembered him, but she welcomed him with the hope that he was there as an emissary of Matías.

During the months that followed, Severo del Valle's visits to the home of the Chi'ens became a habit. He would come at nightfall, when he was through work, tie his horse in front of the house, and appear, hat in one hand and some gift in the other, until gradually Lynn's room filled with toys and baby clothes. Tao Chi'en taught him to play mah-jongg, and they spent hours with Eliza and Lynn moving the beautiful ivory tiles. Lucky didn't join them because to him it seemed a waste of time to play without betting. In contrast, Tao Chi'en played only in the bosom of his family, because in his youth he had sworn never to play for money and he was sure that if he broke that vow he would bring down some misfortune. The Chi'ens became so accustomed to Severo's presence that when he was late they would consult the clock, worried. Eliza Sommers took advantage of his visits to practice her Spanish and remember Chile, that far-off country she still thought of as her homeland but had not set foot in for more than thirty years. They discussed the details of the war, and political changes. After several decades of conservative governments the liberals had triumphed and the struggle to break the hold of the clergy and enact reforms had divided every Chilean family. Most men, however Catholic they might be, were eager to modernize the country, but the women, who were much more religious, turned against their fathers and husbands to defend the Church. As Nívea explained in her letters, no matter how liberal the government, the fate of the poor had not changed, and she added that, as they had forever, upper-class women and the clergy were pulling the strings of power. Separating church and state was no doubt a great step forward, the girl wrote behind the backs of the del Valle clan, which did not tolerate such ideas, but it was still the same families who controlled everything. "Let's start another political party, Severo, one that seeks justice and equality," she proposed, fired by her clandestine conversations with Sor María Escapulario.

In the south of the continent the War of the Pacific raged on, increasingly brutal, while Chilean armies prepared to begin the campaign in the desert of the north, a territory as wild and inhospitable as the moon, where supplying the troops turned out to be a titanic task. The only way to transport soldiers to the places where the battles would be fought was by sea, but the Peruvian navy was not going to permit that. Severo del Valle thought that the war was being won by Chile, whose organization and ferocity seemed unbeatable. It was not just weapons and warlike character that determined the result of a conflict, Severo explained to Eliza Sommers, but the example of a handful of heroic men that could inflame the soul of a nation.

"I believe that the war was decided in May, señora, in a naval battle just outside the port of Iquique. There an obsolete Chilean frigate held out against a far superior Peruvian force. Arturo Prat was in command, a young, very religious, and rather timid captain who never took part in the revels and escapades of military life and who had distinguished himself so little that his superiors had no confidence in his valor. That day, however, he was converted into the hero who galvanized the spirits of all Chileans."

Eliza knew the details; she had read them in an out-of-date copy of the *Times* of London, in which the episode was described as "one of the most glorious combats that has ever taken place. An antiquated wood ship, on the edge of being unseaworthy, bore up for three and a half hours under bombardment from land and a powerful armor-clad ship, and went down with its banner proudly flying." The Peruvian vessel, under the command of Admiral Miguel Grau, a hero of his own nation, set a direct course for the Chilean frigate, piercing her with its ram, at which point Captain Prat leapt onto the attacking ship, followed by one of his men. Both died minutes later, shot on the enemy deck. With the second ramming, several more men leapt onto the Peruvian vessel, emulating their captain, and they too were riddled with bullets. Three-quarters of the crew died before the frigate was sunk. Such unimagined heroism transmitted courage to their compatriots and so impressed their enemies that Admiral Grau repeated with amazement, "How those Chileans fight!"

"Grau is a gentleman. He himself collected Prat's sword and personal belongings and returned them to his widow," Severo recounted, and added that after that battle the sacred motto in Chile was "Fight to victory or to death," as those courageous men had done.

"And you, Severo, aren't you planning to go?" Eliza asked.

"Yes, I will do that very soon," the young man replied, embarrassed, not knowing why he was waiting to perform his duty. In the meantime, Lynn was growing large without losing a shred of her grace or beauty. She stopped wearing dresses she could no longer fasten and made herself comfortable in the bright silk tunics she bought in Chinatown. She went out very little, despite her father's insistence that she take walks. Occasionally Severo del Valle picked her up in his carriage and took her for a ride through the Presidio or along the beach, where they would sit on a shawl to picnic and read: he his newspapers and law books and she the romantic novels she didn't believe in any longer but still read as escape. Severo lived day to day, from one visit with the Chi'ens to the next, with no ambition but to see Lynn. He was no longer writing to Nívea. Many times he had taken pen in hand to confess that he loved another, but he tore up the letters without mailing them because he couldn't find words to break with his sweetheart without wounding her mortally. Lynn, furthermore, had never given him any sign that would offer hope for imagining a future with her. They never spoke of Matías, just as Matías never referred to Lynn, but the question was always in the air. Severo was careful not to mention his new friendship with the Chi'ens in the home of his aunt and uncle, and he assumed that no one suspected it except the fastidious Williams, whom he did not have to inform since he had learned about it the same way he learned everything that happened in that palatial mansion. Severo had been arriving home late with an idiotic smile on his face for two months when Williams led him to the attic and by the light of a spirit lamp showed him a bulky object covered by sheets. When it was uncovered, Severo saw that it was a gleaming cradle.

"It is embossed silver. Silver from the del Valle mines in Chile. All the children in this family have slept here. Take it if you wish," was all he said.

Paulina del Valle was so embarrassed that she stopped going to the tea shop, unable to paste together the shattered pieces of her long friendship with Eliza Sommers. She had to give up her Chilean pastries, which for years had been her greatest weakness, and resign herself to the French cook in her own kitchen. Her commanding vitality, so useful in sweeping aside obstacles and carrying out projects, now was working against her. Condemned to inaction, she was consumed with impatience, her heart jumping up and down in her chest. "My nerves are killing me, Williams," she complained, for the first time in her life feeling indisposed. She reasoned that given the fact she had an unfaithful husband and three irresponsible sons, it was more than likely that scattered here and there were a good number of illegitimate children with her blood, and there was no logic in tormenting herself so. Nonetheless, those hypothetical bastards had no name, no face, while this one was right under her nose. If only it hadn't been Lynn

Sommers! She couldn't forget the visit of Eliza and that Chinese person whose name she couldn't remember; the vision of that dignified couple in her sitting room was very painful to her. Matías had seduced the girl—no subtlety of logic or convenience could refute the truth that her intuition had accepted from the first moment. Her son's denials and his sarcastic comments about Lynn's questionable virtue had merely reinforced her conviction. The baby that girl was carrying in her womb invoked a hurricane of ambivalent sentiments: on the one hand, a mute rage against Matías, and on the other, an inevitable tenderness for that first grandchild. The minute Feliciano returned from his trip, she told him the news.

"These things happen all the time, Paulina, no need to make a tragedy of it. Half the kids in California are bastards. The important thing is to avoid scandal and close ranks around Matías. The family comes first." Feliciano's opinion was clear.

"That baby *is* our family," she argued.

"It isn't even born yet, and you're already taking it in! I know that Miss Lynn Sommers. I saw her posing nude in the sculptor's studio, exhibiting herself in the middle of a circle of men. Any one of them might be her lover. Can't you see that?"

"You're the one who can't see, Feliciano."

"I see that this could turn into blackmail that never ends. I forbid you to have the slightest contact with those people, and if they come anywhere near here, I will handle the matter," was Feliciano's lightning conclusion.

From that day forward, Paulina never mentioned the subject before her son or her husband, but she could not keep it all to herself and ended by confiding in the faithful Williams, who had the virtue of listening to the end and not giving his opinion unless it was requested. If she could help Lynn Sommers, she would feel a little better, Paulina thought, but for once her fortune would not solve anything.

Those months were disastrous for Matías. Not only did the difficulty with Lynn stir up his bile, the pain in his joints had increased so markedly that he could not practice his fencing and he also had to give up other sports. He woke in such suffering that he wondered if the time hadn't come to consider suicide, an idea he had nourished ever since he had learned the name of his illness, but once he got out of bed and began to move around he felt better, and his gusto for life would return with new vigor. His wrists and knees swelled, his hands trembled, and the opium he smoked in Chinatown ceased to be a diversion and became a necessity. It was Amanda Lowell—his best companion in dissipation and his only confidante—who taught him the advantages of injecting morphine: more effective, cleaner, and more elegant than a pipe of opium. A minimal dose, and instantly his agony would disappear and give way to peace. The scandal of the bastard on the way ceased to depress him, and by midsummer he suddenly announced that he was sailing for Europe within a few days to see whether a change of air, the thermal waters of Italy, and English physicians could alleviate his symptoms. He did not add that he planned to meet Amanda Lowell in New York and continue the journey with her, because her name was never spoken in the family, where the memory of the redheaded Scotswoman guaranteed Feliciano indigestion and Paulina apoplectic rage. It was not just his physical discomfort and his wish to get away from Lynn Sommers that motivated Matías's precipitous voyage; there was also the matter of new gambling debts, learned of soon after his departure when a pair of circumspect Chinese appeared in Feliciano's office to advise him, with extreme courtesy, that either he paid the amount his son owed them, including the interest, or something frankly disagreeable would happen to some member of his honorable family. As answer, the magnate had them thrown out of his office and then called Jacob Freemont, the journalist, who was an expert on the underworld of the city. Freemont listened with sympathy—he was a good friend of Matías—and then went with Feliciano to call upon the chief of police, an Australian with a murky reputation who owed him certain favors, to ask him to resolve the matter in his own way. "The only way I know is to pay," the officer replied, and explained that no one opposed the tongs of Chinatown. He had had to collect gutted bodies with their viscera neatly packed in a box beside them. Of course, those were retributions among the Celestials themselves, he added; with whites they at least tried to make it look like an accident. Hadn't Feliciano noticed how many people died in unexplained fires, trampled by horses in a deserted street, drowned in the quiet waters of the bay, or crushed by bricks that in some puzzling way fell from a building under construction? Feliciano Rodríguez de Santa Cruz paid.

When Severo del Valle notified Lynn Sommers that Matías had sailed for Europe with no plan to return in the near future, she burst into tears and kept weeping for five days, despite the sedatives Tao Chi'en gave her, until her mother slapped her in the face and forced her to face reality. She had acted imprudently, and now there was nothing to do but pay the consequences. She wasn't a child any longer; she was going to be a mother, and she should be happy she had a family willing to help her, as other girls in her state ended up thrown into the street and forced to earn a living in the worst way possible, while their bastards were taken to an orphanage. The time had come to accept the fact that her lover had faded into thin air; she would have to be mother and father to the baby and grow up once and for all, for in that house they were sick and tired of putting up with her whims. For twenty years she had been taking with both hands; she shouldn't get the idea she could spend her life lying in bed whimpering, so she should wipe her nose and get dressed, because they were going out for a walk, and they were going to do that twice a day without fail, rain or thunder, and was she listening? Yes, Lynn had listened to the end, her eyes wide with surprise and her cheeks burning from the only slaps she had received in her life. She dressed and obeyed without a word.

From that moment her sanity returned with a crash. She accepted her fate with amazing serenity, never complained again, swallowed Tao Chi'en's remedies, took long walks with her mother, and was even able to laugh when she learned that the project of the Republic statue was shot to hell, as her brother explained, the fault not of the model but of the sculptor, who had fled to Brazil with the money.

At the end of August Severo del Valle finally dared speak of his feelings to Lynn Sommers. By then she felt as heavy as an elephant and did not recognize her own face in the mirror, but to Severo's eyes she was more beautiful than ever. They were returning from a walk, hot and sweaty, when Severo pulled out his handkerchief to wipe her forehead and neck but stopped before he completed the gesture. Somehow he found himself bending down, taking Lynn firmly by the shoulders, and kissing her right on the lips in the middle of the street. He asked her to marry him, and she answered with absolute simplicity that she would never love anyone but Matías Rodríguez de Santa Cruz.

"I'm not asking you to love me, Lynn; the affection I feel for you is enough for both of us," Severo replied in the somewhat ceremonious tone he always used with her. "The baby needs a father. Give me the chance to protect you both, and I promise you that with time I will be worthy of your affection."

"My father says that in China couples are married who have never met, and that they learn to love one another afterward, but I am sure that that would not be the case with me, Severo. I am truly sorry."

"You don't have to live with me, Lynn. As soon as the baby is born I'm going to Chile. My country is at war and I have already put off doing my duty too long."

"And if you don't come back from the war?"

"At least your child will have my name and the inheritance from my father, which I still have. It isn't much, but it will be enough for his education. And you, my beloved Lynn, you will have respectability."

That same night Severo del Valle wrote Nívea the letter he hadn't been able to write before. He told her everything in four sentences, without preamble or excuses, because he understood that she would not tolerate any other way. He didn't even dare ask her forgiveness for the waste of love and time that those four years of their epistolary courtship had meant for her, because such ignoble accountings were beneath his cousin's generosity of heart. He called a servant to take the letter to the post office the next morning and then lay down in his clothes, exhausted. He slept without dreaming for the first time in a long while. A month later Severo del Valle and Lynn Sommers were married in a brief ceremony in the presence of her family and Williams, the one person Severo invited from his own home. He knew that the butler would tell his aunt Paulina, and decided to wait until she took the first step by asking him about it. The marriage was not announced to anyone, because Lynn had requested absolute privacy until after the baby was born and she had recovered her normal appearance. She didn't want to show herself with that pumpkin belly and face covered with splotches, she said. That night Severo said good night to his bride with a kiss on the forehead and left, as always, to sleep in his bachelor room.

That same week another naval battle was waged in the waters of the Pacific and the Chilean ships put two enemy warships out of commission. The Peruvian admiral Miguel Grau, the same gentleman who months before had returned Captain Prat's sword to his widow, died as heroically as Prat had done. It was a disaster for Peru; when they lost control of the sea lanes, their communications were interrupted and their armies fragmented and isolated. The Chileans took command of the sea and were able to transport their troops to sensitive points in the north and to implement the plan to march across enemy territory and occupy Lima. Severo del Valle followed the news with the same passion as the rest of his compatriots in the United States, but his love for Lynn more than outweighed his patriotism and he did not set forward the date for his return voyage.

. . .

In the early morning of the second Monday in October, Lynn woke with a wet nightgown and screamed in horror; she thought she had urinated on herself. "That is not good, her water has broken too soon," Tao Chi'en said privately to his wife, but before their daughter he remained smiling and calm. Ten hours later, when her contractions were barely perceptible and the family was exhausted from playing mah-jongg to distract her, Tao Chi'en decided to try his herbs. The future mother joked defiantly: were these the birth pangs she had been warned about so much? They were easier to bear than the stomach cramps Chinese food gave you, she said. She was more bored than uncomfortable, and she was hungry, but her father would allow her only water and brews of medicinal herbs as he applied his gold acupuncture needles to speed the birth. The combination of drugs and needles had their effect, and by nightfall, when Severo del Valle arrived for his customary visit, he found Lucky at the door, agitated, and the house shuddering from the moans of Lynn and the tumult caused by the Chinese midwife, who was talking at the top of her lungs and running back and forth with rags and jugs of water. Tao Chi'en tolerated the midwife because she had more experience in that field than he, but he did not let her torture Lynn by sitting on her or punching her in the stomach, as she intended. Severo del Valle stayed in the sitting room, back against the wall, trying not to be seen. Every moan from Lynn bored into his soul; he wanted to run from there, as far as possible, but he couldn't move from his corner or speak a word. This was his state when Tao Chi'en came into the room, impassive, dressed with his habitual neatness.

"May I wait here? Am I in the way? How can I help?" Severo babbled, drying the sweat trickling down his neck.

"You are not in the way at all, my son, but you cannot help Lynn. She has to do this job alone. On the other hand, you can help Eliza, who is a little upset."

Eliza Sommers had experienced the fatigue of giving birth, and like every woman, she understood that that was the threshold of death. She knew the courageous and mysterious journey in which the body opens to give passage for another life. She remembered the moment when she began to tumble, unchecked, down a steep slope, contracting, pushing—the terror, the suffering, and the unbelievable amazement when finally the child lets go and comes to light. Tao Chi'en, with all his *zhong-yi* wisdom, was slower than she to realize that something was very wrong in Lynn's case. The resources of Tao's Chinese medicine had provoked strong contractions, but the child was badly positioned, sideways and obstructed by its mother's bones. It was a dry, difficult birth, as Tao Chi'en explained, but his daughter was strong, and it was just a matter of Lynn's keeping calm and not tiring herself more than was necessary. This was a race of endurance, not speed, he added. During one pause, Eliza Sommers, as exhausted as Lynn herself, left the room and met Severo in the corridor. She gestured to him, and he followed, puzzled, to a little room with an altar, a place he had never been before. On a low table stood a simple cross, a small statue of Kuan Yin, the Chinese goddess of compassion, and in the center, a pen-and-ink drawing of a woman in a green tunic and two flowers over her ears. He saw a pair of lighted candles and saucers holding water, rice, and flower petals. Eliza knelt on an orange silk cushion before the altar and asked Christ, Buddha, and the spirit of Lin, Tao's first wife, to come to help her daughter in giving birth. Severo stood behind her, automatically murmuring the Catholic prayers he had learned in his childhood. They stayed there for some time, united by their fear and love for Lynn, until Tao Chi'en called his wife to come help him because he had sent the midwife away and was preparing to turn the baby and pull it out by hand. Severo stayed with Lucky, who was smoking at the door, as little by little Chinatown awakened.

The child was born early Tuesday morning. The mother, dripping with sweat and trembling, struggled to help, but she was not screaming any longer; all she could do was pant, attentive to her father's directions. Finally she gritted her teeth, clung to the bars of the bed, and pushed with brutal determination. A lock of dark hair appeared. Tao Chi'en grasped the head and pulled firmly and gently until shoulders emerged; he turned the small body and removed it with a single rapid movement, while with the other hand he untangled the dark cord about its neck. Eliza Sommers received a small bloody bundle, a tiny girl child with a flattened face and blue skin. While Tao Chi'en cut the cord and busied himself with the second stage of the birth, the grandmother cleaned her granddaughter with a sponge and clapped her back until she began to breathe. When she heard the cry that announced entrance into the world, and verified that the baby had a normal color, she placed her on Lynn's stomach. Exhausted, the mother raised herself on one elbow to welcome her daughter while her body continued to contract; she held the baby to her breast, kissing her and welcoming her in a mixture of English, Spanish, Chinese, and invented words. One hour later Eliza called in Severo and Lucky to meet the baby. They found her sleeping peacefully in the silver cradle that had belonged to the family of the Rodríguez de Santa Cruzes, dressed in yellow silk and a red bonnet that gave her the look of a tiny elf. Lynn was drowsing, pale and calm, between clean sheets, and Tao Chi'en, by her side, was checking her pulse.

"What are you going to name her?" Severo del Valle asked, filled with emotion.

"Lynn and you should decide that," Eliza answered.

"Me?"

"Aren't you the father?" asked Tao Chi'en, winking.

"She will be called Aurora, because she was born at dawn," murmured Lynn without opening her eyes.

"Then her name in Chinese is Lai Ming, which means dawn," added Tao Chi'en.

"Welcome to the world, Lai Ming, Aurora del Valle," and Severo smiled as he kissed the tiny baby on the forehead, certain that this was the happiest day of his life and that this wrinkled infant dressed like a Chinese doll was as much his daughter as if she were actually of his blood. Lucky took his niece in his arms and blew his tobacco and soy sauce breath in her face.

"What are you doing!" cried the grandmother, trying to take Aurora from his hands.

"I'm blowing on her to give her my good luck. What more worthwhile gift do I have to give to Lai Ming?" Her uncle laughed.

When Severo del Valle arrived at the mansion on Nob Hill during dinner and announced that he had married Lynn Sommers a week before and that on this day his daughter had been born, his aunt and uncle were as bewildered as if he had deposited a dead dog on the dining room table.

"And everyone throwing the blame on Matías! I always knew he wasn't the father but I never imagined it was you," Feliciano spit out as soon as he recovered a little from his shock.

"I'm not the blood father but I am the legal father," Severo clarified. "The baby's name is Aurora del Valle."

"This is unpardonable! You have betrayed this family, and after we took you in like our own son," bellowed his uncle.

"I haven't betrayed anyone. I married for love."

"But wasn't that woman in love with Matías?"

"*That woman's* name is Lynn, and she is my wife; I demand that you treat her with the respect she deserves," Severo said curtly, rising to his feet.

"You're an idiot, Severo, a complete idiot!" Feliciano shouted as he strode furiously from the dining room.

The imperturbable Williams, who had come in at that moment to oversee the service of dessert, could not contain a quick smile of complicity before discreetly retiring. Paulina listened, incredulous, to Severo's information that in a few days he would be leaving for the war in Chile. Lynn would continue to live with her parents in Chinatown, and, if things worked out well, he would return when he could to assume his role as husband and father.

"Sit down, nephew, let's talk this over like decent folk. Matías is the baby's father, isn't he?"

"Ask him, Aunt."

"I see it all now. You married to get Matías out of this mess. My son is a cynic, and you're a romantic. . . . But you are going to ruin your life for some quixotic gesture!" exclaimed Paulina.

"You're mistaken, Aunt. I haven't ruined my life; on the contrary, I believe this is the best chance I will ever have to be happy."

"With a woman who loves another man? With a child that isn't yours?"

"Time will help. If I come back from the war, Lynn will learn to love me, and the child will believe I am her father."

"Matías may come back before you do," she noted.

"That won't change anything."

"All Matías would have to do is speak one word and Lynn Sommers would follow him to the end of the earth."

"That is an unavoidable risk," Severo replied.

"You've completely lost your head, Nephew. Those people are not of our social class."

"It is the most decent family I know, Aunt," Severo assured her.

"I see you haven't learned anything from me. To triumph in this world you have to consider the results before you act. You are a lawyer with a brilliant future, and you bear one of the oldest names in Chile. Do you think society is going to accept your wife? And your cousin Nívea, isn't she waiting for you?"

"That's over."

"Well, you stuck your foot in it this time, Severo, I suppose it's too late for regrets. Let's try to fix things as much as we can. Money and social position count for a lot both here and in Chile. I'll help however I can—it's not for nothing that I'm the grandmother of that baby. What did you say her name is?"

"Aurora, but her grandparents call her Lai Ming."

"She's a del Valle, and it is my duty to help her, seeing that Matías has washed his hands of this sorry matter."

"That won't be necessary, Aunt. I've made arrangements for Lynn to have the money from my inheritance."

"You can never have too much money. At least I can see my granddaughter, can't I?"

"We'll ask Lynn and her parents," Severo del Valle promised.

They were still in the dining room when Williams appeared with an urgent message saying that Lynn had suffered a hemorrhage and they feared for her life, that Severo should come right away. He immediately rushed off to Chinatown. When he reached the Chi'en home, he found the small family gathered around Lynn's bed, so still that they seemed to be posed for a tragic painting. For an instant he was struck with wild hope when he saw everything so clean and orderly, with no signs of the birth, no stained rags or smell of blood, but then he saw the expression of grief on the faces of Tao, Eliza, and Lucky. The very air was thin in the room; Severo took a deep breath, gasping, as if he were on a mountain peak. Trembling, he walked to the bed and saw Lynn lying with her hands on her chest; her eyes were closed and her features transparent: a beautiful sculpture in ashen alabaster. He took one hand, hard and cold as ice, leaned over her, and noted that her breathing was barely perceptible and her lips and fingers were blue. He kissed the palm of her hand for an eternal moment, wetting it with his tears, bowed with sorrow. Lynn managed to murmur Matías's name and then sighed twice and departed as lightly as she had floated through this world. Absolute silence greeted the mystery of death, and for a time impossible to measure they waited, motionless, while Lynn's spirit rose from her body. Severo felt a long howl surging from the center of the earth and passing through his body to his lips, but it did not escape. The scream invaded him, filled him, and burst inside his head in a silent explosion. He stayed there, kneeling beside the bed, voicelessly calling to Lynn, not believing that fate had so abruptly taken the woman whom he had dreamed of for years, taken her just when he thought he had won her. An eternity later, he felt someone touch his shoulder, and turned to meet the deadened eyes of Tao Chi'en. "It's all right, it's all right," it seemed he murmured, and behind Tao Severo saw Eliza Sommers and Lucky, sobbing in each other's arms, and he realized that he was an intruder in the family's grief. Then he remembered the child. He staggered to the silver cradle like a drunk and took the tiny Aurora in his arms, carried her to the bed, and held her near Lynn's face, so she could say good-bye to her mother. Then he sat down with her in his arms, rocking inconsolably.

When Paulina del Valle learned that Lynn Sommers had died, she felt a flood of joy, and even whooped with triumph before her shame at feeling such a despicable emotion brought her back to earth. She had always wanted a daughter. From her first pregnancy, she had dreamed of the little girl who would have her name, Paulina, and who would be her best friend and her companion. With the birth of each of her three boys she had felt swindled, but now in the mature years of her life this gift had fallen into her lap: a grandchild that she could raise as a daughter, someone to whom she could offer all the opportunities that love and money can provide, she thought, someone to accompany her in her old age. With Lynn Sommers out of the picture, she could claim the baby in Matías's name. She was celebrating that unforeseeable stroke of good luck with a cup of chocolate and three cream pastries when Williams reminded her that legally Severo del Valle was the father of Aurora, and that he was the one person who had the right to decide her future. Even better, Paulina concluded, because at least her nephew was right on the spot, while bringing Matías back from Europe and convincing him to take responsibility for his daughter would be a long-term project. She could never have anticipated Severo's reaction when she told him her plans.

"For all legal purposes, you are the father, so you can bring the baby here tomorrow morning," said Paulina.

"I won't be doing that, Aunt. Lynn's parents will look after their granddaughter while I go to the war. They want to take care of her, and I agree with that," her nephew responded in a decisive tone she had not heard before

"Are you mad? We can't leave my granddaughter in the hands of Eliza Sommers and that Chinese man!" Paulina exclaimed.

"Why not? They are her grandparents."

"Do you want her to grow up in Chinatown? We can give her an education, opportunities, luxury, a respectable name. They can't do any of that."

"They will give her love," Severo replied.

"So will I! Remember that you owe me a lot, Nephew. This is your chance to repay me and at the same time do something for the child."

"I'm sorry, Aunt, it's decided. Aurora will stay with her maternal grandparents."

Paulina del Valle threw one of the many tantrums of her life. She couldn't believe that the nephew whom she had thought of as her unconditional ally, who had become another son to her, could betray her in such a vile manner. She screamed, cursed, argued in vain, and got herself into such a fit that Williams had to call a doctor to give her a dose of sedatives large enough to knock her out for a long while. When she woke, thirty hours later, her nephew was already aboard the steamship that would carry him to Chile. Her husband and the faithful Williams convinced her that it was not a good idea to resort to violence, as she planned; no matter how corrupt the law was in San Francisco, there was no legal basis for removing the baby from her maternal grandparents' care, especially taking into account that the purported father had left written orders. They also urged her not to use her customary ploy of offering money for the infant, because that could come back like a brick smashed in her teeth. The only possible course to follow was to be diplomatic until Severo del Valle returned; then they could reach some accord, they advised her. She did not want to listen to their arguments, and two days later she appeared in Eliza Sommers's tearoom with a proposal that she was sure the other grandmother could not refuse. Eliza received her dressed in mourning for her daughter but illumined by the consolation of the baby sleeping placidly at her side. Paulina received a jolt when she saw the silver cradle that had belonged to her sons sitting beside the window, but she quickly remembered that she had granted Williams permission to give it to Severo, and she bit her tongue because she wasn't there to fight over a cradle, however valuable, but to negotiate for her granddaughter. "It isn't being right that wins, it's driving the best bargain," she always said. And in this case, it not only seemed evident to her that right was on her side but also that no one could best her in the art of haggling.

Eliza picked up the baby from the cradle and handed her to Paulina. She held that tiny little bundle, so light she seemed no more than a handful of cloth, and thought her heart would burst with a completely new sentiment. "My God, my God," she kept repeating, terrified at the unfamiliar vulnerability that made her weak in the knees and brought a sob to her bosom. She sat in a large chair and rocked the granddaughter half hidden in her enormous lap while Eliza Sommers ordered the tea and pastries she had served in the days that Paulina had been her most assiduous customer. During those minutes, Paulina del Valle managed to recover from her emotion and line up her artillery for the attack. She began by offering her condolences for Lynn's death, and then followed by admitting that her son Matías had to be Aurora's father; all you had to do was look at her to know that, she was a carbon copy of all the Rodríguez de Santa Cruz y del Valles. She was terribly sorry, she said, that Matías was in Europe for reasons of health and could not as yet claim the baby. Then she said that it was her desire to keep her granddaughter, in view of the fact that Eliza worked so hard, had so little time—and fewer resources—and that clearly it would be impossible for her to give Aurora the same quality of life she would have in her own home on

Nob Hill. She said all this in the tone of someone granting a favor, hiding the anxiety that made her hands tremble and a knot form in her throat. Eliza Sommers replied that she appreciated such a generous proposal, but she was sure that between Tao Chi'en and her they could care for Lai Ming, just as Lynn had asked them to do before she died. Of course, she added, Paulina would always be welcome in the little girl's life.

"We must not create any confusion about Lai Ming's paternity," added Eliza Sommers. "You and your son assured us a few months ago that he had nothing to do with Lynn's condition. You will recall that your son made it clear that the baby's father could be any one of his friends."

"These are things you say in the heat of a disagreement, Eliza. Matías spoke without thinking," Paulina stammered.

"The fact that Lynn married Mr. Severo del Valle proves that your son was telling the truth, Paulina. My granddaughter has no ties of blood with you, but I repeat that you can see her whenever you wish. The more people who love her, the better it will be for her."

During the next half hour the two women faced each other like gladiators, each in her own style. Paulina del Valle went from flattery to harassment, from pleading to the desperate stratagem of a bribe, and then when everything else failed, to threats, without moving the other grandmother a half inch from her position—except to take the infant and gently put her back in the cradle. Paulina did not know exactly when her rage went to her head, but she completely lost control of the situation and ended screeching that Eliza Sommers would see who the Rodríguez de Santa Cruzes were, how much power they had in this city, and how they could ruin Eliza, her stupid pastry business, and her Chinaman too, that it was not advisable to make an enemy of Paulina del Valle, and that sooner or later she would take the baby from her, of *that* she could be absolutely sure, because the person hadn't yet been born who could stand in her way. With one sweep of her hand she sent the fine porcelain cups and Chilean pastries flying from the table to land on the floor in a cloud of powdered sugar, and raged out, snorting like a bull. Once in her carriage, with her blood pounding at her temples and her heart kicking beneath the layers of fat captured within her corset, she burst into broken sobs, crying as she hadn't done since she shot the bolt on the door of her room to sleep alone forever in her enormous mythological bed. Just as then, her best tool had failed her: her ability to bargain like an Arab merchant, the talent that had served her so well in other aspects of her life. By wanting too much, she had lost everything.

PART TWO

1880–1896

There is a picture of me when I was three or four, the only one from that era that survived the avatars of fate and of Paulina del Valle's decision to erase any trace of my origins. It is a worn piece of cardboard in a travel frame, one of those antique metal and velvet cases that were so in fashion in the nineteenth century but no one uses anymore. In the photograph you see a very small child dressed in the style of Chinese brides, in a long tunic of embroidered satin over trousers of a different shade; she is wearing delicate little slippers on white felt soles protected by a thin layer of wood. Her dark hair is swept up in a topknot too tall for her size and secured by two thick pins, either gold or silver, joined by a small garland of flowers. The child is holding an open fan in her hand and could be laughing, although the features are barely distinguishable; her face is just a pale moon with eyes like two black smudges. Behind the girl can be seen the huge head of a paper dragon and the glittering stars of fireworks. The photograph was taken during the celebration of the Chinese New Year in San Francisco. I don't remember that moment, and I don't recognize the child in that one surviving portrait.

On the other hand, I have several photographs of my mother, Lynn Sommers, that I saved from oblivion through persistence and good contacts. I went to San Francisco several years ago to meet my uncle Lucky, and while there I spent hours scouring old bookstores and photography studios, looking for calendars and postcards she posed for. My uncle Lucky still sends me some when he comes across them. My mother was very beautiful, that's all I can say about her, because I don't recognize her in those photos either. I don't remember her, naturally, since she died when I was born, but the woman in the calendars is a stranger, I have no connection with her; I can't visualize her as my mother, only as a play of light and shadow on paper. Neither would you think that she's my uncle Lucky's sister; he is a very short Chinese man with a large head, rather rough looking, but a very good person. I look more like my father, I have his Spanish features. Unfortunately I inherited very little of the race of my extraordinary grandfather, Tao Chi'en. If it weren't for the fact that my grandfather is the clearest and most persistent memory in my life—and the oldest love, whom none of the men I've known can measure up to because none can equal him—I would never believe I have any Chinese blood in my veins. Tao Chi'en will live in me forever. I can see him, slim, elegant, always dressed with impeccable correctness, gray hair, round eyeglasses, and an expression of unremitting goodness in his almond-shaped eyes. In my evocations he is always smiling, and at times I hear him singing to me in Chinese. He circles round me, he walks with me, he guides me, just as he told my grandmother Eliza he would do after his death. I have a daguerreotype of my grandparents when they were young, before they married: she is sitting in a chair with a high back and he is standing behind her; both are dressed in the American fashion of the time, looking straight into the camera with a vague expression of fright. That portrait, finally rescued, is on my night table and is the last thing I see before I turn down the lamp every night, but I wish I had had it with me during my childhood, when I had such a great need for those grandparents.

Ever since I can remember, I have been tormented by the same nightmare. The images of that persistent dream stay with me for hours, ruining my day and draining my soul. It is always the same sequence: I am walking through the empty streets of an unfamiliar and exotic city; I am holding the hand of someone whose face I can never glimpse, I see only legs and the tips of shined shoes. Suddenly we are surrounded by children in black pajamas, dancing in a ferocious round. A dark stain, maybe blood, spreads across the paving stones as the circle of the children inexorably closes, more and more threatening, around the person who is holding my hand. We are corralled, pushed, pulled; we are separated. I reach for the friendly hand and find emptiness. I scream, voicelessly, I fall, noiselessly, and then I wake up with my heart racing. Sometimes I go several days without speaking, consumed by the memory of the dream, trying to penetrate the layers of mystery surrounding it to see if I can discover some detail, until then unperceived, that will give me the key to its meaning. Those days I suffer a kind of icy fever in which my body shuts down and my mind is trapped in a frozen land. I was in that state of paralysis for my first weeks in the home of Paulina del Valle. I was five years old when they took me to the mansion on Nob Hill, and no one bothered to explain to me why suddenly my life had taken such a dramatic turn, where my grandmother Eliza and grandfather Tao were, who the monumental lady covered with jewels was who observed me from a throne, her eyes filled with tears. I ran and scooted under a table, and there I stayed like a whipped dog, according to what I've been told. In those days Williams was the Rodríguez de Santa Cruzes' butler—as difficult as that is to imagine—and it was he who the next day had the idea of putting my food on a tray tied to a cord. They pulled the cord little by little, and when I was so hungry I couldn't stand it anymore, I came crawling out after the tray. They managed to extract me from my refuge, but every time I woke up with the nightmare, I ran to hide under the table again. That lasted a year, until we came to Chile, and in the daze of the journey and of getting settled in Santiago that mania passed.

My nightmare is in black and white, silent and unchanging; it has an eternal quality. I suppose that I have enough information now to untangle the keys to its meaning, but that doesn't mean it has stopped tormenting me. Because of my dreams, I am different, like people who because of a genetic illness or some deformity have to make a constant effort to live a normal life. They bear visible signs; mine can't be seen, but it exists. I can compare it to attacks of epilepsy, which come on suddenly and leave a wake of confusion behind. I am afraid to go to bed at night; I don't know what will happen while I'm sleeping, or how I will wake up. I have tried various remedies for my night demons, from orange liqueur laced with a few drops of opium to hypnosis and other forms of black magic, but nothing guarantees me peaceful sleep except good company. Sleeping in someone's arms is, until now, anyway, the only sure cure. I should get married, as everyone has advised me, but I did that once, and it was a calamity; I can't tempt fate anew. At thirty, and with no husband, I am little more than a freak; my friends look on me with pity, even though some envy my independence. I am not alone—I have a secret love, with no ties or conditions, a cause for scandal anywhere but especially here where we happen to live. I am not a spinster, or a widow, or a divorced woman. I live in the limbo of the "separated," where all the wretched creatures end up who prefer public opprobrium to living with a man they don't love. How else can it be in Chile, where marriage is eternal and inescapable? Some extraordinary early mornings, when my lover and I, wet with sweat and limp with shared dreams, are in that semi-unconscious state of absolute tenderness, happy and confident as sleeping children, we fall into the temptation of talking about marrying, of going somewhere else—to the United States, for example, where there is all kinds of room and no one knows us—to live together like any other normal couple, but then we wake up with the sun peering in the window and we don't speak of it again, because we both know that we could not live anywhere but here in this Chile of geological cataclysms and human pettiness, but also of rugged volcanoes and snowy peaks, of immemorial lakes scattered with emeralds, of foaming rivers and fragrant forests, a country narrow as a ribbon, a land of impoverished people still innocent despite so many and such varied abuses. He cannot leave, and I never tire of photographing it. I would like to have children; yes, I would like that, but I have finally accepted that I will never be a mother. I am not sterile, I am fertile in other regards. Nívea del Valle says that a human being is not defined by her reproductive capacity, which is a fine irony coming from her, a woman who has given birth to more than a dozen children. But this isn't the place to talk about the children I won't have, or about my lover, but of the events that determined who I am. I understand that in writing this memoir I must betray others, that's inevitable. "Remember that dirty linen is washed at home," Severo del Valle keeps telling me, he who, like the rest of us, was raised with that maxim. On the other hand, Nívea's advice is, "Write with honesty and don't worry about the feelings of others, because no matter what you say, they'll hate you anyway." So let's get on with it.

Given the impossibility of getting rid of my nightmares, I at least try to draw some benefit from them. I have found that after a miserable night the hallucinations remain, and my nerve ends are raw, an optimum state for creativity. My best photographs have been taken on days like those, when the one thing I want to do is crawl under the table the way I did in those first days in my grandmother Paulina's house. The dream of the children in black pajamas is what led me to photography, I'm sure of it. When Severo del Valle gave me a camera, the first thing that occurred to me was that if I could photograph those demons, I would drive them away. At thirteen, I tried many times. I invented complicated systems of wheels and cords to activate a fixed camera as I slept, until it became obvious that those malicious creatures were invulnerable to the assault of technology. If you observe an ordinary object or body very closely, it is transformed into something sacred. The camera can reveal secrets the naked eye or mind cannot capture; everything disappears except for the thing that is the focus of the picture. The photograph is an exercise in observation, and the result is always a stroke of luck: among the thousands and thousands of negatives that fill several cartons in my studio, very few are exceptional. My uncle, Lucky Chi'en, would feel somewhat defrauded if he knew how little effect his good-luck breath has had on my work. The camera is a simple apparatus, even the most inept person can use it; the challenge lies in creating with it that combination of truth and beauty called art. That quest is above all spiritual. I seek truth and beauty in the transparency of an autumn leaf, in the perfect form of a seashell on the beach, in the curve of a woman's back, in the texture of an ancient tree trunk, but also in more elusive forms of reality. Sometimes, working with an image in my darkroom, the soul of a person appears, the emotion of an event or vital essence of some object; at that moment, gratitude explodes in my heart and I cry. I can't help it. Such revelations are the goal of my work.

Severo del Valle spent several weeks of his voyage weeping over Lynn Sommers and mulling over what the rest of his life might be. He felt responsible for the infant Aurora, and had made a will before he sailed so that the small inheritance he had received from his father, along with his savings, would go directly to her in case something happened to him. In the meantime, she would receive the monthly interest. He knew that Lynn's parents would take better care of her than anyone else, and he expected that however strong her influence, his aunt Paulina would not try to take her by force because her husband would never allow the matter to become a public scandal.

Sitting in the bow of the ship staring at the infinite sea, Severo concluded that he would never get over losing Lynn. He did not want to live without her. The best thing the future could hold for him would be to die in combat; die quickly and soon, that was all he asked. For months his love for Lynn and his decision to help her had occupied all his time and attention, and day after day he had delayed his return while Chileans his age were enlisting en masse to fight. On board ship were several young men with the same intention as his—to join the ranks, since wearing the uniform was a matter of honor—with whom he met frequently to analyze the war news that came over the telegraph. In the four years Severo had spent in California he had cut himself off from his country; he had responded to the call to war as a way of surrendering to his grief, but he did not feel the slightest martial fervor. Even so, as the ship sailed south he was becoming infected by the others' excitement. He started thinking again about serving Chile, as he had wanted to do during the school years when he used to argue politics in the cafés with other students. He imagined that all his former companions would have been fighting for months, while he was wandering around San Francisco killing time before going to visit Lynn Sommers and play mah-jongg. How could he ever justify such cowardice to his friends and relatives? The image of Nívea assaulted him during these musings. His cousin would not understand his tardiness in returning to defend his country, because, he was sure, had she been a man she would have been the first to leave for the front. At least he wouldn't have to explain, for he expected to be shot dead before he saw her again. It would require much greater courage to face Nívea, after having treated her so badly, than to go into combat against the fiercest enemy. The ship plowed on at a maddening pace; at this rate they would reach Chile after the war was over, he conjectured anxiously. He was sure that victory would be theirs despite the numerical advantage of the adversaries and the arrogant ineptitude of the high Chilean command. The commander-in-chief of the army and admiral of the navy were a pair of petty old men who could not agree on the most elementary strategy, although Chileans at least could count on greater military discipline than the Peruvians and Bolivians. "Lynn had to die before I decided to go home to Chile and do my patriotic duty. I'm a louse," Severo groaned with shame.

The port of Valparaíso glittered in the brilliant December light as the steamship anchored in the bay. Sailing into the territorial waters of Peru and Chile, they had sighted several ships of the navies of both countries on maneuvers, but until they anchored in Valparaíso they had seen no evidence of war. The port looked very different from how Severo remembered it. The city was militarized, and camped troops were waiting for transport. The Chilean flag fluttered on every building, and a great flurry of small boats and cranes could be noted around several ships of the fleet; in contrast, there were very few passenger ships. Severo had written his mother the date of his arrival but he didn't expect to see her at the port; for a year or two she had been living in Santiago with her younger children, and the trip from the capital was very tedious. For that reason he didn't trouble to scan the dock for familiar faces, as most of the passengers were doing. He picked up his suitcase, handed a couple of coins to a sailor to look after his trunks, and walked down the gangway, taking deep breaths of the salt air of the city where he had been born. As he stepped ashore he staggered like a drunk; during weeks of sailing he had grown accustomed to the motion of the waves and now he could scarcely walk on solid ground. He whistled over a porter to help him with his luggage and started to look for a carriage to drive him to the home of his grandmother Emilia, where he planned to stay a couple of nights until he was accepted into the army. At that moment he felt someone touch his arm. He turned, surprised, and found himself face to face with the last person in this world he wanted to see: his cousin Nívea. It took a couple of seconds for him to recognize her and to recover from the shock. The girl he had left four years earlier had become a stranger, still short, but much slimmer, and well formed. The one thing that hadn't changed was the intelligent and focused expression on her face. She was wearing a summer dress of blue taffeta and a straw hat with a large white organdy bow tied beneath her chin and framing an oval, fine-featured face with shining, darting, teasing black eyes. She was alone. Severo was unable to say hello; he stood staring at her openmouthed, until he gathered his senses and managed to ask, deeply agitated, whether she had received his last letter, meaning the one in which he had reported his marriage to Lynn Sommers. Because he hadn't written since then, he supposed that his cousin knew nothing about Lynn's death or the birth of Aurora and couldn't guess that he had become a widower and father without having ever been a husband.

"We will talk about that later. For now, let me welcome you home. I have a carriage waiting," she interrupted.

Once the trunks had been placed in the carriage, Nívea instructed the coachman to drive slowly along the sea road, which
would give them time to talk before they reached the house where
the rest of the family was waiting.

"I have behaved like a cad with you, Nívea. The only thing I can
say in my favor is that I never wanted to hurt you," Severo murmured,
not daring to look at her.

"I admit that I was furious with you, Severo, I had to bite my
tongue not to curse you, but I hold no ill will. I believe that you have
suffered more than I. I am truly sorry about what happened to your
wife."

"How did you learn about that?"

"I received a telegram with the news, signed by someone named
Williams."

Severo del Valle's first reaction was one of anger. How had the
butler dared intrude that way in his private life? But then he could
not avoid a flash of gratitude; the telegram had spared him painful explanations.

"I don't expect you to forgive me, only to forget me, Nívea. You,
more than anyone, deserve to be happy—"

"Who told you that I want to be happy, Severo? That's the last
adjective I would use to define the future I aspire to. I want an interesting life, adventurous, different, passionate—in short, almost anything other than *happy*."

"Oh, cousin. It is wonderful to hear how little you have changed!
In any case, within a day or two I will be marching with the army toward Peru, and frankly I expect to die with my boots on, because my
life has no meaning now."

"And your daughter?"

"I see that Williams gave you all the details. Did he also tell you
that I am not the father of the child?" Severo inquired.

"Who is?"

"It doesn't matter. For legal purposes, she is my daughter. She is in the care of her grandparents, and she will not lack for money, I have left her well provided."

"What is her name?"

"Aurora."

"Aurora del Valle, a pretty name. Try to come back from the war in one piece, Severo, because when we marry, that baby will surely become our first daughter," Nívea said, blushing.

"What did you say?"

"I have waited for you all my life; I can certainly go on waiting. There's no hurry, Severo, I have many things to do before I marry. I am working."

"Working? Why?" Severo exclaimed, scandalized, for no woman in his family or any other family he knew worked.

"To learn. My uncle, José Francisco, hired me to organize his library, and he gives me permission to read anything I want. Do you remember him?"

"Only slightly. Isn't he the one who married an heiress and has a palace in Viña del Mar?"

"That's the one, he's kin to my mother. I don't know any man wiser or finer than he, and he is good-looking besides—although not as good-looking as you." She laughed.

"Don't make fun of me, Nívea."

"Was your wife pretty?" she asked.

"Very pretty."

"You will have to go through your mourning period, Severo. Maybe the war will help. They say that very beautiful women are unforgettable. I hope you learn to live without her, even if you don't forget her. I shall pray that you fall in love again, and hope it will be me," Nívea whispered, taking his hand.

And then Severo del Valle felt a terrible pain in his chest, as if a knife had been thrust between his ribs, and a sob escaped his lips, followed by weeping that shook his entire body as he repeated Lynn's name, hiccuping, Lynn, Lynn . . . a thousand times. Nívea pulled him to her breast and put her slim arms around him, patting his back, consoling him as she would a child.

The War of the Pacific began at sea and continued on land, hand-to-hand combat with fixed bayonets and curved knives in the most arid and inclement desert in the world, in the provinces that today are part of northern Chile but before the war belonged to Peru and Bolivia. The Peruvian and Bolivian armies were minimally prepared for such a conflict; they were badly armed, and their supply system failed so dismally that some battles and skirmishes were decided by lack of drinking water or because the wheels of ammunition-laden carts sank in the sand. Chile was an expansionist country with a solid economy, blessed with the best navy in South America and an army of more than seventy thousand men. It had a reputation for civility in a continent of crude caudillos, systematic corruption, and bloody revolutions. The austerity of the Chilean character and solidity of its institutions were the envy of neighboring nations, and its schools and universities attracted foreign professors and students. English, German, and Spanish immigrants had exercised a certain moderating influence on the rash Chilean temperament. The army was instructed by Prussians and had never known peace, because during the years preceding the War of the Pacific they had been in constant armed conflict in the south, fighting Indians in the area known as La Frontera. Though a civilizing influence had reached that far, beyond it lay unpredictable, indigenous lands where until very recently only Jesuit missionaries had ventured. The formidable Araucano warriors who had been fighting without letup since the time of the Conquest had never been bowed by bullets or the worst atrocities, but one by one they were being conquered by alcohol. Fighting against them, the soldiers learned about carnage and cruelty. Peruvians and Bolivians quickly came to fear the Chileans, bloodthirsty enemies capable of shooting or knifing wounded and prisoners. Chileans left such hatred and fear in their wake that they provoked a violent international reaction, followed by an interminable series of diplomatic claims and litigations that only redoubled their adversaries' determination to fight to the death, since there was no escape in surrender. The Peruvian and Bolivian troops, composed of a handful of officers, badly equipped contingents of regular soldiers, and masses of Indians recruited at gunpoint, had very little idea of why they were fighting, and they deserted at the first opportunity. In contrast, the Chilean ranks were filled primarily with civilians, as ruthless in combat as the military, who fought out of patriotic passion and would not surrender. Often conditions were hellish. Marching across the desert, the troops dragged through a cloud of saline dust, dying of thirst, desperate, calf deep in sand, with a merciless sun reverberating over their heads, weighed down by knapsacks and ammunition and clinging to their rifles. Smallpox, typhus, and malaria decimated their numbers; in the military hospitals there were more men ill than wounded in combat. When Severo del Valle joined the army his compatriots were occupying Antofagasta—Bolivia's only maritime province—and the Peruvian provinces of Tarapacá, Arica, and Tacna. In mid-1880 the commander-in-chief of Chile's armed forces died of a stroke in the midst of the desert campaign, plunging the government into total disorder. Finally the president named a civilian in his place, Don José Francisco Vergara, Nívea's uncle, that tireless traveler and voracious reader who was called to take up his sword at the age of forty-six and direct the war. He was among the first to observe that as Chile was advancing toward the conquest of the north, Argentina was silently occupying Patagonia in the south. No one, however, paid any attention; they considered that territory to be as useless as the moon. Vergara was brilliant, with refined manners and an astounding memory. Everything interested him, from botany to poetry; he was incorruptible and totally without political ambition. He planned the war strategy with the same tranquil attention to detail he devoted to his business affairs. In spite of the skepticism of the uniformed troops, and to the surprise of the whole world, he led the Chilean troops straight toward Lima. Just as his niece Nívea had said, "War is too serious a matter to hand over to the military." The phrase made its way from the bosom of the family to become one of those lapidary statements that form the store of a nation's anecdotes.

By the end of the war the Chileans were preparing a final assault upon Lima. Severo del Valle had been fighting eleven months, saturated with filth, blood, and the most inconceivable barbarism. During that time, his memory of Lynn Sommers had been shredded; he no longer dreamed of her but of the destroyed bodies of the men with whom he had shared mess the day before. The war, more than anything, was forced march and patience; moments of combat were almost a relief in the tedium of mobilizing and waiting. When he could sit down to smoke a cigarette he used the time to scribble a few lines to Nívea in the same tone of camaraderie he had always used with her. He did not speak of love, but gradually he was realizing that she would be the only woman in his life and that Lynn Sommers had been nothing more than a prolonged fantasy. Nívea wrote regularly—though not all her letters reached their destination—to tell him of the family, life in the city, her rare meetings with her uncle José Francisco and the books he recommended. She also commented that she was going through an unsettling spiritual transformation, that she was distancing herself from some of the Catholic rites that to her seemed demonstrations of paganism and seeking the roots of a Christianity that was more philosophical than dogmatic. She was worried that Severo, immersed in harshness and cruelty, would lose contact with his soul and be changed into someone she didn't know. The idea that he might have to kill was intolerable to her. She tried not to think about that, but the stories of soldiers stabbed to death, of decapitated bodies, of raped women and children impaled on bayonets were impossible to ignore. Would Severo be involved in such atrocities? Could a man who witnessed such things find peace again, become a husband and father of a family? Could she love him in spite of everything? Severo del Valle asked himself those same questions as his regiment prepared to attack a few miles from the capital of Peru. At the end of December the Chilean contingent was ready for action in a valley south of Lima. They had trained rigorously; they had a large army, mules and horses, ammunition, food and water, and several sailing vessels to transport the troops, in addition to four field hospitals with six hundred beds and two hospital ships flying the flag of the Red Cross. One of the commanders marched to the scene of battle with his brigade intact, after crossing endless swamps and mountains, and arrived looking like a mogul prince, followed by a train of fifteen hundred Chinese with wives, children, and animals. When he saw them, Severo del Valle thought he must be victim of hallucination in which all of Chinatown had deserted San Francisco to be trapped in the same war as he. The colorful commander had recruited the Chinese along the way; immigrants working in slavelike conditions and caught between two fires, without loyalty to any group, they had decided to throw in their lot with the Chileans. As the Christians were celebrating mass before entering battle, the Asians organized their own ceremony; then the military chaplains sprinkled everyone with holy water. "It's a circus here," Severo wrote Nívea that day, never suspecting it would be his last letter. Encouraging the soldiers and directing the embarkation of thousands and thousands of men, animals, cannons, and provisions, was Minister Vergara in person, on his feet beneath a blazing sun from six in the morning until well into the night.

The Peruvians had organized two lines of defense a few kilometers from the city and in locations difficult for the attackers to access. On steep, sandy cliffs they had massed forts, ramparts, batteries of cannon, and sandbag-protected trenches for their riflemen. They had also salted the beach with hidden land mines that exploded on contact. These two lines of defense were linked with the city of Lima by railroad to guarantee transport for troops, wounded, and provisions. As Severo del Valle and his comrades-in-arms knew before initiating the attack in mid-January of 1881, the victory—if there were to be a victory—would come at the cost of many lives.

• • •

That January afternoon the troops were ready for the march upon the capital of Peru. After mess, and after breaking down camp, they burned the shacks where they had slept and divided into three groups with the purpose of taking the enemy defenses by surprise under cover of thick fog. They moved in silence, each with his heavy equipment on his back and rifle at the ready, prepared to attack "head on, Chilean style," as the generals had decided, aware that the most powerful weapon in their arsenal was the daring and ferocity of soldiers drunk with violence. Severo del Valle had seen the canteens of liquor and gunpowder passed around, an incendiary mixture that left a man's gut in flames but spurred him to unthinkable courage. He had tried it once, but afterward suffered vomiting and headaches for two days, so he preferred to go into battle cold. The march through the silence and blackness of the pampa seemed interminable, even with brief moments of pause. After midnight, the large company of soldiers halted for an hour. They planned to storm a coastal town near Lima before dawn, but the contradictory orders and confusion of their commanders spoiled the plan. Little was known about the situation of their advance lines, but apparently the battle had already begun; that forced the exhausted troops to continue without a breather. Following the example of the others, Severo jettisoned his knapsack, blanket, and remaining equipment; he fitted his rifle with the bayonet and began to run forward blindly, shouting at the top of his lungs like a wild beast, for now it was a question not of taking the enemy by surprise but of frightening them. The Peruvians were waiting for them, and as soon as they were within range, they let fly a broadside of lead. Smoke and dust were added to fog, covering the horizon with an impenetrable mantle as the air filled with terror: bugles sounding the charge, war whoops, sounds of battle, the howls of the wounded, the whinnying of horses, and roar of cannon fire. The ground was mined but the Chileans advanced anyway, with the savage cry, "Gut them!" on their lips. Severo del Valle saw two of his companions blown to bits after they stepped on a mine a few meters away. He did not even stop to think that the next explosion might be for him; there was no time to think of anything—the first soldiers were at the enemy line, jumping over trenches, dropping into them with curved knives clamped between their teeth and bayonets fixed, killing and dying amid streams of blood. The surviving Peruvians retreated, and the attackers began to scale the hills, forcing back the defenders. With no idea of what he was doing, Severo del Valle found himself with sword in hand, obliterating one man, then shooting another point-blank in the head as he ran away. Fury and horror had possessed him completely; like all the others, he had become an animal. His uniform was torn and soaked with blood, a piece of someone's gut was hanging from one sleeve, he was hoarse from yelling and cursing; he had lost his fear and his identity, he was nothing but a killing machine, dealing blows without seeing where they fell, his only goal to reach the top of the hill.

At seven in the morning, after two hours of battle, the first Chilean flag fluttered atop one of the peaks, and Severo, on his knees on the hill, saw a large group of Peruvian soldiers retreating in disarray but re-forming in the patio of a hacienda where they faced the frontal charge of the Chilean cavalry. Within a few minutes all hell had broken loose. Severo del Valle, running in that direction, saw the gleam of upheld swords and heard the volleys of shots and cries of pain. By the time he reached the hacienda, the enemy was already fleeing, again pursued by Chilean troops. That was when he heard his commander's voice telling him to get the men of his detachment together and attack the nearby beach town. That brief pause, as lines were being organized, gave Severo a moment to breathe; he fell to the ground, forehead in the dirt, gasping, trembling, his hands frozen on his weapon. In his mind, advancing was a kind of madness; not only was his regiment outnumbered but, confronting troops positioned in houses and buildings, they would have to fight door to door. His mission, however, was not to think but to obey his superior's orders and reduce that Peruvian town to rubble, ash, and death. Minutes later he was running in the lead of his companions as projectiles whistled all around them. They entered the town in two columns, one on each side of the main street. Most of the inhabitants had fled at the cry, "The Chileans are coming!" but those who remained were determined to fight with everything at hand, from kitchen knives to jugs of boiling oil poured from the balconies. Severo's regiment had instructions to go from house to house until the town was emptied out, not an easy task since it was filled with Peruvian soldiers taking shelter behind roof battlements, in trees, windows, and deep-set doors. Severo's throat was raw and his eyes were bloodshot; he could barely see a meter in front of him; the air, dense with smoke and dust, had become unbreathable, and the confusion was so great that no one knew what to do, but simply imitated the men in front of them. Suddenly Severo heard a hail of bullets, and he understood he could not advance any farther—he had to seek shelter. He butted open the nearest door and burst into the room with his sword drawn, blinded by the contrast between the blazing sun outside and interior shadow. He needed at least a few minutes to reload his rifle but didn't have that time: a bloodcurdling scream paralyzed him, and he glimpsed the silhouette of a figure that had been crouched in one corner and now rose before him, brandishing a hatchet. He managed to protect his head with his arms and throw his body backward. The hatchet struck like a lighting bolt on his left foot, nailing it to the floor. Severo del Valle had no idea what had happened, his reaction was pure instinct. With all the weight of his body, he thrust with his fixed bayonet, buried it in the belly of his attacker, and then raked upward with brutal force. A spurt of blood hit him in the face. And only then did he realize that his enemy was a girl. He had gutted her like a sheep, and she had sunk to her knees and was trying to hold in the intestines beginning to spill onto the wood floor. Their eyes met for an immeasurable moment, dumbfounded, wondering in the eternal silence of that instant who the other was, why they were in this position, why they were bleeding, why they had to die.

Severo tried to hold her, but he couldn't move, and for the first time he felt the terrible pain in his foot rising like a tongue of fire from his leg to his chest. At that instant another Chilean soldier erupted into the room. With one glance he evaluated the situation and without hesitation fired point-blank at the woman, who was in any case dead; then he seized the hatchet and with a formidable yank freed Severo. "Come on, Lieutenant, we have to get out of here, the artillery is ready to fire!" Blood was gushing from Severo's foot; he fainted, regained consciousness, and then sank back into darkness. The soldier held his canteen to Severo's lips and forced him to drink a long swig of liquor, then improvised a tourniquet with a kerchief he tied below Severo's knee, grabbed the wounded man's arms, and dragged him from the room. Outside, other hands helped him and forty minutes later, as the Chilean artillery pounded the town with cannon fire, leaving ruin and twisted iron where once there had been a peaceful holiday resort, Severo lay in the patio of the hospital, along with hundreds of mutilated corpses and thousands of wounded abandoned in puddles and besieged by flies, waiting for death or to be saved by a miracle. He was giddy with pain and fear, at times slipping into merciful unconsciousness, and when he did come to he saw the sky had turned black. Following the burning heat of the day came the humid cold of the *camanchaca*, which wrapped night in its mantle of dense fog. In moments of lucidity, Severo remembered the prayers he had learned in childhood and begged for a quick death, as the image of Nívea appeared like an angel; he thought he saw her bending over him, holding him, wiping his forehead with a damp handkerchief, speaking words of love. He repeated Nívea's name, voicelessly pleading for water.

The battle to take Lima ended at six in the evening. In the following days, when a count of dead and wounded could be made, it was calculated that twenty percent of the combatants of both armies had died in those hours. Many more would die afterward as a consequence of infection. Field hospitals were improvised in a school and in tents set up nearby. The wind carried the stench of corruption for miles around. Exhausted doctors and nurses attended the wounded to the extent they were able, but there were more than twenty-five hundred wounded among Chileans ranks and, it was thought, at least seven thousand among the surviving Peruvians. The wounded piled up in corridors and in patios, lying on the ground until their turn came. The most serious were treated first, and Severo del Valle was not yet dying—despite a tremendous loss of strength, blood, and hope—so the stretcher bearers passed him by again and again, giving priority to others. The same soldier who had carried him on his back to the hospital ripped open Severo's boot with his knife, cut off his blood-wet shirt, and with it improvised a binding for the butchered foot, because there were no available bandages, or medicines, or phenol for disinfectant, or opium, or chloroform—everything had been used up or lost in the chaos of the battle. "Loosen the tourniquet from time to time so gangrene doesn't set in your leg, Lieutenant," the soldier counseled. Before he said good-bye, he wished Severo good luck and gave him his most prized possessions: a pouch of tobacco and a canteen with his remaining liquor. Severo del Valle didn't know how long he lay in that patio, perhaps a day, perhaps two. When finally he was picked up to be taken to the doctor, he was unconscious and dehydrated, but when they moved him the pain was so terrible that he woke with a howl. "Hang on, Lieutenant, there's worse to come," said one of the stretcher bearers. Severo found himself in a large room with sand covering the floor, where every so often a couple of orderlies emptied new pails of sand to absorb the blood and in the same buckets carried away amputated limbs to throw on the enormous pyre filling the valley with the odor of burned flesh. Operations on the unfortunate soldiers were performed on four wooden tables covered with metal plates; on the floor were pails of reddened water where sponges were rinsed after stanching blood from severed limbs and piles of rags torn into strips to use as bandages, everything filthy and gritty with sand and sawdust. On a side table were fearsome torture instruments—forceps, scissors, saws, needles—all crusted with dried blood. The cries of the patients filled the air, and the smell of decay, vomit, and excrement was asphyxiating. The doctor was an immigrant from the Balkans who had the hard, sure, quick air of an expert surgeon. He had a two-day growth of beard, eyes red-rimmed with fatigue, and he was wearing a heavy leather apron slick with fresh blood. He removed the improvised bandage from Severo's foot, loosened the tourniquet, and needed only a glance to see that infection had set in and to decide to amputate. There was no doubt at all that he had been cutting off many limbs; he didn't even blink.

"You have any liquor, soldier?" he asked in an obvious foreign accent.

"Water . . ." pleaded Severo del Valle, his tongue dry and swollen.

"Water comes after. Now you need something to dull you a little, but here we don't have a drop of liquor," said the doctor.

Severo pointed to the canteen. The doctor forced him to drink three long swallows, commenting that they had no anesthesia, and used the rest to wet some rags and clean his instruments. Then he signaled the orderlies, who took their places on either side of the table to hold the patient down. This is my hour of truth, Severo had time to think, and he tried to picture Nívea so that he wouldn't die with the image in his heart of the girl he had gutted with his bayonet. A male attendant made a new tourniquet and tied it securely around Severo's leg. The surgeon took up a scalpel, plunged it into flesh some twenty centimeters below the knee, and with a skillful circular motion cut through flesh to the bone. Severo del Valle screamed with pain and immediately lost consciousness, but the orderlies did not let go; they just held him down with greater determination as the doctor used his fingers to pull back skin and muscle, uncovering the bones: then he chose a saw and with three decisive strokes cut through them cleanly. The attendant pulled the cut veins from the stump, and the doctor tied them with incredible dexterity, then loosened the tourniquet slightly as the doctor covered the amputated bone with flesh and skin and stitched it together. The attendants swiftly bandaged the stump, then between them carried Severo to a corner of the room to make way for another patient to be brought, screaming, to the surgeon's table. The entire operation had lasted fewer than six minutes.

In the days following the battle, the Chilean troops had entered Lima. According to official reports published in Chilean newspapers, they did so in an orderly fashion. According to the memory of Lima's inhabitants, it was carnage added to the excesses of defeated, enraged Peruvian soldiers who felt betrayed by their leaders. Part of the civilian population had fled, and affluent families had sought safety on ships in the port, in consulates, and on one beach protected by foreign marines, where the diplomatic corps had set up tents to shelter refugees under neutral flags. Those who stayed to defend their possessions would re-member for the rest of their lives the hellish scenes of drunken soldiers maddened by violence. They sacked and burned houses, raped, beat, and murdered anyone in their path, including women, children, and old people. Finally, one component of the Peruvian regiments laid down their weapons and surrendered, but many soldiers simply fled to the sierra. Two days later the Peruvian general Andrés Cáceres, his leg badly crushed, escaped from the occupied city, aided by his wife and a pair of loyal officers, and disappeared into the seams of the mountains. He had sworn that as long as he had a breath of life he would go on fighting.

In the port of Callao, Peruvian captains ordered their crews to abandon ship and light their powder, sending the entire fleet to the bottom. The explosions woke Severo del Valle, who lay on the filthy sand in one corner of the operating room beside other men who, like him, had just undergone the trauma of amputation. Someone had covered him with a blanket, and at his side was a canteen of water; he reached for it, but his hand shook so hard that he couldn't unscrew it, and so he clutched it to his chest, moaning, until a young canteen worker came to him, opened it, and helped him lift it to his parched lips. He gulped down the entire contents and then, instructed by the girl, who had fought beside the men for months and knew as much about caring for the wounded as the doctors did, he tossed a mouthful of tobacco into his mouth and chewed madly to ease the spasms of postoperative shock. "Killing is easy, soldier, surviving is the hard part. If you're not careful, death will sneak up on you when you're not looking," she warned him. "I'm afraid," Severo tried to say, and maybe she didn't hear what he muttered but sensed his terror, because she removed a small silver medal from her neck and put it in his hand. "May the Virgin look after you," she whispered and bent over and kissed him quickly on the lips before she moved on. Severo was left with the touch of those lips and the medal pressed in his fist. He was shivering, his teeth were chattering, and he was burning with fever; he slept or fainted from time to time, and when he recovered consciousness he was in a stupor from his pain. Hours later the same girl with the dark braids returned and handed him a few moistened rags so he could wipe off the sweat and dried blood; she also brought a tin plate of cornmeal gruel, a chunk of hard bread, and a cup of chicory coffee, a warm dark liquid he didn't even attempt to taste, his weakness and nausea made it seem so disgusting. He buried his head beneath the blanket, surrendering to suffering and despair, moaning and crying like a child until he went to sleep again. "You've lost a lot of blood, my son; if you don't eat you'll die." He was awakened by a chaplain who was going from man to man offering consolation to the wounded and extreme unction to the dying. Severo del Valle remembered that he had come to the war to die. That had been his intention when he lost Lynn Sommers, but now that death was here, hovering over him like a buzzard, awaiting her chance for the last slash of her claws, he was charged with an instinct to live. His desire to save himself was greater than the burning torment that radiated from his leg to every cell of his body, stronger than agony, uncertainty, and terror. He realized that far from caving in to death, he desperately wanted to stay in this world, live in whatever state or condition, however possible, lame, defeated . . .

nothing mattered as long as he lived. Like any soldier, he knew that only one of ten amputees won the battle against blood loss and gangrene— no way to avoid it, it was a question of luck. He decided that he would be one who survived. He thought that his marvelous cousin Nívea deserved a whole man, not a cripple; he didn't want her to see him looking like a beggar, he couldn't bear her pity. Even so, when he closed his eyes, Nívea again appeared at his side; he saw her, untouched by the violence of war or sordidness of the world, bending over him with her intelligent face, her black eyes, and mischievous smile; then his pride would dissolve like salt in water. He hadn't the least doubt that she would love him as much with half a leg as she had loved him with a whole one. He took the spoon in his cramped fingers, tried to control his shaking, forced himself to open his mouth, and swallowed a mouthful of the revolting gruel, already cold and black with flies.

The triumphant Chilean regiments entered Lima in January 1881, and from there attempted to impose the forced peace of defeat on all Peru. Once the barbarous confusion of the first weeks had calmed, the proud victors left behind a contingent of ten thousand men to control the occupied nations, and the remaining men began their voyage to the south to collect their well-deserved laurels, olympically ignoring the thousands of conquered soldiers who had managed to escape to the sierra and who planned to continue fighting from there. The victory had been so crushing that the generals could not imagine that the Peruvians would harry them for three long years. The soul of that obstinate resistance was the legendary General Cáceres, who had by a miracle escaped death and though critically wounded had fled to the mountains, reviving the stubborn seed of courage in a ragged army of ghostly soldiers and Indian conscripts, with whom he waged a cruel guerrilla war of ambushes and skirmishes. Cáceres's soldiers, their uniforms in tatters, often barefoot, undernourished, and desperate, fought with knives, lances, clubs, stones, and a few antiquated rifles, but they had the advantage of knowing the terrain.

They had chosen the right field of battle for engaging a disciplined and well-armed, although not always well supplied, enemy; here you had to be a condor to reach those steep hills. These guerrillas hid on snowy peaks, in caves and gullies, on windswept heights where the air was so thin and the solitude so immense that only they, men of the sierra, could survive. The Chilean troops' eardrums burst and bled, they fainted from lack of oxygen, and they froze in the icy gorges of the Andes. While they could barely climb another step higher because their hearts couldn't take the strain, the Indians of the altiplano bounded like llamas, carrying on their backs a load equal to their own weight, their only sustenance the bitter meat of eagles and the green wad of coca leaves they chewed like a cud. Those were three years of fighting with no respite and no prisoners but with thousands of dead. The Peruvian forces won a single frontal conflict in a village with no strategic value occupied by seventy-seven Chilean soldiers, several of them ill with typhus. The defenders had only a hundred bullets per man, but they fought all night with such bravery against hundreds of soldiers and Indians that in the desolate dawn, when there were but three men left shooting, the Peruvian officers begged them to surrender because it seemed ignoble to kill them. They did not surrender; they kept fighting and died with bayonets in hand, shouting the name of their country. There were three women with them, whom Indian mobs dragged to the center of the bloody plaza, raped, and cut to pieces. During the night one of them had given birth in the church while her husband fought outside; the infant was also killed. The corpses were mutilated, their bellies slit open, the entrails scooped out, and then, as it was reported in Santiago, the Indians ate the viscera roasted on sticks. That bestiality was not exceptional; both sides were equally barbaric in that war. The final surrender and signing of the peace treaty took place in October 1883, after Cáceres's troops were defeated in a last battle, a massacre by knife and bayonet that left more than a thousand dead on the field. Chile claimed three of Peru's provinces. Bolivia lost its one seaport and was forced to accept an indefinite truce, which would be prolonged for twenty years before a treaty was signed.

Severo del Valle, along with thousands of other wounded, was returned to Chile by ship. While many died of gangrene or of the typhus and dysentery rampant in the military field hospitals, he recovered, thanks to Nívea, who the minute she learned what had happened had contacted her uncle, Minister Vergara, and had hounded him until he ordered a search for Severo, rescued him from a hospital where he was but another among thousands of sick men under ominous conditions, and had him shipped home on the first available transport to Valparaíso. Vergara also issued a special permit for his niece that allowed her to enter the military area of the port, and assigned a lieutenant to help her. When Severo del Valle was brought ashore on a stretcher, she didn't recognize him; he had lost over forty pounds and was a sallow-skinned, wild-haired, and bearded corpse with the terrified, delirious eyes of a madman. Nívea, controlling her panic with the Amazon will that had sustained her in all other aspects of her life, greeted Severo with a cheerful, "Hello, Cousin, a pleasure to see you!" Severo was unable to answer. When he saw her, his relief was so great that he covered his face with his hands so she wouldn't see him cry. The lieutenant had a vehicle waiting and in accord with his orders drove the wounded man and Nívea directly to the minister's palace in Viña del Mar, where his wife had prepared a room. "My husband says that you are to stay here until you can walk, my son," she told Severo. The Vergara family physician called on all the resources of science to cure Severo, but when a month later his stump hadn't healed and he was still shaken by feverish paroxysms, Nívea realized that his soul was sickened from the horrors of war, and that the only remedy against such guilt was love. She decided to take extreme measures.

"I am going to ask my parents' permission to marry you," she announced to Severo.

"I'm dying, Nívea," he sighed.

"You always have some excuse, Severo! So when has dying been an impediment to marriage?"

"Do you want to be a widow without ever having been a wife? I don't want you to go through what happened to me with Lynn."

"I won't be a widow, because you're not going to die. Do you think you could ask me humbly to marry you, Cousin? Tell me, for example, that I am the one woman in your life, your angel, your muse, or something in that vein? Invent something, man! Tell me you can't live without me—at least that much is true, isn't it? I admit that I don't enjoy being the only romantic in this relationship."

"You are insane, Nívea. I'm not even whole, I'm a miserable invalid."

"You mean you lost something besides a little piece of your leg?" she asked, alarmed.

"You consider that little?"

"If you have everything else you're supposed to have, that doesn't seem like very much, Severo," she laughed.

"Then marry me, please," he mumbled with profound relief and a sob in his throat, too weak to embrace her.

"Don't cry, Cousin. Kiss me. You don't need your leg to do that," she replied, bending over the bed exactly as he had envisioned her so many times in his delirium.

Three days later they were married in a brief ceremony in one of the handsome salons of the minister's residence, in the presence of their two families. Given the circumstances, they had a private ceremony, but counting just the closest relatives, that came to ninety-four persons. Severo appeared in a wheelchair, pale and thin, with his hair cut à la Byron, his cheeks shaved, and in elegant attire: a shirt with a stiff collar, gold buttons, and silk necktie. There wasn't time to make a bridal gown or arrange a proper trousseau for Nívea, but her sisters and cousins filled two trunks with the linens they had been embroidering for years for their own hope chests. She wore a white satin dress and a tiara of pearls and diamonds lent to her by her uncle's wife. In the wedding photograph she is radiant, standing beside her husband's chair. That night there was a family dinner that Severo del Valle did not attend because the day's emotions had exhausted him. After the guests left, Nívea was led by her aunt to the room she had prepared for her. "I am terribly sorry that your wedding night has to be like this," the good woman stammered, blushing. "Don't worry, Aunt, I will console myself by saying the rosary," the young woman replied. She waited for the house to fall silent, and when she was sure that there was nothing moving but the sea breeze through the trees in the garden, Nívea got up in her nightgown, felt her way down the long hallways of that palace, and went into Severo's room. The nun hired to keep vigil over the patient's sleep was sprawled in a chair, deep asleep, but Severo was awake, waiting for Nívea. She placed her finger to her lips to caution silence, turned down the gas lamps, and slipped into bed.

Nívea had been educated by nuns, and she came from an old-fashioned family in which bodily functions, say nothing of those related to reproduction, were never mentioned, but she was twenty years old, and she had a passionate heart and good memory. She remembered very well the secret games she'd played in dark corners with her cousin, the shape of Severo's body, the tension of never-satisfied pleasure, the fascination of sin. In those days they had been inhibited by modesty and guilt, and both had come out of those corners trembling and weak, their skin aflame. During the years they had been apart, Nívea had had time to replay every instant shared with her cousin and to transform childhood curiosity into profound love. In addition, she had taken full advantage of her uncle José Francisco Vergara's library. He was a man of liberal and modern thought who accepted no boundary to his intellectual curiosity and did not abide religious censorship. As Nívea was classifying his scientific, art, and military books, she had by chance discovered a secret section of shelves where she found a not inconsiderable number of erotic texts and novels on the blacklist of the church, including an amusing collection of Japanese and Chinese drawings of inventive couples in postures that were anatomically impossible but capable of inspiring an ascetic, even more a person as imaginative as she. The most instructive texts, however, were the pornographic novels written by one Anonymous Lady, rather badly translated from English to Spanish, which the girl took with her, one by one, hidden in her handbag, read studiously, and stealthily returned to the same place—a pointless precaution since her uncle was off directing the war, and no one else in his palace ever went into the library. Guided by those books, Nívea explored her own body, learned the rudiments of humanity's most ancient art, and prepared for the day when she could apply theory to practice. She knew, of course, that she was committing a horrendous sin—pleasure always is sin—but she refrained from discussing the subject with her confessor, since it seemed to her that the pleasure she received and would give in the future was well worth the risk of hell. She prayed that death would not take her suddenly and that before she drew her last breath she could manage to confess the hours of delight those books afforded her. She never imagined that her solitary training would help her infuse life into the man she loved, much less that she would have to do it six feet away from a sleeping nun. Starting with that first night with Severo, Nívea arranged to bring a cup of warm chocolate and a few biscuits to the nurse as she went to say good night to her husband, before going to her own room. The chocolate contained a dose of valerian strong enough to speed a camel to dreamland. Severo del Valle had never imagined that his chaste cousin could be capable of such extraordinary exploits. The mending leg, which caused him shooting pains, fever, and weakness, limited him to a passive role, but what he lacked in vigor Nívea made up with initiative and knowledge. Severo had no idea that such acrobatics were possible, and he was sure they were not Christian, but that did not prevent him from enjoying them immensely. If he hadn't known Nívea from childhood, he would have thought his cousin had been trained in a Turkish seraglio, but if he was uneasy about how this maiden had learned such a variety of professional flourishes, he was intelligent enough not to ask. He followed docilely in the voyage of the senses as far as his body could go, surrendering along the way the last shred of his soul. They explored one another beneath the covers in ways described by the pornographers in the library of the honorable minister of war, and in others they invented, spurred by desire and love but limited by the bandaged stump and by the nun snoring in her armchair. Dawn would surprise them throbbing in a knot of arms, their lips joined, breathing in unison, and as soon as the first ray of light peered through the window, Nívea would slip like a shadow back to her room. Their former childish games were transformed into true marathons of lust; they caressed with voracious appetites, kissed, licked, and penetrated, all this in darkness and in the most absolute silence, swallowing their sighs and biting pillows to smother the sounds of joyous licentiousness that lifted them to glory again and again during those all-too-brief nights. The minutes flew by: no sooner had Nívea materialized like a ghost in the room and climbed into Severo's bed than it was morning. Neither of the two closed their eyes, they couldn't lose a minute of those blessed encounters. The next day Severo would sleep like a newborn babe until noon, but Nívea would get up early with the befuddled air of a sleepwalker and carry out her normal routines. In the afternoons Severo del Valle would rest in his wheelchair on the terrace, watching the sun set over the sea, while by his side his wife fell asleep over her embroidery. In front of others they behaved like brother and sister; they never touched and scarcely glanced at one another, but the atmosphere around them was charged. They passed the day counting the hours, waiting with delirious impatience for the moment to hold each other in bed. What they were doing by night would have horrified the doctor, their families, society in general—never mind the nun. Meanwhile, family and friends were going about commenting on Nívea's sacrifice, that pure, Catholic girl condemned to a platonic love, and about the moral fortitude of Severo, who had lost a leg and ruined his life defending his country. Gossipy old ladies wove a tale that a leg wasn't all Severo had lost on the battlefield—it was his male attributes as well. Poor things, they would lament among sighs, never suspecting what a romp that pair of dissolutes were having. After a week of anesthetizing the nun with hot chocolate and making love like gypsies, Severo's stump had healed and his temperature returned to normal. Before two months had passed, Severo del Valle was walking with crutches and beginning to talk about a wooden leg, while Nívea was vomiting up her insides in one of the twenty-three bathrooms in her uncle's palace. When there was nothing to do but confess that Nívea was in a family way, the surprise was so great that it was even suggested that her pregnancy was a miracle. The nun professed to be the most scandalized of all, but Severo and Nívea suspected that despite the massive doses of valerian, the blessed woman had learned a great deal; she had pretended to sleep so as not to deprive herself of the pleasure of spying on them. The one person who was able to imagine how the "miracle" had happened, and to laugh uproariously as he celebrated the couple's cleverness, was Minister Vergara. By the time Severo was able to take his first steps with his artificial leg, and Nívea's belly was not to be disguised, he helped them get settled in another house and gave Severo del Valle a job. "The nation, and the Liberal party, need men of your audacity," he said, although in truth the audacious one was Nívea.

I never knew my grandfather Feliciano Rodríguez de Santa Cruz. He died a few months before I came to live in his house. He suffered apoplexy while presiding at the head of the table during a banquet in his mansion on Nob Hill, choking on a veal pie and red French wine. Several guests picked him up from the floor and laid him, dying, on a sofa with his handsome Arab prince's head on the lap of Paulina del Valle, who to keep up his spirits kept repeating, "Don't die on me, Feliciano, you know widows never get invited anywhere. Breathe, man! If you breathe, I promise that this very day I'll remove the bolt from my door." They tell that Feliciano managed to smile before his heart swelled with blood and exploded. There are countless photographs of that hearty, happy Chilean. It is easy to imagine him alive, because none is posed for a painter or photographer; in every one he gives the impression of having been caught in a spontaneous gesture. He showed shark's teeth when he laughed, waved his arms as he talked, and moved with the certainty and arrogance of a pirate. Paulina del Valle crumbled at his death; she was so depressed that she was unable to attend either his funeral or any of the many homages paid him by the city. Since her three sons were away, it fell to the butler, Williams, and the family lawyers to take charge of the services. The two younger sons arrived a few weeks later, but Matías was wandering around Germany and, using the excuse of his health, did not appear to console his mother. For the first time in her life Paulina lost her coquettishness, her appetite, and her interest in the account books; she refused to go out, and spent days in her bed. She did not allow anyone to see her in that condition; the only people who knew of her grieving were her chambermaids and Williams, who pretended not to notice but from a prudent distant kept watch in order to be of help when she asked. One afternoon Paulina happened to stop in front of the large gold-framed mirror that occupied half the wall of her bathroom and saw what she had turned into: a fat, frowsy witch, her turtle's head crowned by a mat of gray tangles. She screamed with horror. No man in the world—certainly not Feliciano—deserved such abnegation, she concluded. She had touched bottom; it was time to kick up from the depths and rise back to the top. She rang the bell to summon her maids and ordered them to help her bathe, and to send for her hairdresser. From that day on, she began to combat her mourning with an iron will, with no help but mountains of sweets and long baths. Night tended to find her soaking in her tub with her mouth stuffed with pastries, but she did not cry again. Around Christmastime she emerged from her seclusion weighing a few pounds more but perfectly composed; then to her amazement she found that in her absence the world had kept turning and no one had missed her, which was another incentive to get back on her feet once and for all. She was not going to be ignored, she decided; she had just turned sixty and she planned to live thirty years more—even if for the sole purpose of mortifying everyone around her. She would wear mourning for a few months, it was the least she could do out of respect for Feliciano, but he would not want to see her turn into one of those Greek widows who bury themselves in black for the rest of their days. She began planning a stunning wardrobe in pastel colors for the New Year and a pleasure trip through Europe. She had always wanted to go to Egypt, but Feliciano had thought it was a land of sand and mummies where nothing interesting had happened for three thousand years. Now that she was alone, she could fulfill that dream. Soon, however, she realized how much her life had changed and how little she was esteemed by San Francisco society; her fortune was not great enough for her to be forgiven her Latin American origins and her kitchen maid's accent. Just as she had said in jest, no one invited her; she was no longer the first to receive invitations to parties, she was not asked to inaugurate a hospital or a monument, her name was dropped from the social pages, and she was barely greeted at the opera. She was excluded. For another thing, she also found it difficult to augment her income because without her husband she had no one to represent her in financial circles. She made a careful accounting of her holdings and realized that her three sons were throwing money away more rapidly that she could earn it; she had debts everywhere, and before Feliciano's death he had made several terrible investments without consulting her. She was not as rich as she thought, but she was far from defeated. She called for Williams and asked him to contract a decorator to remodel the salons, a chef to plan a series of banquets to celebrate the New Year, a travel agent to talk about Egypt, and a couturier to plan her new wardrobe. That is where she was, employing emergency measures to recover from the shock of widowhood, when she was called on by a child dressed in white poplin, a lace bonnet, and high patent leather shoes, and holding the hand of a woman in mourning. It was Eliza Sommers and her granddaughter Aurora, whom Paulina del Valle had not seen in five years.

"I am bringing you the girl, as you always wanted, Paulina," said Eliza sadly.

"Dear God, what happened?" Paulina del Valle asked, caught entirely off guard.

"My husband is dead."

"I see we are both widows," murmured Paulina.

Eliza Sommers explained that she couldn't care for her granddaughter because she had to take Tao Chi'en's body to China, as she had always promised she would do. Paulina del Valle rang for Williams and asked him to take the little girl out to the garden and show her the peacocks, while the two women talked.

"When do you plan to return, Eliza?" Paulina asked.

"It may be a very long journey."

"I don't want to grow fond of the child and then in a few months have to give her back to you. It would break my heart."

"I promise you that won't happen, Paulina. You can give my granddaughter a much better life than I can. I don't belong anywhere. Without Tao, it makes no sense to live in Chinatown, but neither do I fit among Americans, and I have nothing to do in Chile. I am a foreigner everywhere, but I want Lai Ming to have roots: a family and good education. Severo del Valle, her legal father, should be the one to look after her, but he is far away, and he has other children. Since you always wanted to have the girl, I thought—"

"You did right, Eliza!" Paulina interrupted.

Paulina del Valle heard to the end the tragedy that had befallen Eliza Sommers, and learned all the details about Aurora, including the role Severo del Valle played in her fate. Without realizing, along the way her animosity and pride evaporated and she found herself embracing the woman whom moments before she had considered her worst enemy, thanking her for the incredible generosity of bringing her their granddaughter, and swearing to her that she would be a true grandparent—not as good undoubtedly as she and Tao Chi'en had been—but prepared to devote the rest of her life to looking after Aurora and making her happy. That would be her main mission in this world.

"Lai Ming is a clever girl. Soon she will want to know who her father is. Until recently, she believed that her father, her grandfather, her best friend, and God were all the same person: Tao Chi'en," said Eliza.

"What do you want me to tell her if she asks?" Paulina wanted to know.

"Tell her the truth, that is always the easiest to understand," was Eliza's counsel.

"That my son Matías is her biological father and my nephew Severo her legal father?"

"Why not? And tell her that her mother was named Lynn Sommers, and that she was a good and beautiful young woman," murmured Eliza, her voice breaking.

The two grandmothers agreed right there that to avoid confusing their granddaughter even more, it would be best to make a definitive break with her mother's family, and that she would not speak Chinese again or have any contact with her past. At five, they concluded, children don't reason; with time little Lai Ming would forget her origins and the trauma of recent events. Eliza Sommers promised never to attempt any form of communication with the child and Paulina del Valle promised to adore her as she would have the daughter she always wanted and never had. They said good-bye with a quick hug, and Eliza left by the service door, so her granddaughter would not see her leaving.

I have always regretted that those two good women, my grandmothers, Eliza Sommers and Paulina del Valle, decided my future without giving me any say. With the same tenacious determination that allowed her at eighteen to escape from a convent and despite a shaved head run away with her sweetheart, and at twenty-eight to build a fortune transporting prehistoric ice by ship, my grandmother Paulina set out to erase my past. And had it not been for a slip of fate that changed her plans at the last hour, she would have succeeded. I remember very well the first impression I had of her. I see myself entering a palace high on a hill, walking through gardens with mirrors of water and trimmed hedges; I see marble steps with life-size bronze lions on either side, a double door of dark wood, and an enormous hall lighted by the stained-glass windows of a majestic cupola high in the ceiling. I had never been in a place like that; I was half fascinated, half afraid. Soon I was standing before a chair with gold medallions where Paulina del Valle was sitting, a queen on her throne. Since I saw her so many times in that same chair, it isn't hard to picture how she looked that first day: gowned in a profusion of jewels and enough cloth to curtain a house. Imposing. Beside her, the rest of the world disappeared. She had a beautiful voice, a great natural elegance, and white, even teeth, the effect of a perfect set of porcelain dentures. I'm sure that by then her hair was gray, but she dyed it the same chestnut of her youth and added several skillfully arranged hairpieces so that her topknot always looked like a tower. I had never seen a creature of such dimensions, perfectly matched to the size and sumptuousness of her mansion. Now that finally I know everything that happened in the days preceding that moment, I understand that it isn't fair to attribute my fear to that formidable grandmother alone. When I was taken to her house, terror was already part of my baggage, as much as the little suitcase and Chinese doll I was clinging to. After walking me through the garden and seating me in an immense empty dining room before a goblet of ice cream, Williams took me to the watercolor salon, where I thought my grandmother Eliza would be waiting; instead there was Paulina del Valle, who approached me with caution, as if she were trying to trap an elusive cat, and told me how much she loved me and that from then on I would live in that big house and have lots of dolls, and also a pony and little carriage.

"I am your grandmother," she added.

"Where is my real grandmother?" they say I asked.

"I am your real grandmother, Aurora. Your other grandmother has gone on a long trip," Paulina explained.

I started running. I crossed the hall of the cupola, got lost in the library, and ran into the dining room, where I crawled under the table and curled into a ball, speechless with confusion. The table was huge, with a green marble top and legs carved with figures of caryatids, impossible to move. Soon Paulina del Valle and Williams came in, and a couple of servants intending to wheedle me out of hiding, but I scooted away like a weasel as soon as a hand came near. "Leave her alone, señora, she will come out on her own," Williams suggested, but after several hours went by and I was still dug in under the table, he brought me another tall goblet of ice cream, a pillow, and a cover. "When she falls asleep, we'll get her out," Paulina del Valle had said, but I didn't sleep; instead I squatted and peed, fully aware I was doing something bad but too frightened to look for a bathroom. I stayed under the table even while Paulina was dining; from my battle trench I could see her thick legs, her tiny satin shoes with rolls of fat spilling over them, and the black trousers of the men serving dinner. Once or twice she bent down with great difficulty and winked at me, which I answered by burying my face against my knees. I was hungry, tired, and dying to go to the bathroom, but I was as proud as Paulina del Valle herself, and did not easily give up. Shortly afterward, Williams slid a tray beneath the table holding the third ice cream, cookies, and a huge slice of chocolate cake. I waited for him to go away, and when I felt safe I tried to eat, but the more I reached for the food, the farther away the tray was, which the butler was pulling by a cord. When finally I was able to pick up a cookie, I was outside my refuge, but since there was no one else in the dining room I was able to wolf down the treats in peace and fly back beneath the table as soon as I heard a noise. The same routine was repeated several hours later, as it was growing light, until, following the moving tray, I reached the door where Paulina del Valle was waiting with a yellow pup, which she placed in my arms.

"Here, it's for you, Aurora. This puppy is alone and frightened, too," she said.

"My name is Lai Ming."

"Your name is Aurora del Valle," she repeated categorically.

"Where's the privy?" I muttered, with my legs crossed.

And so began my relationship with the colossal grandmother that destiny had sent my way. I was installed in a room next to hers and was given permission to sleep with the puppy, which I named Caramelo because it was that color. At midnight I was wakened by the nightmare of the children in black pajamas, and without thinking twice I flew to the legendary bed of Paulina del Valle, the way I'd climbed every morning into my grandfather's bed to be pampered. I was used to being welcomed in the strong arms of Tao Chi'en; nothing comforted me as much as the way he smelled of the sea and the soothing words he would whisper in Chinese, half asleep. I didn't know that normal children never crossed the threshold of their elders' rooms, much less climbed into their beds. I had been raised with close physical contact, endlessly kissed and rocked by my maternal grandparents; I didn't know any form of consolation or resting besides being in someone's arms. When she saw me, Paulina del Valle pushed me away, horrified, and I began to keen in chorus with the poor dog; we must have been so pitiful that Paulina del Valle motioned for us to come ahead. I leaped onto her bed and covered my head with the sheets. I suppose I fell immediately asleep; in any case I woke up snuggled against her huge gardenia-perfumed breasts, with the pup at our feet. The first thing I did when I woke amid the Florentine dolphins and naiads was ask about my grandparents, Eliza and Tao. I looked all through the house and the gardens for them, and then stood by the door to wait for them to come get me. I kept doing that all week, in spite of the gifts and outings and cuddling from Paulina. On Saturday I ran away. I had never been outside by myself, and I didn't know where I was, but my instinct told me I had to go down the hill and that was how I got to the center of San Francisco, where I wandered for several hours, terrified, until I saw a pair of Chinese men with a little cartload of washing, and followed them at a careful distance because they looked like my uncle Lucky. They headed toward Chinatown—that's where all of the laundries of the city were located—and as soon as I entered that familiar neighborhood I felt safe, even though I didn't know the names of any streets or my grandparents' address. I was shy and too frightened to ask for help, so I kept walking aimlessly, guided by the smell of food, the sound of the language, and the look of the hundreds of little shops I had so often passed holding my grandfather Tao Chi'en's hand. At some moment I became too tired to go on, and I huddled in the doorway of an old building and fell asleep. I was waked by the shaking and grunts of an old woman whose fine, charcoal-painted eyebrows met over her nose, making her look as if she wore a mask. I screamed, terrified, but it was too late to get away because she was holding on with both hands. She carried me, feet kicking in the air, to an evil little room where she locked me in. The room smelled bad, and I suppose my fear and my hunger made me sick, because I began to vomit. I didn't have any idea where I was. As soon as I was over my nausea, I began yelling for my grandfather at the top of my lungs, and then the woman came back and slapped me so hard it took my breath. No one had ever struck me, and I think I was more surprised than hurt. In Cantonese she ordered me to shut my mouth or she would beat me with a bamboo cane, then she took off my clothes and inspected me, with special attention to my mouth, ears, and genitals, put a clean shift on me, and took away my stained clothes. I was alone again in the room, which was sinking into darkness as the light faded from the one little hole for ventilation.

I believe that adventure marked me, because twenty-five years have gone by and I still tremble when I think of those interminable hours. At that time you never saw little girls alone in Chinatown; their families kept an eagle eye on them because with the least carelessness they could disappear into the cracks of child prostitution. I was too young for that, but girls my age were often kidnapped or bought in order to be trained from childhood in all manner of depravities. The woman returned hours later, when it was black as pitch, accompanied by a younger man. They observed me by lamplight and began a heated discussion in their language, and although I knew it, I understood very little because I was so tired and scared to death. Several times I thought I heard the name of my grandfather, Tao Chi'en. They left, and again I was alone, shivering with cold and terror, I don't know for how long. When the door opened again, the light of the lamp blinded me. I heard my name in Chinese, Lai Ming, and recognized the unmistakable voice of my uncle Lucky. His arms lifted me up and that was the last thing I knew; I was dazed with relief. I don't remember the trip in the carriage or the moment I found myself back in the mansion on Nob Hill, facing my grandmother Paulina. Neither do I remember what happened in the weeks that followed, because I had chicken pox and was very sick. It was a confusing time, with many changes and contradictions.

Now as I tie up the loose ends of my past, I can be absolutely sure that I was saved by the good fortune of my uncle Lucky. The woman who had kidnapped me from the street had gone to a representative of her tong, because nothing happened in Chinatown without the knowledge and approval of those associations. The entire community belonged to one tong or other, closed and zealously guarded brotherhoods that enlisted their members by demanding loyalty and commissions in exchange for protection, contacts for jobs, and the promise that they would return the bodies of their members to China should they die on American soil. That man had seen me many times holding my grandfather's hand, and by a fortunate coincidence he belonged to the same tong as Tao Chi'en. He was the one who had called my uncle. Lucky's first impulse was to take me home so that his new wife, ordered by catalog from China, could look after me, but then he realized that his parents' instructions must be respected. After placing me in the hands of Paulina del Valle, my grandmother Eliza had left to take her husband's body back to Hong Kong for burial.

Both she and Tao Chi'en had always maintained that the Chinese quarter of San Francisco was too small a world for me; they wanted me to be part of the United States. Although he didn't agree with that principle, Lucky Chi'en could not disobey the will of his parents, which was why he paid my kidnappers the agreed-upon sum and took me back to Paulina del Valle's house. I would not see him again for more than twenty years, when I went to find him to track down the last details of my story.

The proud family of my paternal grandparents lived in San Francisco for thirty-six years without leaving much of a trace. I have tried to follow their trail. The mansion on Nob Hill is a hotel today, and no one remembers its first owners. Paging through old newspapers in the library, I discovered many mentions of the family in the social pages, as well as the story of the statue of the Republic and my mother's name. I also found a brief notice of the death of my grandfather, Tao Chi'en, a very laudatory obituary written by a Jacob Freemont, and an expression of condolence from the medical society stating its gratitude for the contributions the *zhong-yi* Tao Chi'en had made to Western medicine. That was rare, because the Chinese population was nearly invisible at that time; they were born, they lived and died, on the fringes of the American consciousness, but the prestige of Tao Chi'en surpassed the limits of Chinatown and of California. He was known even in England, where he gave a number of lectures on acupuncture. Without those printed testimonies, most of the protagonists of this story would have been borne away on the winds of oblivion.

My escapade in Chinatown, when I went looking for my maternal grandparents, was yet another motive for Paulina del Valle's decision to return to Chile. She understood that no sumptuous soirées or extravagances were going to restore her to the social position she had enjoyed while her husband was still alive. She was growing old alone, far from her children, her relatives, her language, and her country. What money she had left would never stretch far enough to maintain the style of life she was accustomed to in her forty-five-room mansion, but it was an enormous fortune in Chile, where everything was less expensive. In addition, a granddaughter who was a stranger to her had fallen into her lap, whom she felt obliged to uproot completely from her Chinese past if she was to make a Chilean señorita out of her. Paulina could not bear the idea that I might run away again, so she hired an English nanny to watch me day and night. She canceled her plans to travel to Egypt and the banquets for the New Year, but she sped up the creation of her new wardrobe and then methodically divided her money between banks in the United States and England, sending to Chile only what was indispensable for setting up house because she considered the political situation unstable. She wrote a long letter to her nephew Severo del Valle, needing to reconcile with him and tell him what had happened to Tao Chi'en and about Eliza Sommers's decision to leave Aurora with her, explaining in detail the advantages in having her, Paulina, raise the little girl. Severo del Valle understood her arguments and accepted her proposal, because he already had two children and his wife was expecting their third—although he refused to give Paulina legal custody, as she wanted.

Paulina's lawyers helped her put her finances in order and sell the mansion, while her butler, Williams, took charge of the practical aspects of organizing the family's move to the south end of the world and of crating all his employer's belongings—she did not want to sell anything so no one could say she needed the money. According to the plan, Paulina would take a steamship with me, the English nanny, and other trusted employees, while Williams would send the baggage to Chile and then be free, after accepting a healthy tip in pounds sterling. That was to be his last duty in Paulina del Valle's service. One week before she left, however, the butler asked permission to speak with her in private.

"Begging your pardon, milady, but may I inquire as to why I have fallen from your favor?"

"What are you talking about, Williams! You know how much I appreciate you and how grateful I am for your services."

"Nevertheless, it is not madam's wish to take me to Chile—"

"Williams, for God's sake! The thought had never occurred to me. What would I do with a British butler in Chile? Nobody has one. They would laugh at both of us. Have you looked at a map? That country is very far from here, and no one speaks English; your life there would not be very pleasant. I have no right to ask such a sacrifice of you, Williams."

"If you will allow me to say so, milady, being separated from madam would constitute an even greater sacrifice."

Paulina del Valle sat looking at her employee, eyes round with surprise. For the first time she realized that Williams was something more than an automaton in a black swallowtail coat and white gloves. She saw a man of about fifty, with broad shoulders and a pleasant face, a thick head of pepper-and-salt hair, and penetrating eyes; he did have the rough hands of a stevedore, and his teeth were yellowed by nicotine, although she had never seen him smoking or chewing tobacco. Neither of them spoke for what seemed a very long time, she observing him and he accepting her scrutiny with no sign of discomfort.

"I could not help noticing, milady, the difficulties that widowhood has thrust upon madam," Williams said finally in the indirect language he always used.

"Are you making fun of me?" Paulina smiled.

"Nothing farther from my mind, milady."

"Uh, ah," she began, clearing her throat to fill the long pause that followed the butler's answer.

"Madam will be asking herself where all this is leading," he continued.

"Let's say that you have succeeded in getting my attention, Williams."

"It occurs to me that in view of the fact that I cannot go to Chile as madam's butler, perhaps it would not be an entirely bad idea if I went, ahem, as her husband."

Paulina del Valle thought the floor would open up and that she, chair and all, would drop to the center of the earth. Her first thought was that the man had lost his sanity, there was no other explanation, but when she reappraised his dignity and calm, she swallowed the insults that had risen to her lips.

"Allow me to explain that point of view, madam," he continued. "I do not, naturally, expect to exercise the role of husband in any sentimental area. Nor do I aspire to madam's fortune, which would be entirely safe—for that madam would undertake the necessary legal precautions. My capacity would be very nearly the same as it is now: that is, to be of assistance in every way I am able, employing the maximum discretion. I surmise that in Chile, as elsewhere in the world, a woman alone encounters many obstacles. I would consider it an honor to be responsible for madam's well-being."

"And what would you gain from this curious arrangement?" Paulina inquired, unable to veil her caustic tone.

"For one thing, I would win respect. For another, I admit that the idea of never seeing madam again has tormented me ever since she began to make plans to leave. I have been at madam's side for half my life, and I have become accustomed to that company."

Paulina was mute for another eternity while she mulled over her employee's strange proposition. The way he had put it, it was a good business deal, with advantages for both: he would profit from a higher level of life than he would ever have otherwise, and she would go about on the arm of a man who, all things considered, was extremely distinguished-looking. In truth, he looked like a member of the British nobility. Just imagining the faces of her relatives in Chile, and the envy of her sisters, made her laugh.

"You are at least ten years younger and sixty pounds lighter than I am. Aren't you afraid of ridicule?" she asked, shuddering with laughter.

"Not at all. As for madam, does she fear being seen with someone of my status?"

"I fear nothing in this life, and I take pleasure in shocking people. What is your name, Williams?"

"Frederick, milady."

"Frederick Williams. A good name, aristocratic as you please."

"I regret to inform madam that it is, shall we say, ahem, the only thing aristocratic about me." And Williams smiled.

And that is how one week later, my grandmother, Paulina del Valle, her newly inaugurated husband, her hairdresser, the nanny, two maids, a valet, a manservant, and I set off by train for New York with a carload of trunks, there to take a British steamer to Europe. We also had Caramelo, who was at the stage in his development when dogs hump everything in sight—in this case, my grandmother's fox cape. The cape had tails all around the edge, and Caramelo, confused by the passivity with which the vixens received his amorous advances, kept chewing the tails off. Furious, Paulina del Valle was at the point of tossing both dog and cape overboard, but I threw such a fit that I saved both their skins. My grandmother occupied a three-room suite, and Frederick Williams one of like size across the passageway. In the daytime she entertained herself by eating every hour, changing clothes for every activity, teaching me arithmetic so in the future I could take charge of her account books, and telling me the story of the family so I would know where I came from, without ever clarifying the question of my father's identity, as if I had popped up in the del Valle clan through parthenogenesis. If I asked about my mother or my father, she answered that they were dead, and that it was all right because having a grandmother like her was more than enough. In the meanwhile, Frederick Williams would be playing bridge and reading English newspapers, like all the other gentlemen in first class. He had let his sideburns grow, had a bushy mustache with waxed tips, which gave him an air of importance, and smoked a pipe and Cuban cigars. He confessed to my grandmother that he was an inveterate smoker, and that the most difficult part of his job as butler had been abstaining in public; now finally he could savor his tobacco and throw away the mint tablets he bought wholesale and that by then had eaten holes in his stomach. In those days when men of high position sported a prominent paunch and double chin, the rather slim, athletic figure of Williams was a rarity in good society, although his impeccable good manners were much more convincing than my grandmother's. At night, before they went down together to the ballroom, they would come by the cabin I shared with the nanny and say good night. They were a spectacle, she combed and made up by her hairdresser, gowned for a ball and shimmering with jewels like an obese idol, and he turned into a distinguished prince consort. At times I would sneak down to the salon to spy, openmouthed, at how Frederick Williams was able to steer Paulina del Valle across the dance floor with all the assurance of someone well accustomed to maneuvering heavy tonnage.

We arrived in Chile a year later, when my grandmother's stumbling fortune was back on its feet thanks to sugar speculation during the War of the Pacific. Her theory had been right: people eat more sweets during bad times. Our arrival coincided with a major theatrical event: the incomparable Sarah Bernhardt in her most famous role, *La Dame aux camélias*. The celebrated actress did not have the same success in Santiago she had in the rest of the civilized world because a sanctimonious Chilean society had no sympathy for a tubercular courtesan; it seemed normal to everyone that she would sacrifice herself for her lover to quiet wagging tongues, and they saw no reason for all that drama and wilting camellias. The famous actress was convinced that she had visited a land of major idiots, an opinion Paulina del Valle fully shared. My grandmother had paraded her entourage through several cities of Europe but had not fulfilled her dream of going to Egypt because she felt sure she wouldn't find a camel that could bear her weight and she would have to visit the pyramids on foot beneath a sun like molten lava. In 1886 I was six years old. I spoke a weird mixture of Chinese, English, and Spanish, but I knew the four fundamental operations of arithmetic and with incredibly precocious skill could convert French francs into pounds sterling, and pounds into German marks or Italian lire. I had stopped crying all the time for my grandfather Tao and grandmother Eliza, but I continued to be regularly tortured by the same inexplicable nightmares. There was a black hole in my memory, something always present and dangerous that I couldn't identify, something unknown that terrified me, especially in the dark or in a crowd. I couldn't stand to be surrounded with people, I would begin to scream like someone possessed, and my grandmother Paulina would have to wrap me in her bearlike grasp to calm me. I still had the habit of taking refuge in her bed when I woke up frightened, and a bond grew between us that I am sure saved me from the madness and terror I would otherwise have sunk into. Affected by her need to console me, Paulina del Valle changed in ways imperceptible to everyone except Frederick Williams. She was growing more tolerant and affectionate, and she even lost a little weight— running around after me, she was so busy that she forgot her pastries. I have no doubt she adored me. I say that with no false modesty, since she gave me so much proof of her love; she allowed me to grow up with as much freedom as was possible in those times, igniting my curiosity and showing me the world. She never allowed sentimentality or complaints: "There's no looking back," was one of her mottoes. She played pranks on me—some a little heavy-handed—until I learned to turn the tables, and that marked the tone of our relationship. Once in the patio I found a lizard that had been run over by a carriage wheel and lain in the sun for several days; it was fossilized and forever preserved in its sorry guise of a squashed reptile. I picked it up and kept it, not sure why, until I devised the perfect use for it. I was sitting at my desk doing my arithmetic, and when my grandmother wandered into the room for some reason, I pretended to have an uncontrollable attack of coughing, and she came over to pound me on the back. I bent way over, with my face in my hands, and to the poor woman's dismay I "spit up" the lizard, which landed in my skirt. She was so shocked when she saw the horror my lungs had apparently spewed forth that she fell back into a chair, but later she laughed as hard as I had, and kept the desiccated little lizard between the pages of a book as a souvenir. It's hard to understand why, as strong as she was, that woman was afraid to tell me the truth about my past. It occurs to me that despite her defiant stance in the face of convention, she was never able to overcome the prejudices of her class. To protect me from rejection, she carefully hid my one-quarter Chinese blood, my mother's modest social position, and the fact that in truth I was a bastard. This is the only thing I can ever criticize my giant of a grandmother for.

In Europe I met Matías Rodríguez de Santa Cruz y del Valle. Paulina did not respect the agreement she had made with my grandmother Eliza Sommers—to tell me the truth—and instead of introducing him as my father, she said he was another uncle, one of the many every Chilean child has, since all relatives or friends of the family old enough to carry the title with a certain dignity are automatically called aunt, or uncle, which was why I always called the good Williams Uncle Frederick. I learned several years later that Matías was my father, when he came home to Chile to die, and he himself told me. The man I met made no particular impression on me; he was thin, pale, and nice-looking. Sitting, he looked young, but much older when he tried to move. He walked with a cane and always had a servant to open doors for him, help him on with his overcoat, light his cigarettes, or hand him the glass of water that was always on a table by his side, because the effort of reaching for something was too much for him. My grandmother Paulina explained that this uncle suffered from arthritis, a very painful condition that made him fragile as glass, she said, and that I was to be very careful when I went near him. She would die years later without ever learning that her eldest son suffered from syphilis, not arthritis.

The del Valle family's stupefaction when my grandmother arrived in Santiago was monumental. From Buenos Aires we had traveled across Argentina to Chile, a true safari when you take into account the volume of luggage that had come from Europe plus the eleven suitcases filled with purchases we had made in Buenos Aires. We traveled in coaches followed by our baggage strapped onto mules and accompanied by armed guards under Uncle Frederick's command because there were bandits on both sides of the border—although unfortunately they did not attack us and we reached Chile with nothing interesting to tell about crossing the Andes. Along the way we had lost the nanny, who fell in love with an Argentine and chose to stay there, and one maid who died of typhus, but my uncle Frederick arranged for us to get domestic help at each stage of our pilgrimage. Paulina had decided to settle in Santiago, the capital, because after living so many years in the United States she thought that the port of Valparaíso, where she had been born, would seem too small. Besides, she was used to being some distance from her clan, and she wasn't up to seeing her relatives every day, a trying custom in every long-suffering Chilean family. Even in Santiago, however, she was not free from family, since she had several sisters who had married among "the best people," as members of the upper class called one another, assuming, I suppose, that the rest of the world fell into the category of "the worst people." Her nephew, Severo del Valle, who also lived in the capital, came with his wife to say hello as soon as we arrived. From the first day we met, I have a much clearer memory of them than of my father in Europe, because they welcomed me with such an extreme show of affection that it frightened me. The most memorable thing about Severo was that despite his lameness and his cane he looked like the prince in illustrations of storybooks—seldom have I seen a more handsome man—and the most memorable thing about Nívea was that she was preceded by an enormous round belly. In those times, procreation was thought to be indecent, and among the bourgeoisie pregnant women were confined to their homes—but not Nívea. She had no intention of hiding her state; she exhibited it, indifferent to the disturbance she caused. In the street, people tried not to look at her, as if she had some deformity, or were naked. I had never seen anything like that, and when I asked what was the matter with that lady, my grandmother Paulina explained that the poor thing had swallowed a melon. In contrast with her handsome husband, Nívea looked like a mouse, but you only had to talk with her a couple of minutes to fall prisoner to her charm and tremendous energy.

Santiago was a beautiful city situated in a fertile valley and surrounded by tall mountains purple in summer and snow-covered in winter, a tranquil, sleepy city filled with the odors of flowering gardens and horse manure. It had the look of a French city, with its old trees, plazas, Moorish fountains, gates, and alleyways, its elegant women and exquisite shops where the finest from Europe and the Orient was sold, its parks and boulevards where the wealthy showed off their coaches and magnificent horses. The streets were crowded with packs of stray dogs and vendors hawking the humble wares in their baskets, and doves and sparrows nested on the tiled roofs. Church bells marked the passage of the hours, except during siesta time, when the streets were empty and people took their rest. It was a stately city, very different from San Francisco with its unmistakable seal of a frontier town and colorful, multiracial air. Paulina del Valle bought a mansion on Ejército Libertador, the city's most aristocratic street, near the Alameda de las Delicias, where every spring the Napoleonic coach, plumed horses, and honor guard of the president of the republic passed on its way to the military parade and patriotic celebrations in the Parque de Marte. The house could not compare in splendor to the mansion in San Francisco, but for Santiago it had an irritating opulence. Even so, it was not the display of prosperity and lack of tact that staggered the city's society, but the pedigreed husband Paulina del Valle "had bought," as they said, as well as the gossip that circulated about her enormous gilded bed with its mythological sea creatures, in which who knows what sins that geriatric pair committed. To Williams they attributed titles of nobility and bad intentions. What reason would a British lord, so refined, so handsome, have for marrying a woman of known bad character, and a lot older than he to boot? He could only be a ruined count, a fortune hunter ready to strip Paulina of her money and then abandon her. Deep down, everyone hoped that was the case, that he would take my arrogant grandmother down a notch or two; nevertheless, no one snubbed Paulina's husband, true to the Chilean tradition of hospitality toward strangers. Besides, Frederick Williams won the respect of pagans and Christians alike with his excellent manners, his prosaic way of confronting life, and his monarchic ideas: he believed that all the ills of society were owing to lack of discipline and of respect for hierarchies. The motto for that man who had been a servant for so many years was, "Everyone in his place and a place for everyone." When he became my grandmother's husband he assumed his role as oligarch as naturally as earlier he had lived his destiny as a servant. He had never attempted then to mix with anyone above him, and now he never had contact with those beneath him: he believed that separation of the classes was indispensable if chaos and vulgarity were to be avoided. In that family of passionate barbarians, which is what the del Valles were, Williams produced stupor and admiration with his exaggerated courtesy and impassive calm, products of his years as a butler. He spoke four words of Spanish, and his compulsory silence was taken as wisdom, pride, and mystery. The one person who could have unmasked the supposed British noble was Severo del Valle, but he never did so because he liked the former servant and admired the aunt who mocked the world by strutting about like a peacock with her stylish husband.

My grandmother Paulina dove into a campaign of public charity to silence the envy and slander her fortune aroused. She knew how one went about it; she had spent the first years of her life in that country, where helping indigents is the obligatory task of women of good breeding. The more one sacrificed for the poor, taking on tasks in hospitals, asylums, orphanages, and tenements, the higher one rose in general regard, which was why good works were shouted to the winds. To ignore this duty brought on so many critical glances and priestly admonishments that not even Paulina del Valle would have escaped a sense of guilt and fear of condemnation. She trained me in these compassionate labors, but I confess that I was always uncomfortable as we drove into a wretched neighborhood in our luxurious carriage loaded with foodstuffs and with two lackeys to distribute the gifts to ragged creatures who thanked us with a great show of humility but with loathing burning in their eyes.

My grandmother had to educate me at home because I ran away from every one of the religious schools she enrolled me in. The del Valle family convinced her again and again that a boarding school was the only way to turn me into a normal child; they maintained that I needed the company of other girls to overcome my pathological shyness and the firm hand of the nuns to subjugate me. "You have spoiled Aurora too much, Paulina, you are making her into a monster," they said, and my grandmother ended up believing what was obvious. I slept with Caramelo on my bed, ate and read whatever I wanted, spent the day playing games I made up—none of it with much discipline because there was no one around who bothered to impose it. In other words, I enjoyed a rather happy childhood. I couldn't bear the boarding schools with their mustached nuns and throngs of schoolgirls; they reminded me of my frightening nightmare of children in black pajamas. Nor could I tolerate the harshness of the rules, the monotony of the daily schedule, or the cold of those colonial convents. I don't know how often the same routine was repeated: Paulina del Valle dressed me in full regalia, recited her instructions in a threatening tone, carried me off, almost literally, and deposited me with my trunks in the care of some husky novice, then escaped as fast as her pounds would permit, awash in remorse. These were schools for wealthy girls, where submission and ugliness prevailed and the end objective was to give us enough instruction that we were not totally ignorant—a veneer of culture had its value in the matrimonial market—but not so much that we would ask questions. The goal was to subdue personal will for the benefit of the collective good, to make us faithful Catholics, sacrificing mothers, and obedient wives. The nuns began by disciplining the body, the source of vanity and other sins: we were not allowed to laugh, run, or play outside. We bathed once a month, covered with long nightgowns so as not to expose our shame before God, who is in all places. The system was based on the theory that learning must be pounded in, so the rod was not spared. We were taught to fear God, the Devil, all adults, the ruler they used to rap our fingers, the pebbles on which we had to kneel while doing penance, our own thoughts and wishes: fear of fear. We were never praised, for fear of instilling pride, but there were more than enough punishments to temper our characters. Inside those thick walls my uniformed schoolmates survived, rather than lived, hair braided so tight that sometimes their scalps bled, and with chilblain rashes on their hands from the eternal cold. The contrast with their homes, where they were treated like princesses during holidays, had to be enough to madden the sanest among us. I couldn't take it. Once I talked a gardener into helping me jump over the fence and run away. I don't know how I reached Calle Ejército Libertador on my own; I was welcomed by a hysterical Caramelo, but Paulina del Valle nearly went into cardiac arrest when she saw me with my muddy clothes and swollen eyes. I spent a few months at home until external pressures forced my grandmother to repeat the experiment. The second time I hid in the bushes on the patio all night, with the idea of perishing from cold and hunger. I imagined the faces of the nuns and of my family when they discovered my body, and wept out of pity for myself: poor child, martyred at such an early age. The next day the school notified Paulina del Valle of my disappearance, and she descended like a tornado to demand an explanation. While she and Frederick Williams were being led by a red-faced novice to the office of the mother superior, I scrambled through the bushes where I had been hiding to the carriage waiting in the patio, climbed in without the coachman's seeing me, and crouched beneath the seat. Frederick Williams, the coachman, and the mother superior had to help my grandmother into the coach; she was screaming that if I did not appear soon, they would see who Paulina del Valle was! When I crawled out of my hiding on the way home, she forgot her tears of distress, grabbed me by the nape of the neck, and gave me a shaking that lasted at least a couple of blocks, until Uncle Frederick managed to calm her. Consistency, however, was not that good lady's forte; when she learned that I hadn't eaten since the day before and had spent the night outdoors, she covered me with kisses and took me to have ice cream. At the third school where she tried to enroll me, I was rejected out of hand because in the interview with the directress I swore I had seen the devil and that he had green hooves. Finally my grandmother declared defeat. Severo del Valle convinced her there was no reason to go on torturing me, since I could easily learn what I needed at home with private tutors. A string of governesses passed through my childhood—English, French, German—who sequentially succumbed to Chile's polluted water and Paulina del Valle's rages; all those unfortunate women returned to the countries of their origin with chronic diarrhea and bad recollections. My education was rather hit-and-miss until an exceptional Chilean teacher came into my life, Señorita Matilde Pineda, who taught me nearly everything important I know—except common sense, because she didn't have any herself. She was passionate and idealistic, she wrote philosophical poetry she was never able to publish, she had an insatiable hunger for knowledge and the overly intelligent person's intransigence regarding other people's weaknesses. She could not abide laziness; in her presence, the phrase "I can't" was forbidden. My grandmother hired Señorita Pineda because she proclaimed herself an agnostic, a socialist, and a supporter of women's suffrage, three reasons that were more than enough to keep her from being employed in any educational institution. "Let's see if you can counteract a little of the conservative and patriarchal hypocrisy of this family," Paulina del Valle instructed during their first interview, backed by Frederick Williams and Severo del Valle, the only ones who glimpsed the talent of Señorita Pineda; everyone else claimed that the woman would nurture the monster I already had inside me. My aunts immediately classified her as being "above herself," and warned my grandmother against that woman of inferior station who "claimed gentility," as they put it. In contrast, Williams, the most class-conscious man I've ever known, liked her. Six days a week, without fail, my teacher came at seven in the morning to my grandmother's mansion, where I was waiting in full armor: starched white dress, clean fingernails, and freshly combed pigtails. We would eat breakfast in a small informal dining room while we talked about important stories in the newspapers; then we would have a couple of hours of regular classes and the rest of the day go to the museum or the Siglo de Oro bookstore to buy books and drink tea with the owner, Don Pedro Tey. We visited artists, took nature walks, performed chemistry experiments, read stories, wrote poetry, and put on classical plays with figures cut out of cardboard. Señorita Pineda was the one who suggested to my grandmother the idea of forming a ladies' club to channel charitable works and instead of donating used clothes or leftover food to the poor create a fund, run it as if it were a bank, and grant loans to women to start some small venture: an egg business, a seamstress shop, some tubs for taking in laundry, a cart for errands; in short, whatever it took to rise out of the absolute poverty in which they and their children were living. Nothing for the men, said Señorita Pineda, because they would use the loan to buy wine, and in any case the government was working on a plan to assist them, whereas no one took women and children into account. "People don't want handouts, they want a way to earn a living with dignity," my teacher explained, something Paulina del Valle easily understood, and she threw herself into that project with the same enthusiasm with which she embraced her most covetous plans for making money. "With one hand I rake money in and with the other I give it out; that way I kill two birds with one stone. I have a good time, and I get to heaven." And my unique grandmother would roll with laughter. She took that initiative even further and not only formed the ladies' club, which she captained with her usual efficiency—the other women were terrified of her—

but also financed schools and neighborhood clinics, then organized a system for collecting unsold but still edible products from the stands in the market and the bakeries to distribute in orphanages and asylums.

When Nívea came to visit, always pregnant and trailed by one or two nursemaids with children in their arms, Señorita Pineda would abandon the blackboard, and while the nurses looked after the clutch of children we would drink tea, and those two would devote themselves to planning a more just and noble society. Even though Nívea had no surplus time or financial resources, she was the youngest and most active of the ladies in my grandmother's club. Sometimes we would go visit her former professor, Sor María Escapulario, who now that she was no longer allowed to exercise her passion for teaching directed a home for aged nuns; her congregation had decided that her progressive ideas were not appropriate for schoolgirls and that she would do less damage caring for doddering old women than sowing rebellion in childish minds. Sor María Escapulario made do with a small cell in a crumbling building but her garden was enchanted; she always welcomed us there with gratitude because she longed for intellectual conversation, a nonexistent commodity in the nunnery. We took her the books she had asked for and we had bought for her in the dusty Siglo de Oro bookshop. We would also bring presents of biscuits or some sweet to go with tea, which she prepared over a paraffin burner and served in chipped cups. In winter we would stay inside in her cell, she sitting on the one chair, Nívea and Señorita Pineda on the cot, and I on the floor, but any time the weather allowed we would walk through her magical garden among century-old trees, climbing jasmine, roses, camellias, and a myriad of flowers in marvelous disarray whose many perfumes made my head spin. I never lost a word of those conversations, even though I understood very little; I've never again heard such impassioned discussions. They whispered secrets, shouted with laughter, and talked about everything except religion, out of respect for Señorita Matilde Pineda, who maintained that God was dreamed up by men to control other men and especially women. Sor

María Escapulario and Nívea were Catholics, but neither seemed fa-
natic, unlike most of the people around me in those days. In the
United States no one talked about religion, while in Chile it was the
main topic of after-dinner conversations. My grandmother and Uncle
Frederick took me to mass from time to time so we could be seen, because not even Paulina del Valle, with all her audacity and fortune,
could give herself the luxury of not attending. Neither her family nor
her society would have tolerated it.

"Are you Catholic, Grandmother?" I asked every time I had to
postpone a walk or reading a book in order to go to mass.

"Do you think it's possible not to be, in Chile?" she would reply.

"Señorita Pineda doesn't go to mass."

"And look at the price the poor woman's paid. As intelligent as
she is, she could be headmistress of a school if she went to mass. . . ."

Against all logic, Frederick Williams adapted very well to the huge
del Valle family, and to Chile. He must have had innards of steel, because he was the only one who didn't get parasites from the drinking
water and who could eat several empanadas without having his stomach burst into flames. No Chilean we knew, except Severo del Valle
and Don José Francisco Vergara, spoke English; the second tongue of
educated people was French, despite the large numbers of British in
the port of Valparaíso, so that Williams had no choice but to learn
Spanish. Señorita Pineda gave him lessons, and after a few months he
could make himself understood in a functional but badly mangled
Spanish and could read the newspapers and carry on a social life in the
Club de la Unión, where he often played bridge with Patrick Egon, the
North American diplomat in charge of the legation. My grandmother
saw to it that he was accepted in the club, hinting of aristocratic origins
in the English court, which no one took the trouble to check because
titles of nobility had been abolished since independence, and, besides,
you had only to look at the man to believe. By definition, the members of the Club de la Unión belonged to "well-known families," and
were "men of position"—women were not allowed past the door—

and had the identity of Frederick Williams been discovered, any of those fine gentlemen would have challenged him to a duel out of shame for having been tricked by a former California butler transformed into the most refined, elegant, and cultivated club member, best bridge player, and irrefutably one of the wealthiest men in town. Williams kept up with the business world in order to counsel my grandmother Paulina, and with politics, a compulsory theme of social conversation. He declared himself an avowed conservative, like almost everyone in our family, and lamented the fact that in Chile there was no monarchy as there was in Great Britain, because to him democracy seemed vulgar and not very efficient. In the inescapable Sunday dinners in my grandmother's home, he argued with Nívea and Severo, the only liberals in the clan. Their ideas were incompatible, but the three admired one another, and I believe that secretly they mocked the other members of the primitive del Valle tribe. On the rare occasions when we were with Don José Francisco Vergara, with whom he could have spoken English, Frederick Williams kept a respectful distance; given his intellectual superiority, Vergara was the one person who intimidated my uncle, and possibly the only one who would have immediately detected his status as a former servant. I suppose that many people wondered who I was and why Paulina had adopted me, but no one mentioned that to me. At those Sunday family dinners there were twenty or so cousins of various ages, and not one ever asked me about my parents; to accept me, it was enough to know I had the same last name.

It was more difficult for my grandmother to adapt in Chile than for her husband, even though her name and fortune opened all doors to her. She was suffocated by the pettiness and prudery, and missed her former freedom. It was not for nothing that she had lived more than thirty years in California, but as soon as she opened the doors to her mansion she became the leader of social life in Santiago, calling on her great style and common sense, knowing all too well how the wealthy are despised in Chile, especially if they put on airs. None of the liveried lackeys she had in San Francisco, only discreet maids in black dresses and white aprons; no spending a fortune on pharaonic soirées, only modest, family-style parties, so she could not be accused of being a social climber or a nouveau riche, the worst insult possible. She did have at her disposal, of course, her opulent carriages, her enviable horses, and her private box in the Teatro Municipal, with a little buffet area where she served ices and champagne to her guests. Despite her years and her pounds, Paulina del Valle set fashions, because she had just returned from Europe and it was assumed that she was au courant with modern styles and events. In that austere and low-key society, she set herself up as the beacon of foreign influences, the one lady in her circle who spoke English, received magazines and books from New York and Paris, ordered fabrics and shoes and hats directly from London, and smoked in public the same slim Egyptian cigarettes as her son Matías. She bought art and at her table served food no one had ever seen, because even the most parvenu families still ate like the unpolished captains of the Conquest: soup, stew, roast meat, beans, and heavy colonial desserts. The first time my grandmother served foie gras and an assortment of cheeses imported from France, only the men who had been in Europe were able to eat them. When one lady smelled the camemberts and port-saluts, she was so nauseated she had to run to the bathroom and vomit. My grandmother's house was a gathering place for artists and young writers of both sexes, who met to show off works generally within the broad frame of classicism. Unless a person was white and had a good name, he or she had to have unusual talent to be accepted; in that regard Paulina was no different from the rest of Chile's high society. In Santiago, intellectuals gathered in cafés and clubs, and only men were included, based on the belief that women were better off stirring the soup than writing verses. My grandmother's initiative in including female artists in her salon was a novelty that bordered on the amoral.

My life changed in that mansion on Ejército Libertador. For the first time since the death of my grandfather Tao Chi'en, I had a sense of stability, of living somewhere that didn't move and didn't change, a kind of fortress with its foundations deep in solid ground. I took over the entire house; there wasn't a cranny I hadn't explored or a corner I hadn't claimed, including the rooftop, where I passed hours watching the doves, and the servants' quarters, even though I was forbidden to go there. The enormous grounds stretched between two streets and had two entrances, the main one on Calle Ejército Libertador and the servants' entrance on the street behind; there were dozens of sitting rooms, bedrooms, gardens, terraces, hiding places, attics, and staircases. One salon was red, another blue, and a third, used only on grand occasions, was gold, and there was a marvelous glassed-in gallery where the family spent a lot of time among huge Chinese flowerpots, ferns, and caged canaries. In the main dining room there were a Pompeian fresco that ran around all four walls, a number of sideboards filled with collections of china and silver, a crystal teardrop chandelier, and a large window embellished with a perpetually playing Moorish mosaic fountain.

Once my grandmother decided not to send me to school and my classes with Señorita Pineda became routine, I was very happy. Every time I asked a question, that magnificent teacher, instead of giving the answer, showed me how to find it. She taught me to organize my thoughts, to do research, to read and listen, to seek alternatives, to resolve old problems with new solutions, to argue logically. Above all, she taught me not to believe anything blindly, to doubt, and to question even what seemed irrefutably true, such as man's superiority over woman, or one race or social class over another. These were subversive ideas in a patriarchal country in which Indians were never mentioned and you had to descend only one rung in the hierarchy of social classes to disappear from collective memory. She was the first female intellectual I met in my life. Nívea, for all her intelligence and education, could not match my teacher. With her intuition and enormous generosity of spirit, Nívea was half a century ahead of her time, but she never posed as an intellectual, not even in my grandmother's famous gatherings, where she stood out with her passionate speeches on suffrage and her theological doubts. In appearance, Señorita Pineda could not have been more Chilean, that mixture of Spanish and Indian that produces short, broad-hipped women with dark eyes and hair, high cheekbones, and a heavy way of walking, as if they were nailed to the ground. Her mind was unusual for her time and situation. She came from a vigorous family in the south; her father worked for the railroad, and of her eight brothers and sisters she was the only one to finish her studies. She was a disciple and friend of Don Pedro Tey, the owner of the Siglo de Oro bookstore, a Catalán gruff in behavior but softhearted, who guided her reading and lent or gave her books because she couldn't afford them. In any exchange of opinions, however banal, Tey would take the opposite side. I heard him assure her, for example, that South Americans are macaques with a tendency toward extravagance, overindulgence, and laziness, but the minute Señorita Pineda agreed, he would immediately change over and add that at least they were better than his Spanish compatriots, who were always irritable and would fight a duel at the drop of a hat. Although it was impossible for them to agree about anything, they got along very well. Don Pedro Tey must have been at least twenty years older than my teacher, but when they began to talk, the difference in ages evaporated: he grew younger in his enthusiasm and she older in presence and maturity.

Within a period of ten years Severo and Nívea del Valle had six children, and would go on procreating until they had fifteen. I have known Nívea for over twenty years, and have never seen her without a baby in her arms; her fertility would have been a curse if she hadn't loved children so much. "I would give anything to have you teach my children!" Nívea would sigh when she met Señorita Matilde Pineda. "But there are so many of them, Señora Nívea, and I have my hands full with Aurora," my teacher would reply. Severo had become a well-known lawyer, one of the youngest pillars of society and a conspicuous member of the Liberal party. He didn't agree with many points of the politics of the president, also a Liberal, and since he was incapable of hiding his criticisms, he was never called on to serve in the government. His opinions would soon lead him to form a dissident group that went over to the opposition when the Civil War broke out, as did Matilde Pineda and her friend from the Siglo de Oro bookshop. My uncle Severo favored me among his dozens of nieces and nephews; he called me his "adopted daughter" and told me that he had given me the del Valle name, but each time I asked if he knew who my real father was, he would answer with an evasive, "Let's just pretend that I am." The subject gave my grandmother a headache, and if I bedeviled Nívea she would tell me to talk to Severo. It was a vicious circle.

"Grandmother, I can't live with so much mystery," I once told Paulina del Valle.

"Why not? People who have hellish upbringings are always more creative," she answered.

"Or end up crazy," I suggested.

"Among the del Valles, Aurora, there are no out-and-out crazies, only eccentrics, as in any respectable family," she assured me.

Señorita Matilde Pineda swore to me that she knew nothing of my origins, and added that there was nothing to worry about, because it doesn't matter where you come from in this life, only where you're going, but when she taught me Mendel's genetic theories she had to admit that there are good reasons to find out who our ancestors are. What if my father were a madman who went around slitting women's throats?

The revolution began the same day I reached puberty. I woke up with my nightgown stained with something that looked like chocolate. I hid in the bathroom, embarrassed, to wash myself off, then discovered I hadn't soiled myself after all, I had blood between my legs. I shot off, terrified, to tell my grandmother about it and for once didn't find her in her huge imperial bed, something unheard of in a person who never got up until noon. I ran downstairs, followed by a madly barking Caramelo, burst like a spooked horse into the library, and found myself face to face with Severo and Paulina del Valle: he dressed for a journey and she wearing the purple satin bathrobe that made her look like a bishop during Holy Week.

"I'm going to die!" I screamed, throwing myself on her.

"This is not a convenient time to do that," my grandmother replied dryly.

For years people had been complaining about the government, and for months now we had heard that President Balmaceda was intending to declare himself dictator, in the process breaking with fifty-seven years of respect for the constitution. That constitution, drawn up by the aristocracy with the idea of governing forever, granted broad powers to the executive. When power fell into the hands of someone with whose ideas they didn't fully agree, the upper class rebelled. Balmaceda, a brilliant man with modern ideas, had not done too badly, actually. He had advanced education more than any previous president, protected Chilean nitrates from foreign companies, and promoted hospitals and numerous public works, especially railroads, although he began more than he succeeded in finishing. Chile had military and naval power; it was a prosperous country, and its currency was the most solid in Latin America. Nevertheless, the aristocracy could not forgive him for having elevated the middle class and for trying to govern with them, and the clergy could not tolerate the separation of church and state, civil marriage, which had replaced the religious, and the law that allowed the dead of any creed to be buried in cemeteries. (It had been a terrible problem to dispose of the bodies of those who had not been Catholic in life, not to mention atheists and suicides, whose corpses often ended up in ravines or the ocean.) Because of those measures, women abandoned the president en masse. Though they had no political power, they ruled in their homes and exercised tremendous influence. The middle class, which Balmaceda had benefited, also turned its back on him, and he responded with the arrogance of one used to commanding and being obeyed, like any other large landowner of the day. His family owned enormous land-holdings, an entire province with its railroad stations, towns, and hundreds of campesinos. The men of his clan had the reputation not of kindly *patrones* but of crude tyrants who slept with a gun under the pillow and expected blind respect from their peons. That may have been the reason Balmaceda thought he could rule the country as he did his feudal estate. He was a tall, good-looking, virile man, with a clear brow and noble bearing, the child of a novelesque love affair, raised on horseback with a whip in one hand and pistol in the other. He had been a seminary student, but he had no calling for the cassock: he was passionate and vain. His nickname was "El Chascón," referring to his obsession with his hair, his mustaches, and his sideburns, and everyone talked about the overly elegant clothes he ordered from London. They ridiculed his grandiloquent speech and declarations of jealous love for Chile, saying that he identified so much with the nation that he couldn't conceive of it without him at the head: "Mine or no one's!" was the phrase attributed to him. Years of governing had isolated him, and in the end he showed erratic behavior that ranged from mania to depression, but even among his worst enemies he was acknowledged to be a good statesman and of irreproachable honesty, like nearly all the presidents of Chile, who, unlike caudillos of other countries in Latin America, left government service poorer than when they went in. Balmaceda had a vision for the future; he dreamed of creating a great nation, but he lived to see the end of an epoch and the collapse of a party that had been too long in power. The nation and the world were changing, and the liberal regime had become corrupt. Presidents designated their successors, and both civilian and military authorities cheated in elections. The government party always won, thanks to so-called brute force, a well-turned phrase if ever there was one. Even the dead and absent voted for the official candidate; votes were bought and beatings brought the undecided into line. The president faced the implacable opposition of the conservatives, a few groups of dissident liberals, all the clergy, and most of the press. For the first time, the extremes of the political spectrum had banded together in a single cause: to defeat the government. Every day opposition protesters thronged into the Plaza de Armas and were dispersed by mounted police with clubs, and in the president's last tour through the provinces, soldiers had to defend him at sword point against angry crowds who booed him and threw rotten tomatoes. Those indications of discontent left him unmoved, as if he didn't realize that the nation was slipping into chaos. According to Severo del Valle and Señorita Matilde Pineda, eighty percent of the people detested the government, and the most decent thing would be for the president to resign; the climate of tension had become unbearable and at any moment would erupt like a volcano. Which was what had happened that morning in January 1891, when the marines rebelled and Congress removed the president from office.

"There's going to be terrible repression, Aunt," I heard Severo del Valle say. "I'm going north to fight. I beg you to look after Nívea and the children because I won't be able to do it for who knows how long."

"You already lost one leg in the war, Severo; if you lose the other, you'll look like a dwarf."

"I don't have any choice, I'd be killed in Santiago, anyway."

"Don't be so melodramatic, this isn't the opera!"

But Severo del Valle was better informed than his aunt, as would be seen a few days later when the terror was unleashed. The reaction of the president was to dissolve Congress, designate himself dictator, and name a man named Joaquín Godoy to organize the repression. Godoy was a sadist who believed that "the rich must pay for being rich, the poor for being poor, and as for the clergy—they should all be shot!" The army remained loyal to the government, and what had begun as a political revolt turned into a frightening civil war as the two branches of the armed forces confronted each other. Godoy, with the clear support of the army chiefs, proceeded to jail any opposition congressman he could lay a hand on. All civil guarantees were terminated and house searches and systematic torture were begun, while the president locked himself in his palace, repelled by his henchman's methods but convinced that there was no other way to subdue his political enemies. "I don't want to know anything about those measures," he was heard to say more than once. On the street where the Siglo de Oro bookstore was located, no one could sleep at night or go outside during the day for the yells of people being beaten at a nearby police station. None of this was discussed in front of the children, of course, but I learned everything because I knew every corner of the house, and since there wasn't much else to do during those months, I entertained myself by spying on the adults' conversations. As the war boiled outside, inside we lived as if we were in a luxurious convent. My grandmother Paulina sent for Nívea and her regiment of children, wet nurses, and nursemaids and locked up the house tight as a drum, convinced that no one would dare attack a lady of her social position who was married to a British citizen. Just in case, Frederick Williams ran up an English flag on the roof, and kept his weapons oiled.

Severo del Valle left to fight in the north in the nick of time; the next day they raided his house, and if they had found him he would have ended up in the detention center of the political police, where rich and poor alike were tortured. Nívea had been a partisan of the liberal regime, like Severo del Valle, but she had become a zealous opponent when the president tried to instate his successor through fraud and to crush the Congress at the same time. During the months of the revolution, pregnant with a pair of twins and caring for six children, she found time and spirit to work for the opposition in ways that had she been caught would have cost her life. Though everything Nívea did was with Williams's full knowledge, she acted behind the back of my grandmother Paulina, who had given definitive orders to stay out of sight and not attract the attention of the authorities. Señorita Matilde Pineda was the exact opposite of Frederick Williams, the former as socialist as the latter was monarchist, but their hatred of the government united them. In one of the back rooms my grandmother never went into, they set up a small printing press with the help of Don Pedro Tey, where they turned out lampoons and revolutionary pamphlets that Señorita Pineda then hid beneath her cape and delivered house to house. They made me swear that I wouldn't say a word to anyone about what went on in that room, and I didn't, because the secret seemed like a fascinating game, and I had no idea of the danger threatening our family. At the end of the Civil War, though, I realized that the peril had been real; despite Paulina del Valle's position, no one was safe from the long arm of the political police. My grandmother's house was not the sanctuary we supposed; her money, connections, and name would not have saved her from a raid of the house, perhaps even prison. The confusion of those months worked in our favor, as well as the fact that most of the population had turned against the government, and it was impossible to control that many people. Even in the bosom of the police there were supporters of the revolution who helped the same people escape that they were supposed to arrest. In every house where Señorita Pineda knocked on the door to deliver her lampoons, she was received with welcoming arms.

For once, Severo and his relatives were on the same side; in this conflict the conservatives had joined with one segment of the liberals. The rest of the del Valle family went into seclusion on their estates, as far as possible from Santiago, and the young men went to fight in the north where a contingent of volunteers was forming, augmented by rebellious naval units. The army, loyal to the government, planned to wipe out the handful of dissident civilians in a question of days, never imagining the resistance they would encounter. The navy and the revolutionaries headed north to take over the nitrate mines, the major source of the nation's revenues, where regiments of the regular army were quartered. In the first serious confrontation the government troops triumphed, and after the battle they killed all wounded and prisoners, as they had often done during the War of the Pacific ten years before. The brutality of that slaughter so inflamed the revolutionaries that when the two forces again met in battle, they scored an overwhelming victory. Then it was their turn to massacre the defeated. By mid-March, the Congresistas, as the rebels were called, controlled five provinces in the north and had formed a government junta, while in the south President Balmaceda was losing followers minute by minute. What was left of the loyal troops in the north had to retreat south to join the bulk of the army. Fifteen thousand men crossed the cordillera on foot, entered Bolivia, passed through to Argentina, and then recrossed the mountains to reach Santiago. They arrived in the capital dropping with exhaustion, bearded, and ragged; they had walked thousands of kilometers through inhospitable extremes of valleys and peaks, infernal heat and eternal ice, on their trek gathering llamas and vicuñas on the altiplano, gourds and armadillos on the pampas, and birds on the towering peaks. They were welcomed as heroes—that feat had not been equaled since the remote times of the fierce Spanish conquistadors—but not everyone participated in the welcome; the opposition had been growing like an avalanche, impossible to contain. Our house sat there with closed shutters, and my grandmother's orders were that no one should stick his nose outside, but I couldn't contain my curiosity, and I climbed up on the roof to watch the parade.

The arrests, sacking, tortures, and regulations had the opposition on tenterhooks; there was no family that was not divided, no one was free from fear. The troops made surprise roundups to conscript young men, swooping down on funerals, weddings, fields, and factories to arrest men of an age to bear arms and take them away by force. Agriculture and industry were paralyzed for lack of a labor force. The extreme power of the military became intolerable and the president understood that he would have to rein them in, but when finally he tried it was too late; the army had become too arrogant, and it was feared that they would unseat Balmaceda in order to install a military dictatorship a thousand times more frightening than the repression imposed by Godoy's political police. "Nothing's as dangerous as power with impunity," Nívea warned us. I asked Señorita Matilde Pineda what the difference was between the government and the revolutionaries, and her answer was that both were fighting for legitimacy. When I asked my grandmother, she answered, None, they were all scoundrels.

Terror knocked at our door when the government arrested Don Pedro Tey and took him to one of Godoy's feared dungeons. It was suspected, rightly, that he was responsible for the antigovernment political lampoons circulating all over the city. One June night, one of those nights of tedious rain and gusting wind when we were eating in the informal dining room, the door flew open, and Señorita Matilde Pineda burst in unannounced, wild-eyed, pale, her cape soaking wet.

"What is it?" my grandmother asked, annoyed by the teacher's lack of courtesy.

Señorita Pineda blurted out that Godoy's ruffians had raided the Siglo de Oro bookshop, beaten anyone who happened to be there, and then taken Don Pedro Tey away in a closed carriage. My grandmother sat with her fork in the air, waiting for something further that would justify the woman's scandalous entrance; she scarcely knew Señor Tey and could not understand why the news was so urgent. She had no idea that the bookseller came almost daily to her house, entering from the street at the rear, and cranked out his revolutionary pamphlets on a printing press hidden beneath her own roof. Nívea, Williams, and Señorita Pineda, on the other hand, could guess what the consequences could be once the poor wretch was forced to confess—and they knew that sooner or later he would do just that because Godoy's methods left no room for doubt. I saw the three of them exchange desperate looks, and although I didn't understand the scope of what was happening, I could imagine the source.

"Because of that machine we have in the back room?" I asked.

"What machine?" my grandmother cried.

"No machine—" I began, remembering the secret pact, but Paulina del Valle did not let me go on, she took me by one ear and shook me with unusual ferocity.

"What machine, I asked you, you devil's seed!" she screamed.

"I say, Paulina. Leave the child alone. She bears no responsibility in this . . . ahem . . . matter. A printing press," said Frederick Williams.

"A printing press? Here? In my house?" my grandmother bawled.

"I'm afraid so, Aunt," murmured Nívea.

"Shit! What will we do now!" And the matriarch fell back into her chair with her head in her hands, muttering that her own family had betrayed her, that we were going to pay the price for such incomparable idiocy, that we were imbeciles, that she had taken Nívea in with open arms and look how she repaid her, that maybe Frederick didn't know that this could cost them their skins, that we weren't in England or in California, that he was going to learn how things were in Chile, and that she didn't want to see Señorita Pineda ever again in her lifetime, and she forbade her to set foot in her house or speak one word to her granddaughter.

Frederick Williams ordered the carriage and announced that he was off to "resolve the problem," which far from calming my grandmother only increased her panic. Señorita Matilde Pineda gave me a good-bye wave and left, and I would not see her again until years later. Williams went directly to the North American legation and asked to speak with Mr. Patrick Egon, his friend and bridge partner, at that hour hosting an official banquet with other members of the diplomatic corps. Egon supported the government, but he was also deeply democratic, like nearly all North Americans, and he detested Godoy's methods. He listened in private to what Frederick Williams had to say and immediately set into motion a plan to speak with the minister of the interior, who received him that same night but explained that it was not in his power to intercede for the prisoner. He was able, nevertheless, to arrange a meeting with the president early the next day. That was the longest night ever lived in my grandmother's house. No one went to bed. I spent the night curled up with Caramelo in a chair in the hall while maids and servants with suit-cases and trunks, nursemaids and wet nurses with Nívea's children asleep in their arms, and kitchen maids with baskets of foodstuffs all raced back and forth. Even a pair of bird cages with my grand-mother's favorite birds ended up in the carriages. Williams and the gardener, a man who could be trusted, dismantled the printing press, buried the pieces at the back of the third patio, and burned all com-promising papers. By dawn, two family carriages escorted by four armed servants on horseback were ready to drive us out of Santiago. The rest of the household personnel had been sent to take refuge in the nearest church, where other coaches would pick them up a little later. Frederick Williams did not want to come with us.

"I am the one who has brought this upon our heads," he said, "and I shall stay here to guard the house."

"Your life is much more valuable than this house and everything else I own. Please, come with us," Paulina del Valle implored him.

"They will not dare lay a hand on me— I am a British citizen."

"Don't be naive, Frederick. Believe me, no one is safe in these times."

But there was no way to convince him. He kissed me on both cheeks, held my grandmother's hands in his for a long time, and said good-bye to Nívea, who was breathing like a conger eel out of water, whether from fear or simply her advanced pregnancy I have no way of knowing. We left as a timid sun began to light the snowy peaks of the cordillera; the rain had stopped and the skies were clear, but a cold wind was whistling through crevices in the carriage. My grand-mother held me tight in her lap, wrapped in her fox cape, the same one Caramelo had ravaged in a fit of lust. Her mouth was tight with anger and fear, but she had not forgotten her baskets of food, and we were barely out of Santiago on the road south before she opened them and unearthed roast chickens, hard-boiled eggs, pastries, cheeses, breads, wine, and barley water, enough to last the entire trip.

The del Valle aunts and uncles, who had fled to the country when the uprising began in January, welcomed us with delight because we were interrupting seven months of numbing boredom, and we brought news. That news was far from good, but it was worse not to have any at all. I got reacquainted with my cousins, and those days that were so nerve-racking for the adults were like a vacation for the children. We had our fill of fresh milk, fresh cheese, and preserves put up during the summer, we rode horses, splashed in the mud when it rained, played in the stables and garrets, put on plays, and organized a chorus that was quite dismal, since none of us had any musical aptitude. The poplar-bordered road to the house curved through a lush valley where there were few traces of the plow and the pastures seemed abandoned. From time to time we saw rows of dry, scrawny sticks my grandmother said were grapevines. If we passed some campesino along the road, he swept off his straw hat and with his eyes to the ground greeted his *patrones.* "Your Mercy," he would say to us. My grandmother was tired and bad-humored when she arrived, but after a few days she opened her parasol and with Caramelo at her heels walked around the property with great curiosity. I saw her examine the twisted sticks of the vines and pick up handfuls of dirt, which she poured into mysterious little bags. The U-shaped, adobe, red-tiled house was heavy-looking and solid, without a trace of elegance but with the enchantment of walls that have witnessed a long history. In summer it was a paradise of trees gravid with sweet fruit, of the fragrance of flowers, the chatter of excited birds, and buzz of diligent bees, but in winter beneath the chill drizzle and lowering skies it resembled a grumpy old lady. The day began very early and ended at sunset, the hour when we gathered in large rooms badly lighted by candles and kerosene lamps. It was cold, but we would sit about round tables covered with a heavy cloth beneath which the servants set braziers of coals to keep our feet warm. We drank red wine mulled with sugar, orange peel, and cinnamon, the only way it could be swallowed. The del Valle uncles produced that crude wine for family consumption, but my grandmother maintained that it was better suited for removing paint than for trickling down human gullets. Every working estate worth its name cultivated grapes and made its own wine, some better than others, but that one was particularly harsh. Spiders wove their delicate lace on the coffered ceiling, and mice scampered around with tranquil hearts because the house cats couldn't climb that high. The whitewashed or indigo blue walls were bare of ornament, but carvings of saints and images of the crucified Christ were everywhere. At the front door was a figure of the Virgin Mary, with wood head, hands, and feet, blue glass eyes, and human hair. She was always honored with fresh flowers and a lighted votive, and we all crossed ourselves as we passed by; no one came or went without greeting the Madonna. Once a week the virgin's clothing was changed; there was a wardrobe filled with Renaissance gowns, and for processions she was robed in jewels and an ermine cape that had seen better days. We ate four times a day in long ceremonies that were never really concluded before the next began, so that my grandmother got up from the table only to sleep and go to the chapel. At seven in the morning we attended mass and Communion conducted by Father Teodoro Riesco, who lived with my aunts and uncles, a rather ancient priest who had the virtue of tolerance: in his eyes no sin was unpardonable, with the exception of Judas's betrayal. Even the horrible Godoy, according to Father Riesco, would find consolation in the bosom of the Lord. "Not that, Father," Nívea would protest. "Look, if Godoy can be forgiven, I would rather pack up all my children and go to hell with Judas." After sunset the family joined with the children, servants, and peons of the estate for prayers. Everyone would pick up a lighted candle and then march in a line to the rustic chapel on the extreme south end of the house. I came to like those daily rites that marked the calendar, seasons, and lives; I enjoyed arranging the altar flowers and cleaning the gold ciboria. The sacred words were poetry:

I am not moved, my God, to love you
because of promises of heaven yet to come,
nor by threat of a hell I fear so greatly
that it alone prevents me from offending you.

You move me, Lord; I am moved
when I see you mocked, and nailed to a Cross,
moved when I see the wounds of your body,
moved by jeers heaped upon you, by your death.

Moved finally, by your love, so greatly
that even if there were no heaven, I would love you
and though there were no hell, I would fear you.

You do not have to give me reason to love you,
because even if I did not hope for what I hope
I would still love you as I love you.

I think that my grandmother's tough heart melted a little, because after that stay in the country she gradually drew closer to religion; she began going to church by choice and not just to be seen, she stopped cursing the clergy out of habit, as she always had, and when we went back to Santiago she ordered the construction of a beautiful chapel with stained-glass windows at her home on Calle Ejército Libertador, where she prayed in her own way. She was not comfortable with Catholicism, so she adapted it to her measure. After nightly prayers we would go back with our candles to the large sitting room to have *café con leche* while the women knit or embroidered and we children listened, terrified, to the ghost stories our uncles told us. Nothing was as fearsome to us as the *imbunche*, an evil creature from Indian mythology. They told us that the Indians stole newborn babies to turn them into *imbunches*; they stitched up their eyelids and anuses, raised them in caves, fed them blood, broke their legs, turned their head backward, and inserted one arm under the skin of their back, and in that way obtained a variety of supernatural powers. Terrified that we would become food for an *imbunche*, we children never stuck our noses outdoors after sunset, and some of us, I for one, slept with our head under the covers, tormented by spine-chilling nightmares. "What a superstitious ninny you are, Aurora! There isn't any such thing as an *imbunche*. Do you think a baby could survive all those tortures?" My grandmother tried to reason with me, but there was no argument that could stop my teeth from chattering.

Since she was always pregnant, Nívea never relied on counting days but calculated instead the proximity of the coming delivery by the number of times she used the chamber pot. When for two nights in a row she got up thirteen times, she announced at breakfast that it was time to send for a doctor, and in fact her contractions began that same day. There were no doctors in that area, so someone suggested they go get the midwife in the nearest village. She turned out to be a *meica*, a Mapuche Indian of indeterminate years, the same brown color from head to toe: skin, braids, even her vegetal dyed clothes. She arrived on horseback, carrying a bag of plants, oils, and medicinal syrups and wrapped in a mantle pinned at the breast with an enormous silver brooch made from antique colonial coins. My aunts were slightly alarmed, since the *meica* seemed only recently emerged from the deepest reaches of Araucanía, but Nívea welcomed her without any sign of mistrust: she had no fear of what lay ahead because she had done it six times before. The Indian woman spoke very little Spanish, but she seemed to know her craft, and once she took off her mantle we could see she was clean. According to tradition, only women who had conceived could go into the room where a woman was in labor, so the young women and children went to the other end of the house and the men gathered in the billiards room with their cues to play and drink and smoke. Nívea was taken to the main bedroom, accompanied by the Indian and a few of the older women of the family, who took turns praying and helping. Two black hens were stewed to prepare a strong broth that would bolster the mother's strength before and after giving birth, and borage tea was brewed to be given should there be any crisis in breathing or heart distress. My curiosity was stronger than my grandmother's threat to give me a whipping if she caught me anywhere near Nívea, and I slipped through the back rooms to spy. I saw the maids going by with white cloths and basins of warm water and oil of chamomile for massaging the abdomen, also blankets and charcoal for the braziers, because nothing was more feared than a *partum chill*, or cold shivers during the birth. I could hear the uninterrupted murmur of women talking and laughing. It didn't seem to me that there was any atmosphere of anguish or suffering on the other side of that door; just the opposite, it sounded like people having a good time. Since I couldn't see anything from my hiding place, and the ghostly breath of the hallways raised the hair on the back of my neck, I soon grew bored and went off to play with my cousins, but later, as night fell and the family had gathered in the chapel, I sneaked back. By then the voices had stilled and I could clearly hear Nívea's emphatic moans, the murmur of prayers, and sound of rain on the roof tiles. I was crouched in a corner of the hall, trembling with terror since I was sure that Indians might come to steal Nívea's baby. And what if the *meica* was one of the witches who made *imbunches* of newborn babies? Why hadn't Nívea thought about that frightening possibility? I was about to run back to the chapel, where there was light and people, but just that moment one of the women came out to look for something; she left the door half open, and I had a clear view of what was happening in the room. No one saw me because the hall was in darkness; in contrast, the room was bright with the glow of two tallow lamps and a multitude of candles. Three braziers in the corners kept the air much warmer than it was in the rest of the house, and a large pot in which eucalyptus leaves were simmering filled the air with the fresh scent of the forest. Nívea, dressed in a short nightgown, a sweater, and heavy wool socks, was squatting over a blanket, clinging with both hands to two thick ropes hanging from the beams of the ceiling and supported from behind by the *meica*, who was quietly whispering words in another language. Her huge, blue-veined belly looked monstrous in the flickering light of the candles, as if it were separate from her body, not even human. Nívea, bathed in sweat, was straining; her hair was stuck to her forehead, her eyes were closed and circled in purple, her lips swollen. One of my aunts was on her knees praying beside a table that held a small statue of San Ramón Nonato, the patron saint of women in labor, the one saint who had not been born in a normal way but taken through a slit in his mother's belly. Another aunt was standing beside the Indian woman with a basin of warm water and stack of clean cloths. There was a brief pause in which Nívea sucked in air and the *meica* moved in front of her to massage her abdomen with her strong hands, as if accommodating the child inside. Suddenly a stream of bloody liquid soaked the blanket. The *meica* caught it up with a rag that also was immediately blood-soaked, then another and another. "*Bendición, bendición, bendición,*" I heard the Indian say in Spanish. Nívea grabbed the ropes and pushed so hard that the tendons in her neck and veins at her temples seemed about to burst. A mute bellow formed on her lips, and then something appeared between her legs, something the *meica* grasped gently and held for an instant, until Nívea gasped, pushed again, and the baby fully emerged. I thought I was going to faint with fright and revulsion. I retreated, reeling down the long and sinister hallway.

An hour later, while the maids were collecting and preparing to burn the stained rags and other items used during the birth—it was thought that this prevented hemorrhaging—and the *meica* wrapped up the placenta and umbilical cord to be buried under a fig tree, the custom in those parts, the rest of the family gathered in the sitting room around Father Teodoro Riesco to give thanks to God for the birth of a pair of twins, two fine boys who, the priest said, would carry on the del Valle name with honor. Two of the aunts held the infants in their arms, warmly wrapped in little wool blankets and with knit caps on their heads, as each member of the family came up to kiss them on the forehead and say, "God be with you," to ward off any gratuitous evil eye. I couldn't do it. I couldn't welcome my cousins as the others had done because to me they looked like two hideous little worms, and the vision of Nívea's bluish belly expelling them like a bloody mass would haunt me forever.

The second week of August, Frederick Williams came to look for us, elegant, as always, and totally calm, as if the risk of falling into the hands of the political police had been nothing but a collective hallucination. My grandmother welcomed her husband like a bride, with shining eyes and cheeks rosy with emotion; she held her hands out to him, and he kissed them with something more than respect. I realized for the first time that this strange pair were united by ties that very closely resembled affection. By then Paulina was nearly sixty-five, an age at which other women were ground down by the imposed sorrows and calamities of life, but Paulina del Valle seemed invincible. She dyed her hair, a coquettish indulgence no lady of her class allowed herself, and she enhanced it with switches; she dressed with the vanity she had always displayed despite her weight, and she used makeup with such subtlety that no one was suspicious of the blush in her cheeks or the blackness of her eyelashes. Frederick Williams was noticeably younger, and it seems that women found him very attractive, because they were always fluttering their fans and dropping handkerchiefs when he was around. I never saw him respond to any of those overtures; in fact he seemed absolutely devoted to his wife. I have often asked myself whether the relationship between Frederick Williams and Paulina del Valle was more than a marriage of convenience, whether it was as platonic as we all supposed or whether there was an attraction between them. Did they ever make love? No one could know, because he never broached the subject, and my grandmother, who in her last years was able to tell me the most personal things, carried the answer to the other world.

We learned through Uncle Frederick that thanks to the personal intervention of the president, Don Pedro Tey had been set free before Godoy could extract a confession from him, which meant that since our family's name had never been entered on the police rolls, we could go back to our house in Santiago. Nine years later, when my grandmother Paulina died and I saw Señorita Matilde Pineda and Don Pedro Tey again, I learned the details of what really happened, information the good Frederick Williams had wanted to spare us. After raiding the bookstore, beating the employees, and throwing hundreds of books onto piles and burning them, they had taken the Catalan bookseller to their sinister barracks, where they applied the usual treatment. At the end of the session, Tey had lost consciousness without having said a single word, so they emptied a bucket of excrement over him, tied him to a chair, and left him there the rest of the night. The following day, as he was being taken back to his torturers, the North American ambassador, Patrick Egon, had come with an aide-de-camp to the president, demanding the prisoner be set free. They had let him go after warning him that if he told a single word of what had happened they would stand him up before a firing squad. He was led, dripping blood and excrement, to the ambassador's carriage, where Frederick Williams and a doctor were waiting, and driven to the legation of the United States to be given asylum. One month later the government fell, and Don Pedro Tey left the legation, making room for the family of the deposed president, which found refuge under the same flag. The bookseller had spent several frustrating months while his wounds from the beating and the bones in his shoulders healed and he could get his book business back on track. The atrocities he had suffered did not deter him; the idea of going back to Catalonia never entered his mind, and he continued working for the opposition—whatever government was in power. When many years later I thanked him for the terrible torture he endured to protect my family, he told me that he hadn't done it for us but for Señorita Matilde Pineda.

My grandmother Paulina wanted to stay in the country until the revolution was over, but Frederick Williams convinced her that the conflict might last for years and that we should not give up the position we enjoyed in Santiago. The truth is that to him the country estate with its humble campesinos, eternal siestas, and stables knee deep in shit and horseflies seemed a much worse fate than prison.

"Do you recall, my dear, that in the United States the Civil War persisted for four years? The same could happen here," he said.

"Four years? By then there wouldn't be a single Chilean alive. My nephew Severo says that in just these few months ten thousand have already died in battle, and more than a thousand have been shot in the back."

Nívea wanted to return to Santiago with us, even though she was still feeling the effects of the birth of the twins, and she was so insistent that finally my grandmother gave in. At first she hadn't spoken to Nívea because of the business of the printing press, but she forgave her completely when she saw the twins. Soon we were all en route to the capital with the same bundles we'd brought with us weeks before, plus two new babies and minus the birds, which had perished from fright along the road. We had several baskets of food and a jug with the remedy Nívea was supposed to drink to prevent anemia, a nauseating mixture of aged wine and the fresh blood of a young bull. It had been months since Nívea had news of her husband, and as she confessed in a moment of weakness, she was beginning to feel depressed. She never doubted that Severo del Valle would return to her side safe and sound from the war; she had a kind of clairvoyance in regard to her own destiny. Just as she had always known she would be his wife, even when he wrote her that he had married another woman in San Francisco, she knew they would die together in an accident. I have heard her say that many times, the words have come to be a family joke. She was reluctant to stay in the country because it would be difficult for her husband to communicate with her there; in the pandemonium of the revolution the mail tended to be lost, especially in rural areas.

Ever since the outset of her love for Severo, when her unbridled fertility was first evident, Nívea realized that if she followed the usual norms of decorum and stayed at home with every pregnancy and each new baby, she would spend the rest of her life trapped in the house, so she decided not to make a mystery of maternity. Just as she sashayed around exhibiting her bulging womb like a shameless country woman, to the horror of "good" society, she had her babies without any fuss, limited her confinement to three days—instead of the forty the doctor recommended—and went everywhere, including her suffragettes' meetings, with her babies and nursemaids in tow. These nannies were adolescent girls recruited in the country and destined to serve for the rest of their lives unless they married or got pregnant, neither of which was very probable. Those self-sacrificing youngsters grew up, withered, and died in someone else's house; they slept in grimy, windowless rooms and ate food left from the main table. They adored the children it was their lot to look after, especially the boys, and when the girls in the family married, they took their nannies with them as part of their dowry, to serve a second generation of babies. In a time when everything relating to maternity was hidden, living with Nívea taught me things at age eleven that no ordinary girl in my surroundings knew. In the country, when animals were bred or dropped their young, they made us girls go in the house and closed the shutters, the basic assumption being that those functions wounded our sensitive souls and put perverse ideas in our heads. They were right; the lascivious spectacle of a magnificent stud mounting a mare, which I saw by chance on my cousin's estate, still makes my blood run hot. Now, today, in 1910, when the twenty-year age difference between Nívea and me has evaporated and more than my aunt she is my friend, I have realized that her annual babies were never a serious obstacle for her; pregnant or not, she continued her erotic cavortings with her husband. In one of our confidential conversations I asked her why she had so many children—fifteen, of whom eleven are living—and she answered that she couldn't help it; none of the methods recommended by knowledgeable French women had worked for her. She was saved from early decrepitude by her unassailable physical strength and a light heart that allowed her to avoid sentimental entanglements. She raised her children following the same method she used for domestic affairs: delegating. As soon as a baby was born, she bound her breasts tightly and handed the infant over to a wet nurse; in her house there were almost as many nursemaids as children. Nívea's ease in giving birth, her good health, and her detachment from her children preserved her intimate relations with Severo. It isn't hard to perceive the passionate affection that unites them. She has told me that the forbidden books she studied with such dedication in her uncle's library taught her fantastic possibilities for making love, including some very undemanding ones for lovers limited in acrobatic capacity, as was the case for both of them: he because of his amputated leg, and she as the result of her ever-swollen belly. I have no idea what the favorite contortions of those two are, but I imagine that the moments of greatest delight are still those they play in the dark, without making a sound, as they did in the bedroom where a nun sat struggling between the half-sleep caused by valerian-laced hot chocolate and the lure of sin.

News concerning the Revolution was strictly censored by the government, but everyone knew everything, even before it happened. We learned about the conspiracy because we were told by one of my older cousins, who slipped into the house in the company of a peon from the country house who acted as both servant and bodyguard. After dinner, he was closeted for a long time in the study with Frederick Williams and my grandmother while I pretended to read in a corner but was tuned into every word they were saying. My cousin was a large, blond, handsome young man with the eyes and curls of a woman, impulsive and likable. He had grown up in the country and had a real talent for breaking horses; that's the only thing I remember about him. He explained that a few young men, of whom he was one, were planning to blow up some bridges to badger the government.

"Which one of you got that brilliant idea? Do you have a leader?" my grandmother asked sarcastically.

"Not yet, we'll elect one when we meet."

"How many are involved in this endeavor, son?" asked Williams.

"About a hundred, but I don't know how many will come. Not everyone knows what we've called them for—we'll tell them afterward, for security reasons. You understand that, don't you, Aunt?"

"Oh, I understand. Are they all proper little gentlemen like you?" my grandmother wanted to know, more and more agitated.

"We have craftsmen, laborers, country people, and a few of my friends, too."

"And are you provided with weapons?" Frederick Williams asked.

"Swords, knives, and I think there are a few carbines. We'll have to get gunpowder, of course."

"That sounds like the height of idiocy!" my grandmother exploded.

They tried to dissuade my cousin, and he listened with feigned patience, but it was obvious that he had made his decision and that this wasn't the moment to change his view. When he left, he was carrying a leather bag containing a few firearms from the collection of Frederick Williams. Two days later we learned what happened at the site of the conspiracy, a few kilometers from Santiago. All that day, rebels showed up at a herder's shack where they thought they were safe; they spent hours arguing, but in view of the fact that they had so few weapons and that every aspect of the plan was leaking water, they decided to postpone the action, spend the night together as good buddies, and scatter the next morning. They never suspected they had been betrayed. At four in the morning they were attacked by ninety cavalry and forty government infantry troops in a maneuver so swift and sure that the surrounded men never lifted a weapon but surrendered, convinced they were safe since they hadn't as yet committed any crime except to hold an unauthorized meeting. The lieutenant colonel in charge of the detachment lost his head in the heat of the moment and, blind with rage, dragged the first prisoner outside and had him shot and bayoneted until he looked like chopped liver, then picked eight more and shot them in the back. The beatings and slaughter continued until by dawn there were sixteen mutilated bodies. The colonel opened the wine cellars of the absent landholder and then handed the women of the campesinos over to troops drunk and emboldened by impunity. They burned the house and tortured the overseer so savagely that they had to prop him in a chair to shoot him. In the meantime, orders flew back and forth from Santiago, but the waiting did nothing to calm the soldiers, it only fired the fever of violence. The next day, after hours of hell, orders came, written in a general's hand: "Execute them all, immediately." And it was done. Afterward they loaded the cadavers onto five carts to haul them off to a common grave, but the outcry was so great that finally they gave the corpses to their families.

At dusk they delivered the body of my cousin, which my grandmother had claimed by pulling strings tied to her social position and influence. He was brought in wrapped in a bloody blanket, and spirited into a room to be doctored up a little before his mother and sisters saw him. Watching from the staircase, I saw a man in a black frock coat come in carrying a small valise; he went into the room with the corpse while the maids jabbered about how he was a master embalmer who could erase the marks of gunshots with makeup, stuffing, and an upholstery needle. Frederick Williams and my grandmother had turned the gold salon into a blazing chapel with an improvised altar and yellow candles in a tall candelabra. By the time the carriages carrying family and friends began to drive up at dawn, the house was filled with flowers and my cousin, clean, well dressed, and free of any trace of his martyrdom, was laid out in a magnificent silver-studded mahogany coffin. The women, in rigorous mourning, were installed in a double row of chairs, weeping and praying. The men were planning revenge in the gold salon, the maids were serving light food as if it were a picnic, and we children, also dressed in black, were choking with laughter and playing at shooting one another dead. The wakes for my cousin and several of his companions lasted three days in their homes, while church bells tolled, uninterrupted, for the many dead. The authorities didn't dare intervene. Despite the strict censorship, everyone in the nation knew what had occurred; the news exploded like a powder keg, and horror shook both revolutionaries and those loyal to the government. The president didn't want to hear the details and denied all responsibility, as he had done with all the atrocities committed by the military and the feared Godoy.

"They killed unarmed men, brutally, like animals. What would you expect, we're a bloodthirsty country." Nívea, much more angry than sad, proceeded to point out that up to this point in the century we'd had five wars. We Chileans, she said, seem inoffensive, and we have a reputation for being timid. We even speak with saccharine politeness—"Would you be so kind, please, as to get me a little water, if it's no bother"—but at the first opportunity we turn into cannibals. You would have to know where we came from to understand our cruel streak, she said; our ancestors were the fiercest and cruelest Spanish conquistadors, the only ones who stuck it out as far as Chile, on foot, their armor red hot in the desert sun, conquering the worst obstacles of nature. They mixed with the Araucans, as fierce as they, the one people on the continent who were never subjugated. The Indians ate their prisoners, and their chieftains, the *toquis*, wore ceremonial masks fashioned from the dried skins of their oppressors, preferably those with beard and mustache because they themselves had no facial hair. That was how they avenged themselves on the whites, who in turn burned Indians alive, ran pikes up their anuses, cut off their arms, and tore out their eyes. "Enough! I forbid any more talk of such barbarity in front of my granddaughter," my grandmother interrupted.

The slaughter of the young conspirators was the spark that ignited the final battles of the civil war. In the days that followed, the revolutionaries put ashore an army of nine thousand men, backed by naval artillery, that advanced toward the port of Valparaíso at full tilt and in apparent disarray, like a horde of Huns, but there was a very clear plan in that chaos: within a few hours they had crushed their enemies. The government reserves lost three of every ten men. The revolutionary army occupied Valparaíso and from there moved quickly to take over Santiago and the rest of the country. In the meantime the president was directing the war from his office by telegraph and telephone, but the reports that came through to him were inaccurate and his orders were lost in the ether because most of the telephone operators belonged to the revolutionary faction. The president heard the news of the defeat at dinnertime. He finished his meal, showing no emotion, then ordered his family to take refuge in the North American embassy, picked up his muffler, his overcoat, and his hat, and, accompanied by a friend, walked to the Argentine legation only a few blocks from the presidential palace. One of the opponents of his government had been given asylum there and they nearly met at the door: one entering, defeated, and the other leaving, triumphant. The persecutor had become the persecuted.

The revolutionaries marched on the capital amid the acclaim of the very citizenry that months before had applauded the government troops. Within a few hours the residents of Santiago had poured out into the streets with red ribbons tied to their arms, most to celebrate but some to hide, fearing the worst from the soldiers and stirred-up crowds. The new authorities put out a call to cooperate in orderly and peaceful fashion, which the mobs interpreted in their own way. They formed gangs with a leader at the head that ran around the city with lists of houses to be sacked, each identified on a map with a precise address. It was said later that the lists were drawn up with malevolence and vengeful spirit by certain ladies in high society. That may be, but it is clear to me that Paulina del Valle and Nívea were not capable of such baseness, despite their hatred for the overthrown government. Just the opposite—they hid a couple of families in their house while the popular furor cooled and the boring calm of the days before the revolution returned—something we all badly missed. The sacking of Santiago was a methodical, even entertaining action—seen from a distance, naturally. Ahead of the "commission," a euphemism for the gangs, went the leader ringing a little bell and giving orders: "You can steal here, boys, but don't break anything." "Save the documents for me here, and then burn the house." "Here you can take anything you want and then smash the rest." The "commission" respectfully followed instructions, and if the owners were present they would greet them politely and then proceed to the sacking with boisterous abandon, like children at a party. They opened desks, removed private papers and documents, which they handed to their leader, then hacked furniture to bits, carried off what they liked, and finally sprinkled the walls with paraffin and set fire to them. From the room he occupied in the Argentine legation, the deposed president Balmaceda heard the roars from the people in the streets. After writing his political testament, and fearing that his family would pay the price for hatred toward him, he shot himself in the temple. The maid who took in his dinner that night was the last to see him alive. At eight in the morning he was found on his bed, properly dressed, his head resting on the bloody pillow. That bullet immediately converted him into a martyr, and in future years he would come to be the symbol of freedom and democracy, respected by even his most ferocious enemies. As my grandmother said, Chile is a country with a bad memory—in the few months of the revolution, more Chileans had died than during the four years of the War of the Pacific.

Severo del Valle showed up in the midst of that chaos, bearded and caked with mud, looking for his wife, whom he hadn't seen since January. He had a major surprise in store to find her with two more children; in the tumult of the revolution she had forgotten to tell him before he left that she was pregnant. The twins had begun to fill out, and in a couple of weeks had taken on a more or less human appearance; they were no longer the wrinkled, bluish little shrews they'd been at birth. Nívea threw her arms around her husband's neck, and that was the first time in my life I had witnessed a long mouth-to-mouth kiss. My grandmother, befuddled, tried to distract me, but to no avail, and I still remember the enormous impact that kiss had on me; it marked the beginning of the volcanic transformation of adolescence. Within a few months I had become a stranger; I couldn't recognize the self-absorbed girl I was turning into. I saw myself trapped in a rebellious and demanding body that was growing and affirming itself, suffering and palpitating. It seemed to me that I was nothing but an extension of my uterus, that cavern I imagined as a bloody hollow in which humors fermented and terrible and unknown flora were developing. I couldn't forget the hallucinatory, candlelit scene of a squatting Nívea giving birth to her babies, of her gargantuan belly studded with a protruding umbilicus, her thin arms clutching the ropes that hung from the ceiling. I would burst into tears without any apparent cause, and I suffered fits of uncontrollable anger, or woke so exhausted I couldn't get out of bed. The dreams of the children in black pajamas returned with greater intensity and frequency; I also dreamed of a gentle man who smelled of the sea, who held me in his arms. I would wake up clinging to my pillow, wishing desperately that someone would kiss me the way Severo del Valle had kissed his wife. I was melting with heat outside and freezing inside; I couldn't settle down enough to read or study but would run through the garden, whirling like someone possessed to keep from howling. I walked into the pond fully clothed, wading through water lilies and frightening the goldfish, my grandmother's pride and joy. Soon I discovered the most sensitive points of my body, and would hide and fondle myself, not understanding why what was supposed to be a sin was so calming. I am going mad, I concluded, terrified, like so many girls who end up being hysterical, but I didn't dare talk about it with my grandmother. Paulina del Valle was also changing; while my body was flowering, hers was drying up, beset by mysterious ills she didn't discuss with anyone, not even her doctor, faithful to her theory that all that was needed to hold decrepitude at bay was to keep going and not make old lady noises. Her weight was a torment, she had varicose veins in her legs, her bones ached, she was short of breath, and her urine came in dribbles, mysteries I divined through small signs but that she held in strictest secrecy. Señorita Matilde Pineda would have helped me greatly during the trials of adolescence, but she had vanished from my life, cast out by my grandmother. Nívea had gone off with her husband, children, and nursemaids, as carefree and happy as when she had arrived, leaving a tremendous void in the house. There were too many rooms and not enough noise; without her and the children, my grandmother's mansion turned into a mausoleum.

Santiago celebrated the fall of the government with an interminable series of parades, parties, cotillions, and banquets; my grandmother, not to be left behind, again opened up the house and tried to resume her social life and soirées, but there was something in the air that the month of September, with its splendid springtime, could not affect. The thousands of deaths, the treachery and sackings, weighed on the souls of both winners and losers. We were all ashamed: the civil war had been an orgy of blood.

That was a strange period in my life; my body changed, my soul expanded, and I began to wonder seriously who I was and where I came from. The catalyst was the arrival of Matías Rodríguez de Santa Cruz, my father—although I didn't yet know he was my father. I welcomed him as the Uncle Matías I had met several years earlier in Europe. Even then I thought he had seemed fragile, but when I saw him again I didn't recognize him; he was little more than a starving bird perched in his invalid's wheelchair. He was escorted by a beautiful, mature, opulent, milky-skinned woman dressed simply in mustard-colored poplin with a faded shawl over her shoulders; her most notable feature was an untamed mat of curls, tangled and gray, held at the neck by a thin ribbon. She looked like an ancient, exiled Scandinavian queen; it took no effort to imagine her at the stern of a Viking ship sailing among icebergs.

Paulina del Valle had received a telegram announcing that her eldest son would be landing in Valparaíso, and immediately put into action a plan to go to the port with me, Uncle Frederick, and the rest of her usual train. We went to meet him in a special car the English railroad manager had placed at our disposal. It was trimmed in varnished wood with fittings of polished brass; the seats were oxblood velvet, and we were attended by two uniformed employees who treated us as if we were royalty. We booked rooms in a hotel facing the sea, and waited for the ship, which was due the next day. When we presented ourselves at the dock, we were as elegant as if we were going to a wedding. I can say that with confidence since I have a photograph taken in the plaza a little before the boat docked. Paulina del Valle is in light-colored silk, all draped and beruffled and wearing rows of pearls; her monumental broad-brimmed hat is crowned with feathers cascading downward like a waterfall, and she is holding an open parasol to protect her from the sun. Her husband, Frederick Williams, is splendid in a black suit, top hat, and cane. I am all in white with an organdy bow in my hair; I look like a birthday present. They lowered the ship's gangplank, and the captain personally invited us to come aboard, escorting us with great ceremony to the stateroom of Don Matías Rodríguez de Santa Cruz.

The last thing my grandmother expected was to run smack into Amanda Lowell. The nasty shock nearly killed her; the presence of her former rival impressed her much more than the pitiful appearance of her son. Of course in those days I didn't have enough information to interpret my grandmother's reaction; I thought she'd been overcome by the heat. The phlegmatic Frederick Williams, on the other hand, didn't turn a hair when he saw La Lowell; he greeted her with a brief but pleasant bow and then concentrated on getting my grandmother comfortable in a chair and getting water for her, while Matías observed the scene with evident amusement.

"Wh-what is this woman doing here!" my grandmother stammered once she could get her breath.

"I imagine you would like to have a family powwow, I'll go for a stroll," said the Viking queen, and exited with her dignity intact.

"Miss Lowell is my friend; let's say she is my only friend, Mother. She has accompanied me to here—without her I could not have traveled. It was she who insisted on my return to Chile, thinking it for me is better to die *en famille* than stretched out in some hospital in Paris," said Matías in an obscure Spanish and with a strange French-English accent.

Then Paulina del Valle looked at her son for the first time, and realized that he was nothing but a skeleton covered with skin like a snake's; his glassy eyes were sunken in their sockets, his cheeks so papery you could see his teeth through the skin. He was propped up in a chair, supported by cushions, his legs covered by a shawl. He looked like a wild, sad little old man, though in fact he couldn't have been more than forty.

"My God, Matías, what's happened to you?" asked my grandmother, horrified.

"Nothing that can be cured, Mother. You understand, *n'est-ce pas*, that I must have reasons very powerful for returning here."

"That woman—"

"I know the whole *histoire* about Amanda Lowell and my father. It happened thirty years ago on the other side of the world. Can you not forget your resentment? By now we are all at an age to shed futile emotions and keep only those that help us live. Tolerance is one of them, Mother. I owe much to Miss Lowell, *beaucoup!* She is my companion for more than fifteen years."

"Companion? What does that mean?"

"What you hear: companion. She is not my nurse, she is not my wife, and no longer she is my lover. She accompanies me in *mes voyages*, in my life, and now, as you can see, she accompanies me at my death."

"Don't talk like that! You're not going to die, son. We're going to give you the proper care, and soon you'll be good as new," Paulina del Valle assured him, but her voice broke, and she couldn't go on.

It had been three decades since my grandfather Feliciano Rodríguez de Santa Cruz had his fling with Amanda Lowell, and my grandmother had seen her only once or twice, and then from afar, but she had recognized her instantly. It was not for nothing that she had slept every night in the theatrical bed she had ordered from Florence to defy her rival; that must have reminded her constantly of the rage she felt toward her husband's scandalous lover. When an elderly, unpretentious woman materialized before her eyes who did not in any way resemble the fabulous filly who had stopped traffic when she swung her hips through the streets of San Francisco, Paulina saw her not as she was but as the dangerous rival she had once been. The anger Amanda Lowell inspired in my grandmother had lain dormant, awaiting its moment to flower, but, hearing her son's words, she searched every corner of her heart and couldn't find it. What Paulina encountered instead was maternal instinct, an emotion she had not been known for but one now flooding her heart with unconditional and unbearable compassion. Compassion not just for her dying son, but also for the woman who had been with him for so many years, who had loved him loyally, had cared for him through the bad times of his illness, and had now traveled across the world to bring him to his mother at the hour of his death. Paulina del Valle sat slumped in her chair, her eyes fixed on her pitiable son as tears rolled silently down her cheeks; she was suddenly diminished, aged, and fragile, and I kept patting her shoulder, understanding very little of what was going on. Frederick Williams must have known my grandmother very well, because he slipped out to find Amanda Lowell and brought her back to the stateroom.

"Forgive me, Miss Lowell," my grandmother murmured from her chair.

"Please forgive *me*, señora," the other woman replied, timidly coming forward until she was facing Paulina del Valle.

They took one another's hands, one standing, the other seated, both with tear-filled eyes, for a time that to me seemed eternal, until

I noticed that my grandmother's shoulders were shaking, and realized that she was quietly laughing. The other woman smiled, first covering her mouth, embarrassed, and then, when she saw Paulina laugh, she uttered a joyful hoot that melded with my grandmother's, and then after a few seconds both were doubled over, infecting one another with hysterical and uncontrollable elation, sweeping away all the years of futile jealousy, shattered rancor, marital deceit, and other abominable memories.

The house on Calle Ejército Libertador sheltered many people during the turbulent years of the revolution, but nothing was as involved and exciting for me as when my father came back to await his death. The political situation had stabilized since the civil war, which put an end to years of liberal governments. The revolutionaries won the changes for which so much blood had been spilled. Before the war, the government imposed its candidate by means of bribery and intimidation and the support of civil and military authorities; now the bribing was done in equal measure by landowners, priests, and the two parties. The system was more fair, because the payoffs of one side compensated for the dirty tricks of the other, and corruption was no longer financed from public funds. This was called free elections. The revolutionaries also devised a parliamentary system based on Great Britain's, though it was not to last very long. "We are the English of America," my grandmother once said, and Nívea immediately replied that the English were the Chileans of Europe. In any case, the parliamentary experiment had no chance to survive in a land of caudillos; the ministers changed so frequently that it was impossible to keep track, and finally the Saint Vitus' dance of politics lost its charm for everyone in our family except Nívea, who to call attention to women's suffrage often chained herself to the gates of Congress with two or three ladies as enthusiastic as she, to the derision of passersby, the fury of the police, and the chagrin of their husbands.

"When women can vote, they will vote in a block. We will have so much leverage that we'll be able to shift the balance of power and change this country," she said.

"Wrong, Nívea," my grandmother refuted. "Women will vote for whoever their husbands or their priests say, women are much dumber than you think they are. Besides, some of us rule from behind the throne—you saw how we made short work of that last government. I don't need suffrage to get what I want."

"Because you have money and an education, Aunt. How many are like you? We have to fight for the vote, that comes first."

"You've lost your head, Nívea."

"Not yet, Aunt, not yet—"

My father was moved into one of the salons on the ground floor, which was converted into a bedroom because he couldn't climb the stairs, and he was assigned a permanent maid, to be with him day and night, like his shadow. The family physician offered a poetic diagnosis—"inveterate turbulence of the blood"—he told my grandmother, because he preferred not to confront her with the truth, but I suppose that to everyone else it was obvious that my father was being consumed by a venereal disease. He was in the last stages, when there is no cataplasm, poultice, or corrosive sublimate that can help, the stage he had meant to avoid at any cost but had to suffer because he hadn't had the courage to commit suicide before it came to that, as he had planned for years. He could barely stir because of the pain in his bones; he couldn't walk, and his mind was failing. Some days he spent tangled in nightmares without ever really waking, murmuring incomprehensible stories, but he had moments of great lucidity, and when the morphine eased his agony he could laugh and talk about the past. Then he would call me to come sit by his side. He passed the day in a large chair by a window, looking at the garden, supported by pillows and surrounded by books, newspapers, and trays of medications. The maid would sit down to knit a short distance away, attentive to his needs, silent and gruff as an enemy, the only person he would tolerate around him because she didn't treat him with pity. My grandmother had arranged a pleasant atmosphere for her son; she had hung chintz curtains and papered the walls in tones of yellow; she kept freshly cut flowers from the garden on all the tables and had hired a string quartet to come several times a week to play his favorite classical melodies, but nothing could disguise the smell of medicine and the certainty that in that room someone was putrefying. At first that living cadaver repelled me, but when I managed to conquer my fear and, forced by my grandmother, began to visit him, my life changed. Matías Rodríguez de Santa Cruz came to the house just when I was waking to adolescence, and he gave me what I most needed: memory. In one of his cogent periods, when he was feeling the solace of drugs, he told me he was my father, and the revelation was so casual that it didn't even shock me.

"Lynn Sommers, your mother, was the most beautiful woman I ever saw. How happy I am that you did not inherit her beauty," he said.

"Why is that, Uncle?"

"Don't call me Uncle, Aurora. I am *ton père*. Your father. Beauty tends to be a curse, because it awakens in men the worst passions. A too beautiful woman cannot escape the desire she arouses."

"Are you sure you're my father."

"*Absolument.*"

"Really! I thought my father was Uncle Severo."

"Severo should have been your father, he is a much better man than I. Your mother deserved a husband like him. I was always the brainless one. That's why you find me as I am, a scarecrow. *En tout cas*, he can tell you much more about her than I can," he assured me.

"Did my mother love you?"

"Yes, but I did not know what to do with that love, and I ran away from it. You are very young to understand these things, *ma chère*. It is enough to know that your mother was wonderful, and that it is sad she died so young."

I agreed with that—I would have liked to know my mother—but I was even more curious about other people from my early childhood who came to me in dreams or in vague memories impossible to pin-point. Though Matías had seen him only once, it was in those conversations with my father that the silhouette of my grandfather, Tao Chi'en, began to form. All he had to do was mention his full name and tell me that he was a tall, handsome Chinese man, and my memories were released, drop by drop, like gentle rain. Once I had put a name to that invisible presence that was always with me, my grandfather ceased to be an invention of my fantasy and became a ghost as real as a flesh-and-blood person. I felt enormous relief when I found out that I hadn't imagined that gentle man who smelled of the sea; he not only existed, he had loved me, and if he had disappeared so abruptly, it was not from any desire to abandon me.

"I understand that Tao Chi'en died," my father informed me.

"How?"

"I think of an accident, but I am not sure."

"And what happened to my grandmother, Eliza Sommers?"

"She went to China. She believed that you would be better off with my family, and she was not mistaken. *Ma mère* always wanted a daughter, and you she raised with more affection than she ever gave my brothers and me."

"What does Lai Ming mean?"

"'*Sais pas*. No idea. Why?"

"Because sometimes it seems to me I hear that word."

Matías's bones were watery from his illness, he tired quickly, and it wasn't easy to get information from him; he tended to lose himself in ramblings that had nothing to do with what interested me, but little by little I was fitting together patches of the past, stitch by stitch, always behind my grandmother's back, who was happy that I was visiting her sick son because she didn't have the spirit to do it. She would go into his room a couple of times a day, give him a quick kiss on the forehead, and stumble out with her eyes filled with tears. She never asked what we talked about, and of course I never told her. Nor did I dare mention the subject to Severo and Nívea del Valle; I was afraid that the least indiscretion on my part would put an end to the talks with my father. Without having discussed it, we both knew that our conversations had to be kept secret, which united us in a strange complicity. I can't say that I came to love my father—there wasn't enough time for that—but in the brief months we lived in the same house he placed a treasure in my hands by giving me details of my history, especially those concerning my mother, Lynn Sommers. He repeated many times that I had the legitimate blood of the del Valles; that seemed very important to him. Later I learned that following a suggestion from Frederick Williams, who had a great influence over every person in that house, he bequeathed me, while he was living, his part of the family fortune, safe in various bank accounts and stocks, to the frustration of a priest who visited every day with the hope of snagging something for the church. This was a grumbly old man with an odor of sanctity—he hadn't bathed or changed his cassock in years—famous for his religious intolerance and his talent for sniffing out the wealthy on their deathbeds and convincing them to leave their fortunes to works of charity. Affluent families would see him approach with real terror, as invariably he announced a death, but no one dared slam the door in his face. When my father realized that the end was near, he called Severo del Valle, with whom he almost never spoke, to reach an agreement about me. They brought a notary public to the house, and both signed a document in which Severo renounced his paternity and Matías Rodríguez de Santa Cruz recognized me as his daughter. In that way I was protected from Paulina's other two sons, Matías's younger brothers, who at my grandmother's death, nine years later, grabbed everything they could.

My grandmother clung to Amanda Lowell with superstitious affection; she believed that as long as she was near, Matías wouldn't die. Paulina was not on intimate terms with anyone, except me at times; she was convinced that most people are hopeless clods and said that to anyone who wanted to listen, which was not the best way to win friends. But that Scots courtesan managed to penetrate the armor my grandmother wore to protect herself. It was impossible to conceive of two women more different. La Lowell wanted nothing; she lived for the day, unfettered, free, fearless; she wasn't afraid of poverty, loneliness, or infirmity. She accepted everything with good grace; for her, life was an entertaining voyage that inevitably led to old age and death. There was no point in accumulating wealth since in the end, she maintained, we all go to the grave in our birthday suit. She had left behind the young seductress who had stirred so many hearts in San Francisco, and long gone was the beauty who had conquered Paris. Now she was a woman in her fifties, with no affectations and no regrets. My grandmother never tired of hearing about her past, or about the famous people she had known, as they leafed through the albums of newspaper clippings and photographs—in several of which she was young and radiant, with a boa constrictor coiled about her body. "The poor creature died of seasickness on a voyage; snakes are not good travelers," she told us. Because she was so cosmopolitan and so attractive—able without intending it to outcharm much younger and prettier women—she became the soul of my grandmother's soirées, enlivening them with her terrible Spanish and her Scots-accented French. There was no subject she couldn't discuss, no book she hadn't read, no important city in Europe she didn't know. My father, who loved her and was greatly indebted to her, said she was a dilettante, that she knew a little about everything and a lot about nothing, but she had more than enough imagination to make up for what she lacked in knowledge or experience. For Amanda Lowell there was no grander city than Paris and no more pretentious society than the French, the only place where socialism with its disastrous lack of elegance would never have a chance to triumph. In that Paulina del Valle was in complete agreement. The two women discovered that not only did they laugh at the same nonsense, including the mythological bed, they were also in agreement in nearly all fundamental matters. One day when they were having tea at a small marble table in the wrought-iron and glass gallery, they lamented not having met earlier. With or without Feliciano and Matías, they would have been great friends, they decided. Paulina did everything possible to get Amanda to stay; she rained gifts on her and introduced her to society as if she were an empress, but La Lowell was a bird that couldn't live in a golden cage. She stayed a couple of months, but finally she confessed in private to my grandmother that she didn't have the heart to watch Matías's decline and that, with all frankness, Santiago seemed a very provincial city despite the luxuries and ostentation of its upper class, which were comparable to those of European nobility. She was bored; her place was in Paris, where she had spent the best part of her life. My grandmother wanted to give her a farewell ball that would make history in Santiago and that the cream of society would attend because no one would dare reject an invitation from Paulina del Valle, even after hearing the rumors circulating about the hazy past of her guest, but Amanda Lowell convinced her that Matías was too ill and that a gala under those circumstances would be in the very worst taste, and, besides, she had nothing to wear for such an occasion. Paulina offered her gowns with the best of intentions, never imagining how she offended La Lowell by insinuating they wore the same size.

Three weeks after the departure of Amanda Lowell, the maid who looked after my father sounded the alarm. The doctor was summoned immediately, and in a thrice the house was filled with people: my grandmother's friends, politicians from the government, family members, a quantity of monks and nuns, including the frayed fortune-grubbing priest who now was hanging around my grandmother with the hope that the sorrow of losing her son would soon dispatch her to a better life. Paulina, however, was not planning to depart this world; she had some time ago resigned herself to the tragedy of her eldest son, and I think she saw the end come with relief—witnessing that slow calvary was much worse than burying him. I was not allowed to see my father because it was supposed that a dying man was not an appropriate spectacle for a little girl and that I had suffered enough anguish with the murder of my cousin and other recent violence, but I was able to say a brief good-bye thanks to Frederick Williams, who opened the door for me at a moment when there was no one else around. He took my hand and led me to the bed where Matías Rodríguez de Santa Cruz lay, of whom nothing tangible remained, barely a handful of translucent bones buried among pillows and embroidered sheets. He was still breathing, but his soul was already traveling through other dimensions. "Good-bye, Papa," I told him. It was the first time I had called him that. He agonized for two days more, and at the dawn of the third day he died like a baby chick.

I was thirteen when Severo del Valle gave me a modern camera that used paper instead of old-fashioned plates, one of the first in Chile. My father had died shortly before, and the nightmares were tormenting me so that I didn't want to go to bed and at night would wander through the house like a lost specter, followed closely by poor Caramelo, who always was a dumb, cowering dog, until my grandmother Paulina took pity and accepted us both in her huge gilded bed. Her large, warm, perfumed body took up at least half, and I would huddle on the other side, trembling with terror, with Caramelo at my feet. "What am I going to do with you two?" my grandmother would sigh, half asleep. It was a rhetorical question, because neither the dog nor I had any future. There was a general consensus in the family that I was "going to come to a bad end." By then the first woman doctor had graduated in Chile, and others had entered the university. That gave Nívea the idea that I could do the same, if only to defy the family and society in general, but it was obvious that I didn't have the least aptitude for studying. Then Severo del Valle appeared with the camera and set it in my lap. It was a beautiful Kodak, precious in the details of every screw, elegant, smooth, perfect, made for the hands of an artist. I still use it, it never fails. No girl my age had a toy like that. I picked it up with reverence and sat looking at it without any idea how to use it. "Let's see if you can photograph the dark shadows in your nightmares," Severo del Valle said as a joke, never suspecting that that would be my one objective for months, and that in the task of deciphering that nightmare I would end up in love with the world. My grandmother took me to the Plaza de Armas, to the studio of Don Juan Ribero, the best photographer in Santiago, a curt man as dry as stale bread on the outside, but generous and sentimental inside.

"I've brought you my granddaughter to be your apprentice," my grandmother said, laying a check on the artist's desk while I clutched her skirttail with one hand and my brand-new camera in the other.

Don Juan Ribero, who was a half head shorter than my grandmother and half her weight, settled his eyeglasses on his nose, carefully read the amount written on the check, and then handed it back to her, looking her up and down with infinite scorn.

"The amount isn't a problem. You set the price," my grandmother wavered.

"It isn't a question of price, but of talent, señora," he replied, guiding Paulina del Valle toward the door.

During that exchange I'd had time to take a quick look around. Ribero's work covered the walls: hundreds of portraits of people of all ages. Ribero was the favorite of the upper class, the photographer of the social pages, but the people gazing at me from the walls of his studio were not bigwig conservatives or beautiful debutantes, but Indians, miners, fishermen, laundresses, poor children, old men, many women like the ones my grandmother helped with her loans from the ladies club. There I saw represented the multifaceted and tormented face of Chile. Those people in the photographs touched something deep inside me; I wanted to know the story of every one of them. I felt a pressure in my chest, like a closed fist, and an uncontainable desire to cry, but I swallowed my emotion and followed my grandmother out with my head high. In the carriage she tried to console me: I shouldn't worry, she said, we would get someone else to teach me to operate the camera, photographers were a dime a dozen; what did that second-

rate lowborn think, anyway, talking in that arrogant tone to her,
Paulina del Valle! And she grumbled on and on, but I wasn't listening;
I had decided that no one but Juan Ribero would be my teacher. The
next day I left the house before my grandmother was up. I told the
coachman to take me to the studio and planted myself in the street,
prepared to wait forever. Don Juan Ribero showed up about eleven,
found me at his door, and ordered me to go home. I was shy then—I
still am—and very proud; I wasn't used to asking for anything because
from the time I was born I was coddled like a queen, but my determination must have been very strong. I didn't move from the door. A
couple of hours later, the photographer came out, threw me a furious
glance, and started walking down the street. When he came back from
his lunch, he found me still there with my camera clutched to my
chest. "All right," he muttered, defeated, "but I warn you, little girl, that
I won't give you any special consideration. Here you come to obey
without talking back and to learn quickly, is that clear?" I nodded
silently, because my voice was stuck in my throat. My grandmother, a
veteran at negotiation, agreed to accept my passion for photography as
long as I would devote the same number of hours to scholarly pursuits
traditional in boys' schools, including Latin and theology, because according to her it wasn't mental ability I was lacking, just discipline.

"Why don't you send me to public school?" I asked, intrigued by
rumors about lay education for girls, something that inspired terror
among my aunts.

"That's for people of a different class, I would never allow that,"
my grandmother said decisively.

So once again teachers filed through the house, several of whom
were priests willing to instruct me in exchange for the juicy gifts my
grandmother lavished on their congregations. I was lucky; in general
they indulged me, because they didn't expect my brain to function as
well as a boy's. Don Juan Ribero, on the other hand, demanded much
more from me; he held that a woman has to work a thousand times
harder than a man to win intellectual or artistic respect. He taught me

everything I know about photography, from the choice of a lens to the laborious process of developing; I never had any other teacher. When I left his studio two years later, we were friends. Now he is seventy-four years old, and he hasn't worked for several years because he's blind, but he still helps me and guides my hesitant steps. Seriousness is his motto. He is passionate about life, and blindness has not prevented him from continuing to survey the world. He has developed a kind of second sight. The way other blind people have someone to read to them, he has various helpers who observe and report to him. His students, his friends, and his children visit him every day and take turns describing what they've seen: a landscape, a scene, a face, an effect of light. They have to learn to observe very closely in order to endure Don Juan Ribero's exhaustive interrogation. As a result their lives change; they can't any longer wander through the world in their old casual way because they have to see with the maestro's eyes. I, too, often visit him. He welcomes me in the eternal penumbra of his apartment on Calle Monjitas, sitting in his comfortable chair in front of the window with his cat on his knees, always hospitable and wise. I keep him informed about technical advances in the field of photography, describe in detail each image in the books I order from New York and Paris, consult him about my doubts. He is up-to-date on everything that happens in this profession; he becomes passionate about different tendencies and theories, and he knows the master photographers in Europe and the United States by name. He has always ferociously opposed the artificial pose, scenes arranged in the studio, the cluttered prints made with superimposed negatives so much in mode a few years ago. He believes in photography as a personal testimony, a way of seeing the world, and that way must be honest, using technology as a medium for capturing reality, not distorting it. When I went through a phase in which I photographed girls in huge glass receptacles, he asked why I did it with such scorn that I did not continue down that road, but when I described to him the portrait I took of a family of itinerant circus artists, naked and vulnerable, he was immediately interested. I had taken sev-

eral photos of that family posed before a rickety covered wagon that
served as transport and living quarters, when a little girl about four or
five had come out, totally naked. That gave me the idea of asking all of
them to take off their clothes. They did it with no ill will and posed
with the same intent concentration as when dressed. It's one of my
best photographs, one of the few that has won prizes. It was soon evident that I am more attracted to people than to objects or landscapes.
When I shoot a portrait there's a relationship with the model that even
if very brief is nonetheless a connection. The plate reveals not only the
image but the feelings that flow between subject and photographer.
Don Juan Ribero liked my portraits, very different from his. "You feel
an empathy for your models, Aurora, you don't try to dominate them,
you try to understand them; that's why you succeed in exposing their
souls," he said. He encouraged me to leave the safe walls of the studio,
take my camera outside, look with my eyes wide open, overcome my
shyness, lose my fear, approach people. I realized that usually I was welcomed, and that the subjects for my lens posed with all seriousness,
even though I was a young girl: the camera inspired respect and confidence, people opened up, gave themselves to it. I was limited by my
youth; it wasn't until many years later that I was able to travel across
the country, witness strikes, go into the mines, hospitals, the shacks of
the poor, forgotten little schools, the cheap boardinghouses, the dusty
plazas where retired old men sat and stared, the fields and fishing villages. "Light is the language of photography, the soul of the world.
There is no light without shadow, just as there is no happiness without
pain," Don Juan Ribero told me seventeen years ago during the lesson
he gave me that first day in his studio on the Plaza de Armas. I have
never forgotten. But I don't want to get ahead of myself. I intend to
tell this story step by step, word by word, as it should be told.

So while I was going along, excited about photography and disturbed
by changes in my body, which was taking on unfamiliar proportions,
my grandmother Paulina wasted no time contemplating her navel but

began mulling over new business projects in her Phoenician merchant's brain. That helped her recover from the loss of her son Matías, and made her feel important at an age when other women have one foot in the grave. She was rejuvenated, her gaze brighter and her step lighter; soon she took off her mourning and sent her husband to Europe on a very secret mission. The faithful Frederick Williams was gone for seven months, and returned laden with gifts for her and for me, and good tobacco for him, the only vice we ever knew him to have. In his luggage he had smuggled thousands of useless-looking little dry sticks about fifteen centimeters long, which turned out to be stock from the best vines of Bordeaux, which my grandmother planned to plant in Chilean soil to produce a decent wine. "We are going to compete with French wines," she had explained to her husband before his voyage. It was pointless for Frederick Williams to rebut that the French had centuries of advantage over us, that conditions there are Edenic, while Chile is a country of atmospheric and political catastrophes, and that a project of such magnitude would take years of work.

"Neither you nor I is young enough to await the results of this experiment," he demurred with a sigh.

"Using that criterion, we'd never get anywhere, Frederick. Do you know how many generations of craftsmen it would take to build a cathedral?"

"Paulina, old girl, we are not speaking of cathedrals. At any moment, either of us could suffer grave cardiac distress."

"This wouldn't be the century of science and technology if every inventor thought about his own mortality, now would it? I want to found a dynasty so the name del Valle will endure in the world, even if it's on the bottom of the glass of every drunk who buys my wine," my grandmother replied.

So the Englishman resigned himself and set off on his safari to France, while Paulina del Valle wove together the threads of the undertaking in Chile. The first Chilean vines had been planted by missionaries in the time of the colony, and they produced a local wine that was quite good—so good, in fact, that Spain banned it to avoid competition with those of the mother country. After independence, the industry expanded. Paulina wasn't the only one who'd had the idea of producing quality wine, but while others bought land in the vicinity of Santiago, for the convenience of not having to travel more than one day, she looked for property farther away, not merely because it was cheaper but because it was better suited to growing grapes. Without telling anyone what she had in mind, she had the soil analyzed and considered the vagaries of water and constancy of the winds, beginning with the lands belonging to the del Valle family. She paid a pittance for vast abandoned properties no one valued because their only source of water was rain. The most savory grape, the one that produces the wines with best texture and aroma, the sweetest and most generous, doesn't grow in rich soil but in stony land; the plant, with a mother's obstinacy, overcomes obstacles to thrust its roots deep into the ground and take advantage of every drop of water. That, my grandmother explained to me, is how flavors are concentrated in the grape.

"Vines are like people, Aurora; the more difficult the circumstances, the better the fruit. It's a shame that I discovered this truth so late, because if I'd known earlier, I would have ridden you and my sons a lot harder."

"You tried with me, Grandmother."

"I've been soft as mush with you. I should have left you with the nuns."

"To learn to embroider and pray? Señorita Pineda—"

"I forbid you to mention that woman's name in this house!"

"All right, Grandmother, but at least I'm learning photography. With that I can earn a living."

"Where did you get such a harebrained idea!" cried Paulina del Valle. "No granddaughter of mine will ever have to earn a living. What Ribero is teaching you is entertainment—that's no future for a del Valle woman. It isn't your destiny to be a photographer taking pictures down on the plaza. You are going to marry someone of your own class and bring healthy children into the world."

"You've done more than that, Grandmother."

"I married Feliciano, I had three sons and a granddaughter. All the rest was just trimming."

"Well, frankly, it doesn't seem like it."

In France, Frederick Williams had hired an expert who came shortly after to assess the technical aspects of the program. He was a hypochondriac, a little man who pedaled over my grandmother's lands on his bicycle with a handkerchief tied around his nose and mouth because he thought that cow dung and Chilean dust would give him cancer of the lungs; he left no doubt, however, in regard to his profound knowledge of viticulture. The campesinos watched with awe as that gentleman in city clothes threaded his velocipede among the sharp rocks, stopping from time to time to sniff the soil like a dog on the scent. Since they couldn't understand a word of his long dia-tribes in the tongue of Molière, my grandmother, in person, in her galoshes and carrying a parasol, had to follow the Frenchman's bicy-cle for weeks to translate. The first thing Paulina noticed was that not all the plants were alike; there were at least three different kinds, mixed together. The Frenchman explained that some matured faster than others, so that if the climate destroyed the most delicate ones, they would get a crop from the others. He also confirmed that the enterprise would take years, because it wasn't simply a question of harvesting better grapes, but of producing a fine wine and marketing it abroad, where it would have to compete with the centuries-old reputations of the wines of France, Italy, and Spain. Paulina learned everything the expert could teach her, and when she felt confident she sent him back home. By then she was exhausted, and she had learned that her plan would require someone younger and lighter on his feet than she, someone like Severo del Valle, her favorite nephew, whom she could trust. "If you keep producing all those babies, you're going to need a lot of money to support them. You're not going to do that lawyering, unless you steal twice as much as the others do, but the wine will make you rich," she tempted him. Just that year, Severo and Nívea del Valle had given birth to an angel—that's what people called her—an infant as beautiful as a tiny fairy, whom they named Rosa. It was Nívea's opinion they had just been practicing with all their previous children in order finally to produce that perfect creature. Maybe God would be satisfied and not send them any more children, because they had a flock of them now. Severo thought the business of the French vines was preposterous, but he had learned to respect his aunt's nose for commercial success and thought that it was worth taking a chance; he didn't know that within a few months the vineyards would change his life. As soon as my grandmother found that Severo del Valle was as obsessed with the vines as she, she decided to make him a partner, leave the vineyards in his care, and take Williams and me to Europe, because, as she said, I was sixteen years old, and it was high time for me to acquire a veneer of cosmopolitanism and a wedding trousseau.

"I'm not planning to marry, Grandmother."

"Not yet, but you'll have to do that before you're twenty, or you'll end up an old maid dressing saints," she concluded categorically.

She didn't tell anyone the real reason for the voyage. She was ill, and she thought that she could be operated on in England. Surgery there had developed apace since the discovery of anesthesia and asepsis. In recent months my grandmother had lost her appetite, and for the first time in her life she was suffering nausea and stomach upsets after a heavy meal. She wasn't eating meat anymore, preferring soft food, sugary puddings, soups, and her pastries, which she couldn't give up even though they fell like stones in her belly. She had heard about the famous clinic founded by a Dr. Ebanizer Hobbs, dead now for more than a decade, where the best physicians in Europe practiced. As soon as winter was over and the trail across the cordillera of the Andes was passable, we undertook the journey to Buenos Aires, where we were to board a transatlantic steamer to London. As usual, we took with us a cortège of servants, a ton of luggage, and several armed guards to protect us from the bandits that lurked in those lonely places, but this time my dog Caramelo couldn't come with us because his legs were giving out. Crossing the mountains by carriage, then horseback, and finally on mules between precipitous cliffs that yawned on both sides like abysmal maws ready to devour us was unforgettable. The path looked like an endless narrow snake slithering through those overwhelming mountains, the backbone of America. Among the rocks grew bushes battered by raw weather and fed by narrow threads of water. Water was everywhere; waterfalls, streams, melting snow. The only sound was of water and the hooves of the beasts on the hard crust of the Andes. When we paused, an abysmal silence fell over us like a heavy mantle; we were intruders violating the perfect solitude of those heights. My grandmother, battling vertigo and the fainting spells that assaulted her almost as soon as we began the upward climb, was sustained by her iron will and the solicitude of Frederick Williams, who did everything in his power to help her. She was wearing a heavy traveling coat, leather gloves, and a pith helmet with heavy veils, as no ray of sunshine, however feeble, had ever touched her skin—thanks to which she planned to go to her grave without a wrinkle. I was dazzled. We had made this trip before, crossing toward Chile, but then I had been too young to appreciate the majesty of this nature. The animals moved forward step by step, picking their way along sheer precipices and high walls of pure rock raked by wind and polished by time. The air was as thin as a transparent veil and the sky a turquoise sea furrowed from time to time by a condor soaring on magnificent wings, absolute lord of those domains. As soon as the sun went down, the landscape was completely transformed; the blue peace of that abrupt and solemn nature disappeared to give way to a universe of geometric shadows that moved menacingly about us, closing us in, enveloping us. One false step and the mules would have tumbled, with us on their backs, into the depths of those ravines, but the guide had calculated the distance well and night found us at a squalid little wood-plank hut, a refuge for travelers. They unloaded the animals and made seats for us on the sheepskin saddles and blankets, lighted by torches dipped in pitch, although lights were almost unnecessary, for an incandescent moon reigned in the giant dome of the skies like a sidereal beacon above the high rock. We had brought firewood with us, which they used to build a fire for warmth and to boil water for *maté* tea. Soon that brew of green, bitter herbs was being passed from hand to hand, everyone sipping from the same silver straw; that restored us and brought color back to the cheeks of my poor grandmother, who asked for her baskets and settled in like a flower vendor in the market to hand around food to dull our hunger. Out came bottles of liquor and champagne, aromatic country cheeses, delicate slices of roast pork, and breads and cakes wrapped in white linen napkins, but I noticed that my grandmother ate very little and did not touch the alcohol. In the meantime the men, skillful with their knives, killed a couple of kids they'd led behind the mules, skinned them, and strung them, crucified, on a pole they hung between two forked sticks. I don't know how the night went—I fell into a deathlike sleep and didn't wake until dawn, when the task began of stirring the coals to make coffee and to dispose of the remains of the kids. Before we started off, we left firewood, a sack of beans, and a few bottles of liquor for the next travelers.

PART THREE

1896–1910

The Hobbs clinic was founded by the celebrated surgeon Ebanizer Hobbs in his own home; it was a large, solid, and elegant residence right in the heart of Kensington, yet they kept tearing down walls, blocking windows, and adding tiles until it became a true horror. Its presence on that elegant street so upset the neighbors that Hobbs's successors had no difficulty buying the adjacent homes to enlarge the clinic, but they kept the Edwardian façades so that from the outside it looked no different from the rows of houses on the block, all identical. Inside it was a labyrinth of rooms, staircases, corridors, and interior windows that didn't look onto anything. It didn't have the typical bullring-style operating room of the old city hospitals—a central circle covered with sawdust or sand and surrounded by galleries for spectators—but small surgery rooms with walls, ceiling, and floors faced with floor tiles and metal plates that were scrubbed with soap and lye once a day because the deceased Dr. Hobbs had been among the first to accept Robert Koch's theory of the propagation of infection and to adopt Joseph Lister's methods for asepsis, which most physicians still rejected out of pride or laziness. It was not easy to change old habits; hygiene was tedious and complicated, and it interfered with the swiftness of operations, which was considered the mark of a good surgeon since it diminished the risk of shock and blood loss. Unlike many of his contemporaries, who believed that infections were produced spontaneously in the body of the patient, Ebanizer Hobbs understood immediately that the germs were outside, on hands, floors, and instruments and in the atmosphere, which is why they sprayed everything from wounds to the air of the operating room itself with phenol. The poor man breathed so much phenol that he died before his time from a renal affection, his skin badly ulcerated, which gave his detractors an opportunity to cling to their own antiquated ideas. Hobbs's disciples, nevertheless, analyzed the air and discovered that germs do not float like invisible birds of prey primed for a sneak attack but are concentrated on dirty surfaces; infection was produced by direct contact, so it was fundamental to clean the instruments thoroughly, use sterilized bandages, and see that surgeons not only zealously washed their hands but when possible wore rubber gloves. These were not the clumsy gloves used by anatomists to dissect cadavers or by some workers to handle chemicals, but a delicate product soft as human skin, made in the United States. They had a romantic origin: a physician, in love with a nurse, wanted to protect her from the eczema caused by disinfectants and had the first rubber gloves made for her; later they were adopted by surgeons for operations. Paulina del Valle had read all this with great interest in the scientific journals lent to her by her relative Don José Francisco Vergara, who, though still the scholar of old, by then had heart trouble and had retired to his palace in Viña del Mar. My grandmother not only carefully chose the doctor she wanted to operate on her, and contacted him from Chile months in advance; she also wrote to Baltimore, ordered several pairs of the famous rubber gloves, and carried them with her, carefully wrapped, in the trunk with her lingerie.

Paulina del Valle sent Frederick Williams to France to check on the wood used in the barrels for fermenting wine, and to explore the cheese industry, because she didn't see any reason why Chilean cows couldn't produce cheeses as tasty as those from French cows, which undoubtedly were equally stupid. During that crossing of the cordillera of the Andes, and later on the ocean liner, I was able to observe my grandmother closely, and I became aware that something basic was beginning to weaken in her, something that wasn't her will, her mind, or her greed, something more like her ferocity. She became gentle, bland, and so absentminded that she used to stroll on the deck of the ship dressed in fine muslin and pearls, but without her false teeth. It was obvious that she had bad nights; she had deep circles beneath her eyes and was always sleepy. She had lost a lot of weight, and her skin hung loose when she removed her corset. She wanted me to stay very close, "So you don't flirt with the sailors," she said, a cruel joke, since at that age my shyness was so absolute that one innocent look in my direction from a man and I would blush like a boiled lobster. The real reason was that Paulina del Valle felt fragile, and she needed me at her side to distract her from death. She didn't mention her health; to the contrary, she talked about spending a few days in London and then going on to France to see about the barrels and cheese, but I guessed from the beginning that she had other plans. That became apparent as soon as we arrived in England and she began her diplomatic labor of convincing Frederick Williams to go on alone; we would stay to shop a while and then join him later. I don't know whether Williams went ahead without suspecting that his wife was ill, or whether he guessed the truth, and understanding her modesty, left her in peace. The fact is that he checked us into the Hotel Savoy, and once he was sure we didn't lack for anything, he took the next ferry across the Channel, but without any enthusiasm.

My grandmother did not want witnesses to her decline, and she was especially reserved in front of Williams. That was part of the coquettishness she acquired once they were married; she'd shown none of that when he was her butler. She'd had no reluctance then to expose to him the worst side of her character, and he saw her dressed any which way, but from the day of their marriage she'd tried to impress him with her best plumage. That autumnal relationship was very important to her, and she didn't want bad health to damage the solid edifice of her vanity, which was why she tried to keep her husband at a distance, and if I hadn't planted my feet she would have shut me out too. It was a battle to be allowed to go with her on those medical visits, but finally she yielded, given my stubbornness and her weakness.

Isabel Allende

She was in pain, and almost couldn't swallow, but she didn't seem frightened, although she sometimes made jokes about the drawbacks of hell and boredom of heaven. The Hobbs clinic inspired confidence from the moment you stepped inside, with its hall filled with bookshelves and oil portraits of the surgeons who had practiced within those walls. We were received by an impeccable matron and led to the doctor's office, a cozy room with elegant brown leather furniture and a fireplace where large logs were crackling. Dr. Gerald Suffolk's appearance was as impressive as his fame. He was a Teutonic type, large and ruddy, with a thick scar on his cheek that instead of making him ugly made him unforgettable. On his desk were the letters he had exchanged with my grandmother, the records of the Chilean specialists she had consulted, and the package with the rubber gloves, which she had sent ahead that morning by messenger. Later we learned that was an unnecessary precaution, since they had been used in the Hobbs clinic for three years. Suffolk welcomed us as if we were on a social call, offering us Turkish coffee scented with cardamom seeds. He led my grandmother to an adjoining room and after examining her returned to the office and leafed through a weighty book while she dressed. The patient soon returned, and the surgeon confirmed the earlier diagnosis of her Chilean doctors: my grandmother had a gastrointestinal tumor. He added that the operation would be risky for someone of her age, and also because it was in the experimental stage, but he had developed a perfect technique for such cases and physicians came from all over the world to learn from him. He expressed himself with such a sense of superiority that one of Don Juan Ribero's maxims came to mind: Conceit is a privilege of the ignorant; the wise man is humble because he knows how little he knows. My grandmother surprised Dr. Suffolk when she demanded that he explain in detail what he intended to do to her; he was accustomed to having patients deliver themselves unto the unquestioned authority of his hands with the passivity of hens, but he seized the occasion to display his erudition with a lecture, more concerned with impressing us with the virtuosity of his scalpel than with the well-being of his unfortunate patient. He drew a sketch of intestines and organs that resembled a demented machine, and pointed out to us where the tumor was located and how he planned to excise it, right down to the type of suture, information that Paulina del Valle listened to imperturbably but so undid me I had to leave the office. I sat in the hall of the portraits to pray quietly. In truth I was more afraid for myself than for her; the idea of being left alone in the world terrified me. It was at that moment, pondering my possible orphanhood, that a man passed by; I must have looked very pale because he stopped. "Is something wrong, *niña?*" he asked in a Chilean-accented Spanish. I shook my head, surprised, not daring to look directly at him, but I must have peeked out of the corner of my eye because I could see he was young, clean shaven, and had high cheekbones, a strong chin, and oblique eyes; he looked like the illustration of Genghis Khan in my history book, though less ferocious. He was the color of honey all over—hair, eyes, skin—but there was nothing honeyed in his tone when he explained that he was as Chilean as we were, and he would assist Dr. Suffolk in the operation.

"Señora del Valle is in good hands," he said, without a shred of modesty.

"What happens if they d-d-don't operate?" I asked, stammering, as I always do when I'm nervous.

"The tumor will keep growing. But don't worry, *niña,* surgery has advanced by leaps and bounds, your grandmother did well to come here," he concluded.

I wanted to know what a Chilean was doing in these parts and why he looked like a Tartar—it was easy to visualize him robed in furs and with a lance in his hand—but I was too upset to say anything. London, the clinic, the doctors, and my grandmother's drama were more than I could manage alone. I couldn't understand Paulina del Valle's reticence regarding her health, or her reasons for sending Frederick Williams across the Channel just when we needed him most. Genghis Khan gave me a condescending pat on the hand and left.

Contrary to all my pessimistic predictions, my grandmother survived the surgery, and after the first week, during which her fever rose and dropped uncontrollably, she stabilized and could begin to eat solid foods. I never left her side except to go to the hotel once a day to bathe and change my clothes, because the smell of the anesthetics, medications, and disinfectants produced a viscous mixture that clung to the skin. I slept in fits and starts, sitting in a chair beside the patient. Ignoring my grandmother's strict injunction, I sent a telegram to Frederick Williams the day of the operation, and he arrived in London thirty hours later. I saw him lose his proverbial composure beside the bed where his wife lay stupefied by drugs, moaning with each breath, toothless, nearly hairless: a parchment-skinned old woman. He knelt beside her and placed his forehead upon the bloodless hand of Paulina del Valle, whispering her name, and when he got up his face was wet with tears. My grandmother, who maintained that youth is not a period in life but a state of mind, and that you have the health you deserve, looked totally defeated in her hospital bed. That woman, whose appetite for life was as colossal as her gluttony, had turned her face to the wall, indifferent to everything around her, immersed in herself. Her enormous strength of will, her vigor, her curiosity, her sense of adventure, even her greed, had been erased by her physical suffering.

During that time I had many occasions to see Genghis Khan, who monitored the state of the patient and turned out to be, as one might have expected, more approachable than the famous Dr. Suffolk or the hospital's strict matrons. He answered my grandmother's concerns with rational explanations instead of vaguely consoling words, and he was the one who tried to ease her discomfort; the others were interested in her temperature and the condition of the incision, but ignored their patient's moans. Did she think it wasn't going to hurt? She should shut her mouth and be grateful they had saved her life. In contrast, the young Chilean physician did not hold back on the morphine: he believed that sustained suffering affected the sick person's physical and moral stamina and retarded or impeded healing, as he clarified to Williams. We learned that his name was Iván Radovic, and that he came from a family of doctors. His father had emigrated from the Balkans to Chile at the end of the fifties; he had married a Chilean schoolteacher from the north, and they had three children, two of whom had followed in his footsteps as doctors. His father, Iván said, had died of typhus during the War of the Pacific, in which he served for three years as a surgeon, and his mother had had to bear the responsibility for the family alone. I was able to observe the clinic's personnel to my heart's desire, and I heard things that were not intended for ears like mine, because no one except Dr. Radovic gave any sign of acknowledging my existence. I was almost seventeen, but I still had my hair tied with a ribbon and wore clothes chosen by my grandmother, who had ridiculous little-girl dresses made for me to keep me a child as long as possible. The first time I wore anything suitable for my age was when Frederick Williams took me to Whitency's without Grandmother's permission and put the whole store at my disposal. When we came back to the hotel, I with my hair in a bun and dressed like a young woman, she didn't recognize me— but that was weeks later. Paulina del Valle must have had the strength of an ox; they opened her stomach, removed a tumor the size of a grapefruit, sewed her up like a shoe, and within a couple of months she was her old self. All that remained of that amazing adventure was a pirate's scar across her belly and a voracious appetite for life and, of course, food. We left for France as soon as she was able to walk without a cane. She completely discarded the diet recommended by Dr. Suffolk; as she said, she hadn't come to Paris from an ass-backward corner of the world to eat baby pap. Using the pretext of studying the manufacture of cheese and the culinary tradition of France, she stuffed herself with every delicacy that country could offer.

Once we were installed in the house Williams had rented on the boulevard Haussman, we contacted the ineffable Amanda Lowell, who had lost nothing of her Viking-queen-in-exile air. In Paris she was in her element; she lived in a shabby but cozy garret with a view of pigeons on the neighboring rooftops and the matchless skies of Paris. We soon verified that her stories about bohemian life and her friendship with famous artists were strictly true; thanks to her, we visited the studios of Cézanne, Sisley, Degas, Monet, and several others. La Lowell had to teach us to appreciate their paintings because we didn't have eyes trained for Impressionism, but before long we were totally seduced. My grandmother acquired a good collection of works that provoked gales of hilarity when she hung them in her home in Chile; no one appreciated the centrifugal skies of van Gogh or the weary showgirls of Lautrec, and it was believed that in Paris they had taken silly old Paulina del Valle for a cleaning. When Amanda Lowell noticed that I was never without my camera and spent hours closeted in the darkroom I improvised in our rented house, she offered to introduce me to the most celebrated photographers in Paris. Like my maestro, Juan Ribero, she believed that photography and painting are not competing arts but basically different: the painter interprets reality, and the camera captures it. In the former everything is fiction, while the second is the sum of the real plus the sensibility of the photographer. Ribero never allowed me sentimental or exhibitionist tricks—none of this arranging objects or models to look like paintings. He was the enemy of artificial composition; he did not let me manipulate negatives or prints, and in general he scorned effects of spots or diffuse lighting: he wanted the honest and simple image, although clear in the most minute details. "If what you want is the effect of a painting, then paint, Aurora. If what you want is truth, learn to use your camera," he would say again and again. Amanda Lowell never treated me like a child; she took me seriously from the beginning. She too was fascinated by photography, which at that time no one called art and for many was just another bit of nonsense among the many bizarre and useless fripperies of a frivolous century. "I'm a little past the age to learn photography, Aurora, but you have young eyes, you can see the world and make others see it the way you do. A good photograph tells a story, it reveals a place, an event, a state of mind; it's more powerful than pages and pages of writing," she told me. My grandmother, in contrast, treated my passion for the camera as an adolescent whim and was much more interested in selecting a trousseau and readying me for marriage. She enrolled me in a school for young ladies, where I attended classes daily to learn to go up and down stairs gracefully, fold napkins for a banquet, select menus to fit the occasion, organize parlor games, and arrange flowers, talents my grandmother considered sufficient for succeeding in married life. She liked to shop, and we spent whole afternoons in boutiques choosing clothes, afternoons I could have better employed exploring Paris with my camera.

I don't know where the year went. When Paulina del Valle had apparently recovered from her illness and Frederick Williams had become an expert on wood for wine casks and on making cheese—from the foulest smelling to the ones with the most holes—we met Diego Domínguez at a ball in the Chilean legation celebrating Independence Day, September 18. I had spent endless hours in the hands of the hairdresser, who constructed atop my head a tower of curls and small braids adorned with pearls, a true feat when you take into account that my hair is stubborn as a horse's mane. My dress was a frothy meringue creation spattered with beads that kept coming off all night and strewing the floor of the legation with glittering little bits like sand. "If your father could see you now!" my grandmother exclaimed, awed, when I was all dressed. She herself was arrayed head to toe in mauve, her favorite color, with a scandalous number of strands of pink pearls around her neck, layered hairpieces in a suspicious shade of mahogany, flawless porcelain teeth, and a cape of black velvet edged with jet from neck to floor. She entered the ball on the arm of Frederick Williams and I on that of a marine from a ship of the Chilean navy that was making a courtesy visit to France, an insipid young man whose face or name I cannot remember, who assumed on his own initiative the task of instructing me on the use of the sextant for navigational purposes. It was an enormous relief when Diego Domínguez took a stance in front of my grandmother to introduce himself with his long array of surnames and ask whether he could dance with me. That isn't his real name—I have changed it in these pages because everything concerning him and his family should be protected. Enough to know that he existed, that his story is a true one, and that I have forgiven him. Paulina del Valle's eyes gleamed with enthusiasm when she saw Diego Domínguez; at last we had before us a potentially acceptable suitor, the son of a well-known family, surely rich, with impeccable manners, and even good-looking. She nodded, he held out his hand to me, and we went out for a spin around the floor. After the first waltz, Señor Domínguez took my dance card and filled in every line, with the stroke of a pen eliminating the expert on sextants and other candidates. At that point I looked at him more closely and had to admit that he looked good; he radiated health and strength, had a pleasant face, blue eyes, and manly bearing. He seemed uncomfortable in his tails, but he moved with assurance and danced well, at least much better than I; I dance like a goose despite a year of intensive classes at the school for young ladies. And my embarrassment increased my clumsiness. That night I fell in love with all the passion and recklessness of first love. Diego Domínguez led me with a firm hand around the dance floor, gazing at me intently, and almost always in silence, because his attempts to establish a dialogue foundered upon my monosyllabic answers. My shyness was torture—I couldn't meet his eyes, and didn't know what to look at with mine; when I felt the warmth of his breath on my cheeks, I grew weak in the knees. I had to fight desperately against the temptation to run from the room and hide under some table. There's no question that I came off very badly, and that unfortunate young man was stuck with me because in a fit of bravado he had filled my card with his name. At one point I told him that he wasn't obliged to dance with me if he didn't want to. He replied with a laugh, the one time he laughed that night, and asked me how old I was. I had never been held in a man's arms, I had never felt the pressure of a male palm at my waist. One of my hands rested on his shoulder and the other in his gloved hand, but not with the dovelike lightness my dancing mistress had imparted—he was holding on with determination. In several brief pauses he offered me goblets of champagne that I drank because I didn't dare turn them down, with the foreseeable result that I stepped on his toes even more often. When at the end of the evening the ambassador of Chile spoke to propose a toast for his distant country and for beautiful France, Diego Domínguez stood behind me, as close as the skirt of my meringue ballgown would permit, and whispered into my neck that I was "delicious," or something of that nature.

In the days that followed, Paulina del Valle called on all her diplomat friends to ask, without a trace of pretense, everything she could extract about the family and ancestors of Diego Domínguez before giving him permission to take me horseback riding along the Champs-Elysées, chaperoned from a prudent distance by her and Uncle Frederick in their carriage. Afterward, the four of us had ice cream beneath some umbrellas, threw bread crumbs to the ducks, and agreed to go to the opera that same week. Between outings and ice creams we arrived at October. Diego had traveled to Europe at his father's behest on the mandatory adventure that nearly every young upper-class Chilean made once in his life as initiation into manhood. After traveling to a number of cities, visiting several museums and cathedrals out of duty, and soaking up the night life and its naughty ramifications—which supposedly would cure him forever of that vice and provide material for boasting to his pals—he was ready to return to Chile and settle down, work, marry, and start his own family. Compared to Severo del Valle, with whom I had been in love since I was a little girl, Diego Domínguez was ugly, and to Señorita Matilde Pineda, he was stupid, but I was in no state to make such comparisons; I was sure I had found the perfect man and could scarcely believe the miracle that he had noticed me. Frederick Williams believed that it wasn't wise to jump at the first man who passed by—I was still very young, and I would have more than enough suitors to choose calmly—but my grandmother maintained that this young man was the best the matrimonial market had to offer, even though he had agricultural holdings and lived a long way from Santiago.

"You can make the trip by ship and railroad without any problem," she said.

"Grandmother, don't go so fast. Señor Domínguez has not hinted to me of any of the things you are imagining," I clarified, blushing to my eartips.

"He'd better do it soon, or I'll have to pin him between the sword and the wall."

"No!" I cried, horrified.

"I'm not going to let anyone play games with my granddaughter. We can't waste time. If that young man doesn't have serious intentions, he should abandon the field right now."

"But, Grandmother, what's the hurry? We've only just met—"

"Do you know how old I am, Aurora? I am getting on. Not many live as long as I have. Before I die, I want to see you well married."

"You'll live forever, Grandmother."

"No, child, it just seems that way," she replied.

I don't know whether she carried out the planned ambush on Diego Domínguez or whether he picked up the hint and made the decision himself. Now that I can look at that episode with a certain distance and humor, I understand that he was never in love with me; he simply felt flattered by my unconditional love and must have weighed in the balance the advantages of such a union. Maybe he desired me, because we were two young people and were available to each other; maybe he thought that with time he would come to love me; maybe he married me out of laziness and convenience. Diego was a good catch, but I was too: I had the income my father left me, and it was supposed that I would inherit a fortune from my grandmother. Whatever his reasons were, the fact is that he asked for my hand and placed a diamond ring on my finger. The danger signs were evident to anyone with two eyes in his head, except for my grandmother—blinded by fear of leaving me alone—and me, madly in love. Uncle Frederick argued from the beginning that Diego Domínguez was not the man for me. Since he hadn't liked anyone who came near me for the last two years, we paid no attention to him, thinking it paternal jealousy. "I find this young fellow to be rather unfeeling," he commented more than once, but my grandmother rebutted him, saying that he wasn't cold, he was respectful, as befitting a perfect Chilean gentleman.

Paulina del Valle went into a frenzy of shopping. In her haste, packages were tossed unopened into trunks, and later, when we took them out in Santiago, it turned out there were two of everything, and half didn't fit. When she learned that Diego Domínguez had to return to Chile, the two of them arranged for us all to go back on the same steamship, which would give us a few weeks to get to know each other better, they said. Frederick Williams put on a long face and tried to divert these plans, but there was no power in this world capable of facing down that lady when she got something in her head, and her current obsession was to get her granddaughter married. I recall very little of the voyage; it went by in a cloud of morning strolls, games of deck tennis and cards, and cocktails and dancing all the way to Buenos Aires, where we parted because Diego had to buy some bulls and drive them along the southern Andean trails to his estate. We had very few opportunities to be alone or to talk without witnesses. I learned the essential things about the twenty-three years of his past and his family, but almost nothing about his tastes, beliefs, and ambitions. My grandmother told him that my father, Matías Rodríguez de Santa Cruz, was dead and that my mother was an American whom we hadn't known because she died when I was born, which was not far from the truth. Diego did not evidence any curiosity to know more; neither was he interested in my passion for photography, and when I made it clear to him that I didn't intend to give it up, he said it wouldn't bother him in the least, that his sister painted watercolors, and his sister-in-law worked cross-stitch. In the long sea crossing we didn't really get to know each other, but we were getting more and more tightly entangled in the web my grandmother, with the best intentions, was weaving around us.

Since there was very little in the first-class section of the ship to photograph, except for ladies' dresses and the dining room floral arrangements, I often went down to the lower decks to shoot portraits, especially of the third-class travelers crowded together in the belly of the ship: laborers and immigrants on their way to America to try their fortune, Russians, Germans, Italians, Jews, people traveling with very little in their pockets but with hearts bursting with hope. It seemed to me that despite the discomfort and lack of services, they were doing better than the passengers in first class, where everything was formal, ceremonious, and boring. Among the emigrants there was an easy camaraderie; the men played cards and dominoes, the women formed groups to tell one another about their lives, the children improvised fishing poles and played hide-and-seek. In the evenings guitars, accordions, flutes, and violins were brought out, and there were happy sessions with singing, dancing, and beer. No one seemed to mind my presence, no one asked questions, and after a few days I was accepted as one of them, which allowed me to photograph them at will. There was no way to develop the negatives on board ship, but I sorted them carefully to do that later in Santiago. During one of those excursions through the lower decks, I ran right into the last person I expected to find there.

"Genghis Khan!" I cried when I saw him.

"I believe, señorita, you've mistaken me for—"

"Forgive me, Dr. Radovic," I apologized, feeling like an idiot.

"Do we know each other?" he asked, puzzled.

"Don't you remember me? I'm Paulina del Valle's granddaughter."

"Aurora? Surely not, I would never have recognized you. How you've changed!"

It's true I had changed. When he had met me I was dressed like a little girl, and now before his eyes he had a grown woman with a camera around her neck and an engagement ring on her finger. On that voyage began the friendship that with time would change my life. Dr. Iván Radovic, a second-class passenger, could not come up to the first-class deck without an invitation, but I could go down to visit him, which I did often. He told me about his work with as much passion as I talked to him about photography; he watched me use the camera, but I couldn't show him anything I'd done because it was at the bottom of the trunks. I did, though, promise to do so when we reached Santiago. That didn't happen, however, because here I was embarrassed to call him—it seemed pure vanity, and I didn't want to take up the time of a man occupied in saving lives. When my grandmother learned he was on board, she immediately invited him to have tea on the terrace of our suite. "With you here, Doctor, I feel safe on the high seas. If I get another grapefruit in my stomach, you will come and cut it out with a kitchen knife," she joked. The invitations to tea were repeated often, followed by card games. Iván Radovic told us he had finished his term in the Hobbs clinic and was going back to Chile to work in a hospital.

"Why don't you open a private clinic, Doctor?" queried my aunt, who had taken a fancy to him.

"I would never have the money and connections that requires, Señora del Valle."

"But I will make that investment, if you like."

"I could never allow you to—"

"I wouldn't be doing it for you, but because it's a good place to put my money, Dr. Radovic," my grandmother interrupted. "Everyone gets sick, medicine is big business."

"I believe that medicine is not a business, señora, but a right. As a physician I am obliged to serve, and I hope that some day good health will be within reach of every Chilean."

"Are you a socialist?" my grandmother asked, with a grimace of distaste; after the "betrayal" of Señorita Pineda she mistrusted socialism.

"I'm a doctor, Señora del Valle. Healing is all that interests me."

We returned to Chile at the end of December 1898, and we found a country in full moral crisis. No one, from rich landowners to schoolteachers and nitrate mine workers, was happy with his lot or with the government. Chileans seemed resigned to character flaws like drunkenness, idleness, and robbery, and to social ills like maddening bureaucracy, unemployment, an inefficient legal system, and a poverty that contrasted sharply with the brazen ostentation of the wealthy that was producing a growing, silent rage extending from north to south. We didn't remember Santiago as being so dirty, with so many wretched people, so many cockroach-infested slums, so many children dead before they could walk. The newspapers asserted that the death rate in the capital was the same as Calcutta's. Our house on Calle Ejército Libertador had been left in the care of a pair of aunts who were poor as church mice, the kind of distant relatives every Chilean family has, and a handful of servants. The aunts had ruled those domains for more than two years and were not overjoyed to see us; Caramelo was there beside them, so old now he didn't recognize me. The garden was overgrown with weeds, the Moorish fountains were dry, the salons smelled of the tomb, the kitchens looked like a pigsty, and there were mouse droppings under the beds, but none of that fazed Paulina del Valle, who had arrived prepared to celebrate the wedding of the century and was not going to allow anything—not age, the Santiago heat, or my retiring personality—to stop her. She had the summer months, during which everyone went to the coast or the country, to get the house ready, because autumn marked the onset of intense social life, and she needed time to prepare for my marriage in September, the beginning of spring, a month of patriotic celebrations and bridal parties, exactly a year after my first meeting with Diego. Frederick Williams took charge of hiring a regiment of masons, woodworkers, gardeners, and maids who put their teeth into the task of renovating that disaster at the pace customary in Chile, which is to say, not overly fast. Summer came with its dust and heat, its scent of peaches and cries of itinerant vendors hawking the delicacies of the season. Because everyone was on vacation, the city seemed dead. Severo del Valle came to visit bringing sacks of vegetables, baskets of fruit, and good news about the vines; he was tanned, heavier, and more handsome than ever. He stared at me openmouthed, amazed that I was the same little girl he had told good-bye two years before; he made me whirl like a top so he could look at me from every angle, and his generous opinion was that I had an air that reminded him of my mother. My grandmother received that comment with a sour face; my past was never mentioned in her presence. For her my life began when I was five, when I stepped over the threshold of her palace in San Francisco; nothing existed before that. Nívea had stayed on their estate with the children because she was about to give birth again and was too big to make the trip to Santiago. The grape harvest promised to be very good that year; they planned to harvest the white grapes in March and the red ones in April, Severo del Valle reported, and added that some red grapes were mixed in with others that were more delicate, more vulnerable to diseases, and later to mature. Even though they bore excellent fruit, Severo said, he planned to uproot them to save problems. Paulina del Valle immediately cocked an ear, and I saw in her eyes the same avaricious light that usually announced a profitable idea.

"In early autumn transplant them to a separate place. Tend them carefully, and next year we will make a special wine from them," she said.

"Why should we fool with them?" Severo asked.

"If those grapes mature late, they must be finer and more concentrated. Surely the wine will be much better."

"We're already producing one of the best wines in the country, Aunt."

"Humor me, Nephew, do what I ask," my grandmother begged in that teasing tone she used before giving an order.

I wasn't able to see Nívea till the very day of my wedding, when she arrived with her newest to hastily fill me in on the basic information any bride should know before her honeymoon but no one had taken the trouble to give me. My virginity, however, did not save me from the assault of an instinctive passion I didn't know how to name. I thought of Diego day and night, and not all those thoughts were chaste. I wanted him, but I didn't know exactly for what. I wanted to be in his arms, wanted him to kiss me as he had once or twice, wanted to see him naked. I had never seen a naked man and, I confess, curiosity kept me awake at night. That was all, the rest of that road was a mystery. Nívea, with her unabashed honesty, was the one person qualified to instruct me, but it wouldn't be until several years later—given time and opportunity for our friendship to deepen—that she would tell me the secrets of her intimacy with Severo del Valle, and describe in detail, rolling with laughter, the postures she'd learned in the books of her uncle José Francisco Vergara. By then I had left my innocence behind, but I was very ignorant in erotic matters, as nearly all women are—and most men as well, Nívea assured me. "Without those books of my uncle's, I would have had fifteen children and never known how it happened," she told me. Her advice, which would have made my aunts' hair stand on end, stood me in very good stead for my second love, but would have been no help at all in the first.

For three long months we lived camped in four rooms of the

house on Ejército Libertador, panting with heat. I wasn't bored, because my grandmother immediately renewed her charitable works, even though all the members of the ladies' club were out of town for the summer. In her absence discipline had deteriorated, and it was up to her to take over the reins of compulsive compassion once more. Again we visited widows, the ailing and mad, delivered food, and supervised loans to poor women. This idea, which even the newspapers had made fun of because no one believed that the beneficiaries—all in the last stages of indigence—would pay back the money, had worked out so well that the government decided to copy it. The women not only scrupulously repaid the loans in monthly payments but backed one another, so that when one couldn't pay, the others paid for her. I think Paulina del Valle actually had the idea that she could charge them interest and turn the charity into a business, but I cut that off short. "There's a limit to everything, Grandmother, even greed," I scolded. My passionate correspondence with Diego Domínguez kept me waiting for the mail. I discovered that in letters I am capable of expressing what I would never dare face-to-face: the written word is profoundly liberating. I found myself reading love poems instead of the novels I had been so fond of; if a dead poet on the other side of the world could describe my feelings with such precision, I had to accept with humility that my love was not exceptional, that I had invented nothing, that everyone falls in love in more or less the same manner. I imagined my sweetheart galloping across his land like a legendary broad-shouldered hero, noble, strong, and handsome, a manly man in whose hands I would be safe; he would make me happy and would give me protection, children, and eternal love. I visualized a cottony, sugary future through which we would float, arms about each other, forever. How would the body of the man I loved smell? Of humus?—like the forests he came from? Like the sweet aroma of the bakery? Or maybe the sea? Like that fleeting tang that had come to me in dreams since my childhood. Suddenly the need to smell Diego became as imperious as thirst, and in a letter I begged him to send me one of the kerchiefs he had worn around his neck, or one of his unwashed shirts. My fiancé's answers to those impassioned letters were calm chronicles of life in the country—cows, wheat, grapes, the rainless summer sky— and sober comments about his family. Naturally, he never sent one of his kerchiefs or shirts. In the last lines he would remind me how much he loved me and how happy we would be in the cool adobe-and-tile house his father was building for us on his property, as earlier he had for his brother Eduardo when he married Susana, and as he would for his sister Adela when she married. For generations the Domínguezes had lived together: love of Christ, the bond among brothers and sister, respect for their parents, and hard work, Diego said, were the foundation of his family.

However long I was occupied in writing and sighing as I read poems, I had time left over, so I went back to the studio of Don Juan Ribero. I went around the city taking photographs and at night worked in the darkroom I had set up at home. I was experimenting with platinum prints, a new technique that produced very beautiful images. The procedure is simple, and costly, but my grandmother bore the expenses. You brush a platinum solution on photographic paper, and that produces images in subtle gradations of tone—luminous and clear, and with great depth—that are not changed by time. Ten years have passed, and those are the most extraordinary photographs in my collection. When I look at them, many memories rise before me with the same impeccable clarity of those platinum prints. I can see my grandmother Paulina, Severo, Nívea, friends, and relatives; in some self-portraits I can also see myself as I was then, just before the events that were to change my life.

When the second Tuesday in March arrived, the house was royally outfitted with a modern gas installation, a telephone, an elevator for my grandmother, wallpaper shipped from New York, brand-new upholstery on the furniture, recently waxed parquet floors, polished brass, washed windows, and the collection of Impressionist paintings in the salons. There was a new contingent of uniformed servants under the command of an Argentine butler Paulina del Valle had stolen from the Hotel Crillón by paying him twice his salary.

"People are going to talk, Grandmother. No one has a butler, it's vulgar," I warned her.

"I don't care. I don't want to have to do battle with Mapuche Indians in house slippers who put hairs in the soup and throw plates down on the table," she replied, determined to impress Santiago society in general and the family of Diego Domínguez in particular.

So the new employees were added to the maids who had been in the house for years and could not, of course, be fired. There were so many people working for us that they had nothing to do but trip over each other, and there was so much gossip and pilfering that finally Frederick Williams had to intervene to establish order, since the Argentine couldn't decide where to begin. That caused a real ruckus, since no one had ever seen the master of the house lower himself to the level of domestic affairs, but he did it to perfection; his long experience in that employ had not been for naught. I don't think that Diego Domínguez and his family, our first visitors, appreciated the elegance of the service; to the contrary, they seemed intimidated by such splendor. They belonged to a very old dynasty of landholders from the south, but unlike most agriculturists in Chile who spend a couple of months on their lands and the rest of the time living off their income in Santiago or in Europe, the Domínguezes were born, raised, and buried in the country. People with a solid family tradition, deeply Catholic, simple, they boasted none of the refinements flaunted by my grandmother, which surely to them seemed slightly decadent and not at all Christian. I was struck by the fact that they all had blue eyes, except for Susana, Diego's sister-in-law, a dark beauty with a languid air, like a Spanish painting. At the table they were confused by the number of knives, forks, and spoons, and the six wine goblets; none of them tasted the duck à l'orange, and they were startled when the baked Alaska was served. When she saw the line of uniformed servants, Diego's mother, Doña Elvira, asked why there were so many military people in our house. They were stunned by the Impressionist paintings, convinced that I had painted those pigs' tracks and my grandmother had the gall to hang them, but they appreciated the brief harp and piano concert we offered in the music salon. The conversation died after the second sentence, until the bulls furnished an opening for talking about cattle breeding—which was of enormous interest to Paulina del Valle, who in view of the numbers of cattle the Domínguezes owned was doubtlessly thinking of starting a cheese business with them. If I had had any doubts about my future life in the country with my fiancé's clan, that visit dissipated them. I fell in love with these people from a long line of country gentry, good-hearted and unpretentious: the sanguine, laughing father, the innocent mother, the amiable and virile older brother, the mysterious sister-in-law, and the young sister, happy as a canary, all of whom had traveled for several days in order to meet me. They accepted me with all naturalness, and I am sure that though they were disconcerted by our way of life, they didn't criticize us; they seemed incapable of a bad thought. Because Diego had chosen me, they considered me part of their family; that was enough. Their simplicity allowed me to relax, something that rarely happens with strangers, and after a while I was talking with each of them, telling about our trip to Europe and my love of photography. "Show me your photographs, Aurora," Doña Elvira asked, and when I did, she couldn't hide her disillusion. I think she was expecting something more comforting than throngs of workers on strike, slums, ragged children playing in irrigation ditches, violent uprisings, patient emigrants sitting on their bundles in the hold of a ship. "But, child, why don't you take pretty pictures? Why go into those places? There are so many nice landscapes in Chile," the sainted lady murmured. I was going to explain that I was interested in those faces lined by hard work and suffering, not "pretty" things, but I realized this was not the proper moment. There would be time ahead for my future mother-in-law and the rest of the family to get to know me.

"Why did you show them those photographs, Aurora? The Domínguezes are mired in the old ways, you shouldn't have frightened them with your modern ideas," Paulina del Valle scolded when they left.

"But, Grandmother, they were already frightened by the luxury of this house and the Impressionist paintings, don't you think? Besides, Diego and his family need to know what kind of woman I am," I replied.

"You're not a woman yet, you're a child. You will change, you will have children, you will have to adjust to your husband's surroundings."

"I will always be the same person, and I don't want to give up my photography. It isn't the same as Diego's sister's watercolors, or his sister-in-law's embroidery. Photography is fundamental to my life."

"Well then, marry first and later do whatever you like," my grandmother concluded.

We didn't wait until September, as planned; we had to get married in mid-April because Doña Elvira Domínguez had a slight heart attack, and a week later, when she was well enough to take a few steps on her own, she made clear her wish to see me become her son Diego's wife before she departed this mortal coil. The rest of the family agreed, because if she died they would have to postpone the wedding at least a year to observe the obligatory mourning period. My grandmother resigned herself to speeding up things and to sacrificing the princely ceremony she'd planned. I drew a deep breath of relief; I had been very nervous at the thought of exposing myself to the eyes of half Santiago as I entered the cathedral on the arm of Frederick Williams or Severo del Valle, floating in a cloud of white organdy as my grandmother had intended.

What can I tell you about my first night of love with Diego Domínguez? Very little, because memory prints in stark black and white; the grays get lost along the way. Perhaps it wasn't as wretched as I recall, but I've forgotten the shadings—all I have left is a general sensation of frustration and rage. After the private wedding in our house on Ejército Libertador, we went to a hotel to spend the night before leaving for a two-week honeymoon in Buenos Aires; Doña Elvira's precarious health did not allow us to go any farther. When I said good-bye to my grandmother, I felt that a portion of my life was coming to a close. When I hugged her, I knew how much I loved her, and how much she had shrunk; her clothes hung from her and I was a half-head taller than she. I had the presentiment that she didn't have much time left; she looked small and vulnerable, a little old lady with a trembling voice and knees weak as cotton wool. Not much re-mained of the formidable matriarch who for more than seventy years had lived life on her own terms and managed the destinies of her family as she pleased. Beside her, Frederick Williams looked like her son. The years hadn't touched him; it was as if he were immune to the decline of ordinary mortals. Up until the day before the wedding, my good uncle Frederick had begged me, behind my grandmother's back, not to marry if I wasn't sure, and each time I replied that I had never been more sure of anything. I had no doubts about my love for Diego Domínguez. As the moment for the wedding grew closer, my impatience increased. I would study myself in the mirror, naked, or barely clothed in the delicate lace nightgowns my grandmother had bought in France, and ask myself anxiously whether he would find me pretty. A mole on my neck, my dark nipples, seemed terrible de-fects. Would he want me as much as I wanted him? I found out that first night in the hotel. We were tired. We had eaten a lot, he'd had more to drink than normal, and I was feeling the effects of three gob-lets of champagne. As we walked into the hotel, we feigned indiffer-ence, but the trail of rice we were leaving behind on the floor be-trayed our state as newlyweds. So great was my embarrassment at being alone with Diego and imagining that outside our door some-one was picturing us making love that I felt nauseated, and I locked myself in the bathroom so long that after a while my new husband tapped gently on the door to ask if I was still alive. He led me by the hand into the bedroom, helped me remove my elaborate hat, took the hairpins from my bun, freed me from my short, fitted suede jacket, unbuttoned the thousand pearl buttons of my blouse, slipped off my heavy skirt and petticoats, until I was dressed only in the fine batiste chemise I wore under my corset. As he was taking off my clothes, I felt myself evaporate like water, I was vanishing, he was reducing me to nothing but bones and air. Diego kissed me on the lips, not as I had imagined so many times during the previous months, but with force and urgency. The kiss became more demanding, and his hands tore at my chemise as I struggled to hold it together because I was horrified by the prospect of his seeing me naked. His hasty caresses and the revelation of his body against mine put me on the defensive; I was so tense that I shook as if I were cold. He asked me, annoyed, what was the matter and ordered me to try to relax, but when he saw that this method was making things worse, he changed his tone, added that I shouldn't be afraid, and promised to be careful. He blew out the lamp and somehow managed to lead me to the bed. The rest happened quickly. I did nothing to help him. I lay as motionless as a hypnotized hen, trying futilely to remember Nívea's counsel. At some moment I was pierced by his sword; I managed to hold back a scream and was aware of the taste of blood in my mouth. My clearest memory of that night was one of disenchantment. Was this the passion that poets wasted so much ink on? Diego consoled me, saying that it was always like that the first time, that we would learn to know each other and everything would go better, then he gave me a chaste kiss on the forehead, turned his back to me without another word, and slept like a baby, while I lay awake in the dark with a cloth between my legs and a searing pain in my vagina and my heart. I was too ignorant to guess the source of my frustration—I didn't even know the word *orgasm*—but I had explored my body and I knew that hiding somewhere was that seismic pleasure capable of turning life upside down. Diego had felt it inside me, that was evident, but I had experienced only anguish. I felt I was the victim of a terrible biological injustice: sex was easy for the man—he could get it even by force—while for us it was without pleasure and with grave consequences. Would I have to add to the divine curse of giving birth with pain that of loving without pleasure?

When Diego awoke the next morning, I had been dressed for a long while and had made up my mind to go back home and find refuge in the familiar arms of my grandmother, but the fresh air and a stroll through the streets of the city center, almost empty at that hour of Sunday morning, calmed me. My vagina was burning where I could still feel the aftermath of Diego's roughness, but step by step my rage was dissipating, and I was prepared to face the future like a woman and not like a runny-nosed, spoiled brat. I was aware of how pampered I had been for the nineteen years of my life, but that stage was over; the night before I had been initiated into my status as a married woman, and I should act and think maturely, I concluded, swallowing my tears. The responsibility for being content was exclusively mine. My husband would not hand me eternal happiness like a present wrapped in tissue paper, I would have to cultivate it day by day with intelligence and effort. Luckily, I loved that man, and I believed, just as he had assured me, that with time and practice things would go much better between us. Poor Diego, I thought, he must be as disillusioned as I. I returned to the hotel in time to close our suitcases and set off on our honeymoon.

Caleufú, the estate set in the most beautiful area of Chile, a wild paradise of cold forest, volcanoes, lakes, and rivers, had belonged to the Domínguez family since colonial times, when land had been divided among the distinguished noblemen of the Conquest. The family had added to its wealth by buying more Indian lands for the price of a few bottles of liquor, until they had one of the most prosperous landholdings in the region. That property had never been divided; by tradition it was passed intact to the eldest son, who had the obligation to give work to or to help his brothers, to support and provide a dowry for his sisters, and to care for the campesinos. My father-in-law, Don Sebastián Domínguez, was one of those people who met every expectation; he was growing old with his conscience at peace and grateful for the rewards life had given him, most of all, the affection of his wife, Doña Elvira. In his youth, as he himself admitted, laughing, he had been a rake, and the proof was several campesinos on his land who had blue eyes, but the gentle, firm hand of doña Elvira had gradually tamed him without his noticing. As patriarch, he was good and kind; the workers on his estate brought their problems to him before anyone else, because his two sons, Eduardo and Diego, were stricter than he, and Doña Elvira never opened her mouth outside the walls of the house. The patience Don Sebastián showed with the people on his lands, whom he treated like slightly retarded children, turned to sternness when dealing with his male offspring. "We are very privileged, which is why we have responsibilities," he would say. "For us there are no excuses or pretexts, our duty is to do God's will and help our people; we will have to answer for that in heaven." He must have been about fifty years old, but he looked younger because he lived a very healthy life. He spent the day on horseback, riding over his property; he was the first up in the morning, and the last to go to bed, he was present at the time for threshing, for breaking new colts, for the roundups, and he helped brand and castrate the cattle. He began his day with a cup of strong black coffee with six spoons of sugar and a slug of brandy; that gave him strength to see to the work in the fields until two in the afternoon, when in the company of his family he ate four full plates and three desserts washed down with abundant wine. There were not very many of us in that enormous house; my in-laws' greatest sorrow was having had only three children. It was God's will, they said. At dinner all of us gathered who during the day had been scattered in different occupations—no one could be absent. Eduardo and Susana lived with their children in a different house two hundred yards from the big house, but the only meal they prepared was breakfast; the others they took at my in-laws' table. Because our wedding date had been set forward, the house intended for Diego and me wasn't ready, and we were living in a wing of his parents' house. Don Sebastián sat at the head of the table in the tallest and most ornate chair; at the other end was Doña Elvira, and on either side were distributed the sons and their wives, two widowed aunts, some cousins or distant relatives, a grandmother so ancient she had to be fed from a baby bottle, and guests—and there were always several. Extra places were set for visitors who dropped in unannounced and sometimes stayed for weeks. They were eagerly welcomed, because in the isolation of the country visits were the major entertainment. Farther to the south lived a few Chilean families deep in Indian territory, also some German colonists without whom the region would have remained semi-savage. It took several days on horseback to travel across the Domínguez holdings, which reached to the border with Argentina. At night there were prayers, and the year's calendar was ruled by religious dates, which were observed with rigor and rejoicing. My in-laws realized that I had been brought up with very little Catholic instruction, but we had no problems in that area because I was very respectful of their beliefs, and they did not try to impose theirs on me. Doña Elvira explained to me that faith is a divine gift: "God calls your name, he chooses you," she said. That freed me from guilt in her eyes; God hadn't as yet called my name, but if He had placed me in that very Christian family it was because He soon would. My enthusiasm for helping her in her charitable works among the tenants compensated for my limited religious fervor. She believed it was owing to my compassionate spirit, a sign of my good character; she didn't know that it was my training in my grandmother's ladies' club and a pedestrian interest in meeting the field laborers so I could photograph them. Outside of Don Sebastián, Eduardo, and Diego, all of whom had gone to a good boarding school and made the obligatory voyage to Europe, no one suspected there was a big world out there. No novels were allowed in that home. I believe that Don Sebastián lacked the heart to censor them, so to prevent anyone's reading a novel on the church's blacklist, he preferred to take the easy way out and forbid them all. Newspapers arrived so long out-of-date that they brought no news, only history. Doña Elvira read her books of prayers and Adela, Diego's young sister, had a few volumes of poetry and some biographies of historic figures and travel journals, which she read over and over. Later I discovered that she somehow obtained mystery novels, tore off the covers, and replaced them with covers from books authorized by her father. When my trunks and boxes came from Santiago and hundreds of books appeared, Doña Elvira asked me with her habitual sweetness not to show them to the rest of the family. Every week my grandmother or Nívea sent me reading matter, which I kept in my room. My in-laws said nothing, confident, I suppose, that this bad habit would pass once I had children and didn't have so many hours of leisure, which was the case with my sister-in-law Susana, who had three darling, and very badly behaved, children. They did not, however, oppose my photography; perhaps they guessed that it would be very difficult to bend my will on that point, and although they never showed any curiosity to see my work, they gave me a room at the back of the house where I could set up my darkroom.

I had grown up in the city, in the comfortable and cosmopolitan atmosphere of my grandmother's house, much more liberated than any Chilean of then or today—even though we are nearing the end of the first decade of the twentieth century, things have not been greatly modernized for girls in this part of the world. The difference in my way of life when I landed in the bosom of the Domínguez family was brutal, even though they did everything possible to make me feel at home. They treated me very well; it was easy to learn to love them. Their affection made up for the reserved and often tight-lipped character of Diego, who in public treated me like a sister and in private scarcely spoke to me. The first weeks of trying to adapt were very interesting. Don Sebastián gave me a beautiful black mare with a white star on her forehead, and Diego sent me with an overseer to ride around the estate and meet the workers and the neighbors, who were located so far away that each visit took three or four days. Then he left me on my own. My husband would go off with his brother and father to the fields or to hunt; sometimes they camped for several days. I couldn't bear the boredom of the house with its endless task of coddling Susana's children, putting up sweets and preserves, cleaning and airing, and sewing and knitting; when my chores in the school or the pantry were over, I would put on a pair of Diego's trousers and gallop off. My mother-in-law had warned me not to ride like a man, astride the horse, because it would cause "female problems," a euphemism I never entirely elucidated, but no one could ride sidesaddle in that land of hills and boulders without breaking her neck in a spill. The landscape left me breathless, surprising me at every turn of the road; I was enthralled. I rode up hill and down valley to luxuriant forests, a paradise of larch, laurel, cinnamon, maniu, myrtle, and the millenary araucarias, fine timber the Domínguezes processed at their sawmill. I was intoxicated by the scent of the damp forest, that sensual aroma of red earth, sap, and roots, the peace of the dense growth guarded by those silent green giants, the mysterious murmur of growing things, the song of unseen waters, the dance of the air through the branches, the whispering of roots and insects, the cooing of gentle ring doves and raucous cries of the chimangos. The trails ended at the sawmill, and beyond that I had to pick my way through thick growth, trusting the instinct of my mare, whose hooves sank into the oil-colored mud, thick and fragrant as vegetal blood. Light filtered through the immense cupola of the trees in bright oblique rays, but there were glacial zones where pumas lay in wait, spying on me with eyes like flames. I carried a shotgun tied to my saddle, but in an emergency I wouldn't have had time to reach it, and in any case I would never have fired. I took photographs of ancient forests, lakes with black sand, tempestuous rivers of singing stones, and impetuous volcanoes that crested the horizon like sleeping dragons in towers of ash. I also took photos of workers on the estate, which I then took to them as gifts, and they received with confusion; they did not know what to do with these images of themselves they had not solicited. I was fascinated by those faces lined by weather and poverty, but they didn't like to see themselves that way, as they were, with their rags and sorrows upon them; they wanted hand-tinted photographs for which they posed wearing the one suit they owned, the one from their wedding day, all well washed and combed, and with their children's noses wiped.

On Sundays, work was suspended and there was mass—when we had a priest with us—or "missions," which the women of the family performed by visiting the peons in their homes to teach them their catechism. In that way, with little gifts and persistence, they combated the native beliefs that were all tangled up with Christian saints. I didn't participate in the religious teaching, but I used the opportunity to get to know the campesinos. Many were pure Indians who still used words in their own tongues and kept their traditions alive; others were mestizos, all of them humble and timid in normal times, but pugnacious and noisy when they drank. Alcohol was a bitter balm that for a few hours alleviated the earthly burdens of the day but over time bored into their guts like a hostile rat. Drunkenness and gunfights were punished, as were other offenses such as cutting a tree without permission or letting animals roam outside the plot allotted to each of them for their own use. The penalty for stealing or insolence to superiors was a beating, but Don Sebastián was repelled by corporal punishment. He had also eliminated the right of the *pernada*, an old tradition from the colonial epoch that allowed *patrones* to deflower the daughters of the campesinos before they were married. He himself had practiced that custom in his youth, but after Doña Elvira appeared on the estate such liberties came to an end. Neither did he approve of visits to whorehouses in nearby villages, and he insisted that his own sons marry young to avoid temptation. Eduardo and Susana had married six years before, when both were twenty, and Diego, then seventeen, had been intended for a distant cousin who drowned in the lake before the engagement could be formalized. Eduardo, the elder brother, was more jovial than Diego. He had a talent for telling jokes and singing; he knew all the legends and stories of the region, liked to talk, and knew how to listen. He was very much in love with Susana; his eyes lit up when he saw her, and he was never impatient with her capricious humors. My sister-in-law suffered headaches that put her in terrible moods. She would lock herself in her room, refuse to eat, and there were instructions never to bother her for any reason, but once the headaches passed, she emerged totally recovered, smiling and affectionate; she seemed a different woman. I learned that she slept alone and that neither her husband nor her children went into her room unless invited; the door was always closed. The family was accustomed to her headaches and depressions, but they considered her desire for privacy almost an offense, just as it amazed them that without my permission I wouldn't allow anyone to go into the little darkroom where I developed my photographs, even though I explained the harm that a ray of light could do to my negatives. At Caleufú no doors or cabinets had a key except for the wine cellars and the strongbox in the office. There was pilfering, of course, but without major consequences, since usually Don Sebastián turned a blind eye. "These people are very ignorant, they don't steal as a vice, not even out of need, it's just a bad habit," he said, although in truth the workers had greater needs than the *patrón* admitted. The campesinos were free men, but in practice they had lived on that land for generations, and it never occurred to them that it could be any other way. They had nowhere to go. Few lived to old age. Many children died in infancy from intestinal infections, rat bites, and pneumonia, the women in childbirth and from consumption, the men from accidents, infected wounds, and alcohol intoxication. The nearest hospital belonged to the Germans, and it boasted a Bavarian doctor of great renown, but that was the last recourse; lesser illnesses were treated with secrets of nature, prayer, and the help of the *meicas*, the female Indian healers, who knew the power of the regional plants better than anyone.

At the end of May winter descended without relief, its curtain of rain washing the landscape like a patient laundress and its early darkness forcing us to gather by four in the afternoon, turning nights into an eternity. I could no longer go out on my long horseback rides or to photograph people around the estate. We were isolated; the roads were mud pits, no one visited us. I entertained myself by experimenting in the darkroom with different techniques for developing film and by photographing the family. I was discovering that everything is related, is part of a tightly woven design. What at first view seems to be a tangle of coincidences is in the precise eye of the camera revealed in all its perfect symmetry. Nothing is casual, nothing is banal. Just as in the apparent vegetal chaos of the forest there is a strict relationship of cause and effect—for each tree there are hundreds of birds, for each bird there are thousands of insects, for each insect there are millions of organic particles—so, too, the campesinos at their labors or the family sheltering from winter inside the house are indispensable parts of a vast fresco. The essential is often invisible: the eye doesn't capture it, only the heart, but the camera at times obtains glimpses of that substance. That is what maestro Ribero attempted to capture in his art, and that is what he tried to teach me: to move beyond the merely documentary and touch the core, the very soul, of reality. Those subtle connections that took shape on the photographic paper moved me profoundly and encouraged me to continue experimenting. In the confinement of winter my curiosity grew; even as my surroundings became more suffocating and constraining and I hibernated among thick adobe walls, my mind grew more restless. I began obsessively to explore the contents of the house and the secrets of its inhabitants. I examined familiar objects with new eyes, as if seeing them for the first time, without taking anything for granted. I let myself be guided by intuition, setting aside preconceived ideas. "We see only what we want to see," Don Juan Ribero always said, and added that my job should be to show what no one had seen before. At first the Domínguezes posed with forced smiles, but soon they became accustomed to my stealthy presence and in the end ignored the camera; then I could capture them off guard, just as they were. The rain carried off the flowers and leaves, the house with its heavy furniture and large empty spaces closed itself to the outdoors, and we were trapped in a strange domestic captivity. We wandered through rooms lighted with candles, avoiding icy currents of air; the furniture creaked with a widow's moans, and you could hear the furtive little footsteps of mice going about their diligent tasks. Everything smelled of mud, of wet roof tiles, of musty clothes. The servants lighted braziers and chimneys, the maids brought us hot water bottles, blankets, and cups of steaming chocolate, but there was no way to trick the long winter. It was then that I succumbed to loneliness.

Diego was a ghost. I try to remember now some moment we shared, but I can see him only as a mime on a stage, voiceless and separated from me by the orchestra pit. I have in my mind—and in my collection of photographs from that winter—many images of him in various activities out in the fields and inside the house, always busy with others, never with me, distant and aloof. It was impossible to be close to him; there was an abysmal silence between us, and my attempts to exchange ideas or ask about his feelings shattered against his obstinate absence. He maintained that we'd said everything there was to say. If we had married, it was because we loved each other; what need was there to delve into the obvious? At first his muteness offended me, but then I realized that that was how he behaved with everyone except his nieces and nephews. He could be happy and tender with the children; maybe he wanted to have children as much as I, but every month we were disappointed. We didn't talk about that, either; it was another of the many subjects related to the body or to love that it wasn't proper to discuss. A few times I tried to tell him how I would like to be caressed, but he immediately became defensive; in his eyes, a decent woman shouldn't feel that kind of need, much less talk about it. Soon his reticence, my embarrassment, and our mutual pride erected a Great Wall of China between us. I would have given anything to talk to someone about what happened behind our closed door, but my mother-in-law was as ethereal as an angel, I had no real friendship with Susana, Adela was barely sixteen, and Nívea was too far away, and I didn't dare put those concerns in writing. Diego and I continued to make love—to put some kind of name to it—now and then, always like that first time. Living together did not bring us closer, but that was painful only to me; he felt very comfortable with things as they were. We didn't argue. We treated each other with strained courtesy, although I would a thousand times over have preferred open warfare to our stubborn silences. My husband fled occasions to be alone with me; at night he stayed up playing cards until I, overcome with exhaustion, went off to bed. In the mornings he leapt from bed with the cock's crow, and even on Sundays, when the rest of the family got up late, he found excuses to leave early. I, on the other hand, indulged his every mood; I hurried to serve him in a thousand details, and did everything I could to attract him and to make his life pleasant. My heart raced in my breast when I heard his steps or his voice. I never tired of gazing at him—he seemed as handsome as the heroes in storybooks. In bed, trying not to wake him, I would run my hand over his broad, strong shoulders, his thick, wavy hair, the muscles of his legs and neck. I loved the odor of his sweat, like earth and horses when he came back from the fields, like English soap after his bath. I buried my face in his clothes to breathe in his man smell, since I didn't dare do that with his body. Now, with the perspective of time and the freedom I've won in recent years, I understand how I humbled myself for love. I put everything aside, from my personality to my work, to dream of a domestic paradise that wasn't to be mine.

All during the long and idle winter, the family had to use different resources of imagination to combat the tedium. All of them had a good ear for music; they played a variety of instruments, and so the evenings went by in improvised concerts. Susana usually delighted us robed in a tunic of frayed velvet with a Turkish turban on her head and her eyes outlined with kohl, singing in a hoarse gypsy voice. Doña Elvira and Adela organized sewing classes for the women and tried to keep the little school going, but only the children of the nearest tenants could defy the weather to come to class. Every day they prayed winter rosaries that attracted young and old alike because afterward they served hot chocolate and cake. Susana had the idea of preparing a play to celebrate the end of the century; that kept us busy for weeks, writing the libretto and learning our roles, setting up a stage in one of the barns, sewing costumes, and rehearsing. The subject, naturally, was a predictable allegory on the vices and misfortunes of the past defeated by the incandescent scimitar of science, technology, and twentieth-century progress. Besides the play, we had contests of target shooting and dictionary words, championships of every kind, from chess to making puppets and constructing villages of matchsticks, but there were still hours to spare. I made Adela my assistant in the darkroom, and we exchanged books on the sly; I lent her the ones I was sent from Santiago, and she gave me her mystery novels, which I devoured with passion. I became an expert detective; usually I guessed the identity of the murderer before page eighty. Our supply was limited, and no matter how we tried to stretch out the reading, the books went fast; then Adela and I played at changing the stories or inventing complicated crimes the other had to solve. "What are you two whispering about?" Doña Adela often asked. "Nothing, Mama, we're planning a murder," Adela would reply, with her innocent little rabbit smile. Doña Elvira would laugh, unable to imagine how true her daughter's answer was.

Eduardo, in his position as firstborn, was due to inherit the estate at Don Sebastián's death, but he had formed a partnership with his brother so they could administer it jointly. I liked my brother-in-law. He was gentle and playful; he made jokes with me and brought me little presents: translucent agates from the riverbed, an inexpensive necklace from the Mapuche reservation, wildflowers, a fashion magazine he had ordered in the village, in that way trying to compensate for his brother's indifference toward me, which was obvious to everyone in the family. He would take my hand and anxiously ask me if I was all right, if I needed anything, if I missed my grandmother, if I was bored at Caleufú. Susana, in contrast, immersed in her odalisque languor, which closely resembled laziness, ignored me most of the time and had an impertinent way of turning her back to me, leaving me with words still in my mouth. Opulent, with her golden skin and large, dark eyes, she was a beauty, but I don't think she was aware of it. She had no one to show off to, only the family, which was why she took so little care in her personal appearance; at times she didn't even comb her hair but lounged the whole day in her bathrobe and lambswool slippers, sleepy and melancholy. Other times, in contrast, she would be as resplendent as a Moorish princess, with her long dark hair caught up with tortoiseshell combs and with a gold necklace defining the perfect line of her throat. When she was in a good humor, she liked to pose for me; once at the table she suggested that I photograph her nude. That provocation fell like a bomb in that very conservative family; Doña Elvira nearly had another heart attack, and Diego, scandalized, jumped up so abruptly he turned over his chair. If Eduardo hadn't made a joke, a real drama would have ensued. Adela, the least attractive of the Domínguez children, with her rabbit face and blue eyes lost in a sea of freckles, was undoubtedly the most likable. Her happiness was as reliable as the morning light; we could count on her to raise everyone's spirits, even in the darkest winter hours when the wind howled over the roof tiles and we were sick of playing cards by candlelight. Her father, Don Sebastián, adored her. He could deny her nothing, and he used to ask her half in jest, half seriously, to grow up to be a spinster and take care of him in his old age.

Winter came and went, leaving two children and an old man dead of pneumonia among the campesinos. The grandmother who lived in the Domínguez house also died; they had calculated that she had lived more than a century, since she had taken her first communion the year Chile declared its independence from Spain, in 1810. All were buried with little ceremony in the cemetery on Caleufú, turned into a bog by the torrential downpours. It didn't stop raining until September, when spring began to burst out everywhere and finally we could go out on the patio to sun our clothing and mildewed mattresses. Doña Elvira had passed those months bundled in shawls, from bed to chair, weaker and weaker. Once a month, very discreetly, she asked me if I didn't "have any news," and since I didn't, her prayers for Diego and me to give her more grandchildren grew more numerous. Despite the long nights of that winter, I was not any more intimate with my husband. We came together in the darkness in silence, almost like enemies, and I was always left with the same feeling of frustration and irrepressible anguish of that first night. It seemed to me we embraced only when I took the initiative, but I could be wrong, maybe it wasn't always like that. With the arrival of spring I again rode out alone toward the forests and volcanoes; galloping through those vast spaces somewhat dampened my hunger for love, as fatigue, and buttocks pummeled by the saddle, overrode repressed desire. I would come back home in the evening soaked from dripping forests and my sweating horse, have a warm bath prepared, and soak for hours in water perfumed with orange leaves. "Be careful, daughter; horseback riding and baths are bad for the womb, they make you sterile," my distressed mother-in-law would admonish me. Doña Elvira was a simple woman, pure goodness and will to serve, her transparent soul reflected in the calm waters of her blue eyes, the mother I would have liked to have. I spent hours by her side, she knitting for her grandchildren and telling me again and again little stories of her life and of Caleufú, and I listening with the pain of knowing that she would not survive much longer. By then I suspected that a baby would not close the distance between Diego and me, but I wanted nothing more than to offer it to Doña Elvira as a gift. When I imagined life there without her, I felt an inconsolable sadness.

The century ended, and Chileans were struggling to jump on the bandwagon of the industrial progress in Europe and North America, but the Domínguezes, like many conservative families, were alarmed by the loss of traditional customs and the tendency to imitate foreign ways. "Tools of the devil," Don Sebastián would say when he read about technological advances in his out-of-date newspapers. His son Eduardo was the only one interested in the future: Diego lived in his own world, Susana always had a headache, and Adela hadn't yet emerged from her cocoon. As remote as we were, however, ripples of progress reached us, and we could not ignore the changes in the society. Santiago was caught up in a frenzy of sports, games, and walks in the fresh air more befitting the eccentric English than the relaxed descendents of the hidalgos of Castille and León. A blizzard of art and culture from France enlivened the atmosphere, and a heavy clank of German machinery interrupted Chile's long colonial siesta. An arriviste and educated middle class was developing that sought to live like the wealthy. The social crisis rocking the foundations of the nation with strikes, disorders, unemployment, and charges of mounted police with unsheathed swords was a distant rumble that had no effect on the rhythm of our life on Caleufú; even though on the estate we kept living like the great-grandparents who had slept in those same beds a hundred years before, the twentieth century was descending on us, too.

My grandmother Paulina had declined badly, Frederick Williams and Nívea del Valle wrote me; she was succumbing to the many indispositions of old age and to a premonition of her death. They realized how much she had aged when Severo del Valle brought her the first bottles of wine from the grapes that matured late and that, they learned, produced a smooth, voluptuous wine with very little tannin called a *carmenere*, as good as the best in France, which they baptized Viña Paulina. Finally they had in hand a unique wine that would bring them fame and wealth. My grandmother tasted it delicately. "It's a shame I can't enjoy it—let the others drink it," she said, and then never mentioned it again. There was no explosion of joy, no arrogant comments of the kind that usually accompanied her entrepreneurial triumphs; after a lifetime of defiance, she was becoming humble. The clearest sign of her weakness was the daily presence of the infamous priest in the stained cassock, who hovered around the dying to snatch their fortunes. I don't know whether by her own initiative or at the suggestion of that old augurer of fatalities, my grandmother banished to the cellar her famed mythological bed, in which she had spent half her life, and replaced it with a soldier's cot and horsehair mattress. That to me seemed a very alarming symptom, and as soon as the mud on the roads dried, I announced to my husband that I had to go to Santiago to see my grandmother. I expected some opposition but, to the contrary, in less than twenty-four hours Diego had arranged my trip by cart to the port, where I would take a boat to Valparaíso, from there to continue by train to Santiago. Adela was wild to go with me, so much so that she sat in her father's lap, nibbled his ears, tugged at his sideburns, and pleaded, until finally Don Sebastián could not deny her that new whim, even though Doña Elvira, Eduardo, and Diego were not in agreement. They didn't have to state their reasons; I assumed that they didn't consider the atmosphere they had perceived in my grandmother's house to be appropriate, and thought that I wasn't mature enough to take care of the girl properly. But we set out for Santiago accompanied by a pair of German friends who were traveling on the same boat. We wore scapulars of the Sacred Heart of Jesus on our chests to protect us from all evil, amen; we also had money sewed into a little bag under our corsets, precise instructions not to speak with any strangers, and more luggage than needed for a trip around the world.

The two months Adela and I spent in Santiago would have been wonderful if my grandmother hadn't been ill. She welcomed us with feigned enthusiasm, full of plans for going on outings, to the theater, and by train to Viña del Mar to take the air on the coast, but at the last moment she sent us with Frederick Williams, and she stayed behind—as she did when we made a trip by carriage to visit Severo and Nívea del Valle at the vineyards, which by then were producing the first wines for export. My grandmother thought that Viña Paulina sounded too local and wanted to change it for something in French to sell it in the United States, where, according to her, no one understood about wine, but Severo was opposed to that kind of ruse. I found Nívea with threads of gray in her bun, surrounded by her youngest children, a little heavier but no less lively, impertinent, and mischievous. "I believe that finally I'm getting the change; now we'll be able to make love without fear of having another baby," she whispered in my ear, never imagining that several years later Clara, the clairvoyant, would come into the world, the strangest of the children born into the numerous and bizarre del Valle clan. Little Rosa, whose beauty evoked so many comments, was five. I regret that a photograph can't capture her coloring; she looks like a sea creature with her yellow eyes and hair as green as old brass. She was already an angelic thing, a little slow for her age, who wafted through life like a spirit. "Where did she come from?" her mother joked. "She must be the daughter of the Holy Ghost." That beautiful little girl had come to console Nívea for the loss of two of her younger children who had died of diphtheria, and the long illness that had ravaged the lungs of a third. I tried to talk with Nívea about that—they say there is no suffering more horrible than the loss of a child—but she changed the subject. The most I could get her to tell me was that for centuries and centuries women had suffered the pain of giving birth and of burying their children, and that she was no exception. "It would be very arrogant of me to suppose that God blessed me by sending me many children and that all of them would live longer than I," she said.

Paulina del Valle wasn't a shadow of the woman she had been; she had lost interest in food and in business, she could barely walk because her knees were so bad, but she was more lucid than ever. The vials of her medications were lined up on her night table, and three nuns took turns looking after her. My grandmother intuited that we would not have many more opportunities to be together, and for the first time in our relationship was ready to answer my questions. We paged through photograph albums, as she explained them one by one; she told me about the origins of the bed commissioned in Florence, and about her rivalry with Amanda Lowell, which from the perspective of her age seemed more comic than anything, and she talked to me about my father and about Severo del Valle's role in my childhood, but she steadfastly avoided the subject of my maternal grandparents and Chinatown. She told me that my mother had been a very beautiful American model, and that was all. Some afternoons we would sit in the glass gallery to talk with Severo and Nívea del Valle. While he talked about the years in San Francisco and his experiences in the war, she would recall details about what happened during the revolution, when I was only eleven. My grandmother never complained, but Uncle Frederick advised me that she had severe stomach pains and that it was a tremendous effort for her to get dressed each morning. Faithful to her belief that you are the age you appear, she kept dyeing the few hairs left on her head, but she didn't parade about like a peacock in her empress's jewels, as she had before. "She hasn't many left," her husband whispered to me mysteriously. The house seemed as run-down as its mistress; missing paintings had left pale rectangles on the wallpaper, there were fewer carpets and furniture, the tropical plants in the gallery were a withered, dusty tangle, and the birds were silent in their cages. What Uncle Frederick had written about my grandmother's sleeping on a soldier's cot was true. She had always occupied the largest bedroom in the house, and her famous mythological bed rose in the center like a papal throne; from there she had directed her empire. Every morning found her in that bed, surrounded by the aquatic polychrome figures that a Florentine craftsman had carved forty years before, studying her account books, dictating letters, inventing new business ventures. Beneath the covers her bulk diminished, and she could create an illusion of fragility and beauty. I had taken countless photographs of her in that gilded bed, and I wanted to photograph her now in her modest viyella nightgown and grandmotherly shawl in the bed of a penitent, but she roundly refused. I noticed that the beautiful French furniture covered in quilted silk had disappeared from her room, along with the large rosewood desk with inlaid Indian mother-of-pearl, and many rugs and paintings, and that now the only adornment was a large crucifix. "She is giving her furniture and jewels to the church," Frederick Williams explained, in view of which we decided to replace the nuns with nurses and find a way to prevent, even if by force, the visits of the apocalyptic priest, because in addition to carrying things off he was contributing to a climate of fear. Iván Radovic, the one doctor Paulina trusted, was fully in accord with these measures. It was good to see that old friend again—true friendship withstands time, distance, and silence, as he said—and to confess to him, between giggles, that in my memory he was always in the disguise of Genghis Khan. "It's the Slavic cheekbones," he justified with good humor. He still vaguely resembled a Tartar chieftain, but association with patients in the hospital for indigents where he worked had softened him. Besides, in Chile he didn't look as exotic as he had in England; he could have been a taller and cleaner Araucan *toqui*. He was a quiet man who listened with intense attention, even to the incessant chatter of Adela, who immediately fell in love with him and, being accustomed to beguiling her father, used the same technique to cajole Iván Radovic.

Unfortunately for her, the doctor saw her as an innocent and ingenuous little girl, but little girl nonetheless. The abysmal cultural ignorance of Adela and the sauciness with which she reeled off the most outlandish nonsense didn't bother him; I think he was amused, although her naive fits of flirtatiousness could make him blush. The doctor invited confidence; I found it easy to talk to him on subjects I rarely mentioned to other people for fear of boring them—photography for instance. He was interested in that because it had been used in medicine for several years in Europe and the United States. He asked me to show him how to handle a camera; he wanted to develop an archive of operations he'd performed, and patients' visible symptoms, to use in his lectures and classes. With that aim, we went to call on Don Juan Ribero, but we found the studio closed and posted with a FOR SALE sign. The barber next door informed us that the maestro wasn't working anymore because he had cataracts on both eyes, but he gave us Don Juan's address, and we went to visit him. He was living in a building on Calle Monjitas that had known better days: large, antiquated, and sighing with ghosts. A maid led us through several connecting rooms lined ceiling-to-floor with Ribero's photographs to a sitting room with ancient mahogany furniture and chairs with worn plush upholstery. The lamps were not lit and it took several seconds for our eyes to adjust to the half-light and see the maestro sitting with a cat on his knees before a window reflecting the last rays of the afternoon sun. He stood and walked forward with great certainty to say hello; nothing in the way he moved betrayed his blindness.

"Señorita del Valle! Forgive me, now you are Señora Domínguez, isn't that right?" he exclaimed, holding both my hands.

"Aurora, maestro, the same Aurora as always," I replied, giving him a hug. Then I introduced Dr. Radovic, and explained his wish to learn photography for medical purposes.

"I can't teach anymore, my friend. Heaven has punished me where it hurts most, in my vision. Imagine, a blind photographer. What an irony!"

"You don't see anything, maestro?" I asked, alarmed.

"Not with my eyes, no, but I still survey the world. Tell me, Aurora, have you changed much? How do you look now? The clearest image I have of you is of a thirteen-year-old girl with her feet planted before the door of my studio like a stubborn mule."

"I'm still the same, Don Juan. Shy, silly, and hardheaded."

"No, no. Tell me, for example, how your hair is combed, and what color you're wearing."

"The señora is dressed in an airy white dress with lace around the neckline; I don't know what the fabric is because I don't understand such things, and she has a yellow ribbon around her hat. I assure you she looks very pretty," said Radovic.

"Don't embarrass me, Doctor, I beg you," I interrupted.

"And now the señora's cheeks are pink," he added, and they both laughed.

The maestro rang a little bell, and the maid came in with a tray of coffees. We passed a very entertaining hour talking about the new techniques and cameras used in other countries, and how much the science of photography had advanced. Don Juan Ribero was up-to-date in everything.

"Aurora has the intensity, the concentration, and the patience every artist requires. I suppose the same things are needed to be a good physician, isn't that so? Ask her to show you her work, Doctor; she's modest and won't do it unless you insist," the maestro suggested to Iván Radovic as we said good-bye.

A few days later there was occasion to do just that. My grandmother had waked up with terrible stomach pain, and her usual sedatives hadn't helped, so we called Radovic, who came quickly and administered a strong compound of laudanum. We left my grandmother resting in bed, and once we were outside the room, he told me that we were dealing with another tumor but that she was too old to attempt another operation; she wouldn't survive the anesthesia. All we could do was try to control the pain and help her die in peace. I wanted to know how much time she had left, but it wasn't easy to determine that because, despite her age, my grandmother was very strong, and the tumor was growing very slowly. "Be prepared, Aurora, the end could come within a few months," he told me. I couldn't help crying. Paulina del Valle represented the only roots I had; without her I would be cast adrift, and the fact that I had Diego for a husband didn't lessen my feeling of coming disaster, it increased it. Radovic handed me his handkerchief and stood quietly, looking away from me, troubled by my tears. I made him promise he would give me warning in time to come in from the country and be with my grandmother in her last moments. The laudanum took effect, and she quickly relaxed. When she was asleep, I showed Iván Radovic out. At the door he asked whether he could stay a bit; he had a free hour, and it was very hot outside. Adela was taking her siesta, Frederick Williams had gone to his club to swim, and the enormous house on Calle Ejército Libertador seemed like a docked ship. I offered him a cool drink, and we sat in the gallery of the ferns and bird cages.

"Whistle something, Dr. Radovic," I said.

"Whistle? Why?"

"According to the Indians, whistling brings the wind. We need a breath of air to survive this heat."

"Well, while I whistle, why don't you bring me your photographs?" he asked. "I would like very much to see them."

I brought several boxes and sat beside him to try to explain my work. First I showed him some photographs I'd taken in Europe, when I was still more interested in aesthetics than content, then the platinum prints of Santiago and the Indians and campesinos on the estate, and finally the photos of the Domínguez family. He studied them as attentively as he examined my grandmother, with a question from time to time. He paused on those of Diego's family.

"Who is this very beautiful woman?" he wanted to know.

"Susana, Eduardo's wife, my sister-in-law."

"And I take it that this is Eduardo?" he asked, pointing to Diego.

"No, that's Diego. Why did you think he is Susana's husband?"

"I don't know, he seemed. . . ."

That night I spread the photographs on the floor and stared at them for hours. I went to bed very late, distressed.

I had to tell my grandmother good-bye because it was time to return to Caleufú. In Santiago's sunny December, Paulina del Valle was feeling better—winter there had been very long and lonely for her, too—and she promised that she and Frederick Williams would come for a visit after New Year's instead of summering at the beach, as everyone did who could escape the dog days in Santiago. She felt so well that she went with us by train to Valparaíso, where Adela and I caught the boat south. We were back in the country before Christmas, because we couldn't miss the most important festival of the year for the Domínguezes. For months in advance, Doña Elvira supervised gifts for the campesinos, either made at home or bought in town: clothing and toys for the children, fabric for dresses and knitting yarn for the women, tools for the men. On that day they gave out animals, sacks of flour, potatoes, *chancaca*, or dark sugar, beans and rice, *charquí*, or dried meat, *maté* tea, salt, and squares of quince paste, which was prepared in huge copper kettles over outdoor cook fires. The workers on the estate came from the four cardinal points, some traveling for days with their wives and children for the celebration. Steers and goats were slaughtered, potatoes and fresh corn boiled, and pots of beans simmered for hours. My job was to decorate the long tables set up in the patio with flowers and pine branches, and to prepare the jugs of sweet, watered wine that was not strong enough to intoxicate the adults and that the children could drink mixed with toasted flour. A priest came and stayed for two or three days, baptizing babies, confessing sinners, marrying unwed couples, and recriminating adulterers. On the stroke of twelve on December 24, we attended midnight mass before an improvised outdoor altar, because there were too many people to fit in the small chapel, and at dawn, after a delicious breakfast of *café con leche,* fresh baked bread, butter, marmalade, and summer fruit, Baby Jesus was carried in a joyful procession so each person could kiss his porcelain feet. Then Don Sebastián announced the family chosen for outstanding moral conduct and awarded the Child to them. For a year, until the following Christmas, the crystal urn containing the small statue would occupy a place of honor in that campesino hut, bringing them blessings. While it was there, nothing bad could occur. Don Sebastián worked it out so that each family had an opportunity to shelter Jesus beneath their roof. That year we also had the allegorical play about the arrival of the twentieth century, in which all the members of the family participated—except Doña Elvira, who was too weak, and Diego, who preferred to take charge of technical aspects such as footlights and backdrops. Don Sebastián, in an excellent mood, agreed to play the part of the Old Year, shuffling off grumbling, and one of Susana's children—still in diapers—represented the New Year.

At word of free food, several Pehuenche Indians showed up. They were very poor—they had lost their lands, and government plans for progress ignored them—but out of pride they did not arrive with empty hands: under their mantles they brought a few apples, which they offered caked with sweat and dirt, a rabbit smelling of putrefaction, and a few gourds of *muchi,* a liquor they made from a small violet-colored fruit they chew, spit into a ladle, and mix with saliva, and then let ferment. The ancient chief came forward with his three wives and his dogs, followed by twenty or so members of his tribe. The men never lowered their lances, and in spite of three centuries of abuse and defeats, they had not lost their fierce aspect. The women were not in the least timid, they were as independent and powerful as the men; there was an equality between the sexes that Nívea del Valle would have applauded. They offered ceremonious greetings in their tongue, addressing Don Sebastián as "brother," along with his sons, who welcomed them and invited them to join in the feast, although they also kept close watch, since the Indians would steal at the first excuse. My father-in-law maintained that they had no sense of property because they were used to communal living and sharing, but Diego alleged that those Indians who were so quick to take what wasn't theirs never allowed anyone to touch anything of their own. Fearing that they would get drunk and become violent, Don Sebastián, as an incentive, offered to give the chief a cask of liquor as they left, not to be opened on his property. The Indians sat in a large circle to eat, drink, share a pipe, and to deliver long speeches no one listened to; they didn't mix with the campesinos of Caleufú, although all the children raced around together. That celebration gave me a chance to photograph Indians to my heart's content, and to make friends with a few of the women with the idea that they would let me visit them on the other side of the lake, where they had camped for the summer. When the grazing was exhausted, or they grew bored with the scenery, they would pull their tent poles from the ground, roll up the cloth, and leave in search of new campsites. If I could spend a little time with them, maybe they would get used to the camera, and to me. I wanted to photograph them in their daily tasks, an idea that horrified my in-laws—since there were all kinds of hair-raising stories about the customs of these tribes, upon which the patient labor of the missionaries had applied very little veneer.

My grandmother Paulina did not come to visit me that summer, as she had promised. She could tolerate the trip by train and by ship, but the two days by oxcart from the port to Caleufú frightened her. Her weekly letters were my main contact with the outside world, and as the weeks went by, my nostalgia grew. My mood changed; I became unsociable, more taciturn, trailing my frustration behind me like a heavy bridal train. My loneliness brought me closer to my mother-in-law, a gentle, discreet woman totally dependent on her husband, with no ideas of her own, incapable of coping with the slightest problems of living, but who made up for lack of intellect with enormous goodness. My silent tantrums melted in her presence; Doña Elvira had the virtue of focusing me and of placating my sometimes suffocating anxiety.

Those summer months we were busy with harvests, new calves and kids, and putting up preserves. The sun set at nine P.M., and the days were eternal. By that time the house my father-in-law had built for Diego and me was ready: solid, new, beautiful, encircled with roofed galleries on four sides, and sweet with the scent of fresh clay, newly hewn wood, and basil, which the campesinos planted along the walls to frighten off bad luck and witchcraft. My in-laws gave us some furniture that had been in the family for generations; Diego bought the rest in town without asking my opinion. Instead of the wide bed in which we had slept until then, he bought two bronze single beds and placed a night table between them. After lunch the family retired to their rooms for an obligatory rest until five in the afternoon, because it was thought that heat paralyzed digestion. Diego would lie in a hammock under the grape arbor to smoke for a while and then go to the river to swim. He liked to go alone, and the few times I wanted to go with him, he was annoyed, so I didn't insist. Seeing that we didn't share those hours of the siesta in the intimacy of our room, I targeted them for reading or working in my little darkroom, because I couldn't get used to sleeping in the middle of the day. Diego didn't ask me for anything; he never questioned me, his interest in my activities and feelings was no more than the barest good manners, he was never impatient with my changing moods, my nightmares, which had returned with greater frequency and intensity, or my sullen silences. We would go for days without exchanging a word, but he didn't seem to notice. I wrapped myself in my muteness like an armor, counting the hours to see how long we could draw out that contest, but in the end I would give in, because the silence weighed much more on me than on him. Before, when we had shared the same bed, I would move close to him, pretending to be asleep. I would press myself against his back and interlace my legs with his; in that way I sometimes bridged the abyss that was deepening between us. In those rare embraces I was not seeking pleasure, since I didn't know that was possible, only consolation and companionship. For a few hours I lived the illusion of having recap-

tured him, but then dawn would come, and everything would again
be as it always was. When we moved to the new house, even that precarious intimacy evaporated; the distance between our beds was much
wider and more hostile than the raging waters of the river. Sometimes,
however, when I awakened screaming, pursued by the black pajama-
clad children of my dreams, he would get up and put his arms around
me until I grew calm. Those were perhaps the only spontaneous contacts between us. He was worried by those nightmares; he believed
they might degenerate into madness, and he bought a vial of opium
and sometimes gave me a few drops dissolved in orange liquor to help
me sleep and have happy dreams. Except for activities shared with all
the other family members, Diego and I were almost never together.
Often he would go off on some jaunt, crossing the cordillera toward
the Argentine Patagonia, or to town to buy provisions; sometimes he
would be away two or three days without explanation, and I would
sink into anguish, imagining an accident, but Eduardo would calm me
with the argument that his brother had always been that way, a solitary
man brought up in the magnitude of nature, accustomed to silence.
From the time he was young he had needed great spaces; he had the
soul of a wanderer, and had he not been born within the closely
woven net of that family, he might have been a sailor. We had been
married a year, and I felt guilty; not only had I not given him a child, I
hadn't been able to interest him in me, much less win his love. Something basic was lacking in my womanhood. I supposed that he had
chosen me because he was of an age to marry, his parents had pres-
sured him to look for a bride, and I was the first, maybe the only, person he had come across. Diego didn't love me. I had known that from
the beginning, but with the arrogance of first love and my nineteen
years, that hadn't seemed an insurmountable obstacle. I had thought I
could seduce him with persistence, virtue, and flirtation, as girls did in
romantic tales. In the anguish of identifying what was lacking in me, I
devoted hours and hours to shooting self-portraits, some before a large
mirror I had brought to my studio, others standing before the camera.

I took hundreds of photographs; in some I am dressed, in some I'm naked; I examined myself from every angle, and the only thing I discovered was a crepuscular sadness.

From her invalid's chair, Doña Elvira observed family life without missing a detail, and she was aware of Diego's prolonged absences and my desolation; she put two and two together and reached some conclusions. Her delicacy, and the very Chilean habit of not talking about emotions, prevented her from confronting the problem directly, but in the many hours we were alone together the closeness between us grew stronger and stronger; we came to be like mother and daughter. So, discreetly, gradually, she told me about the difficulties she had had with her husband in the beginning. She had married very young and hadn't had her first child until five years later, after several miscarriages that left her battered in heart and soul. In those days Sebastián Domínguez was immature and had little sense of responsibility in his married life; he was impetuous, a carouser, and a fornicator—she didn't use that word, of course, I doubt if she knew it. Doña Elvira had felt isolated, far from her family, alone and frightened, convinced that her marriage had been a terrible mistake from which her only escape was death. "But God heard my pleas; we had Eduardo, and overnight Sebastián changed completely. There is no better father or husband than he is; we have been together for more than thirty years, and every day I give thanks to heaven for the happiness we share. You must pray, daughter, that will help very much," she counseled. I prayed, but it must not have been with the proper intensity and persistence, because nothing changed.

My suspicions had begun months before, but I dismissed them, disgusted with myself; I couldn't accept them without exposing something evil in my own character. I kept telling myself that such conjectures could only come from the devil, thoughts that took root and grew like lethal tumors in my brain, ideas I had to combat mercilessly, but the termite of rancor was stronger than my good intentions. First it was the photographs of the family I had showed to Iván Radovic. What wasn't evident to the naked eye—because of our habit of seeing only what we want to see, as my maestro Juan Ribero used to tell me—was there in black and white in the photos. The unmistakable language of body, gestures, gazes, was stark in the prints. After those first suspicions, I turned more and more to the camera. Using the pretext of making an album for Doña Elvira, I was constantly photographing the family, pictures I developed in the privacy of my studio and studied with perverse attention. In that way I put together a miserable collection of vague proofs, something so subtle that only I, poisoned by wrath, could see. With the camera before my face, like a mask that made me invisible, I could focus on a scene and at the same time maintain a glacial distance. Toward the end of April, when temperatures began to drop, clouds crowned the peaks of the volcanoes, and nature began to go into seclusion in preparation for autumn, I considered that with the signs revealed in the photographs I had enough, and I began the odious task of watching Diego like any jealous woman. When finally I realized what that claw buried in my throat was, and could give it its dictionary name, I felt I was sinking in quicksand. Jealousy. The person who hasn't felt it cannot know how much it hurts, or imagine the madness committed in its name. In my thirty years I have suffered it only once, but I was burned so brutally that I have scars that still haven't healed, and I hope never will, as a reminder to avoid that feeling in the future. Diego wasn't mine—no person can belong to another—and the fact that I was his wife gave me no right over him or his feelings; love is a free contract that begins with a spark and can end the same way. A thousand dangers threaten love, but if the couple defends it, it can be saved; it can grow like a tree and give shade and fruit, but that happens only when both partners participate. Diego never did; our relationship was damned from the start. I realize that today, but then I was blind, at first with pure rage and later with grief.

Spying on him, watch in hand, I began to be aware that my husband's absences did not coincide with his explanations. When supposedly he had gone out hunting with Eduardo, he would come back hours earlier or later than his brother; when the other men in the family were at the sawmill or at the roundup branding cattle, he would suddenly show up in the patio, and later, if I raised the subject at the table, I would find that he hadn't been with them at any time during the day. When he went to town for supplies he would come back without anything, presumably because he hadn't found what he was looking for, although it might be something as common as an ax or a saw. In the countless hours the family spent together, he avoided conversation at all cost; he was always the one who organized the card games or asked Susana to sing. If she came down with one of her headaches, he was quickly bored and would go off on his horse with his shotgun over his shoulder. I couldn't follow him on horseback without his seeing me or raising suspicion in the family, but I could keep an eye on him when he was around the house. That was how I noticed that sometimes he got up in the middle of the night, and that he didn't go to the kitchen to get something to eat, as I had always thought, but dressed, went out to the patio, disappeared for an hour or two, then quietly slipped back to bed. Following him in the darkness was easier than during the day, when a dozen eyes were watching us, it was all a matter of staying awake and avoiding wine at dinner and the bedtime opium drops. One night in mid-May I noticed when he slipped out of bed, and in the pale light of the oil lamp we always kept lit before the cross, I watched him put on his pants and boots, pick up his shirt and jacket, and leave the room. I waited a few instants, then quickly got out of bed and followed him, with my heart about to burst out of my breast. I couldn't see him very well in the shadows of the house, but when he went out on the patio his silhouette stood out sharply in the light of the full moon, which for moments at a time shone bright in the heavens. The sky was streaked with clouds that cloaked everything in darkness when they hid the moon. I heard the dogs bark and was afraid they would come to me and betray my presence, but they didn't; then I understood that Diego had tied them up earlier. My husband made a complete circle of the house and then walked rapidly toward one of the stables where the family's personal mounts were kept, the ones not used in the fields; he swung the crossbar that fastened the door and went inside. I stood waiting, protected by the blackness of an elm a few yards from the barn, barefoot and wearing nothing but a thin nightgown, not daring to take another step, convinced that Diego would come out on horseback, and I wouldn't be able to follow him. I waited for a period that seemed very long, but nothing happened. Suddenly I glimpsed a light through the slit of the open door, maybe a candle or small lantern. My teeth were chattering, and I was shivering from cold and fright. I was about to give up and go back to bed when I saw another figure approaching from the east—obviously not from the big house—and also go into the stable, closing the door behind. I let almost fifteen minutes go by before I made a decision, then forced myself to take a few steps. I was stiff from the cold and barely able to move. I crept toward the door, terrified, unable to imagine how Diego would react if he found me spying on him, but incapable of retreating. Softly I pushed the door, which opened without resistance because the bar was on the outside and it couldn't be secured from the inside, and slipped like a thief through the narrow opening. It was dark in the stable, but a pale light flickered far at the back, and I tiptoed in that direction, almost not breathing—unnecessary precautions since the straw deadened my footsteps and several of the horses were awake; I could hear them shifting and snuffling in their stalls.

In the faint light of a lantern hanging from a beam and swayed by the wind filtering between the wooden timbers, I saw them. They had spread blankets out in a clump of hay, like a nest, where she was lying on her back, dressed in a heavy, unbuttoned overcoat under which she was naked. Her arms and her legs were spread open, her head tilted toward her shoulder, her black hair covering her face, and her skin shining like blond wood in the delicate, orangeish glow of the lantern.

Diego, wearing nothing but his shirt, was kneeling before her, licking her sex. There was such absolute abandon in Susana's position and such contained passion in Diego's actions that I understood in an instant how irrelevant I was to all that. In truth, I didn't exist, nor did Eduardo or the three children, no one else, only the two of them and the inevitability of their lovemaking. My husband had never caressed me in that way. It was easy to see that they had been like this a thousand times before, that they had loved each other for years; I understood finally that Diego had married me because he needed a screen to hide his love affair with Susana. In one instant the pieces of that painful jigsaw puzzle fell into place; I could explain his indifference to me, the absences that coincided with Susana's headaches, Diego's tense relationship with his brother Eduardo, the deceit in his behavior toward the rest of the family, and how he arranged always to be near her, touching her, his foot against hers, his hand on her elbow or her shoulder, and sometimes, as if coincidentally, at her waist or her neck, unmistakable signs the photographs had revealed to me. I remembered how much Diego loved her children, and I speculated that maybe they weren't his nephews but his sons, all three with blue eyes, the mark of the Domínguezes. I stood motionless, gradually turning to ice, as voluptuously they made love, savoring every stroke, every moan, unhurried, as if they had all the rest of their lives. They did not seem like a couple of lovers in a hasty clandestine meeting but like a pair of newlyweds in the second week of their honeymoon, when passion is still intact, but with added confidence and the mutual knowledge of each other's flesh. I, nevertheless, had never experienced intimacy of that kind with my husband, nor would I have been able to invent it in my most audacious fantasies. Diego's tongue was running over Susana's inner thighs, from her ankles upward, pausing between her legs and then back down again, while his hands moved from her waist to her round, opulent breasts, playing with her nipples, hard and lustrous as grapes. Susana's soft, smooth body shivered and undulated; she was a fish in the river, her head turning from side to side in the desperation of her pleasure, her hair spread across her face, her lips open in a long moan, her hands seeking Diego to guide him over the beautiful topography of her body, until his tongue made her explode in pleasure. Susana arched backward from the ecstasy that shot through her like lightning, and she uttered a hoarse cry that he choked off with his mouth upon hers. Then Diego took her in his arms, rocking her, petting her like a cat, whispering a rosary of secret words into her ear with a delicacy and tenderness I never thought possible in him. At some moment she sat up in the straw, took off her coat, and began to kiss him, first his forehead, then his eyelids, his temples, lingering on his mouth; her tongue mischievously explored Diego's ears, swerved to his Adam's apple, brushed across his throat, her teeth nibbling his nipples, her fingers combing the hair on his chest. Then it was his turn to abandon himself completely to her caresses; he lay facedown on the blanket and she sat astride him, biting the nape of his neck, covering his shoulders with brief playful kisses, moving down to his buttocks, exploring, smelling, savoring him, and leaving a trail of saliva as she went. Diego turned over, and her mouth enveloped his erect, pulsing penis in an interminable labor of pleasure, of give and take in the most profound intimacy conceivable, until he could not wait any longer and threw himself on her, penetrated her, and they rolled like enemies in a tangle of arms and legs and kisses and panting and sighs and expressions of love that I had never heard before. Then they dozed in a warm embrace, covered with blankets and Susana's overcoat like a pair of innocent children. Silently I retreated and went back to the house, while the icy cold of the night spread inexorably through my soul.

A chasm opened before me; I felt vertigo pulling me downward, a temptation to leap and annihilate myself in the depths of suffering and fear. Diego's betrayal and my dread of the future left me floating with nothing to cling to, lost, disconsolate. The fury that had shaken me at first lasted only briefly, then I was crushed by a sensation of death, of absolute agony. I had entrusted my life to Diego, he had promised me his protection as a husband; I believed literally the ritual words of marriage: that we were joined until death us did part. There was no way out. The scene in the stable had confronted me with a reality that I had perceived for a long time but had refused to face. My first impulse was to run to the big house, to stand in the middle of the patio and howl like a madwoman, to wake the family, the servants, the dogs, and make them witnesses to adultery and incest. My timidity, however, was stronger than my desperation. Silently, feeling my way in the dark, I dragged myself back to the room I shared with Diego and sat on my bed shivering and sobbing, my tears soaking into the neck of my nightgown. In the following minutes or hours I had time to think about what I had seen and to accept my powerlessness. It wasn't a sexual affair that joined Diego and Susana, it was a proven love; they were prepared to run every risk and sweep aside any obstacle that stood in their way, rolling onward like an uncontainable river of molten lava. Neither Eduardo nor I counted; we were disposable, barely insects in the enormity of their passion. I should tell my brother-in-law before anyone else, I decided, but when I pictured the blow such a confession would be to that good man, I knew I wouldn't have the courage to do it. Eduardo would discover it himself some day, or with luck, he might never know. Perhaps he suspected, as I did, but didn't want to confirm it in order to maintain the fragile equilibrium of his illusions; he had the three children, his love for Susana, and the monolithic cohesion of his clan.

Diego came back sometime during the night, shortly before dawn. By the light of the oil lamp he saw me sitting on my bed, my face puffy from crying, unable to speak, and he thought I had woken with another of my nightmares. He sat beside me and tried to draw me to his chest, as he had on similar occasions, but instinctively I pulled away from him, and I must have worn an expression of terrible anger, because immediately he moved back to his own bed. We sat looking at each other, he surprised and I despising him, until the truth took form between the two of us, as undeniable and conclusive as a dragon.

"What are we going to do now?" were the only words I could utter.

He didn't try to deny anything or justify himself; he defied me with a steely stare, ready to defend his love in any way necessary, even if he had to kill me. Then the dam of pride, good breeding, and politeness that had held me back during months of frustration collapsed, and silent reproaches were converted into a flood of recriminations that I couldn't contain, that he listened to quietly and without emotion, attentive to every word. I accused him of everything that had gone through my mind and then begged him to reconsider; I told him that I was willing to forgive and forget, that we could go far away somewhere no one knew us, and start over. By the time my words and tears were exhausted, it was broad daylight. Diego crossed the distance that separated our beds, sat beside me, took my hands, and calmly and seriously explained that he had loved Susana for many years and that their love was the most important thing in his life, more compelling than honor, than the other members of his family, than the salvation of his very soul. To make me feel better, he said, he could promise that he would give her up, but it would be an empty promise. He added that he had tried to do that when he went to Europe, leaving her behind for six months, but it hadn't worked. Then he had gone so far as to marry me, to see whether in that way he might break that terrible tie to his sister-in-law, but far from helping him in the decision to leave her, marriage had made it easier because it diluted the suspicions of Eduardo and the rest of the family. He was, however, happy that finally I had discovered the truth because it was painful to him to deceive me. He had nothing to say against me, he assured me. I was a good wife, and he deeply regretted that he couldn't give me the love I deserved. He felt miserable every time he slipped away from me to be with Susana; it would be a relief not to lie to me anymore. Everything was in the open now.

"And Eduardo doesn't count?" I asked.

"What happens between him and Susana is up to them. It's the relation between you and me that we must decide now."

"You have already decided, Diego. I don't have anything to do here, I will go back home," I told him.

"This is your house now, we are husband and wife, Aurora. What God has joined together you cannot put asunder."

"You are the one who has violated holy commandments," I pointed out.

"We can live together like brother and sister. You won't want for anything, I will always respect you, you will be protected and free to devote yourself to your photographs, or whatever you want. The only thing I ask is, please not to create a scandal."

"You can't ask anything of me, Diego."

"I'm not asking for myself. I have thick skin, and I can face it like a man. I'm asking for my mother's sake. She couldn't bear it."

So for Doña Elvira's sake, I stayed. I don't know how I was able to get dressed, splash water on my face, comb my hair, have a cup of coffee, and leave the house for my daily chores. I don't know how I faced Susana at lunch, or what explanation I gave my in-laws for my swollen eyes. That day was the worst; I felt beaten, dazed, on the verge of tears at the first word from anyone. That night I had a fever, and my bones ached, but the next day I was calmer. I saddled my horse and raced off toward the hills. Soon it began to rain, but I kept galloping on until my poor mare couldn't go any farther; then I got off and pushed my way on foot through the undergrowth and mud beneath the trees, slipping, and falling, and getting back up, screaming at the top of my lungs as the rain poured down. My soaked poncho weighed so much that I threw it off and went on, shivering from the cold but burning inside. I rode back at sunset; I had lost my voice and had a fever. I drank a cup of hot tea and got into bed. I remember very little of the rest, because in the following weeks I was busy fending off death and hadn't the time or spirit to think about the tragedy of my marriage. The night I had spent barefoot and half naked in the stable, and the gallop through the rain, had brought on a pneumonia that nearly killed me. They took me by cart to the German hospital, where I was placed in the hands of a Teutonic nurse with blond braids whose tenacity saved my life. That noble Valkyrie could lift me like a baby in her strong woodcutter's arms, and just as ably spoon chicken broth into me with the patience of a wet nurse.

At the beginning of July, when winter had definitively set in and all you could see was water—torrential rivers, floods, bogs, rain and more rain—Diego and two of the campesinos came to the hospital to get me and take me back to Caleufú wrapped in blankets and furs like a package. They had improvised a roof of waxed canvas over the cart, installed a bed, and there was even a lighted brazier to combat the dampness. Sweating in my cocoon of covers I made the slow journey home, Diego riding alongside on horseback. At times the wheels became mired; the oxen weren't strong enough to pull the cart out, and the men had to lay planks over the mud and push. Diego and I did not exchange a single word during that long day's journey. At Caleufú, Doña Elvira came out to welcome me, weeping with joy, nervous, bestirring the maids to get the braziers, the hot water bottles, the soup with calf's blood to bring back my color and my wish to live. She had prayed so much for me, she said, that God had taken pity. Using the excuse that I still felt very vulnerable, I asked her to let me sleep in the big house, and she put me in a room near hers. For the first time in my life I had a mother's care. My grandmother Paulina del Valle, who loved me so dearly and had done so much for me, was not given to shows of affection, although at heart she was very sentimental. She said that tenderness, that honeyed mixture of love and compassion so frequently represented on calendars by enraptured mothers beside their babies' cradles, was tolerable when applied to defenseless creatures like kittens, for example, but supreme foolishness when it came to human beings. There had always been an ironic and brassy note in our relationship; we scarcely ever touched, except when I slept with her as a child, and in general we treated each other with a certain brusqueness that was very comfortable to us both. I would fall back on a mocking tenderness when I wanted to get my way, and I always won, because my prodigious grandmother was easy to soften up—more to escape demonstrations of emotion than for any weakness of character. Doña Elvira, on the other hand, was a simple being to whom the sarcasm my grandmother and I used would have been offensive. She was naturally affectionate. She would take my hand and hold it in hers, and kiss and hug me; she liked to brush my hair, she personally gave me my marrow bone and codfish tonics, applied camphor plasters for my cough, and made me sweat out my fever by rubbing me with eucalyptus oil and wrapping me in warm blankets. She worried over me, seeing that I ate well and got enough rest, and at night she gave me the opium drops and stayed at my side praying until I fell asleep. Every morning she asked if I'd had nightmares, and asked me to describe them in detail, "because by talking about those things you lose your fear." Her health wasn't good, but she found strength from God knows where to nurse me and stay with me, while I pretended to be more fragile than I truly was in order to prolong that idyll with my mother-in-law. "Get better soon, child, your husband needs you at his side," she would say, concerned, although Diego kept saying I should spend the rest of the winter in the big house. Those weeks beneath her roof recovering from pneumonia were a strange experience. My mother-in-law gave me the care and warmth I would never have from Diego. That gentle and unconditional love acted like a balm, and little by little I was getting over wanting to die and feeling such animosity toward my husband. I had come to understand Diego and Susana's feelings and the inexorable fatalism of what had happened. Their passion had to be a force of nature, an earthquake that tossed them about at will. I imagined how they had fought against that attraction before succumbing to it, how many taboos they had to overcome in order to be together, how terrible the torment of each day must be, pretending a brother-and-sister relationship to the world while they were burning with desire inside. I stopped asking myself how it was possible that they could not conquer the lust and selfishness that kept them from seeing the disaster they could cause among those closest to them because I intuited how tortured they must be. I had loved Diego desperately, I could understand what Susana felt for him. Would I have done the same as she in the same circumstances? I didn't think so, but that was impossible to know. Although my sense of failure was as strong as ever, I was able to let go of my hatred, to stand back and put myself in the skin of the other protagonists in that misery. I had more compassion for Eduardo than sorrow for myself. He had three children, and he loved his wife; the drama of that incestuous infidelity would be worse for him than for me. For my brother-in-law's sake, too, I had to hold my tongue, but the secret wasn't weighing now like a millstone around my neck because the horror of what Diego had done had been mitigated, washed by the hands of Doña Elvira. My gratitude to that woman was added to the respect and affection I had felt from the beginning. I clung to her like a lapdog; I needed her presence, her voice, her lips on my forehead. I felt obliged to protect her from the cataclysm brewing in the bosom of her family. I was willing to stay at Caleufú, hiding my humiliation as a rejected wife, because if I left and she discovered the truth she would die of grief and shame. Her life turned around that family, around the needs of each of the persons who lived within the walls of their compound: that was her entire universe. My agreement with Diego was that I would play my part as long as Doña Elvira lived, and after that I would be free; he would let me leave and would never contact me again. I would have to live with the stigma—calamitous for many—of being "separated," and would not be able to marry again, but at least I wouldn't have to live with a man who didn't love me.

• • •

In mid-September, when I was running out of excuses to stay in my in-laws' house and the moment had come to move back to live with Diego, Iván Radovic's telegram arrived. In a couple of lines he informed me that I should return to Santiago because my grandmother was nearing the end. I had expected that news for months, but when the telegram came I felt as if I'd been clubbed; I was stupefied with sorrow and surprise. My grandmother was immortal. I couldn't visualize her as the tiny, bald, fragile old woman she truly was, only as she had been: an astute, bewigged Amazon with a gluttonous appetite. Doña Elvira took me in her arms and told me that I mustn't feel alone, that I had another family now, that I belonged at Caleufú and she would try to look after me and protect me as Paulina del Valle had done before. She helped me pack my two suitcases, again hung the scapular of the Sacred Heart of Jesus around my neck, and swamped me with advice. To her, Santiago was a den of iniquity and the trip a perilous adventure. It was the time they started up the sawmill again after the paralysis of winter, which afforded Diego a good excuse not to come with me to Santiago, even though his mother insisted he should. Eduardo took me to the boat. The whole family stood waving good-bye at the door of the big house at Caleufú: Diego, my in-laws, Adela, Susana, the children, and various servants. I didn't know that I would not see them again.

Before I left I went through my darkroom, which I hadn't been in since that fateful night in the stable, and found that someone had removed the photographs of Diego and Susana, but since that person knew nothing about the developing process, the negatives hadn't been touched. Those pathetic vestiges of evidence had no purpose now, so I destroyed them. I put the negatives of the Indians, the people around Caleufú, and the other members of the family into my suitcases, because I didn't know how long I would be away and I didn't want them to be damaged. I made the trip with Eduardo on horseback, with my luggage strapped onto a mule, stopping at small settlements to eat and rest. My brother-in-law, that large bearlike man, had the same gentle

nature as his mother, the same nearly childish naïveté. Along the way
we had time to talk as we never had before. He confessed that from
the time he was a child he had written poetry. "How can you not
when you live in the midst of such beauty?" he added, indicating the
landscape of woods and water around us. He told me there was nothing he wanted; unlike Diego, he had no curiosity about other places in
the world, Caleufú was enough for him. When he'd traveled to Europe
in his youth, he had felt lost and deeply unhappy; he couldn't live away
from that land he loved. God had been very generous with him, he
said, setting him down in the middle of an earthly paradise. We said
good-bye in the port with a quick hug. "May God protect you, Eduardo," I whispered in his ear. He seemed a little taken aback by that
solemn farewell.

Frederick Williams was waiting for me at the station, and he took
me by carriage to the house on Ejército Libertador. He was surprised
to see me so thin, and my explanation that I had been very sick did
not satisfy him. He kept looking at me out of the corner of his eye,
insistently asking about Diego, whether I was happy, what the family
of my in-laws was like, if I had adapted to life in the country. From
being the most splendid in that neighborhood of small palaces, my
grandmother's mansion had become as decrepit as its mistress. Shutters were swinging from their hinges, and the walls looked faded. The
garden was so abandoned that spring hadn't touched it, it was still
caught in wintry sadness. Inside the desolation was worse; the once
beautiful salons were nearly empty; furniture, carpets, and art had disappeared, and nothing remained of the famous Impressionist paintings
that had caused such a scandal several years before. Uncle Frederick
explained that in preparing for death, my grandmother had given
nearly everything to the church. "But I believe that her monetary resources are intact, Aurora, because she still keeps count of every
penny, and her account books are under the bed," he added with a
mischievous wink. She, who had gone to church only to be seen,
who detested the swarms of obsequious nuns and priests with their

hands out who were always buzzing around the rest of the family, had in her will set aside a considerable sum for the Catholic church. Always sharp in business dealings, she was prepared to buy at her death what she'd had little need of in life. Williams knew my grandmother better than anyone, and I think he loved her almost as much as I; against all the predictions of the envious, he did not steal her fortune and abandon her in her old age but looked after the interests of the family for years. He was a husband worthy of her, willing to stay to her last breath, and he would be of great help to me, as he later demonstrated. Paulina was not very lucid; the drugs she had to take to ease her pain kept her in a limbo without memory or desires. In those months she had been reduced to pure skin because she couldn't swallow and was being fed milk through a rubber tube introduced through a nostril. She had almost no hair on her head, and her large dark eyes had narrowed to two little dots in a map of wrinkles. I bent down to kiss her, but she didn't know me and turned her face away; at the same time, however, her hand felt in the air for her husband's, and when he took it an expression of peace lighted her face.

"We are not allowing her to suffer, Aurora, we are giving her a goodly amount of morphine," Uncle Frederick informed me.

"Have you notified her sons?"

"Yes, I sent them a wireless two months ago, but we have received no answer, and I doubt that their arrival will be opportune. Paulina's time is growing short."

And that was true. Paulina del Valle died silently the next day. Her husband, Dr. Radovic, Severo, Nívea, and I were at her side; her sons appeared much later with their lawyers to fight for the inheritance that no one was disputing. The doctor had removed my grandmother's feeding tube, and Williams put gloves on her because her hands were icy. Her lips turned blue, and she was very pale; her breathing was less and less perceptible, with no sign of distress, and at one point it simply stopped. Radovic took her pulse; a minute passed, maybe two, then he announced that she was gone. There was a gentle quiet in the room; something mysterious was happening. Maybe my grandmother's spirit had left her body and was circling like a confused bird above her body, telling us good-bye. I felt desolate at her parting, an old, old feeling I knew well but could not name or explain until a couple of years later when the mystery of my past finally was clarified and I realized that the death of my grandfather Tao Chi'en, many years before, had plunged me into similar anguish. The wound had been there beneath the surface and now had opened with the same searing pain. The sense of being absolutely alone, an orphan, that I experienced at my grandmother's death was identical to what had gripped me when I was five years old, when Tao Chi'en vanished from my life. I suppose that the old sorrows of my childhood—loss after loss—buried for years in the deepest layers of my memory rose up with their menacing Medusa heads to devour me: my mother dead at my birth, my father unaware of my existence, my maternal grandmother's depositing me in the hands of Paulina del Valle without explanation, and especially, the sudden loss of the person I loved most in the world, my grandfather Tao Chi'en.

Nine years have gone by since that September day when Paulina del Valle died; that and other misfortunes are behind me, and now I can remember my magnificent grandmother with a peaceful heart. She did not disappear into the boundless blackness of absolute death, as it first seemed, part of her stayed behind and is always near me, along with Tao Chi'en, the two very different spirits that accompany me and give me counsel—the first in practical matters, and the second in resolving emotional questions—but when my grandmother stopped breathing on that army cot where she spent her last months, I had no way to know that she would return, and I was overcome with grief. If I were capable of exteriorizing my emotions, I might suffer less, but they get locked inside me, like a huge block of ice, and years can pass before that ice begins to melt. I didn't weep when she died. The silence in the room seemed an error of protocol, because a woman who had lived like Paulina del Valle ought to die operatically, singing, accompanied by an orchestra; instead her farewell was silent, the one discreet thing she did in all her life. The men left the room, and Nívea and I carefully dressed her for her last voyage in the Carmelite habit she had kept hanging in her closet for more than a year, but we couldn't resist the temptation to clothe her first in her best French mauve silk lingerie. When we lifted her body, I realized how slight she had become; all that was left was a brittle skeleton and some loose skin. In silence I thanked her for everything she had done for me; I spoke the words of affection I would never have dared voice if she could hear me. I kissed her beautiful hands, her reptilian eyelids, her noble forehead, and I asked her forgiveness for the tantrums I threw as a child, for having come too late to say good-bye, for the dried lizard I'd spit out in a false attack of coughing, and other heavy-handed jokes she'd had to put up with, while Nívea seized the excuse offered by Paulina del Valle's departure to weep noiselessly for her dead children. After we dressed my grandmother, we sprinkled her with *eau de gardenia* and opened the drapes and windows to let spring blow in, as she would have liked. No mourning gallery, no black clothes, no covering the mirrors; Paulina del Valle had lived like an eccentric empress, and she deserved to be celebrated in September light. Which was what Williams thought, too; he went personally to the market and filled the carriage with fresh flowers to decorate the house.

When relatives and friends arrived—dressed in mourning and with handkerchief in hand—they were scandalized, for they had never seen a wake with bright sunlight, wedding flowers, and no tears. They went off mumbling darkly about plots, and years later there are still people who point me out, convinced that I rejoiced when Paulina del Valle died because I thought I could clamp onto her fortune. I inherited nothing—because her sons quickly sewed that up through their lawyers—but after all, I didn't have to, since my father left me enough to live decently, and I can earn the rest with my work. Despite my grandmother's endless advice and teaching, I never developed her nose for profitable business dealings; I will never be rich, and I'm happy about that. Frederick Williams did not have to fight the lawyers, either, because he was much less interested in money than evil tongues had been whispering for years. Besides, his wife had given him a lot in her lifetime, and he, a cautious man, had put it in a safe place. Paulina's sons could not prove that their mother's marriage to the former butler was illegal, and they had to resign themselves to leaving Uncle Frederick in peace. Neither could they appropriate the vineyards because they were in Severo del Valle's name, in view of which the would-be heirs set their lawyers onto the priests, to see if they could recover the wealth they'd obtained by frightening the sick woman with the cauldrons of hell, but up till now no one has won a case against the Catholic Church, which has God on its side, as everyone knows. In any case there was money to spare, and the sons, various relatives, and even the lawyers have lived on it to the present day.

The one joy during those depressing weeks was the reappearance in our lives of Señorita Matilde Pineda. She read in the newspaper that Paulina del Valle had died, and she worked up her courage and came to the house she'd been thrown out of during the days of the revolution. She arrived with a bouquet of flowers, accompanied by the bookseller Pedro Tey. She had matured during those years, and at first I didn't recognize her; he, on the other hand, was the same small, bald man with heavy satanic eyebrows and burning pupils.

After the cemetery, the masses, the requested novenas, and the distribution of alms and charitable bequests indicated by my deceased grandmother, the dust of the spectacular funeral settled, and Frederick Williams and I found ourselves alone in the empty house. We sat together in the glass gallery to lament my grandmother's absence in private, because neither of us is much for tears, and to remember her in her many glories and her few imperfections.

"What do you plan to do now, Uncle Frederick?" I wanted to know.

"That depends on you, Aurora."

"On me?"

"It has not escaped my attention, dear child, that you seem a bit off your feed," he said, with that subtle way he had of asking a question.

"I've been very sick, and losing my grandmother has made me very sad, Uncle Frederick. That's all, I'm all right, really."

"I regret that you underestimate me, Aurora. I would have to be a very foolish man indeed, or have very little feeling for you, not to have been aware of your state of mind. Tell me what is happening to you, and perhaps I can be of assistance."

"No one can help me, Uncle."

"Put it to the test," he said, "and we shall see."

And then I realized that I had no one else in the world in whom I could confide, and that Frederick Williams had proved to be an excellent counselor, the one person in the family with common sense. I could easily tell him my tragedy. He listened to the end, giving me all his attention, not interrupting once.

"Life is long, Aurora. At this moment everything looks black, but time heals and erases nearly all things. This stage is like walking blindly through a tunnel; it seems to you there is no way out, but I promise there is. Keep going, child."

"What's to become of me, Uncle Frederick?"

"You will have other loves; perhaps you will be blessed with children, or be the finest photographer in the country," he told me.

"I feel so confused, and so alone!"

"You are not alone, Aurora; I am with you now, and I shall be as long as you have need of me."

He persuaded me that I need not go back to my husband, that I could find a dozen excuses to put off my return for years, although I was sure that Diego would not encourage me to come back to Caleufú since it was to his advantage to have me as far away as possible. And as for the gentle, kind Doña Elvira, there was nothing to do but comfort her with faithful correspondence. It was a matter of winning time; my mother-in-law's heart was weak, and according to the doctors' prognosis she would not live much longer. Uncle Frederick assured me that he was in no hurry to leave Chile; I was his only family, and he loved me like a daughter or granddaughter.

"Don't you have anyone in England?" I asked him.

"Not a soul."

"You know there is all kind of gossip about your background; people say you're a ruined nobleman, and my grandmother never denied that."

"Nothing further from the truth, Aurora!" he exclaimed, laughing.

"So you don't have a family coat of arms hidden somewhere?" I laughed, too.

"Look, dear child," he replied.

He took off his jacket, unbuttoned his shirt, pulled up his undershirt, and showed me his back. It was crisscrossed with horrendous scars.

"A flogging. A hundred strokes in an Australian penal colony for stealing tobacco. I served five years before I escaped on a raft. I was picked up on the high seas by a Chinese pirate ship, and they worked me like a slave, but as soon as we got within sight of land, I escaped again. So, in one way or another, I finally reached California. My accent is the only thing about me related to British nobility, and I learned that from a true lord, my first employer in California. He also instructed me in the office of being a butler. Paulina del Valle engaged me in 1870, and I have been in her service since that date."

"Did my grandmother know that story, Uncle?" I asked when I got over my surprise and could speak.

"Of course. Paulina found it very amusing that people mistook a convict for an aristocrat."

"Why were you sent to prison?"

"For stealing a horse when I was fifteen. They would have hanged me, but I was fortunate; they commuted my sentence and I ended up in Australia. Have no fear, Aurora, I have never stolen a farthing since; the flogging cured me of that vice, but they could not cure me of my taste for tobacco." He laughed.

So the two of us stayed together. Paulina del Valle's sons sold the mansion on Ejército Libertador, which today is a girls' school, and auctioned off what little was left in the house. I saved the mythological bed by dismantling it before the heirs arrived and hiding it in the storeroom of Iván Radovic's public hospital, where it stayed until the lawyers tired of digging through corners, looking for the last vestiges of my grandmother's possessions. Frederick Williams and I bought a country house on the outskirts of the city, on a road to the mountains. We have twelve hectares of land bordered by trembling aspen, invaded with fragrant jasmine, and washed by a modest stream, where everything grows unbidden. There Williams breeds dogs and thoroughbred horses and plays croquet and other boring games the English find entertaining. And there I have my winter quarters. The house is past its prime, but it has a certain charm, and space for my darkroom and for the famous Florentine bed, which rises with its polychrome sea creatures in the middle of my room. I sleep there, guarded by the watchful spirit of my grandmother Paulina, who appears in time to take her broom after the black-pajamaed children of my nightmares. Santiago will surely grow toward Estación Central, the railway depot, and leave us in peace in this bucolic countryside of aspen and hills.

Thanks to Uncle Lucky, who blew his good-luck breath onto me when I was born, and to the generous protection of my grandmother and my father, I can say I have a good life. I have the means and the freedom to do what I want; I can devote myself fully to traveling the length of Chile's abrupt geography with my camera around my neck, as I have been doing for the last eight or nine years. People talk behind my back, it's inevitable; several relatives and acquaintances cut me off, and if they see me in the street, they pretend not to know me; they cannot tolerate a woman who left her husband. Those slights do not keep me awake; I don't have to please everyone, only those who truly matter to me, and they are not many. The dismal results of my relationship with Diego Domínguez should have immunized me forever against precipitous and fervent love affairs, but that wasn't how it was. It's true that I went about for several months with a wounded wing, dragging myself day after day with a feeling of absolute defeat, of having played my one card and lost everything. It is also true that I am condemned to being a married woman without a husband, which prevents me from "remaking" my life, as my aunts call it, but this strange condition gives me a lot of confidence. A year after Diego and I were separated, I fell in love again—which means that I have thick skin and heal quickly. My second love was not a gentle friendship that with time turned into a tried-and-true romance, it was simply a passionate impulse that took us both by surprise, and by chance worked out well . . . that is, it has up till now; who knows how it will be in the future? It was a winter day, one of those days of green, persistent rain, of jagged lightning and heaviness of heart. Paulina del Valle's sons and their lawyers had come again to toss manure by the shovelful, bringing their interminable documents, each with three copies and eleven seals, which I signed without reading. Frederick Williams and I had left the house on Ejército Libertador and were still living in a hotel because the repairs on the house where we live now weren't finished. Uncle Frederick ran into Iván Radovic, whom we hadn't seen in a long time, and they made a date for the three of us to go see a Spanish light opera company that was on tour through South America. When the day came, however, Uncle Frederick had taken to his bed with a cold, and I found myself waiting alone in the vestibule of the hotel, my hands freezing and my feet aching because my high-buttoned shoes were too tight. There was a waterfall running down the windowpanes, and the wind was shaking the trees like feather dusters. It was a night that did not invite venturing out, and for a moment I envied Uncle Frederick his cold, which allowed him to stay in bed with a good book and cup of hot chocolate; nevertheless, when Iván Radovic walked in, I forgot the weather. He arrived with his overcoat soaked, and when he smiled at me, I realized that he was much more handsome than I remembered. We looked into each other's eyes, and it was as if scales had fallen from them. I think we saw each other for the first time; at least I looked him over earnestly, and I liked what I saw. There was a long silence, a pause which in other circumstances would have been awkward but at that moment seemed a form of dialogue. He helped me on with my cape, and we slowly walked to the door, hesitant, still in our mutual daze. Neither of us wanted to challenge the storm raking the heavens, but neither did we want to go separate ways. A porter ran up with a huge umbrella and offered to see us to the carriage that was waiting at the door, so we went out without a word, unsure what we wanted to do. I had no flash of romantic clairvoyance, no extraordinary presentiment that we were soul mates; I did not visualize the beginnings of a love story, nothing like that; I simply took note of the way my heart was beating, of how hard it was to breathe, of my hot and prickly skin, and of my tremendous desire to touch that man. I fear that there was nothing spiritual about my role in the encounter, only lust, although at that time I was too inexperienced and my vocabulary too limited to put the dictionary name to that excitement. The word is the least of it; what is interesting is that that visceral jolt overcame my shyness, and in the shelter of the carriage, from which there was no easy escape, I took his face in my hands and without thinking twice I kissed him on the mouth, just as years before I had seen Nívea and Severo del Valle kiss, decisively and greedily. It was a simple action, with no turning back. I won't go into details about what followed, because it is easy to imagine, and because if Iván reads these pages, we would have a colossal fight. It must be said, our battles are as memorable as our reconciliations are passionate; this is not a quiet, saccharine love, but what can be said in its favor is that it is steadfast; obstacles do not seem to diminish it, only strengthen it. Marriage is a commonsense affair, something neither of us has much of. The fact we are not married enhances our love. That way each of us can do what we do; we have our own spaces, and when we are about to erupt, there is always the escape of living apart for a few days and then coming back together when we yearn for kisses. With Iván Radovic I have learned to speak up and show my claws. If I found he had betrayed me—may God forbid—as happened with Diego Domínguez, I would not drown myself in tears as I did then, I would kill him without a moment's remorse.

No, I am not going to talk about how close my lover and I are, but there is an episode I have to tell because it has to do with memory, and *that*, after all, is the reason I'm writing these pages. My nightmares are a blind journey through the shadowy caverns where my oldest recollections lie locked in the deep strata of consciousness. Photography and writing are a tentative way of seizing those moments before they vanish, of fixing those memories in order to give meaning to my life. Iván and I had been together several months; we had already become accustomed to the routine of seeing each other discreetly, thanks to good Uncle Frederick, who harbored our love from the beginning. Iván had to give a medical lecture in a city in the north, and I went with him under the pretext of photographing the nitrate mines, where the working conditions are very unhealthful. The English managers refused to negotiate with the workers, and there was a climate of growing violence that would explode a few years later. When that happened, in 1907, I happened by chance to be there, and my photographs are the only irrefutable documents that the slaughter at Iquique occurred, because government censorship erased from the face of history the two thousand dead that I saw in the plaza. But that is another story, and has no place in these pages. The first time I went to that city with Iván, I could not suspect the tragedy I would later witness; it was a brief honeymoon for us both.

We registered separately in the hotel, and that night, after each of us finished the work of the day, he came to my room, where I was waiting with a magnificent bottle of Viña Paulina. Until then our relationship had been an adventure of the flesh, an exploration of the senses that for me was fundamental because as a result I managed to overcome the humiliation of having been rejected by Diego and to understand that I was not an incomplete woman, as I feared. In every meeting with Iván Radovic I had been gaining more confidence, conquering my shyness and repressions, but I hadn't realized that our glorious intimacy was turning into love. That night we embraced with the languor of the good wine and the day's fatigue, slowly, like two wise grandparents who have made love nine hundred times and can no longer surprise or deceive one another. What was special about it for me? Nothing, I suppose, except that series of happy experiences with Iván, which that night reached the critical number necessary to crumble my defenses. After an orgasm, when I came back to myself in the strong arms of my lover, I felt a sob shaking my body, and then another and another, until I was rocked by an sea swell of accumulated weeping. I cried and cried, surrendered, abandoned, more sure in those arms than I could remember ever having been. A dam burst inside me, and an ancient pain overflowed like melted snow. Iván did not ask questions or try to console me; he held me firmly against his chest, let me cry until my tears ran out, and when I tried to explain, he closed my lips with a long kiss. At that moment I had no explanation for anything, I would have had to invent it, but now I know—because it has happened several times more—that when I feel absolutely safe, sheltered and protected, the memory of those first five years of my life begins to come back, the years that my grandmother Paulina and everyone else cloaked in a mantle of mystery. First, in a flash of clarity, I saw the image of my grandfather Tao Chi'en whispering my name in Chinese: Lai Ming. It was a brief instant, but luminous as the moon. Then awake, I relived the recurrent nightmare that has tormented me forever, and I realized that there is a direct relationship between my beloved grandfather and those demons in black pajamas. The hand that lets go of mine in the dream is the hand of Tao Chi'en. The one who slowly falls is Tao Chi'en. The stain that spreads relentlessly across the paving stones of the street is the blood of Tao Chi'en.

I had been living officially with Frederick Williams a little more than two years, but always more dedicated to my relationship with Iván Radovic, without whom I could not envision my destiny, when my maternal grandmother, Eliza Sommers, reappeared in my life. She came back whole, with the same aroma of sugar and vanilla, invulnerable to the ravages of trouble or oblivion. I recognized her at first glance, although many years had gone by since she came to leave me at the home of Paulina del Valle, and in all that time I had not seen a photograph of her and her name had been spoken only rarely in my presence. Her image was tangled in the gears of my nostalgia and she had changed so little that when she materialized in our doorway, suitcase in hand, it seemed that we had said good-bye only the day before, and that everything that has happened since was illusion. The one novelty was that she was shorter than I had remembered, but that could be the effect of my own height; the last time we were together I was a child of five, and had to look up at her. She was still as stiff-backed as an admiral, with the same young face and the same severe hairdo, though now the hair was streaked with white. She was even wearing the same pearl necklace I had always seen her wear and now know she never takes off even to sleep. She was brought by Severo del Valle, who had been in touch with her all those years but had not told me because she wouldn't let him. Eliza Sommers had given her word to Paulina del Valle that she would never try to contact her granddaughter, and she had kept her word religiously until Paulina's death freed her from that promise. When Severo wrote to tell her, she packed her trunks and closed her house, as she had done many times before, and set sail for Chile. When she was widowed in 1885, in San

Francisco, she undertook the pilgrimage to China with the embalmed body of her husband, to bury him in Hong Kong. Tao Chi'en had lived most of his life in California, and was one of the few Chinese immigrants to obtain American citizenship, but he had always expressed his wish that his bones end in Chinese soil; that way his soul would not be lost in the enormity of the universe, unable to find the gates to heaven. That precaution was not sufficient, though, because I am sure that the ghost of my ineffable grandfather Tao Chi'en still wanders these worlds; otherwise I can't explain how it is that I feel him with me. It's not just imagination; my grandmother Eliza has confirmed some clues, such as the scent of the sea that sometimes envelops me, and the voice that whispers a magical word: my name in Chinese.

"Hello, Lai Ming," was the greeting from that extraordinary grandmother when she saw me.

"Oi poa!" I exclaimed.

I hadn't spoken those words—"maternal grandmother" in Cantonese—since the remote days when I lived with her on the upper floor of an acupuncture clinic in the Chinese quarter of San Francisco, but I hadn't forgotten them. She put one hand on my shoulder and scrutinized me from head to foot, then nodded her approval and finally hugged me.

"I am happy that you are not as beautiful as your mother," she said.

"My father said the same thing."

"You are tall, like Tao. And Severo tells me that you are also clever like him."

In our family we serve tea when a situation is slightly uncomfortable, and since I feel self-conscious almost all the time, I serve a lot of it. That beverage has the virtue of helping me steady my nerves. I was dying to grab my grandmother by the waist and waltz her around the room, to babble everything about my life, and to list for her the reproaches I had mumbled to myself all those years, but none of that was possible. Eliza Sommers is not the type of person you treat familiarly; her dignity is intimidating, and it would be weeks before she and I finally could talk with ease. Fortunately the tea, and the presence of Severo del Valle and Frederick Williams—who came back from one of his walks around the property decked out like an explorer in Africa—relieved the tension. As soon as Uncle Frederick took off his pith helmet and smoked glasses and saw Eliza Sommers, something changed in his attitude: he puffed out his chest, raised his voice a notch, and fluffed out his feathers. His admiration doubled when he saw the steamer trunks and suitcases with souvenirs labels of her travels and learned that that tiny woman was one of the few foreigners who had gone to Tibet.

I don't know whether the only reason my *oi poa* came to Chile was to meet me—I suspect that she was planning to go on to the South Pole, where no woman had as yet set foot—but whatever the reason, her visit was essential for me. Without her my life would still be obscured with nebulae; without her I would not be writing this memoir. It was my maternal grandmother who provided the missing pieces for fitting together the jigsaw puzzle of my life, who told me about my mother, about the circumstances of my birth, and gave me the final key to my nightmares. It was also she who later would go with me to San Francisco to meet my uncle Lucky, a prosperous Chinese merchant, fat, short-legged, and absolutely delightful, and to unearth the documents I needed to tie together the loose ends of my story. The relationship between Eliza Sommers and Severo del Valle is as deep as the secrets they shared for many years; she thinks of him as being my true father, because he was the man who loved her daughter and married her. All Matías Rodríguez de Santa Cruz did was accidentally supply some genes.

"Who conceived you is not really important, Lai Ming; anyone could do that. Severo is the one who gave you his name and took responsibility for you," she assured me.

"In that case, Paulina del Valle was my mother and my father; I carry her name and *she* took responsibility for me. All the others passed like comets through my childhood, leaving not much more than a faint trail of stardust," I rejoined.

"Before her, Tao and I were your father and your mother. We raised you first, Lai Ming," she insisted, and rightly, because those maternal grandparents had such a powerful influence on me that for thirty years I have carried their gentle presence inside me, and I am sure they will be there for the rest of my life.

Eliza Sommers lived in another dimension, beside Tao Chi'en, whose death was a major inconvenience but not an obstacle to loving him as she always had. My grandmother Eliza is one of those beings destined to have one spectacular love; I don't believe she has room for another man in her widow's heart. After burying her husband in China beside the tomb of Lin, his first wife, and performing the Buddhist funeral rituals he wished, she was free. She could have returned to San Francisco to live with her son Lucky and the young wife he had ordered by catalog from Shanghai, but the idea of becoming a feared and venerated mother-in-law was to her the equivalent of giving in to old age. She did not feel alone, or frightened of the future, since the protective spirit of Tao Chi'en was always with her. In fact, they are closer than before, since now they are never separated for a single instant. She acquired the habit of talking with her husband in a very low voice—in order not to be taken for a mental case—and at night of sleeping on the left side of the bed in order to leave space for him on the right, which was their custom. The adventurous spirit that had impelled her to flee Chile when she was sixteen, hidden in the belly of a sailing vessel bound for California, awakened in her again once she became a widow. She recalled an epiphany when she was eighteen, right at the height of the gold rush, when the neighing of her horse and the first light of dawn woke her in the immensity of a wild and solitary landscape. That morning she discovered the exaltation of freedom. She had spent the night alone beneath the trees, surrounded by a thousand dangers: pitiless bandits, unfriendly Indians, snakes, bears, and other wild animals, yet for the first time in her life she was not afraid. She had been brought up wearing a corset, bound in body, soul, and imagination, frightened even of her own thoughts, but that adventure had released her. She had to develop a strength that she may always have had but until then ignored because she had no need for it. She had left the protection of her hearth when still a young girl, and pregnant, following the trail of an elusive lover; she had stowed away on a ship, on which she lost the baby and nearly her life as well. She reached California dressed as a man, and prepared to scour the territory from tip to tail, with no weapons or tools but the desperate spur of love. She had been able to survive alone in a land of machos where greed and violence were the rule; in the process she acquired courage and a taste for independence. She would never forget the intense euphoria of adventure. Also for love, she had lived for thirty years with Tao Chi'en as his discreet wife, a mother and pastry maker, fulfilling her duty, her only horizon her home in Chinatown—but the germ planted in those early years as a nomad lay intact in her spirit, ready to burst into bud at the propitious moment. When Tao Chi'en died, the polestar of her life, the moment to drift on the tide had come. "At heart I have always been a rover; what I want is to travel with no fixed course," she wrote her son Lucky. She decided, however, that first she had to carry out the promise she had made her father, Captain John Sommers: not to abandon her aunt Rose in her old age. From Hong Kong she had gone to England, prepared to stay with the aged lady in her last years; it was the least she could do for a woman who had been like a mother. Rose Sommers was more than seventy years old, and her health had begun to fail, but she kept writing her novels—all more or less the same—and was now the most famous romance writer in the English language. There were people who traveled great distances to get a glimpse of her tiny figure walking her dog in the park, and it was said that Queen Victoria consoled her lonely life as a widow by reading Rose's syrupy stories of love triumphant. When Eliza arrived, whom she had cared for like a daughter, it was an enormous comfort to Rose Sommers; among other reasons because her hand was growing unsteady, and it was more and more difficult for her to clasp a pen. From then on she dictated her novels, and later, when she was also becoming less lucid, Eliza pretended to take notes but in fact did the writing, without the editor or the readers ever suspecting; all she had to do was repeat the formula. When Rose Sommers died, Eliza stayed on in her little house in the bohemian quarter—very valuable because the area had become stylish—and inherited the fortune accumulated from her adoptive mother's little romances. The first thing she did was visit her son Lucky in San Francisco and meet her grandchildren, who to her seemed rather ugly and boring; then she set off for more exotic places, finally realizing her destiny as a wanderer. She was one of those travelers who make an effort to get to places from which other people escape. Nothing satisfied her as much as seeing labels and seals from the most obscure countries on the planet on her luggage; nothing gave her as much pride as contracting some foul disease or being bitten by some foreign vermin. She traveled for years with her explorer's trunks, but always returned to the little house in London, where Severo del Valle's correspondence would be waiting with news about me. When she learned that Paulina del Valle had shuffled off this coil, she decided to return to Chile, where she had been born but which she hadn't given a thought to for more than a half century, for a reunion with her granddaughter.

It's possible that during the long voyage on the steamship my grandmother Eliza recalled her first sixteen years in Chile, this geographically narrow and proud nation, her childhood in the care of a generous Indian woman and the beautiful Miss Rose, and her peaceful and secure life before the intrusion of the lover who left her pregnant, abandoned her to chase after gold in California, and was never again seen. Since my grandmother Eliza believes in karma, she must have concluded that the long voyage was necessary in order for her to meet Tao Chi'en, whom she would love in each of her reincarnations.

"That is not a particularly Christian idea," Frederick Williams commented when I tried to explain to him why Eliza Sommers didn't need anyone.

My grandmother Eliza brought me as a gift a beat-up trunk, which she delivered to me with a naughty twinkle in her dark eyes. It contained yellowed manuscripts signed by "An Anonymous Lady." Those were the pornographic novels Rose Sommers had written in her youth, another well-guarded family secret. I read them carefully—for purely didactic reasons, of course—to the direct benefit of Iván Radovic. That entertaining literature—where did a Victorian spinster get such audacity?—and Nívea del Valle's confidences have helped me combat my shyness, which at first was a nearly insurmountable obstacle between Iván and me. It is true that on the day of the storm, when we were supposed to go to the operetta but didn't, I made the move to kiss Iván in the carriage before the poor man could defend himself, but that was as far as my daring went; after that we lost a lot of precious time arguing over my tremendous insecurity and his scruples, because he didn't want "to ruin my reputation," as he put it. It wasn't easy to convince him that my reputation was rather battered before he appeared on the horizon, and would go on being battered because I did not plan ever to go back to my husband or to give up my work or my independence, all of which are frowned on in this country. After the humiliating experience with Diego, I thought I was incapable of inspiring desire or love. Added to my total ignorance in sexual matters was a sense of inferiority; I thought I was ugly, inadequate, not very feminine, and I was ashamed of my body and of the passion Iván aroused in me. Rose Sommers, that distant great-grandmother I'd never known, handed down a fantastic gift when she gave me the playful freedom so necessary in making love. Iván often takes things too seriously; his Slavic temperament tends toward the tragic. Sometimes he sinks into despair because we can't live together until my husband dies, and by then surely we will be ancient. When those clouds darken his mind, I go to An Anonymous Lady's manuscripts, where I discover some new trick for giving him pleasure, or at least to make him laugh. For the purpose of entertaining him in our private time, I have been losing my inhibitions and acquiring a security I've never had. I don't feel seductive yet—the positive effect of the manuscripts hasn't gone that far—but at least I am not afraid to take the initiative in encouraging the adventurous side of Iván, who might otherwise be mired in the same routine forever. It would be a waste to make love like an old married couple when we're not even married. The advantage of being lovers is that we have to work hard at our relationship, because everything conspires to drive us apart. Our decision to be together has to be renewed again and again; that keeps us on our toes.

This is the story my grandmother Eliza Sommers told me.

Tao Chi'en never forgave himself for the death of his daughter Lynn. It was futile for his wife and Lucky to keep repeating that no human power is capable of changing the course of fate, that as a *zhong-yi* he had done everything possible, and that medical science was still powerless to prevent or contain the fatal hemorrhages that kill so many women during childbirth. For Tao Chi'en it was as if he had walked in circles to find himself right where he'd been more than thirty years before in Hong Kong when his first wife, Lin, gave birth to a baby girl. She, too, had begun to bleed, and in his desperation to save her, he had offered heaven anything he had in exchange for Lin's life. The baby had died a few minutes later, and he had believed that was the price for saving his wife. He never imagined that much later, on the other side of the world, he would have to pay again with his daughter Lynn.

"Don't talk that way, Father, please," Lucky berated him. "It isn't a matter of trading one life for another, those are superstitions unworthy of a man of your intelligence and culture. My sister's death has nothing to do with that of your first wife, or with you. These calamities happen all the time."

"What use are all my years of study and experience if I couldn't save her?" Tao Chi'en lamented.

"Millions of women die in childbirth. You did everything that could be done for Lynn."

Eliza Sommers was as crushed as her husband by the pain of having lost her only daughter, but she bore in addition the responsibility of caring for the tiny orphan. While she fell asleep on her feet out of pure exhaustion, Tao Chi'en never shut his eyes. He spent the night meditating, walking around the house like a somnambulist, and secretly weeping. They had not made love for days, and considering the states of mind in that home, it didn't seem they would anytime in the near future. After a week Eliza chose the only solution that came to her: she placed her granddaughter in Tao Chi'en's arms and announced to him that she was incapable of tending her, that she had spent more than twenty years of her life like a slave, looking after their children, Lucky and Lynn, and that she didn't have the strength to start all over with little Lai Ming. Tao Chi'en found himself in charge of a newborn baby, who had to be fed watered milk every half-hour from an eyedropper because she could barely swallow, and be rocked constantly because she screamed with colic night and day. The little thing was not even pleasant to look at; she was tiny and wrinkled, her skin yellow with jaundice, her features squashed by the difficult birth, and there was not a hair on her head, but after twenty-four hours of caring for her, Tao Chi'en could look at her without being terrified. After twenty-four days of carrying her in a pouch strung around his neck, feeding her with the eyedropper, and sleeping with her, she began to seem pretty to him. And after twenty-four months of giving her a mother's care he was completely enamored of his granddaughter and convinced that she would be even more beautiful than Lynn, despite there not being the least basis for that supposition. The child was not the mollusk she had resembled at birth, but she was far from looking like her mother. Tao Chi'en's routines, which previously had been composed of his practice and the few hours he shared with his wife, changed completely. His schedule centered around Lai Ming, that demanding infant who was glued to his side, whom he had to tell stories to, sing to sleep, force to eat, take on walks, buy the prettiest dresses in American stores as well as those in Chinatown, and introduce to everyone on the street because there had never been such a clever little girl, according to the grandfather, whose judgment was clouded by affection. He was sure that his granddaughter was a genius, and to prove it he talked to her in Chinese and in English, to which he was adding the Spanish jargon her grandmother spoke, creating a monumental confusion. Lai Ming responded to Tao Chi'en's stimuli like any two-year-old child, but to him it seemed that his occasional successes were irrefutable proof of superior intelligence. He reduced his office hours to a few in the afternoon; that way he could spend the morning with his granddaughter, teaching her new tricks, like a trained macaque. Only grudgingly did he allow Eliza to take her to the tearoom in the afternoons while he worked, because he had it in his head that he could begin to train her for medicine from early childhood.

"There are six generations of *zhong-yi* in my family; Lai Ming will be the seventh, seeing that you do not have the least talent for it," Tao Chi'en told his son Lucky.

"I thought that only men could be physicians," Lucky commented.

"That was in the past. Lai Ming will be the first female *zhong-yi* in history," Tao Chi'en replied.

But Eliza Sommers did not permit him to fill their granddaughter's head with medical theory at such an early age. There would be plenty of time for that; for the moment they needed to get the girl out of Chinatown a few hours a day to Americanize her. On that point at least, the grandparents were in agreement. Lai Ming should belong to the world of the whites, where undoubtedly she would have more opportunities than among Chinese. In favor of this plan, the girl had no Asian features; she had come out looking as Spanish as the family of her father. The possibility that Severo del Valle would return one day with the proposition of reclaiming his purported daughter, and take her to Chile, was intolerable, so it was never mentioned. It was simply assumed that the young Chilean would respect their pact because he had given ample proof of nobility. They did not touch the money he had provided for the girl but deposited it in an account for her future education. Every three or four months Eliza wrote a brief note to Severo del Valle, telling him about his "protégée," as he called her, to make it clear that they did not recognize his claim of paternity. There was no reply for a year, because he was immersed in his mourning, and the war, but later he was able to answer occasionally. They had not seen Paulina del Valle again, because she did not return to the tearoom and never acted on her threat to take away their granddaughter and ruin their lives.

And so five years of harmony went by in the home of the Chi'ens, until, inevitably, the events that were to destroy the family were set in motion. Everything began with the visit of two women who announced themselves as Presbyterian missionaries and asked if they could speak alone with Tao Chi'en. The *zhong-yi* received them in his consulting room, because he thought they had come for reasons of health; there was no other explanation for why two white women would unexpectedly appear in his house. They looked like sisters; they were young, tall, rosy-cheeked, with eyes bright as the waters in the bay, and both displayed the attitude of radiant assurance that tends to accompany religious zeal. They introduced themselves by their given names, Donaldina and Martha, and proceeded to explain that the Presbyterian mission in Chinatown had until that moment maneuvered with great caution and discretion in order not to offend the Buddhist community, but now it could count on new members determined to implant the minimum norms of Christian decency in that sector which, as they put it, "was American territory, not Chinese, and thus violations of law and morality could not be tolerated." They had heard about the Singsong Girls but had encountered a conspiracy of silence in regard to the traffic in children for sexual purposes. The missionaries knew that American authorities were taking bribes and looking the other way. Someone had told them that Tao Chi'en would be the only person with enough courage to tell them the truth, and to help them. That was why they were there. The *zhong-yi* had waited decades for that moment. In his slow labor of rescuing those miserable adolescents, he had counted solely on the silent aid of a few Quaker friends who took responsibility for getting the young prostitutes out of California and starting them in a new life far from the tongs and madams. It had been his role to buy the girls he could afford to pay for in the clandestine auctions and to take to his home those who were too ill to work in the whorehouses. He tried to heal their bodies and comfort their souls, but he did not always succeed; many died in his care. In his home there were two rooms, almost always occupied, where the Singsong Girls were given shelter, but Tao Chi'en felt that as the Chinese population in California increased, the problem of the slaves grew worse every day, and he could do very little to change that by himself. Those two missionaries had been sent from heaven; first of all, they had the backing of the powerful Presbyterian Church, and, second, they were white. They would be able to mobilize the press, public opinion, and the American authorities to put an end to that inhuman traffic. So he told them in detail how the girls were bought or kidnapped in China, how Chinese culture disdained girls, and how it was not unusual in that country to find newborn baby girls drowned in wells or tossed into the street to be chewed on by rats and dogs. Their families had no love for them, which was why it was so easy to acquire them for a few cents and bring them to America, where they could be exploited for thousands of dollars. They were transported like animals in huge crates in the holds of ships, and the ones who survived dehydration and cholera entered the United States carrying false marriage contracts. They were all brides in the eyes of immigration officers, and their young age, their lamentable physical condition, and the expression of terror on their faces apparently did not arouse suspicion. They were not important. What happened to them "was up to the Celestials," it was of no concern to the whites. Tao Chi'en explained to Donaldina and Martha that the life expectancy of the Singsong Girls, once they started in the trade, was three or four years. They serviced up to thirty men a day, and they died of venereal diseases, abortion, pneumonia, hunger, and rough treatment. A twenty-year-old Chinese prostitute was a curiosity. No one kept a record of their lives, but since they entered the country with a legal document, their deaths had to be recorded, though it was highly improbable that anyone would ask after them. Many went mad. They were cheap; they could be replaced in a blink of an eye. No one invested in their health or in making them live. Tao Chi'en reported to the missionaries the approximate number of young slaves in Chinatown, when the auctions were held, and where the brothels were located—from the most wretched, in which the girls were treated like caged animals, to the most luxurious, ruled by the celebrated Ah Toy, who had become the major importer of new flesh into the country. She bought youngsters of eleven in China and on the voyage to America handed them over to the sailors, so that when they arrived they would already know how to say "pay first" and tell gold from brass, so they wouldn't be tricked by false coins. Ah Toy's girls were selected from among the most beautiful, and they were more fortunate than the others, whose fate was to be auctioned like cattle and to service the most degenerate men in any way they demanded, however cruel and humiliating. Many became wild creatures, acting like ferocious beasts that had to be chained to the bed and kept dazed with narcotics. Tao Chi'en gave the missionaries the names of three or four Chinese businessmen who had money and prestige, among them his own son Lucky, who might help them in their task, the only ones who agreed with him about eliminating that kind of traffic. Donaldina and Martha, with trembling hands and teary eyes, took notes on everything Tao Chi'en said, then thanked him. As they said good-bye they asked if they could count on him when the time came to act.

"I will do what I can," the *zhong-yi* answered.

"And so will we, Mr. Chi'en. The Presbyterian mission will not rest until it puts an end to this perversion and saves those poor girls, even if we have to hack down the doors of those dens of evil," they assured him.

When Lucky Chi'en found out what his father had done, he saw bad omens on every side. He knew Chinatown much better than Tao, and he realized that his father had committed an irreparable indiscretion. Thanks to his accomplishments and good nature, Lucky had friends at all levels of the Chinese community; for years he had been engaged in lucrative business dealings and winning—with moderation, but regularly—at the fan-tan tables. Even though he was young, he had become a figure beloved and respected by all, including the tongs, which had never bothered him. For years he had helped his father rescue the Singsong Girls, with the tacit agreement that he would not get involved in a major intrigue; he knew very clearly the absolute circumspection needed to survive in Chinatown, where the golden rule was not to have anything to do with whites—the feared and despised *fan-wey*—and to solve all matters, particularly in the case of crime, among compatriots. Sooner or later it would be learned that his father had informed the missionaries, and they, in turn, had told the American authorities. There was no surer formula for attracting disaster, and all his good luck would not reach far enough to protect them. This is what Lucky told Tao Chi'en, and that was what happened in October 1885, the month I had my fifth birthday.

My grandfather's fate was sealed the memorable Tuesday on which the two young missionaries, accompanied by three husky Irish policemen and the elderly crime reporter Jacob Freemont, barged into Chinatown in broad daylight. All activity in the street stopped dead, and a crowd formed behind the party of *fan-wey*, a rare sight in that neighborhood, which marched resolutely to a dilapidated house with a narrow, grated door where two Singsong Girls, faces painted with rice powder and rouge, were offering themselves to clients with mewing voices and exposed, puppy-dog breasts. When they saw the white people approaching, the girls retreated inside with squeals of fear, and in their place appeared a furious old woman who responded to the police with a string of insults in her tongue. At a sign from Donaldina, an ax glinted in the hands of one of the Irish officers, and he proceeded to chop the door down before the stupor of the bystanders. The intruders burst through the narrow doorway; there were sounds of screams, running, and orders in English, and within fifteen minutes the attackers emerged herding a half-dozen terrorized girls, the old woman—dragged kicking by one of the policemen—and three men stumbling along at gunpoint. A menacing rumble rose up in the street, and a few of the curious moved forward threateningly, but stopped short when several shots echoed in the air. The *fan-wey* shoved the girls and others under arrest into the closed police van, and the horses trotted off with their cargo. The rest of the day everyone in Chinatown talked about nothing but what had happened. Never had the police invaded the quarter for reasons other than those having to do directly with other whites. The American authorities had a great tolerance for the "customs of the yellows," as they classified them, and no one bothered to investigate the opium dens or gaming houses, much less the slave girls, whom they considered another of the grotesque perversions of the Celestials, like eating roast dog with soy sauce. The one person who was not surprised, but complacent, was Tao Chi'en. The illustrious *zhong-yi* was nearly attacked by a pair of thugs from one of the tongs in the restaurant where he always had lunch with his granddaughter, when in a voice loud enough to be heard above the uproar he had expressed his satisfaction that at last the city authorities had taken action in the matter of the Singsong Girls. Even though most of the diners at the other tables thought that in a nearly all-male population the young slave girls were an indispensable consumer item, they hurried to defend Tao Chi'en, because he was the most respected figure in the community. Had it not been for the timely intervention of the owner of the restaurant, there would have been a real row. Indignant, Tao Chi'en stormed out, holding his granddaughter by one hand and in the other his lunch wrapped in a piece of paper.

Maybe the episode of the brothel would have had no major consequences if two days later it hadn't been repeated in similar form on a different street: the same Presbyterian missionaries, the same newspaperman, Jacob Freemont, and the same three Irish policemen. This time, however, they brought four additional officers as backup, and two large German shepherds tugging at their chains. The operation lasted eight minutes, and Donaldina and Martha led away seventeen girls, two madams, a pair of bouncers, and several clients who came outside buttoning their trousers. Word of what this Presbyterian mission and the *fan-wey*'s government proposed flashed like gunpowder through Chinatown and reached even the filthy cells where the slaves barely survived. For the first time in their wretched lives there was a breath of hope. Threats to beat them if they rebelled, or chilling stories of how the white devils would carry them off and suck their blood, had no effect; from that moment the girls sought a way to reach the ears of the missionaries, and in a matter of weeks the police invasions multiplied, publicized by articles in the newspapers. This time the insidious pen of Jacob Freemont was finally put to good service, stirring the consciences of the citizens with his eloquent campaign on behalf of the horrible fate of the tiny slaves right in the heart of San Francisco. The aging journalist would die shortly after, without learning the measure of the impact of his articles; in contrast, Donaldina and Martha would see the fruit of their zeal. Eighteen years later I met them on a trip to San Francisco; they still have rosy skin and the same messianic fervor in their gaze; they still walk through Chinatown daily, ever vigilant, but no one calls them accursed *fan-wey*, and no one spits at them as they pass by. Now they are called *lo-mo*, "loving mother," and people bow when they greet them. They have rescued thousands of souls and eliminated the brazen traffic in girls, although they have not succeeded in erasing other forms of prostitution. My grandfather Tao Chi'en would be very satisfied.

On the second Wednesday of November, Tao Chi'en went, as he did every day, to pick up his granddaughter Lai Ming at his wife's tearoom on Union Square. The girl stayed with her grandmother Eliza in the afternoons until the *zhong-yi* finished with the last patient in his office and then came to get her. It was only seven blocks from the house, but Tao Chi'en had the habit of strolling down the two principal streets in Chinatown at that hour, as the paper lanterns were being lighted in the shops and people were finishing work and shopping for food for dinner. He walked hand in hand with his granddaughter through the markets, where exotic fruits from across the sea were artistically arranged and glazed ducks hung from hooks, admiring the mushrooms, insects, shellfish, organ meats, and exotic plants that could be found nowhere but there. Since no one had time to cook at his house, Tao Chi'en carefully chose the dishes he would take home for dinner, nearly always the same because Lai Ming was very picky about eating. Her grandfather tempted her, giving her bites of delicious Cantonese dishes being sold in the street stands, but usually they ended up with the same varieties of chow mein and pork ribs. That day Tao Chi'en was wearing a new suit for the first time; it had been made by the best Chinese tailor in the city, who took only the most distinguished men as clients. Tao had followed American style for many years, but after obtaining his citizenship he tried to dress with meticulous elegance as a sign of respect for his adopted country. He looked very handsome in his perfect dark suit, shirt with stiffly starched collar and morning coat tie, overcoat of English cloth, top hat, and ivory kid gloves. Young Lai Ming's outfit contrasted with the Western garb of her grandfather; she was wearing cutoff trousers and a quilted silk jacket in brilliant tones of yellow and blue, so thick that the little girl moved along woodenly, like a bear, her hair pulled into a tight pigtail and with a black cap embroidered in Hong Kong style. The two of them attracted attention in the ill-assorted, almost exclusively male crowd clad in typical black trousers and tunics, so universal the Chinese population seemed uniformed. People stopped to greet the *zhong-yi*, because if they weren't his patients at least they knew him by sight and by name, and the merchants would give some little treat to the granddaughter just to ingratiate themselves with the grandfather: a phosphorescent scarab in its miniature wooden cage, a paper fan, a sweet. At dusk in Chinatown there was always a festive atmosphere, the noise of shouted conversations, haggling, and vendor's cries; on the air were the smells of fried foods, spices, fish, and garbage, because all waste was thrown into the middle of the street. The grandfather and granddaughter visited the places where they usually did their shopping, chatting with the men on the sidewalk playing mahjongg; they went into the dark cubby of the herbalist to pick up some medicines the *zhong-yi* had ordered from Shanghai and stopped briefly at a gaming house to look at the fan-tan tables from the doorway, because Tao Chi'en was fascinated with the betting but avoided it like the plague. They drank a cup of green tea in Uncle Lucky's shop, where they admired the latest shipment of antiquities and carved furniture, and then turned around to make their peaceful way home. Out of nowhere a young boy in a state of great agitation ran up to the *zhong-yi* to ask him to come with him, hurry, because there had been an accident: a man had been kicked in the chest by a horse and was spitting blood. Tao Chi'en followed as quickly as he could, still holding his granddaughter's hand, down a side alley and then another and another, plunging into narrow passageways in the demented topography of the quarter until they found themselves alone in a blind alley barely lighted by the paper lanterns glowing like fantastic fireflies in a few windows. The boy had disappeared. Tao Chi'en realized then that he had fallen into a trap, and he tried to turn back, but it was too late. From the shadows surged several men armed with clubs and surrounded him. The *zhong-yi* had studied martial arts in his youth and always carried a knife in the belt beneath his morning coat, but he could not defend himself without letting go of Ming's hand. He had a few instants to ask what they wanted, what was the matter, and to hear the name of Ah Toy as the men in black pajamas, their faces covered with kerchiefs, danced around him—then came the first blow, on his back. Lai Ming felt herself being dragged away and tried to cling to her grandfather, but the beloved hand had let go. She saw the clubs rising and falling upon her grandfather's body, saw a stream of blood spurt from his head, saw him fall facedown, saw how they kept beating him until he was nothing but a bleeding heap on the paving stones.

"When they brought Tao on an improvised stretcher, and I saw what they had done to him, something shattered to a thousand pieces inside me, like a crystal goblet, and my capacity ever to love again all spilled out. I dried up inside. I have never been the same person since. I feel affection for you, Lai Ming, and for Lucky and his children; I was fond of Miss Rose, but love I can only feel for Tao," my grandmother Eliza Sommers confessed to me. "Without him nothing much matters; every day I live is a day less in the long wait to be reunited with him." She added that she had felt great sorrow for me because at five I had to witness the martyrdom of the person I loved most, but she had supposed that time would erase that trauma. She thought that my life with Paulina del Valle, far from Chinatown, would be enough to make me forget Tao Chi'en. She never imagined that the scene in the alley would live forever in my nightmares, or that the scent, the voice, and the soft touch of my grandfather's hands would pursue me in my waking hours.

Tao Chi'en was returned alive to his wife's arms; eighteen hours later he regained consciousness, and after a few days he could speak. Eliza Sommers had summoned two American physicians who on several occasions had called on the *zhong-yi*'s knowledge. Sadly, they examined him; his spinal column had been shattered, and in the unlikely case that he lived, he would be paralyzed. There was nothing science could do for him, they said. They could only clean his wounds, set some of his broken bones, stitch his head wound, and leave him massive doses of narcotics. All that while, the granddaughter, forgotten by everyone, huddled in a corner near her grandfather's bed, silently calling, *oi goa! oi goa!* not understanding why he didn't answer, why she couldn't go near him, why she couldn't sleep in his arms, as she always did. Eliza Sommers administered her husband's drugs with the same patience she tried to get him to swallow soup from a funnel. She did not allow herself to be dragged down by despair; tranquil and without tears she kept watch over her husband for days, until he could speak through swollen lips and smashed teeth. The *zhong-yi* knew beyond any question of doubt that under those conditions he could not, he did not want to, live. That was what he told his wife, asking her not to feed him or give him liquids. The deep love and absolute intimacy they had shared for more than thirty years allowed them to intuit each other's thoughts; there was little need for words. If Eliza was tempted to plead with her husband to live, immobilized in bed, just so she would not be left alone in the world, she swallowed the words, because she loved him too much to ask such a sacrifice. For his part, Tao Chi'en did not have to explain anything; he knew that his wife would do what had to be done to help him die with dignity, as he would for her had things been different. He also thought it wasn't worth the effort to insist that she take his body to China—now it did not seem very important and he didn't want to add one more burden to the load Eliza must bear, but she had decided to do it anyway. Neither of the two had the heart to discuss what seemed obvious. Eliza simply told him that she was incapable of letting him die of hunger and thirst; that could take many days, perhaps weeks, and she couldn't allow him to suffer such a long agony. Tao Chi'en told her how to do it. He said to go to his office, look in a certain cabinet, and bring him a blue vial. She had helped him in the clinic in the first years of their relationship and still did when his assistant couldn't come; she knew how to read the Chinese

characters on the containers and how to give an injection. Lucky
came into the room to receive his father's blessing and left immediately, shaken with sobs. "Neither Lai Ming nor you need worry, Eliza,
because I will not desert you; I will always be nearby to protect you.
Nothing bad can happen to either of you," Tao Chi'en murmured.
Eliza picked up her granddaughter in her arms and carried her to her
grandfather to say good-bye. The child looked at that swollen face
and drew back, frightened, but then she focused on the black eyes
looking at her with the same eternal, unchanging love, and she recognized him. She clung to her grandfather's neck and kissed him and
called his name desperately, her warm tears dropping on him until
she was pulled away by her grandmother, taken outside, and placed in
her uncle Lucky's arms. Eliza Sommers went back to the room where
she had been so happy with her husband and softly closed the door
behind her.

"What happened then, *oi poa?*" I asked.

"I did what I had to do, Lai Ming. Then I lay down beside Tao
and kissed him for a long time. His last breath stayed with me. . . ."

EPILOGUE

———

Ⅰf it weren't for my grandmother Eliza, who came from far away to light the dark corners of my past, and for the thousands of photographs that have collected in my house, how could I tell this story? I would have to create it from my imagination, with no material but the elusive threads of the lives of many others and a few illusory recollections. Memory is fiction. We select the brightest and the darkest, ignoring what we are ashamed of, and so embroider the broad tapestry of our lives. Through photography and the written word I try desperately to conquer the transitory nature of my existence, to trap moments before they evanesce, to untangle the confusion of my past. Every instant disappears in a breath and immediately becomes the past; reality is ephemeral and changing, pure longing. With these photographs and these pages I keep memories alive; they are my grasp on a truth that is fleeting, but truth nonetheless; they prove that these events happened and that these people passed through my destiny. Thanks to them I can revive my mother, who died at my birth, my stalwart grandmothers, and my wise Chinese grandfather, my poor father, and other links in the long chain of my family, all of mixed and ardent blood. I write to elucidate the ancient secrets of my childhood, to define my identity, to create my own legend. In the end, the only thing we have in abundance is the memory we have woven. Each of us chooses the tone for telling his or her own story; I would like to choose the durable clarity of a platinum print, but nothing in my destiny possesses that luminosity. I live among diffuse shadings, veiled mysteries, uncertainties; the tone for telling my life is closer to that of a portrait in sepia.

About the author

About the book

Read on

Insights,
Interviews
& More . . .

Life at a Glance

© William Gordon

ISABEL ALLENDE was born in 1942 in Lima, Peru, and raised in Chile. She fled Chile after the 1973 military coup and assassination of her uncle, President Salvador Allende, and worked in Venezuela from 1975 to 1987, when she moved to the United States. She now lives in California.

Isabel has worked as a TV presenter, a journalist, and a playwright. Her first book for adults, the acclaimed *House of the Spirits,* was published in Spanish in 1982 and has been translated into twenty-seven languages. Since then, she has written eleven more novels, a collection of stories, and four memoirs, and her books have become bestsellers across four continents.

In 2004, Isabel was inducted into the American Academy of Arts and Letters. ❧

Isabel Allende on Destiny, Personal Tragedy, and Writing

"Life is nothing but noise between two unfathomable silences." Can you describe that noise, what it is, and what it means to you?

We have very busy lives—or we make them very busy. There is noise and activity everywhere. Few people know how to be still and find a quiet place inside themselves. From that place of silence and stillness the creative forces emerge. There we find faith, hope, strength, and wisdom. Since childhood, however, we are taught to *do* things. Our heads are full of noise. Silence and solitude scare most of us.

You often talk and write about destiny. What is destiny for you?

We are born with a set of cards and we have the freedom to play them the best we can, but we cannot change them. I was born female in the forties into a conservative Catholic family in Chile. I was born healthy. I had my shots as a child. I received love and a proper education. All that determines who I am. The really important events in my life happened in spite of me. I had no control over them: the fact that my father left the family when I was three; the 1973 military coup in Chile that forced me into exile; meeting my ▶

> 66 The really important events in my life happened in spite of me. I had no control over them. 99

husband Willie; the success of my books; the death of my daughter; and so forth. That is destiny.

Just before your daughter Paula went into a coma she said, "I look everywhere for God but can't find him." Do you, can you, have faith in God after such a tragedy?

Faith has nothing to do with being happy or not. Faith is a gift. Some people receive it and some don't. I imagine that a tragedy like losing a child is more bearable if you believe in God because you can imagine that your child is in heaven.

There is a lot of autobiographical writing in your books, but no actual autobiography. Do you imagine ever writing an autobiography?

Yes, I suppose that one day I will write another memoir. I think that my book *Paula* has a lot about me. It is a kind of personal memoir, is it not?

Do you think that fiction has a moral purpose? Or can it simply be entertainment?

It can be just entertainment, but when fiction makes you think it is much more exciting. However, beware of authors who pound their "moral messages" into you.

You have written letters all your life, most notably a daily letter to your mother. You've also worked as a journalist. Which form or experience of writing helped you most when you started writing books?

The training of writing daily is very useful. As a journalist I learned to research, to be disciplined, to meet deadlines, to be precise and direct, and to keep in mind the reader and try to grab his or her attention from the very beginning.

Does writing each book change you?

Writing is a process, a journey into memory and the soul. Why do I write only about certain themes and certain characters? Because they are part of my life, part of myself, they are aspects of me that I need to explore and understand.

You loved science fiction as an adolescent. Do you think it inspired your love of creating other worlds?

Science fiction reinforced the idea—planted by my grandmother—that the universe is very strange and complex. Everything is possible and we know very little. My mind and my heart are open to the mystery.

You always start writing on January 8, but when do you finish? How long does it take you to write your books?

I write approximately a book per year. It takes me three or four months to write the first draft, then I have to correct and edit. I write in Spanish, so I also have to work closely with my English translator Margaret Sayers Peden. And then I have to spend time on book tours, interviews, traveling, etc.

Do you have a favorite among your books?

I don't read my own books. As soon as I finish one I am already thinking of the next. I can hardly remember each book. I don't have a favorite but I am grateful to my first novel *The House of the Spirits,* which paved the way for all the others, and to *Paula,* because it saved me from depression.

You grew up in Chile but now live in the United States. Which country has had the most influence on your writing and why?

It is very easy for me to write about Chile. I don't have to think about it. The stories just flow. My roots are in Chile and most of my books have a Latin American flavor. However, I have lived in the United States for many years, I read mainly English fiction, I live in English, and certainly that influences my writing. ▶

Isabel Allende on Destiny, Personal Tragedy, and Writing *(continued)*

The United States was, to a Chilean, an enemy country in the seventies. How did you overcome that and learn to love it?

I know that most Americans are not responsible for the evil that their government has done or does today abroad. Most people in this country have good intentions. They think of themselves as decent citizens and moral human beings. They want to do good. But there is great ignorance and indifference. The United States has supported in other countries the kind of brutal tyranny that it would never tolerate in its own territory. If Americans were better aware of the atrocities that have been committed in their name and with their tax money they would be horrified.

Emigrants "lose their crutches" and their past is "erased." Is that both positive and negative?

When one moves to another country as an immigrant one loses everything that is familiar. To survive one needs to draw strength from within and make double the effort of the locals to get half the results. I think that it is important to remember the past and be proud of one's roots. ❧

A Conversation with Isabel Allende

What was your relationship to photography prior to writing this book? Were (or are) you a photographer?

I am not a photographer but my husband is. For many years I have been in touch with the art of photography. I'm especially fascinated by black-and-white and by old photos. They reveal the soul of the models. No wonder many tribal people are afraid of cameras, believing that pictures steal the soul.

Do you appreciate the symbolic or otherwise artistic use of photography in any particular novels?

Photography has been the subject of many novels but I didn't look for inspiration in fiction. I researched the photographic techniques of the eighteen hundreds, including the life and art of Louis Daguerre, the inventor of photography. The poor man ended up crazy from exposure to mercurial fumes.

Aurora del Valle is such a compelling character. With her complex ethnic background—she is Chilean, Chinese, and English—she must have been a challenge to bring to life on the page. What inspired you to write about a character who is the child of three continents? ▶

  ❝ I'm especially fascinated by black-and-white and by old photos. They reveal the soul of the models. ❞

7

I find the mixture of races very interesting, maybe because I have traveled extensively. Each place and its people are different, but when all is said and done our similarities outnumber our differences. It is astonishing to me that there is so much racial hatred and so much violent nationalism and religious fundamentalism in the world. Why is it that we tend to exclude those who are not from our own ethnic group? Diversity is the strength of any species.

In Portrait in Sepia, *as in many of your novels, history is more than just a backdrop. Settings include: the War of the Pacific, when Chile fought Peru and Bolivia; the Chilean Revolution of 1891; and San Francisco's Chinatown. How do you decide to pair a particular character with a particular event? Does one give rise to another?*

Usually when I start a book I don't know what it will be about or who the characters will be. I only have a time and a place that I have thoroughly researched. In the case of *Portrait in Sepia* I knew that I wanted to write about the second half of the nineteenth century in Chile, a time of war and Chilean imperialism that shaped the national character. By the time I sat down to write the book I had a lot of information but I didn't have a story. Some characters from my previous novel, *Daughter of Fortune,* kept creeping back into my pages and they brought the story to me. I know it sounds crazy, but the truth is that for me the plot unfolds itself slowly in the process of writing many hours every single day for months. One thing leads to another, the characters behave like real people, and my job is to show up in front of my computer and let the story evolve.

Margaret Sayers Peden has been your English-language translator for many years. Do you collaborate closely with her on the translations? What is your working relationship like?

Margaret and I have been working together since my second novel in 1983. We know each other so well that we have developed a sort of psychic relationship. She says that I should be careful what I write because it may happen to her! She lives in Missouri and I live in California, but we are constantly in touch by e-mail and telephone. She sends me every thirty or forty pages of the translation, which I read carefully and send back to her with my comments. She doesn't need my input. She does a splendid job.

Aurora struggles to understand a mystery from her past that has cast a shadow on her life. To what extent do our memories of the past define who we are? Can we be free of our pasts?

Memory is very important and can sometimes define our personality, but I think that most healthy and normal people can live with their past and draw strength and knowledge from it. For a writer memory is essential. In my life the past is always in my mind but not in a negative way. I don't want to be free from it. I want to use it in my writing and in my life.

Portrait in Sepia ends with a memorable epilogue in which Aurora reflects on the story she has just told. One passage reads: "I write to elucidate the ancient secrets of my childhood, to define my identity, to create my own legend. In the end, the only thing we have in abundance is the memory we have woven." How are your own reasons for writing similar to—or different from—Aurora's?

That paragraph is me talking. Aurora feels about her photography as I do about my writing.

Many of the characters in this novel are part of a family of characters that also appears in House of the Spirits and Daughter of Fortune. Do you think you'll ever revisit the del Valles and the Sommerses in future novels?

I can't predict what I will be writing in the future. Each year on January 8 I try to start a book. I have no idea what the next one will be. I am totally focused on the current project. The idea of writing a sequel to *The House of the Spirits* has been in the air for many years. People—including some publishers—keep suggesting to me that it could be interesting, but at the present moment I am not planning anything of the sort. ᴄᴍ

Have You Read?
More by Isabel Allende

The following books are also available in Spanish from Rayo, and can be found at www.harpercollins.com.

ISLAND BENEATH THE SEA

Born a slave on the island of Saint-Domingue, Zarité—known as Tété—is the daughter of an African mother she never knew and one of the white sailors who brought her into bondage. Although her childhood is one of brutality and fear, Tété finds solace in the traditional rhythms of African drums and the voodoo loas she discovers through her fellow slaves.

When twenty-year-old Toulouse Valmorain arrives on the island in 1770, he has powdered wigs in his trunks and dreams of financial success in his mind. But running his father's plantation, Saint Lazare, is neither glamorous nor easy. Although Valmorain cruelly purchases young Tété to be his bride, it is he who will become dependent on the services of his teenage slave.

Against the merciless backdrop of sugarcane fields, the lives of Tété and Valmorain grow ever more intertwined. When the bloody revolution of Toussaint Louverture arrives at the gates of Saint Lazare, the couple flees the brutal conditions of the French colony that will become Haiti for the raucous, free-wheeling enterprise of New Orleans. There Tété finally forges a new life, but her connection to Valmorain is deeper than anyone knows and not easily severed. With an impressive richness of detail, and narrative wit and brio second to none, Allende crafts the riveting story of one woman's determination to find love amid loss, to offer humanity though her own has been battered, and to forge her own identity in the cruelest of circumstances.

INÉS OF MY SOUL

This magisterial work of historical fiction recounts the astonishing life of Inés Suarez, a daring Spanish conquistadora who toiled to build the nation of Chile—and whose vital role has too often been neglected by history.

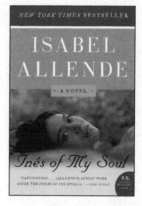

It is the beginning of the Spanish conquest of the Americas, and when Inés's shiftless husband disappears to the New World, she uses the opportunity to search for him as an excuse to flee her stifling homeland and seek adventure. After a treacherous journey to Peru, she learns of his death in battle. She meets and begins a passionate love affair with a man who seeks only honor and glory: Pedro Valdivia, war hero and field marshal to the famed Francisco Pizarro. Together, Inés and Valdivia will build the new city of Santiago and wage a ruthless war against the indigenous Chileans. The horrific struggle will change them forever, pulling them toward their separate destinies.

Inés of My Soul is a work of breathtaking scope, written with the narrative brilliance and passion readers have come to expect from Isabel Allende.

"Riveting. . . . It simply captivates. . . .
A colorful and clear-eyed portrait of a
woman and a country."
—*Chicago Sun-Times*

"A powerfully evocative narrative. . . .
Allende is at her best here."
—*Newsweek*

ZORRO

Born in southern California late in the
eighteenth century, Diego de la Vega is
a child of two worlds. His father is an
aristocratic Spanish military man turned
landowner; his mother a Shoshone
warrior. Diego learns from his maternal
grandmother, White Owl, the ways of
her tribe, while receiving from his father
lessons in the art of fencing and in cattle
branding. It is here, during a childhood
filled with mischief and adventure, that
Diego witnesses the brutal injustices dealt
to Native Americans by European settlers
and first feels the inner conflict of his
heritage.

At the age of sixteen, Diego is sent to
Barcelona for a European education. In
a country chafing under the corruption
of Napoleonic rule, Diego follows the
example of his celebrated fencing
master and joins La Justicia, a secret
underground resistance movement
devoted to helping the powerless and
the poor. With this tumultuous period
as a backdrop, Diego falls in love, saves
the persecuted, and confronts for the first

time a great rival who emerges from the world of privilege.

Between California and Barcelona, the New World and the Old, the persona of Zorro is formed, a great hero is born, and the legend begins. After many adventures—duels at dawn, fierce battles with pirates at sea, and impossible rescues—Diego dc la Vcga, aka Zorro, returns to America to reclaim the hacienda on which he was raised and to seek justice for all who cannot fight for it themselves.

"Allende's discreetly subversive talent really shows. . . . You turn the pages, cheering on the masked man."
—*Los Angeles Times*

DAUGHTER OF FORTUNE

Orphan Eliza Sommers goes on a search for love, but ends up on a journey of self-discovery. Brought up in the British colony of Valparaíso in Chile by the well-intentioned spinster Miss Rose (and her stuffier brother Jeremy), Eliza falls unsuitably in love with the humble but handsome clerk Joaquín. When he heads to California to take part in the 1849 Gold Rush Eliza follows him. But in the rough-and-tumble life of San Francisco our unconventional heroine finds that personal freedom might be a more rewarding choice than a traditional gold band on the wedding finger.

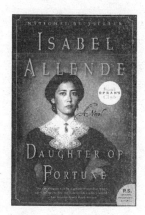

"Brilliant."
—*New York Times Book Review*

"Like a slow, seductive lover, Allende teases, tempts, and titillates with mesmerizing stories." —*Washington Post*

THE INFINITE PLAN

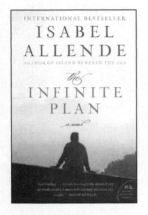

Selling more than 65,000 copies and topping bestseller lists around the world, *The Infinite Plan* tells the engrossing story of one man's quest for love and for his soul. Gregory Reeves is the son of Charles, an itinerant preacher. As a boy Gregory accepts the endless journeying and poverty which is his family's lot, never questioning the validity of his father's homespun philosophy of life—the infinite plan. But as manhood approaches he finds himself possessed by a yearning to escape. Hankering after worldly wealth, he longs to break away from the teeming Hispanic barrio of downtown Los Angeles where his family has finally settled. Gregory's quest, so different from his father's, takes him first to law school at Berkeley, next to the killing fields of Vietnam, and then into a headlong (and hedonistic) pursuit of the American Dream.

"Spellbinding. . . . Allende has caught the mood of our spiritually troubled times with uncanny precision and insight."
—*Miami Herald*

APHRODITE: A MEMOIR OF THE SENSES

Under the aegis of the Goddess of Love, Isabel Allende uses her storytelling skills brilliantly in *Aphrodite* to evoke the delights of food and sex. After considerable research and study she has become an authority on aphrodisiacs, which include everything from food and drink to stories and, of course, love. Readers will find here recipes from Allende's mother, poems, stories from ancient and foreign literature, paintings, personal anecdotes, fascinating tidbits on the sensual art of food and its effect on amorous performance, tips on how to attract your mate and revive flagging virility, passages on the effect of smell on libido, a history of alcoholic beverages, and much more.

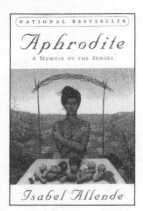

"Allende turns the joyous preparation and consumption of fine food into an erotic catalyst."
—*New York Times Book Review*

MY INVENTED COUNTRY: A MEMOIR

Isabel Allende evokes the magnificent landscapes of her country, a charming, idiosyncratic Chilean people with a violent history and an indomitable spirit, and the politics, religion, myth, and magic of a homeland that she carries with her even today. The book circles around two life-changing moments. The assassination of her uncle Salvador Allende Gossens on September 11, 1973, sent her into exile and transformed her

into a literary writer. And the terrorist attacks against her adopted homeland the United States on September 11, 2001, brought forth an overdue acknowledgment that Allende had indeed left home. *My Invented Country,* mimicking the workings of memory itself, ranges back and forth across that distance between past and present lives. It speaks compellingly to immigrants and to all of us who try to retain a coherent inner life in a world full of contradictions.

"The book gets my undivided attention when it expounds on the relationship of the author to that country of hers, invented, imaginary, fictional, to the story of her family, which is itself invented memory, and to her vocation as a narrator."   *—Los Angeles Times*

PAULA: A MEMOIR

With an enchanting blend of magic realism, politics, and romance reminiscent of her classic bestseller *The House of the Spirits,* Isabel Allende presents a soul-baring memoir that seizes the reader like a novel of suspense.

Written for her daughter Paula when she became ill and slipped into a coma, *Paula* is the colorful story of Allende's life—from her early years in her native Chile, through the turbulent military coup of 1973, to the subsequent dictatorship and her family's years of exile. In the telling, bizarre ancestors reveal themselves, delightful and bitter childhood memories surface, enthralling anecdotes of youthful years are narrated, and intimate secrets are softly whispered.

In an exorcism of death and a celebration of life, Isabel Allende explores the past and questions the gods. She creates a magical book that carries the reader from tears to laughter, and from terror through sensuality to wisdom. In *Paula,* readers will come to understand that the miraculous world of her novels is the world Isabel Allende inhabits—it is her enchanted reality.

"Spellbinding. . . . In flawlessly rich prose, [Allende] shares with us her most intimate feelings."
—*Washington Post Book World*

THE SUM OF OUR DAYS

In *The Sum of Our Days*, internationally acclaimed author Isabel Allende reconstructs the painful reality of her own life in the wake of the tragic death of her daughter, Paula. Narrated with warmth, humor, exceptional candor, and wisdom, this remarkable memoir is as exuberant and full of life as its creator. Allende bares her soul as she shares her thoughts on love, marriage, motherhood, spirituality and religion, infidelity, addiction, and memory—and recounts stories of the wildly eccentric, strong-minded, and eclectic tribe she gathers around her and lovingly embraces as a family.

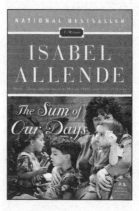

Have You Read? *(continued)*

"Terrific. . . . Funny, insightful, moving, and filled with Allende's unique voice."
—*USA Today*

The Jaguar and Eagle Trilogy

CITY OF THE BEASTS

Riveting reading for Allende fans young and old, ecothriller *City of the Beasts* takes fifteen-year-old Alexander Cold on the trip of a lifetime. Parting from his family and ill mother, Alexander joins his fearless grandmother, a magazine reporter for *International Geographic*, on an expedition to the remote and dangerous world of the Amazon. Their mission, along with the others on their team—including a celebrated anthropologist, a local guide and his young daughter Nadia, and a doctor—is to document the legendary Beast of the Amazon.

Alexander is amazed to discover under the dense jungle canopy much more than he could have imagined about the hidden worlds of the rain forest. Drawing on the strength of the jaguar, the totemic animal Alexander finds within himself, and the eagle, Nadia's spirit guide, both young people are led by the invisible People of the Mist on a thrilling and unforgettable journey to the ultimate discovery.

"Part thrilling survival adventure, part coming-of-age journey. . . . Blends magical realism with grim history and contemporary politics in a way that shakes up all the usual definitions of savagery and civilization."
—*Booklist* (starred review)

KINGDOM OF THE GOLDEN DRAGON

Not many months have passed since teenager Alexander Cold followed his bold grandmother into the heart of the Amazon to uncover its legendary Beast. This time reporter Kate Cold escorts her grandson and his closest friend Nadia, along with the photographers from *International Geographic,* on a journey to another remote niche of the world—this time in the Himalayas. The team's task is to locate its fabled Golden Dragon, a sacred statue and priceless oracle that can foretell the future of the kingdom.

In their scramble to reach the statue before it is destroyed by the greed of an outsider, Alexander and Nadia must use the transcendent power of their totemic animal spirits: Jaguar and Eagle. With the aid of a sage Buddhist monk, his young royal disciple, and a fierce tribe of Yeti warriors, Alexander and Nadia fight to protect the holy rule of the Golden Dragon.

"Imagining this utopian land and animating Buddhist beliefs is clearly fun for Allende, and her joy translates onto the page."   —*San Francisco Chronicle*

FOREST OF THE PYGMIES

Alexander Cold knows all too well that his grandmother Kate is never far from an adventure. When *International Geographic* commissions her to write an article about the first elephant-led safaris in Africa, they head—with Nadia Santos and the magazine's photography crew—to the blazing red plains of Kenya. Days into the tour a Catholic missionary approaches their camp in search of his companions, who have mysteriously disappeared. Kate, Alexander, Nadia, and their team, agreeing to aid in the rescue, enlist the help of a local pilot to lead them to the swampy forests of Ngoubé. There they discover a clan of Pygmies who unveil a harsh and surprising world of corruption, slavery, and poaching. Alexander and Nadia, utilizing the magical strengths of their totemic animal spirits, Jaguar and Eagle, launch a spectacular and precarious struggle to restore freedom and return leadership to its rightful hands.

"Captures the romance of exotic travel. . . . Has at least two things Allende's adult fiction is known for: passion and politics."
                    —*Philadelphia Inquirer*